The Heart of the Home

Grace Thompson is a much-loved Welsh author of saga and romance novels, and a mainstay of libraries throughout the United Kingdom and beyond.

Born and raised in South Wales, she is the author of numerous series, including the Valley series, the Pendragon Island series, and the Badger's Brook series. She published her 42nd novel shortly after celebrating her 80th birthday, and continues to live in Swansea.

Also by Grace Thompson

Holidays at Home

Wait Till Summer
Swingboats on the Sand
Waiting for Yesterday
Day Trippers
Unwise Promises
Street Parties

A Badgers Brook Saga

The House by the Brook
A Girl Called Hope
A New Beginning
The Heart of the Home
False Friends

A Pendragon Island Saga

Corner of a Small Town
The Weston Girls
Unlocking the Past
Maisie's Way
A Shop in the High Street
Sophie Street

The Valley Sagas

A Welcome in the Valley
Valley Affairs
The Changing Valley
Valley in Bloom

GRACE THOMPSON

The
Heart of the Home

CANELO

First published in the United Kingdom in 2005 by Severn House Publishers Ltd

This edition published in the United Kingdom in 2021 by

Canelo
31 Helen Road
Oxford OX2 0DF
United Kingdom

A CIP catalogue record for this book is available from the British Library.

Print ISBN 978 1 78863 383 3
Ebook ISBN 978 1 91085 930 8

Look for more great books at www.canelo.co

Printed and bound in Great Britain by Clays Ltd, Elcograf S.p.A.

One

Meriel watched with amusement as her father showed a prospective buyer around a newly offered property. The young couple seemed ill at ease, trying to appear knowledgeable and in control and her darling Dadda was flattering them on their perspicacity, appearing surprised at some of their comments as though none of their observations had occurred to him before.

She smiled as he described the very small kitchen as bijou and remembered asking him once what the word meant. 'I'm not really sure,' he had replied with a twinkling grin. 'But it sounds good. If I'm pushed I say it's like a small and perfect jewel. And,' he added, 'I always remind them that the kitchen, where all the caring is done, is the heart of the home. Although really, the heart of the home is love.'

With his well-practised charm and his genuine desire to help, he had the young couple sitting down discussing the way they would furnish the house within half an hour. He had even planned the garden for them. Walter John Evans, Estate Agent and Auctioneer, was a clever man who was definitely in the right job.

Meriel watched with some regret as the couple set off to discuss their choice with their families. She was twenty-two and so far there had been no sign of that special man with whom she could settle and make a home of her own.

She was just too comfortable at home, working for her father in a job she loved. She hoped that the plan she was incubating, to move away and make a fresh start, would open up her life before it was too late.

She had lived all her life in the town of Barry on the South Wales coast. It had been a Mecca for holidaymakers for many years and was a perfect place to grow up. There were so many attractions beside one of the finest sandy beaches; she knew she would find it a wrench to leave but if one of the two interviews she had arranged ended with the offer of a job she would go. Although, she admitted, she was already reminding herself that she could always return. The door would always be open and her job there to come back to whenever she needed it.

A couple of days later she walked along a road on which large buildings rose high on one side, blocking out the weak November sun. She was looking for an hotel but from the neglected facades along the row she wasn't very hopeful of it being a thing of beauty. There were one or two where some attempt had been made to brighten the property; fresh paint, windows open to the afternoon air and fresh net waving in the slight breeze from the sea. She guessed, from the indications on the front doors, that these had been converted into flats. When she saw Golden Acres, with its peeling gaudy-blue paint, the rotting wood on the windows, the fallen fences, her heart sank. This was not going to be easy to sell.

She had an appointment with the owner but as she was early she walked around to the back lane and examined the property by peering through the space that had once held a gate. As was often the case, it looked worse than the front, she thought with fading hope. As she turned to walk back, she heard voices interspersed with a woman's tinkling laughter. A couple came out of the next gateway, arm in arm, and stopped to kiss passionately. Embarrassed, Meriel slipped into the garden of the property she was about to visit.

She heard the couple walk away, peeped out once and saw them embrace and kiss again. When she guessed they had reached the end of the lane she stepped out and almost knocked the woman off her feet. She wore no shoes, her tiny feet with their red varnished toenails looked incongruous, like those of a child. She hadn't made a sound as she returned. The woman appeared to be in her thirties, very small but with a generous figure. Blonde hair fell in wild waves around her pretty face, her make-up was heavily applied and she carried her shoes by their three-inch heels.

'Oh, I'm sorry,' Meriel said.

'Had a good ol' look, did you?' the woman retorted, tapping the side of her nose, her bright red lips clammed tight with disapproval. 'Hiding behind fences, listening to other people's conversations, there's a name for people like you! You should be ashamed.'

Taken aback, Meriel could only begin to protest. 'I wasn't—'

Without another word the woman walked up the path of the next door building and Meriel heard her slam the door.

Meriel composed herself with difficulty, angry at being unfairly accused of nosiness, or even voyeurism, and went around to the front where she was to meet the vendor. He turned out to be a very young man who looked hardly more than sixteen. He explained that he had inherited the house from his grandmother and wanted to raise as much money as he could from its sale, for when he was ready to

3

buy a home of his own. 'I don't want the responsibility of it,' he explained. 'I rent two rooms in a house and someone to deal with the washing and all that, so I don't want a place of my own yet. Certainly not a place this big!'

'There are one or two nice pieces of furniture,' Meriel noted as they walked through the sad rooms. 'If you wish, we could add them to our next general sale.'

The boy nodded. 'I don't really care,' he said. 'I hardly knew her and I don't feel the need to keep any mementoes.'

Meriel felt a pang of pity for the old lady, the grandmother he had hardly known. It made her all the more grateful for her parents and the happiness she had enjoyed. After giving an assessment of the price they might reasonably expect to achieve, she went into a phone box and reported back to her father.

'Dadda, it's a mess,' she said. 'But if someone was prepared to spend money and get the work done it would make three good flats.' She told him what her valuation had been and asked him to come and confirm her estimate.

She decided she would go and sit in the car and fill in the rest of the details in her notebook while it was fresh in her mind, but as she left the phone box she bumped into the blonde woman again. She now wore a hooded coat over her suit and the high heels had been changed for some flat, brown wedge-heeled shoes but it was definitely the same woman.

'Has someone sent you to spy on me?' she demanded.

'No, of course not. I'm an estate agent and valuer and I—'

'Don't talk rot. Whoever heard of a woman doing a job like that? You must think I'm stupid. Just clear off and mind your own business.'

Meriel opened her bag and handed her a card. 'W J Evans is my father,' she said, thankful she had been allowed to complete a sentence.

A man approached them and called, 'Is anything wrong?' He too had added an overcoat to his apparel but she recognized him as the man from the lane.

'No. Go away you fool,' the woman hissed.

Thankful to leave them behind, Meriel got into the car and drove away. What they had been doing that made them so aggressive she daren't think. It was clearly something they didn't want others to know.

The following day she went with her father to discuss selling the run-down property. They took a builder with them and met the owner there. Walter managed to arrange a sale between the two of them to the delight of the builder and the obvious relief of the owner. Meriel looked around anxiously as she passed the neighbouring house which appeared to be in a worse state than the one they had just sold, but was relieved to see no sign of the irate blonde or her boyfriend.

–

Meriel had a lot on her mind that day. She had arranged an interview for a job with an estate agent in a small town called Cwm Derw. Telling her parents she was intending to leave home was not going to be easy, she had tried to prepare them but they seemed unconvinced that she would actually go. She knew how hard it was for them to face but she knew she had to go before it was too late.

Walter watched her, aware of her dilemma but saying nothing. He loved working with his only child and he'd miss her dreadfully, but he knew he had to let her go without any arguments, so she knew she was loved but had her freedom. Love could so easily be used as a key with which to lock a door.

The following morning, Meriel said her piece then glanced at her father, saddened by his attempt to hide his disappointment. 'But Dadda, it isn't as though I'm going to the other side of the world,' she said, touching his arm affectionately. 'I just need to spread my wings for a while, get some fresh experience.' Her parents still looked doubtful as she continued, 'You and Mam have done a good job. You've prepared me, given me the confidence to move on, stand on my own feet. I'm so grateful for the wonderful start you've given me. No one could have had better parents than I've had.'

'Yet you want to leave us,' her mother said. 'Why do you have to go? Isn't the work with Dadda interesting enough for you?'

'I don't want to be stuck in a rut, Mam.' Meriel turned to her father. 'I'm not going far, Dadda. I've applied for a job not far away. It's in a small town, and you and Mam can easily visit in a day. The few miles will be nothing in your smart new car,' she said with a smile. They asked her where she was going but she refused to say. 'I expect this will be the first of several interviews so I won't tell you until I have the offer of a job. Right?'

She picked up her gloves and reached for her handbag. 'Time I was leaving. I don't want to be late for my interview or I won't be leaving after all.'

'Just don't go too far or stay away too long. Promise?' Walter handed her the keys of his Hillman Minx. 'Take my car, it will get you there quicker.'

'Your new car? Thanks, Dadda! That's wonderful!' she said in surprise, staring at the keys on her palm. She kissed them both, hugged her mother and hurried from the house. If her father were any kinder she'd burst into tears and cancel the whole idea of leaving.

'Don't forget, love,' her father called, 'this interview is for you to make up *your* mind about the job, as well as for them to decide whether or not you will suit them.'

She drove away from Barry, through the pretty villages in the Vale of Glamorgan without haste, passing Aberthaw, Boverton, St Donat's, Southemdown, before she turned northward to Cwm Derw. She had allowed herself plenty of time, even without the newer, more powerful car. She drove through lanes that, even in the early winter of 1949, had a sort of beauty; soothing and restful. The colours were sombre, the autumn leaves now fallen and soggy on the ground, but she never found the wintertime melancholy, she looked upon it as the unwinding after a hectic summer, nature slumbering, a world at rest.

She was making a real change in her life; leaving the sales, auctions and estate management agency in which she had worked alongside her father since she had left school and going to a new position among strangers. In moments of panic she wondered why she was doing it, why she had felt the need for such a drastic change. But she knew that if she didn't, she might stay there for too long, until it was impossible to get out of the rut, interesting though the rut might be.

She felt the need to add to her experiences before it was too late for her to leave. There weren't many who

7

would accept her. This interview was one of only two she had been offered and the other had made it clear she would remain in the office while men did the real work. Most estate agents still believed that the public looked with more confidence towards a man in the business of selling and auctioning property.

The first agency at which she had arranged an interview was in the High Street of Cwm Derw – Valley of Oaks, and she parked the car outside the post office and walked across. The name of the agency was Ace Estate Agency. The outside looked rather run-down, with chipped paint and shabby, ill-fitting blinds. Inside, a young man stood behind the counter, apparently staring through the window at nothing at all. Dreaming of home time, she thought with a cynical smile; like some of the people her father had interviewed to take her place over the past weeks.

The bell rang cheerfully as she opened the door and at once the young man came out of his daydream and smiled at her.

'My name is Meriel Evans, I have an appointment to see Mr Dexter.' She spoke sharply, and hoped her interview wasn't with this uninteresting and obviously bored young man.

'That will be my father, George Dexter,' the young man said. 'I'm Teifion Dexter. I'll go and fetch him.'

Meriel sat down near the counter and looked around the walls – where photographs of farms and houses were interspersed with a few posters, old and new, giving details of properties offered for sale. From what she could see the office wasn't a busy one. What would she do all day? She couldn't imagine standing staring into space waiting for the doorbell to ring as Teifion Dexter had been doing. She reminded herself of her father's last words. 'Remember this is for you to make up your mind about the job, as well as for them to decide whether or not you will suit them.'

George Dexter came in and stared at her for a long time. Meriel stared boldly back. He was rather heavily built and he wore an expensive suit and shirt, both of which seemed a little too small. His greying hair was slicked back with Brylcreem and a thin moustache decorated his upper lip. There were several rings on his hands and a gold watch was just visible on his wrist. She immediately had visions of him standing in the street, with an open suitcase in front of him, selling illegal items while looking out for a policeman. A spiv, no doubt about it, her mam would say.

She was ushered into a back room and when she had eased off her coat, George Dexter asked her a few questions which he had written on a piece of paper.

'So,' he said when the list of questions was finished, 'you know the business well, having worked with your father since school.'

'Before that really. Every Saturday and during school holidays I helped out with filing and typing letters and so on. I also attended many farm and house auctions, and my valuations are almost always in line with his.'

'And you're sure you'll be happy living away from home?'

'I am twenty-two,' she said mildly.

'Have you arranged accommodation?'

'No point until I know if I have the job, whether I suit you – and the position you offer suits me.' She looked at him wryly. 'It has to be what we both want, doesn't it?'

George stared at her. She sounded as though she might be a bit 'chopsy', this one.

'I don't imagine it will be difficult to find a temporary place while I look around for something permanent,' she told him. 'Should we decide we suit each other.'

'Evans,' he mused. 'It's not an uncommon name, would I know your father?'

'Walter Evans,' she said, 'we live in Barry.' She was surprised at the odd smile that creased his face and the sharpened light in his dark eyes.

'Does he know where you have applied for work?'

'Not yet. Until I have something permanent it seems pointless to discuss it.'

'I would like to offer you the position,' he said, offering his hand across the desk.

'Thank you, as long as we understand I'm not a filing clerk without a thought in my head we'll get along fine. And from the look of the over-stuffed shelves, I would want to rearrange some of the files and remove some of the oldest to somewhere less visible. It doesn't give a good impression to a client, seeing untidiness, does it?'

Definitely chopsy, he thought. This could be fun.

'Would you like me to help find a room?' he asked.

'I'd prefer to do that myself, but thank you.'

That sharpness was there: so far but no further, over-confident without a doubt. She was better by far than the others he had interviewed and if she did her job well and was polite with clients, he didn't think an occasional sharp remark would bother him. He pictured Walter Evans's face when his daughter told him who was to be her new boss. This was really too good an opportunity to miss. His dark eyes glittered with amusement but also with malice. For a while at least, a reliable assistant would give him more time to enjoy himself with Frieda; his son Teifion sadly lacked the necessary flair. Who knows, someone as stroppy as Meriel Evans might even defy her father's inevitable protests, and stay.

After the details were discussed, and he had agreed to pay her a pound more than he had intended, she left the office, and returned to where Teifion was writing something in a ledger. She waited until he put down his pen and said, 'It seems that you have a new assistant.'

'Good. I'm sure we'll work together happily.' He held out his hand and she shook it. He held hers for a fraction longer than necessary, and said, 'There's a modest bed and breakfast not far away. It's run by Elsie and Ed Connors. You might find it suitable while you're looking for something better.'

So, Meriel thought, he had been listening to what had been said. She thanked him and left.

The bed and breakfast he mentioned was not far from where she had left her father's Hillman Minx, in a quiet road behind the post office. As she knocked on the front door, she looked around at the neat and well-kept front. Inside was the same. Clean and comfortable. It was Ed Connors who showed her the room and he explained that his wife was unwell and needed a lot of rest. 'But when you come to stay she'll be here to meet you, she likes to introduce herself to our guests,' he told her.

She took the room which looked out onto the quiet street. She didn't want to get involved in renting something more permanent until she had been at the Dexter's agency for a month or so. No point settling in before she was sure she wanted to stay in this small town.

When she reached home she called, 'Mam! Dadda! I was offered the job and I've taken it.'

Walter Evans came out of the living room and hugged her. 'Darling girl, of course they offered you the job. There isn't anyone better suited. I hope this new boss of yours realizes how lucky he is.'

Her mother, Lynne, was more practical. 'Have you found somewhere to stay?'

'Not really. I've booked into a small guest house for a month, while I make sure I'll be happy there.'

Lynne hugged her. 'I hope you *hate* it,' she said, her smile making a joke of the remark. 'Seriously, I hope you enjoy meeting people and making new friends. But remember, you can always come back here. If you aren't completely happy, come home to us. Remember, the business will be yours one day.'

As she handed back the keys to her father's car and thanked him for trusting her with it, he exchanged them for another set. 'Mam?' She stared at her mother, surprise on her face. 'Don't tell me you have a car. I thought you hated driving.'

'Look outside,' Walter said, nodding towards the front window. A small Austin was parked against the kerb and he tapped the keys he held on her open palm. 'She's yours, you'll need transport if you're to do the valuations.' As she ran out to examine her exciting gift he turned to Lynne. '*And* she can come home to see us often,' he added sadly.

'Tell me the name of the firm,' Walter asked as she came in filled with excitement at the surprise gift.

'It's Ace Estate Agency in Cwm Derw.' She started as her parents groaned in disbelief.

'Not George Dexter?' her father pleaded.

'Yes, and his son Teifion is there too, a bit useless I suspect, but… what is it? Is there something I should know about this firm?'

Without explaining why, they pleaded with her not to go but she was adamant. If she turned this down, she might not get another opportunity and she badly wanted to leave home and stand on her own efforts. She was puzzled by their reaction particularly as they refused to even hint at the reason for their dismay.

–

Trying out her new acquisition the next day was an excuse to drive around all her favourite places, and visit friends to say goodbye and give them her temporary address.

The Barry Island sands were empty that November day, the sea sullen and unwelcoming. The headlands at each side of the bay were grey, lacking the bright patches of colour from the small sturdy plants that grew in defiance of the barren rocks and the wild weather. She strolled along the deserted promenade, past shops and entertainments now closed up until the spring. She looked at the line of poplars that indicated the cricket ground, also unused and silent.

She would miss being able to come to the seaside at a moment's whim, and see the holiday resort in all its moods. But there was no point in getting melancholy, she was stretching her wings and flying the nest. There was more to life than sea and sand. But she stopped and turned back for one more glance before getting into the car and driving off. She called on several friends and promised to write, and then she went to the road on which large houses overlooked the docks.

Leo Hopkins was one person she would sorely miss. He was her father's assistant and had been for many years. It was Leo, eight years older than her, who had taught her so much about the business. Her father told her what to do but Leo was patient enough to tell her why she was doing it. It was mainly because of his help that she had become expert at valuations, although her father would never allow her to deal with important sales on her own. That was one of the reasons for the move; a new start, giving her employer the clear understanding that she had no intention of being an office clerk.

Mrs Hopkins opened the door and told her Leo was in the garden. She went through the house to where Leo was planting a few bulbs.

'These were forgotten,' he told her. 'Dad left them in the shed, so although it's a bit late, I thought I'd put them in.'

She watched him for a moment, then said, 'Leo, I've got the job. I start Monday.'

Shock registered briefly, a nerve ticked in his cheek as the words he dreaded to hear were uttered. 'I'm pleased, if you're sure it's what you want. But why so soon? I thought you'd start in the new year. Things are very quiet during the last weeks of the year. Better they paid you when you could be kept busy.'

'I'll be busy all right. I've had a look at their filing system and the way they keep addresses of enquirers and I've promised to revise the way the office is run. I think George Dexter's wife has been doing the office work and she's been very slap-dash. Perhaps because they seem to be the only auctioneers in the area, they've become complacent.'

'George Dexter?' Concern showed in his blue eyes. 'Does your father know who you'll be working for?'

'Yes and they obviously don't like each other. He won't tell me why, probably some professional jealousy. He tried to make me change my mind but I won't.'

'There must be other firms who would be glad to have someone like you.'

'Not so many. Most still think it's a job for men. Even though women did almost everything during the war, often men still think of us as second class and slightly stupid. You wouldn't believe the attitude of most people who I approached about a vacancy. This is the only offer I've had and I have to give it a try, Leo. You can understand that, can't you?'

Leo didn't reply. He went on loosening the earth even though the bulbs had all been planted. She rested her hand on his shoulder. 'Thanks to you, I know how things ought to be done. I appreciate all you taught me.'

'Pity I did. You wouldn't have wanted to leave if I hadn't bothered.'

Now it was her turn to remain silent. She was saved from replying by Mrs Hopkins calling to tell her tea was made. Below them the water of the docks was stirred by a rising wind. She was aware of how cold she had become.

'Don't forget, Meriel, I'm here if you have any problems,' Leo said as they walked back into the cosy warmth of the house.

The table was neatly set and the food attractively displayed. Since the death of her husband, Mrs Hopkins had concentrated all her love on her son. Her two daughters had moved far away and Meriel had the somewhat disturbing feeling that his mother depended on Leo far too much. Perhaps he too ought to leave while he still could, she thought sadly.

She was puzzled by the dislike between her parents and George Dexter, and equally so by their refusal to discuss it. Mrs Hopkins insisted she knew nothing about it, although the way she looked away from her when she denied any knowledge of the quarrel made Meriel doubt this. All Leo would tell her was that the two men had argued when they were young and dislike hadn't faded with time. There was no hint of why.

As she was leaving, he hugged her and kissed her cheek and the warmth and security his closeness engendered made her almost regret her decision to go. She was inexplicably sad as she drove away and headed for home. Saying goodbye to Leo had been harder than she had expected. She had always loved him but only in the way she loved all those close to her. Now there was something more and it was unsettling. Her decision to leave home seemed to have stirred up emotions stronger than anything else had in her whole life.

–

Meriel's first days at Dexter's Ace Estate Agency and Auctioneers were strange. When she had mentioned her father, George had made it clear he didn't want to discuss their past differences. Her second and greater disappointment was that he didn't seem to expect her to do anything apart from sit in the office and attend to any enquiries. When she asked to make a start on the untidy files and consider changes to the various forms they used which were seriously out of date, he said he had to wait for his wife to return. 'Frieda will explain everything to you better than I can, and at present she's in Brighton with her sister.'

'But I can't sit and do nothing,' she complained. 'Couldn't I just look through what you do so your wife and I can discuss any changes when we meet?'

Despite the fact much of their work was with farms and farm stock two people came during her first week and, despite the fact that Christmas was just over a month away, asked for their home to be placed on the market. One family had decided to emigrate to Australia, while the second was selling a house after the death of his mother. It was Teifion who went with his father to decide on the valuation while Meriel sat and waited in the hope of another enquiry. She spent some time looking at the advertising pages of the local papers, noting what was selling and gathering information about prices in the town.

That lunchtime she drove around to look at the first place and made a vague assessment of its value by comparing it with another being sold on the same street. While George and Teifion were looking at the second property, a client came in and she gave him details of the few houses they had on their list and also told him about the property she had seen that day.

By the time George and Teifion came back the man was almost convinced the place was for him; he knew the street and the actual house. They took him to see the house and he agreed straight away to put an offer in. Their valuation had been the same as hers and they were delighted with her success.

By the end of her first week, Meriel was feeling hopeful of the job being suitable. Once she had proved they could trust her they would give her more important and inter-esting work to do. 'Maybe I won't wait a month before finding somewhere to live,' she told Teifion.

On Sunday, instead of going home as her parents had hoped, she walked around the neighbourhood. There were only two other houses for sale, both were being sold privately, with home-made boards set up in their gardens. Perhaps she would call and try to convince the owners of the advantages of employing the services of professionals.

She drove away from the main roads and down a narrow country lane where ditches and grass verges lined both sides. There were a few houses on one side and woodland on the other. She stopped when she caught sight of a house set back from the rest. Its windows were bare of curtains, its chimney without smoke. At this time of year that must mean it's empty.

At first she wondered whether the owner might be selling and therefore a prospective client, but then, as she drew near and saw the place something happened. The house seemed to call her, and she almost ran the last few yards to peer through its windows, her heart racing. The floors were huge slabs of Welsh slate. The living room had a fireplace with the fire laid, just waiting for a match, a solitary couch seemed to be the only furniture. Large windows offered a superb view over the surprisingly neat garden at the front and, at the back, facing the lane, was the kitchen with a gas stove and a long, oak table. Standing on the back porch, tall trees hiding the lane from sight, she had the impression that the house and its garden were part of the woodland. There was no For Sale notice, only a house name. She saw it was called Badgers Brook.

She felt stomach-churning excitement. It was too large and the rent would be ridiculously high. There would be the cost of furnishing, and even considering it for a moment was ridiculous. But she knew without doubt that she desperately wanted to live there.

'Looking for someone, are you?' a shrill voice called. A woman aged between fifty and sixty stepped out of the hedge and tilted her head questioningly.

'I just wondered about the house. It's obviously empty and might be for rent.'

'I'm Kitty Jennings, me and Bob live in the first house on the lane. It's Geoff Tanner you want. Him at the ironmongers. He'll tell you whether or not he wants to rent it.'

'Thank you, I think I know the place, in Steeple Street, isn't it? I'll call on Monday and ask him.'

'Call now, he and Connie won't mind. Love visitors they do.'

'I couldn't, not on a Sunday.'

'I'll come with you if you like. My little Sunday joint won't take much cooking, no bigger than a couple of conkers! It can wait an hour.' Without waiting for agreement, she ran off and Meriel heard her calling to her husband. 'Bob? I'm just popping to see Connie and Geoff, I won't be long.' And she was back, dragging on a coat, plonking a hat on her head.

'I have a car, so we won't be long,' Meriel said, taking out her keys.

'Ooh, there's a treat!' Kitty said with a wide smile.

Geoff and Connie were in their kitchen preparing vegetables for their Sunday roast. Connie answered Kitty's knock and invited them in. 'Put the kettle on, Geoff, we've got visitors,' she called as she ushered them through the shop and into the warm kitchen.

Introductions completed, Meriel asked them about Badgers Brook.

'Where did you hear about it being for rent?' Geoff asked, putting aside the sprouts he had been cleaning. 'We haven't advertised it and you say you're a newcomer to the town?'

'I work at the Ace Estate Agency on the High Street. Do you know George Dexter? I was just driving past, saw it and felt I had to live there.' Meriel lowered her eyes, she felt silly making such a remark. She was a business woman and not given to fanciful thoughts.

'It's large for one person,' Connie said.

'I know and I don't even know how long I'll be staying. Dexter's might not be suitable for me, or I for them. It's far too early to be sure that I'll be staying. But even though it's probably too expensive and definitely too large I just know I'll be happy there. Silly, isn't it?'

'Stay and share our meal and then we'll take you for a look around,' Geoff offered.

Meriel looked at once at Connie, unsure whether she would be happy coping with an uninvited guest. Connie was smiling as she held out her hand. 'Please stay, we'd love to show you Badgers Brook.'

Adding a few more potatoes and extra vegetables, the meal they prepared was generous and tasty. Geoff had given Kitty a lift home in the firm's van and had returned, having opened the windows and doors of Badgers Brook, to freshen the rooms of the empty house.

Despite being November and with the windows and doors of the house being open for a couple of hours, the place felt warm and welcoming. There were no disappointing aspects, and she felt happy as she wandered through the rooms. She imagined herself living there, longed to show the place to her parents and friends. Before she left, as she thanked Connie and Geoff for their hospitality, she had agreed to move in.

Being auctioneers as well as dealing with the sale of buildings and farm contents, Meriel knew she would have no difficulty buying the pieces of furniture she would need. A week later she had already acquired cupboards, a chest of drawers and six chairs, as well as two large couches.

'Are you sure you'll need all those chairs?' Teifron teased. 'You must be very restless if you're going to use them all!'

She looked at him in surprise. She had no idea why she had bought so many chairs. She was going to live there alone, so a couple would surely suffice. She didn't anticipate hordes of visitors, she didn't know anyone apart from Connie and Geoff and Kitty Jennings.

–

As she began to settle into Badgers Brook, one of the first people she met was Lucy Calloway. Lucy worked at the hairdresser's shop owned by Mr and Mrs Ernest James. Mrs Jennie James had once been Lucy's closest friend but since her marriage to the owner, the friendship had declined. She was looking for a change of occupation, she whispered to Meriel one day as she set her lovely auburn hair into a long outward roll, but couldn't decide where to go or what to do. 'I just feel I need a change,' she explained.

At twenty-nine, she had little hope of marrying and having a family to care for and she didn't like the idea of a future that saw her staying in exactly the same place as now. She had been engaged to Gerald Cook throughout the war but his lack of enthusiasm for marriage finally persuaded her to end it. Still living with her parents and going to the hairdresser's every day was becoming so predictable, so utterly boring.

After she had cut and set Meriel's hair they went to the café for lunch and she described her tedious life. 'I admire your bravery in leaving home. I did try once, shared a flat with Jennie Jones, who became Jennie James when she married my boss. It was a disaster, but I should have tried again. I might have avoided my present monotony.

'Every Tuesday, Mrs Richards and Mrs Elsie Maybury sit here trying to outdo each other in swank, Friday late night there's Mrs Nerys Bowen from the dress shop, and on Fridays and Saturday morning the young girls come to get their hair set ready for dates and the dances.' She gave a deep sigh. 'It seems a long time since I enjoyed weekends packed with fun. So it's a pleasant surprise to see someone new in town. Perhaps we can go out sometime, to the pictures or something?' She offered to show her the town and introduce her to a few people. Then on discovering there was a film which they both wanted to see, they began meeting often and soon found they had a great deal in common. In less than two weeks they both felt they had found a new and close friend.

–

A week after moving in Meriel was glad she had bought all those chairs. Curiosity about the new tenant brought several visitors. They went away pleased with her genuine welcome and told others and before she knew it she was on Christian name terms with practically everyone in the vicinity of the lane and the High Street.

Most visitors brought small gifts, and offered overwhelming invitations to spend some of the Christmas period with them, but she and Lucy had their own plans for Christmas and it was at Badgers Brook. Both young women had decided to step away from their traditional family Christmases and start traditions of their own.

Although George still didn't allow her to deal with 'out of office' appointments on her own, he was encouraging and obviously pleased with her expertise. His wife had still not returned from her sister in Brighton, so the files were still in a mess, although Meriel was beginning to work out the best way of updating the chaotic system. She began to fill her quiet moments with assessments of other changes, ways in which the office was run which would improve efficiency.

George listened to her recommendations with growing interest.

'The trouble is we've done things the same way for so long we can't see how out of date we are. I'm sure you and Frieda will agree on what's best.' He laughed and added, 'She's not so set in her ways as me.'

'Countrywide, there's been an encouraging, although small, growth in the number of people buying their own homes in the past year,' she said. 'Soon we'll be into a new decade. The fifties!' She pointed to the date on one of the forms they regularly used.

George groaned on seeing the date printed was 1939. 'I didn't think anyone would notice, and we ordered so many when we were warned that paper might be scarce during the war, it seemed a pity to waste them,' he confessed.

Warming to her theme, Meriel went on, 'The fifties! Imagine that. We'll be saying goodbye to all the shortages of wartime and look forward to great things. There's a feeling of excitement in the air, a confidence that the best times are on the way. Perhaps, one day, we'll see a larger part of the business dealing with house purchase.'

George looked at her, caught up in her excitement, seeing a boom in his business, good profits that enabled him to buy the house near the sea his wife wanted so badly. But when he spoke he said doubtfully, 'Perhaps you're right, as long as it doesn't become "Boom and Bust" as the Americans warn. Anyway, for the moment we'd better get these accounts posted or we'll never survive to see it!'

The furniture was well used in Badgers Brook. There were very few evenings when no one called. They came with excuses to call at first, telling her of the various activities taking place in the area or bringing something to help feed her endless visitors, but soon gave up the pretence and just walked in and sat around the fire or filled her kitchen making tea, often bringing a tiny share of their food rations to help.

During the first week of December she phoned her parents from the phone box on the lane and insisted they came to Badgers Brook for Christmas instead of her going home.

'It's such a magical place, you'll love it,' she gushed. 'And the people are so friendly you won't want to go back home.'

So it was decided. The changes she had brought about were making her life just perfect. Spending Christmas in this beautiful house, a promising new job, new friends, and her parents coming to meet them would make it even better. The following morning she finally met George Dexter's wife, Frieda, and everything fell apart.

Frieda Dexter was George's second wife and fifteen years his junior. Small, pretty in a china doll kind of way, her makeup was carefully applied to be unobtrusive, and her hands wore soft-pink varnish to match exactly the lipstick and the clothes she wore. She had a demure shyness about her that George adored. How lucky he'd been to win her heart.

She didn't see Meriel at first, as the taxi driver dropped her suitcase on the front step. After she had walked in and held out her arms for George's hug, smiled shyly at Teifion, she looked up and recognition, already shown by the paralysing horror on Meriel's face, was repeated on her own. They had met in the lane behind that dilapidated row of large houses several weeks ago. Her clothes and make-up were completely different but there was no mistaking her.

Unaware of the shock on both faces, George introduced them. They didn't shake hands and almost immediately Frieda left the front office and disappeared into the back room.

Meriel asked for an early lunch and went to sit in the café, drank tea she didn't want and ate a sandwich she couldn't taste. What should she do? Pretend they hadn't met in the lane behind the hotel, a lane a very long way from Brighton? Or carry on as though nothing had happened between them? That would surely be impossible, but the alternative was to leave the job, leave Cwm Derw and forget she had ever seen Badgers Brook.

–

When George went into the back office, Frieda was staring at the books and files, noting the changes Meriel had begun.

'Why have you allowed her to mess up our system?' she demanded, her voice still soft and almost pleading. 'She's muddled everything so only she knows where to find things. Miss Indispensable, that's what she wants to be, muddling everything so only she knows where to find things.'

'I don't think it's like that, she's very experienced and I like some of her ideas.'

'It's a clever idea, darling, but not one that gets past me.' When she looked up, she said slowly and carefully, 'George, darling, she will have to go.'

'What? How can you make such a decision? You've only just met her.'

'Her reputation comes before her. I recognized her straight away, which is why she suddenly went out for lunch. She's the daughter of Walter Evans, isn't she?'

'Yes, and that's part of the appeal, him worrying about what I'll tell her! She's worked with her father most of her life and has knowledge we can use. Best of all, Frieda, it will mean we can spend more time together. She's our ticket to better things, so why don't you want her here?'

'Because she's a devious and troublesome liar.'

'Come on, she can't be that terrible. We're in the same business, I'd have heard and I've only been told good things about her. We're very lucky to have her. You must be mistaken, darling.'

'Why d'you think her father let her go?'

'She told me she wanted more experience.'

Frieda shook her pretty head. 'She was told to leave. She really can't stay. Trust me on this, George, she will bring us nothing but trouble.'

'But I can't tell her to leave without explaining why. What has she done? You have to tell me.'

'I can't.'

'Frieda, tell me.'

'Please, darling,' Frieda whispered breathlessly, choking on her sobs. 'Don't press me on this.' Tears threatened and George hugged her and backed off the subject.

Teifion had invited Meriel to go with him to the pictures that evening and after taking her back to Badgers Brook, he went home and walked in on a row between his father and stepmother. After George stormed out of the house, Teifion made Frieda a cup of tea and begged to be told what was going on.

'It's that girl. I don't want her here.'

'Meriel? But she's marvellous. She knows the job and is full of new ideas to help our business to grow. I've learned so much from her already.' After some cajoling Frieda agreed to tell him what she knew on condition he told no one.

'There's no proof you see, so you can't repeat it, but she stole from one of her father's friends, and tried to convince everyone that another member of his family was guilty. There was an uproar but no police were involved. I don't know all the facts, but they were friends of mine and I do know that her father paid to hush it all up.'

As Frieda knew he would, Teifion immediately told his father, and the following day, two weeks before Christmas, George regretfully told Meriel she wasn't suitable and gave her two weeks' money in lieu of notice.

Her first reaction was to get in the car and drive to Barry to tell Leo. When her tears had subsided she made him promise not to tell her parents until she had decided what she would do.

'I can't come home, not before I try to find something else,' she explained. 'My flight into independence has to last longer than a few weeks.'

'I'll say nothing as long as you promise to keep me informed. I need to know you're all right and not so miserable that rather than come home to us you'll take on a job where you won't be happy. I want you to be happy, Meriel.'

She knew he wanted her to admit defeat and return home but she was even more determined as she drove back to the haven of Badgers Brook. It soothed her with its calm, peaceful atmosphere, confidence flowing into her as she felt utterly certain it wanted her to stay.

–

Christmas was no longer the joyous occasion Meriel had hoped for, but her parents still came. Lucy helped her to prepare for their visit and they managed to buy sufficient food. Peter Bevan, who had once sold vegetables from a horse and cart but now owned a shop in the town, managed to get her a pheasant and a couple of rabbits as well as a share of the available fruit and vegetables.

They planned that their neighbours and friends would gather at Badgers Brook for an evening meal on Boxing Day. Rabbit casserole, roasted pheasant, with oddments of off-ration cheese – begged from Haywards, the grocer – were the main ingredients and when the table was set for ten places, it looked like a feast.

They had invited Betty Connors, the sister of Ed Connors at the B & B. She owned the local pub, the Ship and Compass, and was pleased to have company for a while on her rare day off. They had miscounted and two people had to sit on the hearth and use a stool for a table but the inconvenience simply added to the fun.

Meriel tried not to think about her lack of employment, but simply enjoy the occasion. As he left, Geoff thanked her for her hospitality and said, 'I think an auctioneer at the other side of town is looking for an assistant. Give him a try.'

As soon as Christmas was over she did, but the man looked at her apologetically and turned her down. It seemed that Frieda had passed on stories of her dishonesty. Because of Frieda's own misbehaviour and lies, she seemed determined to drive Meriel from the town, knowing she had witnessed something she shouldn't have seen.

Walter and Lynne were worried about their daughter. They had heard the rumours and tried to deny them, but mud always sticks. They presumed it was George who had started them.

'Typical of the man, having fun humiliating a capable young woman because of her parents. If she hadn't been our daughter he wouldn't have employed her. As it is he did so for the childish pleasure of giving her the sack!' Lynne sighed. 'Troubles never really go away, do they? They lie dormant, then hover and reappear just when everything seems perfect.'

–

So, 1950 will arrive with all its hope and promise and I'll be without a job, Meriel thought, and all because I walked around the lane to view that hotel. Why was life so unfair? It would be so easy to give up and go home, but she knew she wouldn't, she couldn't. She had made friends here and felt a part of the community, something she hadn't felt when she had been safe in the cocoon of her sheltered life and her loving parents. There she had continued to live the life of a child, accepting their opinions without question – until recently when restlessness awoke in her. But she had stepped away and with Mr Micawber's confidence that 'Something will turn up', she decided to stay in Cwm Derw and continue to live at Badgers Brook.

Two

New Year, 1950, was a time of celebration. It was the beginning of a new decade and everyone seemed thankful to leave behind the forties, and the long shadows of war, and were looking forward to better times. As New Year was a Sunday, the whole weekend and the days that followed were an excuse for many parties. It was a time to reassure everyone that good times were coming and the painful memories of the many tragedies so many families had suffered were beginning to fade.

The tenants of Badgers Brook were one of the last to invite friends round and call it a New Year party, even though it was a week after the start of the New Year. True to tradition, a few were invited and many turned up. As it was Sunday, even Betty Connors from the Ship and Compass came and she brought her brother, Ed, and his wife, Elsie, who ran the local bed and breakfast establishment. Leo brought his mother and although the intention was to drive home later, they didn't need much persuasion to stay.

It was after two a.m. before the party ended. Walter and Lynne slept in the spare room while Leo and his mother settled into Meriel's and Lucy's rooms, leaving them to sleep downstairs.

Nothing was said about Meriel losing her job and she was thankful that, in the lively crowd, she could avoid conversation easily. She would find a job first, then tell them. She knew that, being so badly hurt by her treatment, she'd have found it difficult to resist their pleading for her to return home.

It was Leo who helped serve breakfast, a sorry meal of stale bread – toasted and spread with a mixture of margarine mixed with the top of the milk, whisked to make an imitation butter. It was helped down with some home-made plum jam brought by Stella, from the post office.

Lucy met a few of Meriel's friends and the time went very fast. After another huge meal, and having been given packets of food to take with them, they left. Walter and Lynne kissed them both on the cheek, and wished them a 'Happy New Year' as they departed.

'I just know the fifties are going to be great,' Meriel said.

Lucy enthusiastically agreed. 'This weekend is the start and it will get better and better, I just know it.'

'I hate lying to Mam and Dadda,' Meriel admitted as they drove back to Cwm Derw. 'But if I tell them I don't have a job, my not wanting to go back home would be impossible for them to understand. They'd be hurt, wouldn't they?'

'I wish I'd made the break during the war. It was easier to explain about leaving home then. I had my chance and I didn't take it. Most of my friends escaped by joining the forces or the Land Army or the NAAFI. I was too nervous. Then taking the flat with Jennie didn't work out, and now I feel I'm stuck at home for the rest of my life.'

'Won't you marry?'

'I'm twenty-nine years old, that's something else I've left a bit late. Jennie and I were having such fun you see.

When life is good you don't look ahead and think of it ending.'

'As an experienced hair stylist you could move away, get a job somewhere else.'

'My wages aren't enough to buy independence.'

'Mine would be – if I could find a job! But my experience is not something many people want. I'm a woman doing a man's job – which makes me unacceptable. Crazy, but there it is. So although I've more to offer than many of the men in similar jobs, my knowledge of the work is useless, unless I go back to my father's business – which incidentally will be mine one day.'

'Isn't it a pity we can't be our own boss,' Lucy said.

'It sounds silly, but besides wanting to break away from the security of home, I'd find it hard now to leave Badgers Brook.'

'There is something special about the place.'

'It's soothing and friendly. It's the strangest thing, it's the coldest month of the year yet there's always a welcoming warmth when I walk in. Even though there hasn't been a fire lit for three days it won't be cold. Come back and we'll find something for supper. You'll see what I mean.'

While Lucy prepared a meal from the package of food Meriel's mother had given them, Meriel dealt with the fire. It had been laid ready and the first match soon had it roaring up the chimney. They sat and ate cold, roast goose with mashed potatoes and a few leeks and tinned carrots from trays on their laps, the warmth making them sleepy.

'It's so good to be home.' Meriel sighed. 'I wish Leo were nearer though. He's so easy to talk to and he always manages to get to the nub of a problem and say all the right things. It helps me to see things more clearly.'

'I sometimes wish I could see Gerald, although too much time has passed for us to get back together. If we met again I might not feel the same as I once did anyway.'

'There's nothing like that about Leo. He's my father's friend, and my friend, not a love interest,' Meriel protested sleepily.

Lucy returned to the hairdresser's shop on Tuesday morning and Meriel went job hunting with a determination to accept anything that would help pay the rent. She began by considering her options which included using the car. Deliveries were something she might try, but where to start? She parked outside the post office and began calling on shops and businesses. By offering her services to several shops she found sufficient to at least pay the rent and feed herself and her continuing stream of visitors.

Over the next couple of weeks, she delivered groceries, office supplies, the occasional bouquet, even bread when the baker's boy fell ill. The money slowly filled her purse but she was frustrated at the way her plans had fallen apart. 'They didn't fall apart, they were pushed, by stupid Frieda Dexter,' she grumbled to Lucy one day when they were on their way to the pictures.

'Talk of the devil,' Lucy whispered, gesturing to the people ahead of them in the queue. 'Or his son!' she added with a giggle. Teifion Dexter was on his own a few yards ahead of them, moving slowly as the patient queue of people shuffled towards the ticket desk. He saw them and managed to sit next to Meriel.

She leaned firmly away from him toward Lucy but he said, 'Don't be angry with me, I didn't want you to leave and I don't think Dad did either. It was Frieda. She has sudden likes and dislikes and there's no arguing with her.'

34

'It was most unfair and you know it. A few enquiries would I have proved her wrong. My reputation is excellent.'

'I know.'

'I didn't see you supporting me at the time!'

'Sorry, but it was difficult.' he said. 'I couldn't disagree with my father and my stepmother. Loyalty isn't compatible with honesty, is it?' he added sadly.

'That's very perspicacious of you,' she replied.

'Er, is it?' he asked, pretending not to understand.

'He's such a bore,' Meriel said as they drove back home. 'I think he's been belittled all his life by his father and hasn't the sense to get away. He still tries desperately to please him. I think he wants a kick up the you-know-what!'

'Why did you really leave Dexter's?' Lucy asked. 'No one believes the story about you stealing.' After a brief hesitation, Meriel told her about meeting Mrs Dexter, dressed like a tart, and with a man, outside a seedy hotel when she was supposed to be with her sister in Brighton.

'But she took such a chance telling you to go. How did she know you wouldn't tell Mr Dexter the truth?'

'She was confident she would be believed. D'you know, Lucy, that woman is two different people: the brazen, tarty creature I first met, and the demure, butter-wouldn't-melt Mrs George Dexter. If you had seen the way she was dressed when I first saw her, red lipstick and heavy eye make-up, wild hair and awful clothes including a startlingly short skirt and high-heeled red shoes, and then compare that with the vision of shy, simpering loveliness she displays for her husband, well, you wouldn't believe it and neither would he. How could he look at her and not laugh at what I told him? He's daft on her.

35

She knew she was safe. But whatever she does, she isn't going to drive me away from Cwm Derw.'

–

Walter Evans knew something was wrong and over the past weekend, as they had sat together, shared anecdotes and laughed at each other's experiences, he had waited patiently for Meriel to tell him. News always got around, through the various firms in the same line of business as himself, and he knew Meriel had been asked to leave. There was much speculation about her sudden dismissal. What he had heard he had ignored or had flared in her defence. He knew how easily supposition became rumour, and how quickly rumour became accepted as the truth. No, he wanted to be told by Meriel before he believed any of the stories he'd heard. Whatever he was told he knew that George Dexter's long-standing dislike of him was the real reason for his adored daughter being hounded and disgraced. But he could do nothing until Meriel told him exactly what had happened.

–

Leo Hopkins was late one morning and explained that his mother had been unwell during the night. Later, Walter called him into his office and asked him to make an excuse to call on Meriel. 'Will you go there, see what you can find out? I don't want her to know, so can you just be in the area on business and look her up?'

It was arranged that Leo would call at Badgers Brook on the pretence of visiting a distant cousin living a few miles further west. But his mother's illness and extra work delayed him and several days passed before the opportunity arose. They were days in which Walter continued to worry and to wonder why his daughter, with whom he had always shared complete honesty, wouldn't tell him the truth.

Leo eventually walked into Badgers Brook as Meriel was returning home at six o'clock. Lucy was already there, having planned an evening listening to music played on a gramophone given to Meriel by Betty Connors. The music met him at the door, 'Tico Tico', played by Ethel Smith on her electric organ, and he laughed as Lucy opened the door swinging to the lively beat.

He was invited to stay for a meal and although he tried to persuade them to talk they were as tight-mouthed as the proverbial clam. He left about eight o'clock and instead of driving back to Barry he called into the Ship and Compass. A young man was drinking alone, whom he heard being called by name when ordering a drink. George Dexter's son, he thought.

'Teifion? Can I join you?' he asked.

It was soon apparent that Teifion had been drinking for a while. He was maudlin and his voice was slurring over some words. Leo encouraged him to talk, playing the role of sympathetic listener.

'My father has never understood me,' Teifion said. 'All my life I've tried to please him but I've let him down.'

'He expects too much of you,' Leo said soothingly. 'Too much of everybody, not just you.' He listened some more and when he thought the moment was right he said, 'Telling Meriel to go must have been hard for you too. I bet you couldn't understand what she'd done wrong.'

'She didn't do anything wrong,' Teifion said, struggling with the words. 'She shouldn't have been sacked. She didn't do anything bad. She's a lovely, lovely woman. Truth is, the real villain is—'

'Teifion!' George came into the bar and called to his son before marching across pulling him out of his seat.

As he was led out, Teifion called back. 'See? I'm always letting him down. I'm useless, aren't I, Dad?'

Leo smiled, he already knew the name Teifion had been about to utter. He went back to Walter and told him the truth – albeit distorted – that Teifion had almost blurted out what had happened, but not quite.

–

On three separate occasions Meriel was asked to advise on buying a house. Geoff's niece, Joyce, was getting married and, while they intended to rent two rooms to start, Joyce had discussed the possibility of buying a place of their own with Geoff and Connie. They sent her to Badgers Brook to talk to Meriel. Kitty and Bob also sent someone to her for guidance before going to Dexter's to see what houses were available to rent or buy. Meriel was able to show them their various choices, work out general costs and promised further help if they needed it. She also valued the properties they had seen and recommended a price on which to begin their negotiations. A third person called to explain that he wanted to sell his mother's house and buy something larger. Business seemed to be coming to her and she wondered idly how she could benefit.

There were few evenings when there were no knocks on the door; people continued to call for the most feeble excuses and stay for a while. A stranger called one day, having heard of her reputation, and said they wanted to sell their house as they were moving to London. Meriel loved the business of property deals and she offered to help but couldn't bring herself to suggest they went to George Dexter. 'Come back tomorrow and I'll see what I can arrange,' she said, without an idea of what she was going to do.

She was still making notes on all property for sale or to rent in the area, mainly out of habit, and the following morning she was surprised to notice a house with a shop front that she hadn't seen before. It was sadly neglected and had obviously been empty for some time. She went to the butcher next door to ask who owned it and walked around the outside. There was a small front garden, and its overgrown privet – once a neat edge to the property – had recently been cut back to reveal the property of which she had not previously been aware.

A feeling of excitement filled her as she began to see possibilities. Lucy's words, about it being a pity they couldn't be their own boss, burst out from the back of her mind. She discovered the name of the owner and went at once to see him. That evening she and Lucy went to have a look.

The dampness hit them like a blow as they opened the door and stepped inside. Oddments of linoleum covered the wooden floor and wallpaper was slowly leaving the walls. The woodwork was all dark brown and the windows were streaked with dirt, reducing the light to an eerie gloom.

An examination of the floor suggested that once the floor covers had been discarded the place might dry out satisfactorily. She thought the place suffered mainly from the lack of fresh air blowing through. It had probably been closed up for years. She climbed into the loft and examined the beams and slates with a torch she had brought. It all appeared to be remarkably sound. They struggled to look outside where the garden was seriously overgrown.

'What d'you think, Lucy?' she asked, her blue eyes glowing with excitement in her dirt-smudged face.

'You mean take it? Live here?'

'No, I mean you and I could open our own business here, be our own boss. What d'you think?'

Lucy laughed, convinced her friend was joking.

'I'm serious, Lucy. I think we could make a success of it, and it's very cheap because it's been empty for so long.'

'But I don't know anything about business, I've done nothing except work in the hairdresser's shop. And Jennie doesn't even let me deal with the books. How can you even consider me as your partner?'

'We get on well together and you're very bright, quick to understand, interested in anything I say. Most importantly you're very good with people. I know we can make a success of things.'

'What would I do?'

'Everything I do. We'll deal with clients, value property, plan advertising, do everything together. I don't just want you as a drudge to do the boring bits. I know we'd make a good team. Come on, what do you say?'

'It's very exciting. But I'd be afraid of letting you down.'

'Impossible.'

They discussed the idea for a while and Lucy became more and more excited. 'Something is telling me this is right for us,' she said. 'The shop appearing when we need it, the people coming to you for advice, my restlessness—'

'That's how I feel, that this was meant for us.'

'I was saving up for when Gerald and I were married, I'll willingly offer all I have.' They discussed finances for a while, each honest in their commitment. 'But isn't there a lot of work to do before we can make plans?' Lucy asked. 'We don't just open the shop and sit there smiling, hoping someone will come in.'

'In the last half an hour my plans have been made! In fact I can find us several clients straight away. It's up to you whether you want to take a chance on me.'

'The mess? The damp? The forest that was once a garden?'

'It looks awful but the work is superficial. A builder and a decorator could make it liveable in a few weeks. Lighting fires will help dry it out. All it needs is a bit of love. We could lease the rest of the house eventually, that will provide a small income to help us while we get established.'

Lucy hugged her, aware that the moment was an important one.

'Well?' Meriel urged.

'Well, a week's notice should suffice, so I'll say nothing until it's ours! Oh Meriel, it sounds wonderful. Are you sure I'm the one to help you?'

'Absolutely sure.' She hesitated then added, 'There is one thing I'd like to do, ask my father to come and look at it. He won't change my mind,' she added hurriedly. 'But he'd help us decide on the work that's needed. He might have a few ideas about how we arrange the office, that sort of thing.'

'I agree. You'll have to tell him you lost your job though.'

'I suppose I should. We'll see. Could I just suggest that I sacked them rather than they sacked me?'

'Tell him the truth, it's always best,' Lucy advised.

They spent several hours in the telephone box on the lane, arranging an appointment to view, making an appointment with the bank manager, and a brief call to tell Meriel's parents what they were planning.

'Write everything down,' Walter told her. 'I want to look at your ideas and assessments before I see the place. From what you've told me I already believe you two can make a success of this, so don't worry that I'm going to look at it and try to discourage you.'

He laughed then as Lucy, who was also listening, whispered, 'Fat chance.'

'All right, I know you too well to believe I could stop you. You're too much your father's daughter for me even to try and change your mind once it's made up.'

Meriel and Lucy went back to Badgers Brook filled with excitement to write down their plans. Meriel wrote to her father, Lucy helping to compose the letter. Two days later his reply arrived, promising to come and inspect the property, which was at 43 Forge Street. He dealt with the purchase and managed to get a small reduction and he also arranged for quotes from builders and decorators. He promised them a typewriter, some office files, a desk and a couple of chairs.

Lucy was thrilled. It became impossible to keep the news to herself and, just before the deal was complete, it burst out of her when her ex-friend, Jennie, now her boss, came in to collect the day book with its appointments and money.

'You're leaving us?' Jennie said, in surprise. 'But why? I thought you were happy here?'

'I'm going in to business, a partnership with someone called Meriel Evans, isn't it amazing?'

'Meriel Evans, isn't she a customer?'

'Yes, it's how we met and became friends.'

Jennie frowned. 'I remember now, she was sacked for dishonesty wasn't she?'

'No she wasn't! That woman told lies and I know why but I can't tell you!'

'What d'you mean, Lucy? I'm your friend, you can tell me anything,' Jennie coaxed.

'Not this, I can't. Just remember that Meriel isn't dishonest but Mrs George Dexter is!' She refused to say any more, being careful not to tell her the full story or explain exactly what they were planning. She suspected that George Dexter would try to prevent it if he heard rumours. 'So I'll be leaving towards the end of February. That will give you plenty of time to find my replacement.'

'Oh no. I can't have that. I'll make up your wages and you can leave right now!'

'What?' Lucy was aghast.

'I'll get your cards and money, if you'll just wait here.'

'Jennie! You can't do this.'

'Watch me! And don't think I won't be glad to find someone else. Mediocre you are, Lucy Calloway. You never had any flair.'

Ten minutes later Lucy was holding back tears as she hurried home through the drizzle of the early February evening, clutching a wage packet and her employment card. When she had thought of leaving she'd imagined it would be with a gift and a thank you, as she was showered with good wishes; not this, sent away with Jennie saying she was glad to be rid of her. She knew even more clearly how Meriel must have felt.

She told something of her new venture to her parents but declined to tell them any details. Again she was careful to avoid any hint of what they were planning getting to

George Dexter. If she had tried to explain the reason for their secrecy they would have accused her of everything from paranoia to watching too many mystery films.

When Meriel finally told her father exactly what had happened to her at Dexter's, he was very angry. 'I can understand the woman's alarm, but to say you were dishonest. That's criminal! In our business, going into people's homes, being trusted with their private finances, such lies could mean the end of a career! How could George Dexter had believed such a thing?'

'He probably didn't. He's just daft about his baby-doll wife,' Meriel said glumly. 'She's much younger than him and such a pretty thing to carry around like a badge of success, how could he risk losing her? Far better to let me go.'

'What d'you want me to do?'

'Nothing, Dadda. I'll build a business to rival his, that's the best way of getting revenge.'

'I'll go and see him.'

'No, please don't. No one will believe him anyway and already people are coming to me for advice, even though I'm not yet in business. You'll see, I'll beat him with my business prowess.'

Walter nodded, but he knew he couldn't let it rest. His daughter hadn't deserved George's treatment of her, whatever his reasons. George's hatred of him should be left in the past where it belonged, not be used to harm his daughter. How could the man hold on to his anger and resentment for so long?

When they had first looked at the property on Forge Street together he had instantly agreed with the purchase, even though it would leave Meriel with very little money. He recommended a small mortgage or taking a third partner. 'Then you'll have plenty to pay for the repairs and modernization,' he had explained.

'No, Dadda,' Meriel had insisted. 'It has to be just Lucy and me.'

'I can help in small ways, can't I?' he said as they peered through the white-washed windows. 'Print leaflets and pay for some advertising to get you started,' he said. Glancing at her he quickly added, 'That's all I mean to do, just a few small things to start you off. You two will soon be on the way. Just remember I'm always available if you have any problems.'

Leo came and helped them to clear the place of abandoned rubbish and help pull the wallpaper off the walls ready for decoration. He even used some of his time off to paint and paper the office enabling them to open at least a week sooner than planned.

They hadn't taken out a mortgage. Instead, Walter had lent them the money, assuring them it was strictly a loan and he looked forward to repayment when they could afford it. He also promised to only visit when invited.

'I feel sure they'll succeed,' he told Lynne. 'Our Meriel is a business woman through and through. I think she made a good choice taking on Lucy, too, even though I doubted it at first. She's reliable and very determined to do her best. I just hope they'll tell us if they have any problems.'

'I'm sure they will, darling. You and Meriel are as close as father and daughter can be.'

Now, as Meriel held the keys of the property in her hand, he hugged his daughter and Lucy, saying, 'Good luck, you two. I know this will be a success.'

-

Meriel and Lucy celebrated their acquisition by going to Gwennie Flint's and buying a fish and chip supper, rushing back to Badgers Brook with the hot, steaming packages like excited children.

'You know we'll be seriously broke, don't you?' Lucy said. 'Are you sure you wouldn't consider leaving here and living behind the shop?'

'No, this is where I live and where I'm happy. There hasn't been a day when I haven't run the last steps to get inside. I love this place and it's my haven when things go wrong.'

'Then I think one of us should work to bring in survival money. And,' she added before Meriel could disagree, 'I think it should be me, as you're the one with the knowledge.'

'Go on?'

'First of all, I would like to learn to drive, then I can be more use generally, but if I learned now, couldn't I do what you've been doing? Deliver flowers and groceries and all that?'

'It costs money and time. We don't have enough of either at present, but I do agree with you. Being able to drive is essential.'

–

George watched the progress with increasing anger. Of all people. Walter's daughter hadn't the right to muscle in on his town and challenge him on a business level. A part of him secretly wished he'd ignored Frieda's complaints and kept her on. She was good at what she did and her ideas for his office had already been implemented. But to please his adored wife he had sent her away and now she had the audacity to open up in opposition. Somehow she had to be stopped.

'Teifion,' he called to his son the following morning. 'What are we to do about Meriel Evans and this Lucy Calloway?'

'What can we do? She has the right to open an estate agency, although I doubt she'll make a success of it, competing with you is a bit optimistic.'

'You know she's stealing my clients? Going to see people and persuading them I'm not the best one to deal with their sale?'

Frieda came into the office, sobbing prettily. Beside her was a suitcase, which, George explained, was because this had upset her so much she was going to her sister's in Brighton for a rest.

'After all the lies she told and now trying to rob your father of his customers, you have to do something, Teifion,' she sobbed. 'It's your firm too and one day when your father retires, you'll find there's nothing to inherit unless she's stopped.'

'I wouldn't want to hurt her – or Lucy,' Teifion said anxiously.

Guessing the attraction, George said, 'Get them out of that office and you can offer Lucy a decent, secure job here, with you. You'd like that, wouldn't you, son?' As Teifion hesitated, he added coldly, 'Need I remind you that the alternative is for you to have nothing to inherit?'

Over the following days Meriel suffered a few setbacks. The builder called at the office and instead of being dressed to continue with the work he was doing, he asked for full payment.

'There's been a few rumours, like,' he said, embarrassment covering his face with a red glow. 'Some say I won't get my money and I can't risk that. Only a small family business mine is, see, and I can't take risks.'

She argued for a while then, anxious for the work to be completed, offered him a post-dated cheque on condition he finished two days sooner than promised. 'Well, thank you Mr George Dexter,' she said to an amused Lucy. 'I think we won that round.'

An order for a sign to be made to go over the shop front was returned by post together with a complaint about the time already wasted on the project. An enquiry led to them being told that the order had been cancelled by telephone. This time it was Lucy who dealt with it, insisting that the work was done and delivered without delay after being so unbusinesslike not checking such a change of plan with them.

Having heard of these irritations, which Meriel told him in a light-hearted way, pleased at the way the tables had been turned, Walter went to Cwm Derw but not to see Meriel. Unable to resist a moment longer, he went to see George Dexter.

The result of the conversation left George devastated. Walter hadn't tiptoed around but had told him he knew exactly what had happened to cause Frieda to ask Meriel to leave. At first George bluffed and refused to listen but as Walter added a clear description of the hotel and its location, he collapsed like a deflated balloon.

'You knew, didn't you?' Walter said.

George nodded.

'I didn't know for certain, but so many little details have crowded in and built a picture that I didn't want to see. What you've told me only confirms it. What shall I do? I love having her as my wife, being envied by my friends. The humiliation if she leaves me is something I can't imagine.'

'I'll say nothing, but you have to make sure you don't hurt my daughter any more than you already have. No rumours, except about her excellence, help her get started and we'll forget this conversation. Right?'

George nodded, then offered his hand. So when George heard that Lucy needed to learn to drive, he sent his son to teach her. That should keep Walter quiet, he thought, as his ever-willing son ran to do what he asked.

Meriel and Lucy were delighted at the way everything was falling into place for them, unaware of the hatred George Dexter was really feeling. George discussed the situation with Teifion and persuaded him that one serious effort would rid them of Meriel for good, leaving his way open to offer Lucy a job. He flattered his son, tried to turn him against Meriel and increase his sympathy for his stepmother. 'Just one more effort and it will all slip into place,' he promised. 'I know you can do it. You'll be head of the company and Lucy will be your partner. Working with Meriel has been useful. Just think, it will be perfect, son.' He watched the expressions passing over Teifion's face. Heavens above, the boy is so weak, he thought with disgust. How could I have produced a son like him? He piled on the persuasions, increasing his allowance, buying him a new and better car, promising him Lucy as a partner in the business. Then, as doubt still shadowed Teifion's face, he began to warn him of what might happen if he refused to do what he demanded. With his face white with anguish but fearful of upsetting his father any further, he agreed.

–

As Meriel predicted, Lucy took to driving without any difficulty. She really wanted and needed to drive, and, with her quick mind, the new skill was easily accomplished. She took over the deliveries from Meriel and in the first three weeks after they opened they had arranged the sale of two properties and the purchase of a third.

By the end of the first week they had their name over the door of their clean and smart new office, Evans and Calloway. Decorators had been working on the rest of the house and they hoped that they would soon be advertising for tenants.

'Shall we ask Dexter's to find us some tenants?' Lucy joked.

Meriel growled, then showed her friend the new advertising on which she had added, "Letting agents for houses, flats and rooms". 'Well, once the upstairs is finished we'll have at least one flat on our books,' she said.

Teifion had called regularly for Lucy, to give her driving lessons, but had never come in. Neither had he spoken to Meriel since the time they had met in the picture house. So it was a surprise when he came into their office when Lucy was out, and invited Meriel out for a meal.

'I'm grateful for the help you've given Lucy,' she said firmly, 'but there's nothing that would tempt me to spend even a minute with anyone called Dexter.' She opened the door to the street. 'Goodbye, thank you for calling.'

'Please, Meriel. None of this is my fault, and anyway, wasn't it a good thing, giving you the opportunity to start your own business?'

'You really think I'm glad your father sacked me and told lies about my honesty? If I'd been less well known he could have ruined my life. Go away!'

He didn't go. He sat down on the chair where clients sat and stared at her. He really was rather good-looking, she thought with a flash of weakness. His expression showed no sign of regret, in fact his brown eyes were shining with a hint of amusement. The little-boy-lost expression no longer there. 'Come on, say yes,' he coaxed. 'You know we could become friends. Just you and me, no George Dexter and no Walter Evans. You' – he said slowly – 'and me.' Meriel wondered cynically whether the idea had come from George, but curious, she went anyway.

They met at the edge of town. She parked her car and he drove her to a place a long way from Cwm Derw in a small village close to the sea in the Vale of Glamorgan. The fourteenth-century thatched building where they stopped surprised her. 'We're eating here?' she asked doubtfully.

'A drink first, then we'll go to the place where I've booked a table.'

The fascinating inn, with its history proudly told by the barman and displayed on posters on the ancient walls, interested her and they were late leaving. When they reached the restaurant the tables were all occupied but the waiter found them a place near the kitchen doors where people dashed in and out with steamily laden plates and wafting tempting smells towards them, but also those piled up with the messy dregs of meals. It was hardly a pleasant place in which to eat.

With little interest, wishing she hadn't come, Meriel chose a meat pie and smiling, Teifion asked for the same. She looked at him, puzzled by the look of nervousness. He seemed restless and edgy. Was he going to be a nuisance on the drive home? She wasn't too worried. She had success-fully discouraged more than one over-eager boyfriend in the past.

A bottle of wine finally appeared and Meriel sipped appreciatively. She was hardly aware of him topping up her glass as they talked easily, sharing details about their lives previous to their meeting. She wasn't aware of George sitting at another table watching and nodding encouragement to his son. It wasn't until she stood to leave that she realized she had enjoyed the wine a little too much. Looking around she noticed they were the last to leave.

Outside, the car park was deserted and very dark. Then Teifion began to fondle her in a way that alarmed her and she pushed him away. 'Stop that!' she shouted, and staggered as she walked away, her legs stiff and awkward, her leaden feet stumbling over the uneven ground. He opened the car door and held her close as he helped her in and again she pushed him away. This time he tripped over her leg and fell. Instead of apologizing, she giggled.

He got into the driving seat and said, 'Get in, you stupid woman, or I'll go without you.'

'Stupid woman?' she said with a frown. 'Who are you calling stupid?'

'You, and myself, for imagining you'd be good company. No wonder you steal from friends, you need it for alcohol. You disgust me!' he shouted.

To her utter disbelief he slammed the door and began to move off. He hesitated then, but behind her, he could see his father gesturing for him to leave. With a wide-eyed terrified glance towards her, he started to drive away. Meriel stared in disbelief, not aware of George and his friend getting into their car. 'Come back at once!' she yelled. The car reversed and the window rolled down. 'Phone your father,' Teifion said, his voice trembling with embarrassment. He threw a handful of coins towards her and drove away.

Meriel stared at the coins strewn at her feet, then at the now empty road. He was leaving her miles from home and she did not know where she was. Tearfully she telephoned her father.

–

Badgers Brook was silent when she went inside, seeming to disapprove of her behaviour. Walter was non-judgemental. 'Can you tell me how much you drank, love?'

'We had a bottle of wine and I can't remember Teifion topping it up but he must have done. But I couldn't have drunk that much, there was more than half a bottle left when we came away.'

'I think you might have had a Mickey Finn,' he told her, his eyes bright with anger. 'Something stronger added when you weren't looking. You could have been seriously hurt. Even if you'd got a lift or a taxi, you'd have had to drive the car back from the other side of town.' he added grimly. 'Was that to make sure no one saw you together? Or to make sure someone did? Whatever the reason, what he did could have resulted in a serious accident. It seems that George Dexter and his son haven't forgiven you for finding out Frieda's nasty little secret.' He knew that the hatred between himself and George went back a lot further than that, and seemed unlikely to end.

He helped her to her room and, leaving a candle burning on the landing windowsill in case she got out of bed in the night, he went down and lay on a couch.

He didn't know what to do. He'd agreed to say nothing about Frieda's secret 'other life' but this evening's behaviour negated any such promise. His darling daughter might have been seriously hurt. George's campaign of spite had to be stopped. It might have been Teifion spiking the drink while pretending friendship but the idea was almost certainly his father's.

Teifion wasn't capable of thinking out such a malicious idea, although his pathetic need to impress his father obviously made him willing to carry it out. 'Why, oh why had Meriel chosen Cwm Derw to settle?' he said aloud.

He waited until he heard Meriel get up and made a tray of tea, leaving it outside her room. 'All right, love? I'm just going out for a paper, I'll come back and see how you are, then we can go and collect the car.'

He went out, knocked on George's door and when George opened it he pushed him roughly inside and followed. 'Touch my daughter again and you'll regret it.'

George blustered and insisted he didn't understand, but Walter, although a successful businessman, had come up the hard way and he could have fought with the man and won, but he didn't. He simply warned him of the consequences if Meriel was harmed in any way, and from the look on his face, George understood.

'Call yourself a man? Causing distress to a young woman of twenty-two? Putting her in extreme danger?'

At the top of the stairs Teifion cringed with shame. What sort of a man was he, doing his father's dirty work, too afraid to refuse, trying to pretend to like it? How weak was he, allowing himself to be persuaded to do such a terrible thing?

He went to the office to offer to bring back Meriel's car, but saw it standing outside. With racing heart he went in and tried to apologize, but Meriel and Lucy threw him out, one each side of him, like a couple of crazy policemen. Feeling more embarrassed and miserable than ever before in his whole life, he stood there for an age, trying to decide on his next move.

Going back inside he asked Meriel the true reason behind his father's dislike of her. Meriel refused to tell him, but Lucy had no such qualms.

'He doesn't deserve protecting, after what he's done to you,' she said to her friend, and told Teifion exactly why Meriel had been told to leave.

'I can't tell you how ashamed I feel. How could I have been persuaded to do such a terrible thing? I've been so anxious to get my father's approval I've become a little mad, I think. He threatened to leave everything to Frieda, leave me penniless. I – I believed him and couldn't face it. I'm so ashamed, but also in an odd way I feel free of him. Please believe me, Meriel, when I promise I will never ever do anything so stupid or cruel again. I feel as though I've just woken up from a nightmare.'

Meriel and Lucy stared at him throughout his speech without a word. When he finally stopped, Lucy said brightly, 'Bye then. Close the door after you.'

At the door he paused. 'I can't expect you to forgive me, it stretches the imagination for someone my age to have acted so stupidly, but if I can ever do anything for you, anything at all, you only have to ask,' he said in a choking voice.

Neither girl replied.

Teifion went back to his father. 'Is it true?' he demanded, after repeating what Lucy had told him. He didn't need a reply, it was clear from his father's expression that he wasn't going to deny it. Two hours later he had taken a room in the guest house of Elsie and Ed Connors, and began looking for a job.

When Meriel learned of his leaving Dexter's she took no pleasure in the news. 'It's that stupid father of his,' she said to Lucy. 'How can he be so besotted with that woman he can treat me, a stranger, so badly and watch as his son walks away?'

Lucy sighed. 'Lucky Frieda. It must be good to be loved so much and treated as someone very special.'

'Love? Rubbish! George Dexter uses her like a status symbol, better than the latest Rolls Royce she is, making him feel a heck of a great guy. I don't think love comes into it at all.'

Lucy stared dreamily out of the window remembering how close she had once been to love, a home of her own and children. The damned war had lost her the only chance she'd ever have. 'If only Gerald had thought as much of me, we'd have married and I'd have a couple of children by now.'

'Why don't you look him up?'

'Too long ago.'

'You think he might be married? Do you know what happened to him?'

'Nothing much. I see his mother occasionally and apparently he went back to his job working with his father repairing motorbikes. And he still lives at home. Not very exciting, eh?'

'Not like you, running a business and… look out, pretend to be busy, there's someone coming in.'

Lucy began adding a few scribbles in her desk diary, so anyone looking would imagine they were doing better than they were. A young couple came in looking for a couple of rooms to rent.

'Yes, we can certainly help you with rooms, but we also have something far better. Will you follow me?' Happily, Lucy took them to see the flat above the shop, fingers crossed that they would manage the higher rent once they saw the clean and spacious, neatly furnished accommodation.

Lucy showed them around, dreamily describing how ideal the place was for newlyweds, in her mind seeing herself living there with the man in airforce uniform she had once loved so much.

They had a visitor later that morning. Leo called and invited both girls out to lunch. Not having seen him for a while, Meriel was aware for the first time of changes in the man she had known for so many years. He had always been neatly but poorly dressed, in clothes that were never a good fit. Second-hand or passed on from his father or someone's older brother, she had assumed. With his mother and three sisters bemoaning the shortage of clothing coupons, Meriel had guessed he had been too generous towards them and had shared his allowance with them.

He was good-looking in a schoolboy kind of way, his hair was mid brown, very straight and difficult to style, always falling across his eyes. There was a serious expression in his grey eyes and he had the earnestness of a pupil listening to a teacher when he was in conversation. She always believed he was really interested in everything she had to say.

Now, although that hadn't changed, his appearance had. Since clothes rationing ended the previous year he had begun to dress well. Today, he wore a pair of grey trousers and a good quality Harris tweed jacket. His shirt was immaculate and his shoes shone like glass.

He was attentive to them both, making sure they enjoyed the brief break from their work. Afterwards, Lucy said, 'You know I said it must be nice to be thought of as someone very special? Well that's how Leo thinks of you.'

'Ridiculous!' Meriel said at once. 'He still thinks of me as a child.'

'Not any more he doesn't!' Lucy was adamant.

Meriel laughed and shook her head but the thought remained with her for a long time. Teifion ashamed and wanting to make amends, and now Leo of all people noticing she was a woman. Whatever next?

Three

Lucy and Meriel allowed themselves one day off a week, to do whatever they wanted to. Meriel sometimes went home to see her parents, but Lucy usually travelled on buses, through the towns and villages within a few miles of Cwm Derw, wandering around, her mind on houses, her eyes glancing at any property bearing a 'For Sale' notice. These were usually home-made and she would often knock and introduce herself and occasionally find them a new client.

She also placed advertisements in shop windows and on village notice boards. She found when she went again these had usually been taken down even though she had paid the threepence a week for their display. George Dexter, she guessed, as she replaced them and requested they stayed.

Although she still lived at home, Lucy didn't see much of her family. When she was not at the pictures or out with Meriel on trips looking for prospective clients she spent the evenings in her room, reading, or listening to her gramophone, which she had bought at a house sale she and Meriel had attended. She avoided the rest of the family, only going downstairs to make a cup of tea or cocoa.

It was a long time since she felt a part of the household, even her name was different from the others. She paid her weekly contribution by leaving the money on the mantelpiece where it would be picked up, presumably by her stepfather who managed the household's expenses, some time when she was not there to see.

She scarcely remembered her father; her memories were not of a man, moving and talking and laughing, but as a white face on a white pillow, huge eyes that stared into space but seemed not to see. She had vague images of him lying in bed in the darkened front room, where the curtains were almost fully closed, covered except for his pale face, quiet and with an aura of sickness and indifference that discouraged her from staying with him.

She remembered most clearly the day he had died; the house hushed and darkened, whispering people coming and going, filling the house with mourners dressed in black, the house smelling of flowers and mothballs. She had been just seven when he died and her mother had hastily married Douglas Lloyd.

She and Douglas did not get along. He had walked into the house and had expected to take over the running of the place, be masterful. Her mother had loved it and Lucy had rebelled. Although until then a mild-mannered child, her protests were loud and distressing and completely unquenchable. After a while, with her mother and her new stepfather delighting in the prospect of a new child, she gave up trying and, left to her own devices, she had slipped out of the family circle, a lodger no one particularly wanted. Three babies arrived and Lucy felt like a complete outsider from the sound of her stepsister's first cry. Three sisters and all too far away in age to be her friend, and to make things worse, she had been expected to look after them while her mother and stepfather went out most evenings.

She wasn't resentful, she quite liked her three step-sisters, Dawn, Diana and Deborah, but she did feel sad and lonely in spite of the full household. Douglas, her stepfather, rarely spoke to her, calling her 'the girl' when he referred to her, which was rare. She stayed because there was nowhere else to go, her wage as a hairdresser was too small to allow her to rent a place of her own. Her one attempt to share, with Jennie James, had been a failure.

None of her stepsisters were married either. The devotion of her mother and the over-zealous protection of their father made it impossible for them to meet and make friends with people of their own age. Neither parent had felt so protective towards her and, although it had caused some dismay in the past, Lucy was now grateful for their indifference – which had given her freedom – of a sort.

The sad truth was that she longed for someone to share her life. Freedom was all very well, but it could mean loneliness as well. There was no one to whom she was number one, no one hugged her and talked to her about their intimate dreams and ambitions. She had dreams but they lacked excitement with no one to share them. Although she lived in a house with five other people and was never far away from another human being, she always saw herself as sitting outside a circle, looking in, invisible to the rest.

She still thought about Gerald Cook and wondered how they would be if they should meet again. Would he smile and show pleasure? Or back away, afraid of her expecting too much? Foolishly she sometimes practised how she would smile at him, act casually, walk on as though he was of no consequence to her, a person left far away in her past and almost forgotten. Then there were other moments when she imagined seeing him and running towards him to be swept up in his arms and… she fought away those dreams. They only led to greater loneliness. Even when they had been engaged, Gerald had never been demonstrative, more afraid of what people would think than willing to show his feelings.

She knew that she had been fortunate meeting Meriel and being offered a share of a new business which she was already enjoying more than anything else she had done. She had only one regret at becoming Meriel's partner; it was now impossible for her to leave home and find a place of her own. Her income was seriously reduced and her savings were gone. She managed on the little she earned with her deliveries, although much of that was pooled with the small amount of commission they managed to collect.

As she walked towards the bus stop to return to Cwm Derw she thought again of Gerald, whom she had once dreamed of marrying and around whom her thoughts had once been centred to the exclusion of everything else. She no longer suffered the miseries of rejection, his interest had faded slowly and the realization he no longer wanted her had been less painful that it might otherwise have been. Her regrets were not for Gerald the man, but for what he had represented. She grieved for the home and children they might have had.

She wondered vaguely if he had changed and whether he had found that special someone. Her communication with Gerald's family had been reduced to a Christmas card but she knew that if she hadn't sent one, they wouldn't have bothered to send one to her. Best to let it go, she decided. It's 1950 and it's 'off with the old' even if there's no 'on with the new'.

She was walking along a country road and stopped suddenly, all thoughts of Gerald and his family fading as she saw a man struggling to erect a For Sale board. She pulled a leaflet from her bag, silently thanking Meriel's father for providing them, and walked across to him.

The man was pleasant enough but he shook his head at the mention of business.

'It's the Lord's day and not a time for talking about money matters,' he said. He spoke kindly as though presuming she must have simply forgotten it was a Sunday. 'I wouldn't even be fixing this today if it hadn't fallen. I worried it could have caused an accident, leaning out over the hedge.'

'Can I call and see you tomorrow?' she asked. 'It's just that we have a few people on our books looking for a house and we might be able to arrange a sale quite quickly.'

Though still polite, he raised a hand like a barrier to her words, and said, 'Tomorrow, young lady, not on the Lord's day.'

'Thank you.' She smiled at him and replaced the leaflet in her bag. 'May I come tomorrow morning and discuss ways we can help, and—?'

'I will pleased to talk to you – tomorrow.'

'Tomorrow,' she said, backing away. She turned and smiled at him again before disappearing around the corner.

The man continued with his work. He was tall and alarmingly thin, dressed formally in a navy suit and white shirt. His neat collar and tie seemed too large for his skinny neck. On his head he wore a rather battered homburg, he was hardly dressed for fixing signs, Sunday or not. Lucy was grinning as she got on to the bus for Cwm Derw. He was an intriguing character with kindly blue eyes and

63

an expression of resignation and tolerance as though the world had shown him its worst and he'd expected no less. She looked forward to the following day's visit.

It was almost three o'clock and the weather had been overcast all day giving the impression it was later than it actually was. A chill March wind gusted occasionally cutting through her clothes. She didn't go home; in spite of the gloom it was too early to incarcerate herself in her room. Instead she walked down the lane to Badgers Brook where she found Meriel and several friends enjoying tea and home-made biscuits, sitting around the log fire – a pleasant sight on such a dull afternoon.

To her surprise, she saw Teifion, standing near the window. He looked ill at ease and was obviously unwelcome. She presumed he had come to apologize to Meriel again, for the way he had abandoned her a long way from home. It was clear that Meriel did not intend to listen. He stood away from the others who seemed to have gathered closer together to isolate him further.

People immediately shuffled around to make room for her. Kitty Jennings, Meriel's immediate neighbour, went to the kitchen and returned with a cup of tea, and a tin of biscuits was passed around. The conversation passed briefly to what Lucy had been doing but she didn't mention the prospect she had half arranged for the following day. Teifion Dexter might be carrying a flag of truce but she didn't trust him for a moment. 'I've something exciting to tell you later,' she whispered to Meriel.

Teifion watched as Meriel mouthed the words, 'A prospect?' Lucy nodded excitedly. 'Never! Not on a Sunday?'

Teifion left soon after but Meriel didn't get up and didn't show him to the door. 'He hadn't been invited,' she explained to Lucy, 'he isn't welcome and doesn't deserve my usual politeness.'

'Came to apologize – again – had he?'

'I don't know for certain, but from the little he said I think my father must have gone to see George Dexter. I didn't want him to, but if it means he'll leave us alone from now on I won't complain.'

–

Teifion drove home with anger in his heart. He had left home because of the stupid way he had done what his father had asked of him, left his home and his job, and after all that, Meriel's refusal to forgive him seemed unfair. His regrets were genuine and she ought to understand that.

Foolishly he had imagined being welcomed into the friendly group at Badgers Brook and being accepted for the way he had changed. After walking away from his home, family and his safe, secure occupation, he had felt a rosy glow, but Meriel's attitude had washed that feeling away and left him feeling only humiliation and growing anger. He was sorry for what he had done, so how dare she behave so meanly.

He thought of the word 'prospect' that had passed between Lucy and Meriel and after a moment of hesitation, decided that if she wasn't going to allow him the chance to apologize and try to explain, then it wouldn't do any harm to please his father and take the client from them. After all, a prospect was just that, a possibility, until an agreement had been reached.

–

Meriel and Lucy opened the office the next morning and at ten o'clock Lucy set off by bus, leaving the car in case Meriel needed it, to find the man who had been so adamant that the Lord's day was not a day for discussing business, hoping he would be willing to listen to her.

A few moments later, Teifion followed the bus by car, staying well back in case Lucy saw him, and catching up only when the bus had been lost to his sight for a while. He saw her hesitate beside a hedge with a home-made sign and walk up the path. He cruised past and parked close by. She came out about fifteen minutes later and Teifion saw she was smiling. He allowed a few minutes to pass then knocked on the door.

He would never again be persuaded to act as unkindly as before, his father's hold over him had been broken that evening, but he wasn't averse to stealing their sale. Hardly recognizable, but still deep within him was his need for his father's approval.

–

When Lucy learned from Meriel a couple of days later that the sale had been given to Ace, George Dexter's agency, she was angry. 'If you go and talk to him, reminding him that he broke his word, and that's a kind of dishonesty, we might still retrieve it,' Meriel said. 'Surely that's worse than discussing business on a Sunday?'

Lucy went there straight away, leaving Meriel in the office, and knocked loudly on the door. When the door opened she faced a small, red-haired woman.

It took some persuading to be allowed inside but eventually the woman told her the reason her husband had changed his mind was because the second caller had explained that besides being an estate agent, his father was also an experienced auctioneer.

'My partner has been dealing with auctions for several years,' Lucy assured her. 'She has had training in all aspects of the property business. But why do you want to auction the property? There's a risk we might not reach the valuation we agree on.'

'It's all the stuff in the shed,' the woman explained. She led Lucy through the house and opened the door of a large brick building. 'My husband is often given things to sell to raise money for our church and he's been neglectful and allowed it to build up.'

That was an understatement, Lucy thought, as she gazed at the jumble of furniture, toys and odds-and-ends that were stacked untidily.

'If you will allow us to sort through and label everything, maybe discard a few things, clean and repair others, I'm sure we could make quite a few extra pounds for your church with this.'

'Really? The other man, Mr – er—' she queried.

'Mr Dexter?' Lucy offered.

'Yes, that was his name. Mr Teifion Dexter. He thought it best to empty the shed and discard the items to make the property more attractive.'

'Did he! And of course he offered to dispose of them for you.'

'Well, yes.'

'He'd sell it and keep the money he raised.' Lucy said no more but her words were convincing because she believed them to be true. With the larger auctions Dexter's could have added the best of the furniture, and many of the oddments would also have found buyers.

'I'll talk to my husband when he gets home,' the woman promised.

Lucy thanked her, gave her their business card and left with her fingers crossed.

'There were all sorts of things in that shed,' she told Meriel when she got back to the office. 'Besides furniture, there were boxes of china, toys and even a hair drier, would you believe.'

'A hair drier?'

'And other things connected with hairdressing.'

'You'd be able to value that stuff. I do hope they give us a chance to go through it all, goodness knows what we'll find. Enough to make them a bit more money for certain. Just imagine, our first auction! It's so exciting.'

'I might buy the drier myself,' Lucy said thoughtfully.

'What on earth for? You aren't thinking of leaving me, are you?' Meriel was alarmed.

'Not leave, but if I used the back room, I might be able to earn more money than I do making deliveries and I could do the office work in between customers.' She laughed. 'Very popular we'll be, first stealing work from Dexter's and then me taking clients from Jennie James's hairdresser's shop!'

'We are rather desperate,' Meriel admitted. 'There isn't really enough work to go round, but I don't intend to give up.'

'Let's see what we find in the shed,' Lucy replied. She frowned as she thought about it. 'Sets and cutting only, no perms, that wouldn't be too difficult to organize – if we get the drier, and if it works.'

It was Lucy who saw the man they now knew as Mr William Roberts-Price, when he called to tell them they would be dealing with the house sale.

'I had a word with the young man at Dexter's, and his father, and I'm satisfied that they were in the wrong trying to cheat you out of my sale and also that I was wrong to be so easily convinced.' He sat at the desk opposite Lucy and they were filling out the details, with Lucy making a list of things she needed to do when he broke off in the middle of a sentence and started over her shoulder. She turned and saw he was staring at Meriel. 'Oh, I don't think you've met my partner,' she said, curious at his nervous stuttering as she introduced Meriel. He seemed anxious to leave, and the information was quickly taken and he hurried from the office with hardly another glance at Meriel who had come to stand beside Lucy at the desk.

'Strange man,' Lucy said.

Meriel shrugged. 'So long as he allows us to act for him I don't care, do you?'

'He changed as soon as he saw you, Meriel. I wonder why?'

'Oh, perhaps I remind him of someone. I certainly don't know him.'

They began at once to make the initial preparations for the house sale. A letter was delivered by a rather dowdy young woman who looked about twenty, later that afternoon, telling them they could clear the contents of the shed the following day.

'Wonderful,' Meriel said. 'But how are we to man the office and go to the shed to clear the junk? That job will need both of us.'

Kitty Jennings, Meriel's neighbour at Badgers Brook, offered a solution. That evening, when they talked about the problem they faced she at once offered to sit there and take messages. 'Bob will come as well and between us we should be able to cope,' she said cheerfully. 'Bit of fun it'll be, won't it, Bob, love?' And so it was arranged.

Early the following morning, with Lucy driving and armed with notepads, pencils, measuring tape, dusters and polishing cloths, they set off. The house appeared to be empty and after knocking a few times they opened the door and went inside. Everything was neat and clean but rather sparse. The furniture was functional, mostly built-in wardrobes and cupboards, which on examination contained only a few clothes and those were very old-fashioned. There were very few ornaments, and no personal items in sight.

'More like a house of correction than a home,' Lucy whispered. They dealt with the measurements and assessment of the house first, feeling a sadness enveloping them so they were relieved to escape to the rather more cheerful muddle in the shed. They had brought a flask of tea and they sat in the tidy garden beside the precisely clipped trees and mown grass with its straight edging and wondered at the lack of flowers.

'They don't believe life is to be enjoyed, do they?' It was Meriel's turn to whisper. There was something about the place that forbade inappropriate laughter.

Fortunately the day was dry so they dragged out the contents of the shed into the garden and listed everything of value. Some of the furniture was of good quality and they discussed the prices they might bring with enthusiasm. The boxes containing china were weakened by damp and in danger of losing their contents so the breakables were taken out and placed in some empty tea chests.

Lucy had been right about the hairdressing equipment and she recognized some of it as having come from the hairdresser's where she had worked.

'Jennie must have bought new, but these seem to be in reasonable condition. But I'd have to have them checked and overhauled,' she said happily.

They were just beginning to replace the sorted items back into the shed, having discarded a lot of broken and unsaleable pieces, when an angry voice called over to them.

'What d'you think you're doing? I'm going to call the police!' A young man in army uniform ran towards them and glared at the stuff spread over the garden.

'It's all right, Mr and Mrs Roberts-Price know we're here.'

'We're agents, selling the house and we're sorting out the contents of the shed,' Lucy added, as the man came close, glaring at them both.

'Stay there and don't move,' the young man warned. He had red hair and his face was almost the same colour, as anger brought heat to his skin.

Meriel wasn't having that. 'We will not! My partner and I will continue with our work. We don't have time to play games!' Turning her back on the man she carried a smoker's chair back into the shed and rather more reluct-antly, Lucy began to lift an oak flower-pot stand.

'I said stop what you're doing!'

'Please stop shouting,' Meriel said with a sigh. 'Now, Lucy, d'you think we could manage this oak hall stand between us?'

The man ran off and came back with a notebook. 'I demand to know who you are and what you're doing in my parents' house.'

Meriel pointed to her handbag. 'Pass me my bag and I'll give you our card,' she said snapping her fingers, and obediently the man passed her the bag. She thrust a card at him and continued to repack the shed.

'Where is my father?'

'I have no idea, now please stop interrupting us or we'll be here till midnight.'

By this time Lucy could hardly lift a thing, her muscles useless as she struggled to hold back her laughter, and when the man finally went into the house they both collapsed and leant against the walls of the shed, helpless in the throws of wild giggles.

'Meriel, how can you talk to a stranger like that?' Lucy gasped. 'The poor man didn't know how to deal with you.'

'You've heard of attack being the best form of defence? That was it in action! My father taught me other things besides selling houses, you know!'

They had already finished sorting and repacking the shed and Meriel was in the car when Mrs Roberts-Price returned. Lucy was standing beside the abandoned rubbish and checking through the list she had made. The young man came over with his mother to speak to Lucy and, rather embarrassed, explained that he'd been away on manoeuvres and out of touch with his parents for a few weeks and didn't know about the sale.

After introducing himself as Noah, and adding that he had a sister called Martha, Lucy smilingly assured him they weren't upset, trying not to laugh again as she remembered the peremptory way Meriel had dealt with his protest. 'We'll prepare a list of the items we think we can sell and pop it in the post this evening. You'll get it tomorrow,' she assured them, before joining Meriel.

'Thank goodness Mrs Roberts-Price arrived or we might have been locked in the shed!' Lucy said to her friend, as she started the engine. 'Could we arrange the sale here, in their garden, d'you think?' she suggested as they drove away. Meriel nodded.

'Better than trying to move it, and hiring a hall would take some of the profit. Yes, that's a good idea, Lucy. We'll sell it on site, and that bossy brat of theirs can do the carrying!'

Kitty and Bob had managed well, dealing with a few enquiries and even arranging an appointment for a prospective buyer to call the following morning.

'It was fun,' Kitty told them, 'and any time you need to be out of the office, just ask and we'll help, won't we, Bob?'

'We certainly will, and if you like I'll make you a display board for that wall, in case you get a lot more clients. Best to be prepared, eh?'

They stayed late that evening, arranging lists of the items they had found in the shed, then typing them out with a carbon copy for their file. When the letter was posted they sat for a while and went through their achievements so far. There had been very few sales.

'The truth is, there isn't the work for two estate agents in this small town,' Meriel said. 'Dexter's have been here so long they're the automatic choice for the locals. I don't know what we can do to change that.'

'If only we could let people know that they cheat.'

'That's difficult ground, Lucy. It's an impossible thing to prove, following you and persuading the man to change from us to Dexter's, and possibly intending to cheat the Roberts-Prices out of the sale of the shed contents. Who would believe us?'

'The best thing we can do is impress people with our expertise. Sell the Roberts-Price's house quickly and make them some extra money from the auction. News gets around fast, specially in a small town like Cwm Derw.'

Fortunately someone came into the office the following day and after looking around the Roberts-Prices' house, and being assured that the shed would be cleared of the contents, they agreed to buy.

Leo Hopkins came to the auction and bought a hall stand for a little more than they hoped to get. 'It's a birthday present for my mother,' he told Meriel. Most of the stuff went that day and later, Elsie and Ed Connor, who owned the bed and breakfast establishment, bought all the china and some of the other items that were left. Lucy acquired the hair drier and a box of sundry items in case she decided to start hairdressing and Meriel bought even more chairs and a side table for Badgers Brook.

'Not more chairs?' Lucy laughed. 'How many visitors do you expect?'

'Lots!' was the reply. 'It's that sort of house.'

–

George Dexter drove past the house soon after the sale had ended. He stopped and looked back at the house and, as he was parked, he was overtaken by a stream of cyclists. Eight in all, each bicycle loaded with pannier bags and saddle bags, obviously touring the area. They stopped and one of the men walked back to ask him if there was a place where they might spend the night. 'We lost our way, then there were a couple of punctures so we're a long way from the youth hostel where we intended to stay,' he explained. 'We all have sleeping bags, it's just a bit of someone's floor we need.'

George mentioned Elsie and Ed Connor's Bed and Breakfast. 'But I don't know whether they'll have room for all of you,' he said doubtfully. Then he pointed to the recently sold house. 'Religious family in there, they wouldn't turn you away I'm sure. Shall I knock and ask them for you?'

The young man in uniform opened the door but he shook his head. 'We've no room, I'm afraid. There are only three bedrooms and they're in use.'

George returned to the cyclists and shrugged. Then a thought occurred to him and he smiled. 'I've just thought of the perfect place.' He directed them all to Badgers Brook. 'There's a woman there who is sure to help. Good Samaritan she is. She won't turn you away.'

When Lucy saw the group of people walking up the path carrying assorted bags she called Meriel. She opened the door to their knock, listened to their request and called Meriel again, this time more urgently.

Meriel shook her head, but a reminder, that the day was ending and they were still a long way from their original destination made her give in. 'But I have to ask my landlord before I let you come in,' she said.

Lucy offered to go and see Geoff. She grabbed her coat and after making Meriel promise she wouldn't let the eight strangers inside before she returned, she hurried off up the lane towards the town. She fortunately found Geoff and Connie at home.

Geoff had no complaints, but he insisted on coming to see them and make sure Meriel would be safe with the house full of strangers. 'I'll stay with her tonight,' Lucy said at once. 'I'll call to tell Mam I won't be home tonight, and go straight back.'

Geoff gave her a lift in the firm's van, firstly to her parents where she left a note and gathered a few clothes, then back to Badgers Brook. Kitty and Bob were there as well as Stella and Colin from the post office. Meriel laughed. 'What a place this is for spreading news! I wonder who else will turn up to help?'

'Lucky you bought all those chairs,' Geoff said.

Lucy went straight to the kitchen to start making the inevitable tea and standing at the sink was Gerald Cook.

'Good heavens! Lucy! Fancy meeting you. How are you? Great to see you. What are you doing here, I thought you'd still be with your mam and dad? Still at the hairdresser's?' He was embarrassed and the questions came in a breathless stream.

'Hello, Gerald.' His unexpected appearance startled her, and a shyness overcame her, but newly acquired confidence forbade her showing it. Her response was not what he would have expected. 'You're still with *your* mam and dad, I suppose,' she replied with a sweet smile. 'Never the adventurous kind, were you?'

'I'm only there to help out. I'd have been off long ago if Dad hadn't needed my help. The garden and the bicycle repairs. That's how I joined this club.'

'Going to start a new life in Australia, weren't you? Or was it America?' Her heart was racing and she wondered where her sarcasm came from. She had been without him too long for resentment, in fact she was amused at his reaction to her casual greeting. She had hardly felt a tinge of a thrill when she saw him standing there. Whatever she had once felt, he was now a rather boring part of a previous life and no longer had the ability to hurt her.

'What are you doing now?' he asked, moving aside for her to refill the kettle.

'Oh, I'm working for an estate agent,' she replied.

Meriel came into the room then and, after a brief and very casual introduction, she said, 'Lucy is too modest. We are partners in a successful and fast-growing estate agency – Evans and Calloway.'

'Really? I'm impressed, Lucy. Where did you learn this new skill?'

Lucy was about to say she was still learning, but again that confidence and the need to impress changed her mind. 'I'm a business woman, Gerald,' she said with a casual shrug. 'It's something that comes naturally to me.'

'That's right,' Meriel added. 'Lucy is amazingly clever. She'd succeed at any business she undertook, luckily for me, she chose this one.'

They both walked away from him then, carrying trays holding cups and a milk jug into the living room where people were sprawled around the floor. 'Shout when the kettle boils, will you?' Lucy called back. After all the months of waiting for him to make up his mind, followed by the disappointment of their parting, she felt like a new woman and she was enjoying it.

She stayed the night with Meriel but neither of them slept well. With so many strangers in the house they couldn't relax. They woke early the following morning and tiptoed their way through the recumbent bodies covering the floor. One of them rose and waved sleepily. 'Morning, Gerald,' Lucy whispered. He followed them into the kitchen and helped set a tray for three and when Meriel said they would need to go to the baker for bread, to provide a breakfast before the cyclists set off on the next leg of their journey, he at once offered to go.

During the night Lucy had explained about the engagement and its end and thanked Meriel for supporting her as she had boasted in a very uncharacteristic way, to let Gerald know he hadn't been the cause of prolonged grief. While he set off on his cycle with a couple of emptied pannier bags to collect the loaves they talked some more.

'I suppose I was unfair when I made veiled criticism about his still living at home. I'm still with my parents and hating it.'

'Then leave.' Meriel smiled. 'You're here more than you are at home, what you give your mother each week will go into the pot and we would be slightly better off. The rent is cheap and the gas bill is about all we'd have to find. Wood keeps the fire going and we can do some of the cooking on that to save gas.'

Lucy's eyes glowed as she stared at her friend. 'I expected to live at home until I married, but that's less and less likely and I could be there for the rest of my life, playing second fiddle to my three stepsisters. But—'

'Come on, Lucy, you trusted me enough to leave the hairdressers where you'd worked since you left school. You might as well share Badgers Brook, you're hardly at home apart from sleeping and it is the most peaceful place you can imagine. The bird song is your wake-up call and the night sounds of gently rustling leaves and owls and foxes become a part of wonderful dreams.'

There were stirrings from the living room and at the same time the back door opened as Gerald returned with the bread. Lucy gave Meriel a hug, then held out a hand. 'Meet your new lodger, unless Geoff has any objection.'

'I'll ask Geoff the moment I see him,' Meriel called, as she ran to relieve Gerald of the freshly baked, delicious smelling loaves.

'If he's the man who came last night,' Gerald called, having heard the last few words, 'you can ask him in less than a minute, he's on his way.'

Meriel opened the back door and heard the double slam of van doors, then Geoff came up the path followed by his wife, Connie, who was carrying her inevitable picnic basket.

'Just in time for breakfast,' Meriel called.

Geoff and Connie willingly agreed to Lucy sharing the house, and with the departure of the cyclists and the bustle of moving furniture to prepare for Lucy's move, the day had the air of celebration. 'Like everything we do in this friendly house,' Meriel explained happily.

–

A man called at the office the following morning and, glancing around, asked, 'Oh, I see the men are out of the office. When can I speak to the proprietor, please?' To Meriel's surprise, Lucy's voice changed.

'Would that be Mr Evans or Mr Calloway you'd be wanting, sir?' Lucy asked in a slightly stupid tone.

'Either, as long as it's a man who knows what he's doing.' He spoke with a hint of irritation.

'He? Oh sorry, sir, we can't help you there. There's only us two women and between us we don't make up the quality of one man.'

Alarmed at the possibility of losing a client, Meriel stood up and offered her hand. 'I'm Meriel Evans and this is my partner, Lucy Calloway.'

The man threw back his head and laughed. 'I'm sorry, but it's unusual to find two pretty women dealing with house sales.'

'I'm sorry too,' Lucy said. 'I'm usually very sensible, I don't know what came over me, except that it's a wonderful day, I've just found the perfect place to live and I found the opportunity irresistible.'

He sat at the desk and explained. 'I'm looking for a business premises, a workroom at the back and small shop at the front, in a place where there are lots of passers-by. Can you help?' he asked. He kept staring at Meriel until she felt a slight glow in her cheeks, he really was rather charming. She pushed back her long auburn hair and was thankful Lucy had trimmed and washed it the previous evening. It was a great advantage having a hairdresser as a friend!

Meriel pretended to look through the papers for something suitable but Lucy admitted there was nothing on their books that moment. 'We'll make a note of your name and address and let you know the moment something comes in,' she said.

'In that case, can I take you two ladies to lunch – just to make sure you keep me in mind,' he added, staring at Meriel with interest brightening his pale hazel eyes. Meriel had no hesitation in accepting.

Although he was talking to both of them his gaze hardly left Meriel's face through most of the hour. Her greatest disappointment was when he referred to his wife, but she later gathered that the wife had left and a divorce was imminent. The day was certainly looking up.

The reason for his enquiry about premises was unclear. The friend who was the possible client would call them, they were told, and later, when they talked about the man, they both admitted that the explanation was as vague as the man was handsome. 'And worst of all,' Meriel added, 'was that he didn't give us his name or address. Which was odd because we both asked several times and offered him a pad on which to write it but he avoided doing so. Who on earth was he? And more importantly, what did he want with us?'

George Dexter had learned from Teifion that the house of the Roberts-Price family contained some valuable old pieces and he wanted to have a look. They might be persuaded to sell a few and if they did he wanted to be the recipient. Using the excuse of the stranded cyclists he called the following morning and told them a place had been found for them to stay. Mrs Roberts-Price invited him in and showed him into a cold, sparsely furnished front room. It was apparent the room was only used for the occasional visitor. A three-piece suite, table, an aspidistra in a pot on a matching pillar, and a couple of ornamental tea caddies on the mantelpiece was all it contained. He wasn't going to see much unless he could find an excuse to look at the other rooms. He sat there in the cold soulless place while she went to find her husband.

He stood up and looked around the walls and saw behind where he was sitting a small low table on which was a brass-bound family Bible. Idly, without real interest, he opened it and saw page after page of entries relating to the families, old faded spidery writing and many photographs, some stuck in, others loose. Then he noticed a marker and opened that page to see a small notepad labelled, Prayers Are Asked For – followed by a list of names and the reason for the prayers. The top one was for Our Dear Lost Child, still sadly missed. George presumed a child had died and they hadn't been able to write the actual word. He heard footsteps returning and closed the heavy book and returned to his seat.

He didn't stay long, he just told them that the cyclists had been offered a place to stay and would now be on their way.

The serious-faced man glanced at the table as George stood to leave and asked, 'You were interested in our family Bible, Mr Dexter?'

'Sorry, but I did glance at it, I was intrigued by the prayer list. The lost child, you had a baby who died, did you? That's very sad.'

'No, lost doesn't mean dead, Mr Dexter. Now, we must get on. Thank you for taking the trouble to call, but any items for sale will be dealt with by Evans and Calloway.'

As he left, his disappointment at not finding anything to buy was forgotten as he puzzled over the lost child. What did it mean? You don't lose children. They can die, or be adopted or taken from you for various reasons. He wondered which of those things was represented by the nameless child at the top of the prayer list.

He checked the time and realized he had to hurry as he was auctioneer at a farm sale in less than two hours. As he was about to get into his car a voice called and he looked back to see the couple waving, beckoning him back. Conscious of the time and also filled with hope of a deal, he slammed the car door and went to rejoin them.

'We have changed our minds. We still have a few things we won't need at our new place, and feel they should be handled separately from the church gifts, to avoid confusion.'

With hope rising he followed them into the house. As he staggered down the stairs, carrying the top of a marble washstand, for which he had paid ten shillings, Mr Roberts-Price followed close behind him with a beautiful gilded mirror, dusty from being hidden away in a cupboard. His wife was dragging the lower part of the washstand from the bedroom. Trying to avoid getting his clothes dirty George lost his grip, slipped and fell. He landed against the corner of the marble washstand top and the mirror hit him on the side of his head.

-

Teifion was at an hotel having attended a reunion of some ex-RAF friends when the manager told him he was wanted on the telephone. The explanation that he was needed urgently to conduct the sale caused him to panic. Less than two hours? He couldn't get home in time, he was too far away and he knew that he wasn't able to drive well enough to even try. He opened his diary and tried everyone who might be willing to help but no one was available at such short notice. In desperation he telephoned the office of Evans and Calloway. It was Meriel who answered and without much hope he asked if she would take over the auction on behalf of his father. 'Of course. And I'm sure he'll remember if we should ever be in the same situation,' she said. She quickly took down the details and, taking Lucy with her, she drove to the farmhouse where the goods were on display, the lot numbers all marked and listed. With only a short time to go she and Lucy introduced themselves and hurriedly inspected the items for sale. The house and outbuildings went quickly and they reached a higher price than George Dexter had estimated, to two brothers who intended to farm there. Then they went outside. People huddled around in groups, their catalogues marked with the pieces they hoped to buy, and slowly they worked their way through the lots. They were cold and very tired by the time they had finished but pleased with their achievements. Apart from a few unwanted items, mostly damaged and practically valueless, everything was gone, carried with difficulty by the purchasers, or taken away in cars, vans, trucks and horses and cans.

A man called to them as they stood clearing the final items. It was the mysterious man who had called, taken them out and purported to want a shop premises for a friend. This time he introduced himself.

'Hello again. I thought you two managed the auction very well. Almost as good as a man would have done,' he teased.

In her 'silly' voice, Lucy replied, 'Thank you kindly, sir.'

'My name is Harry Power and I work for Mr Lewin of Bracken Court. He is preparing for a very important sale and wondered whether to put it in your hands instead of his usual auctioneer.'

Meriel and Lucy didn't try to hide their delight and after details had been exchanged, Harry Power invited them out to tea and promised to contact them again soon.

They declined the invitation to tea. 'This isn't our auction, we're doing it to help out someone who has had an accident,' Meriel explained. 'We need to get home and do the accounts and deliver them to the person concerned.'

Lucy smiled as she noticed Meriel had avoided mentioning George Dexter and the Ace Estate Agency.

The money was put into the bank ready for George the following day, their fee written alongside the final amount. Meriel also put a note through George's door telling him exactly what had been sold and for how much. She had never worked on behalf of another auctioneer before and didn't want there to be any conflict.

The following day Lucy told her mother she was leaving home. It didn't take her long to move. They expressed regret at her leaving but Lucy didn't think they'd have any sleepless nights. She kissed Dawn, Diana and Deborah and promised to keep in touch and almost ran to the car where Meriel had been waiting. The move into her new life was complete.

'D'you think you'll see Gerald, now you've met up again?' Meriel asked her later.

Lucy shook her head. 'Unlikely and if I'm honest I'm a little disappointed that he went off without even promising to keep in touch. It probably shows a side of me that isn't very nice, but I hoped he'd ask, so I'd have the pleasure of turning him away, and be able to show off a bit more and remind him of what he missed when he left me. Isn't that terrible.'

'Sounds normal to me!' Meriel said, with a laugh.

As they sat beside the fire and discussed the progress of the estate agency, George came round, bandaged and supported by a silver-topped cane, banging on their door and demanding to know by what right had they stolen his client.

Four

The smile on Meriel's face froze. She had expected George Dexter to greet her with appreciation and thanks for helping him out of a difficulty. Taking over the auction at such short notice was surely a reason to be grateful, so why the anger?

'How dare you steal business like that? I'll make sure everyone knows what you've done. This town won't tolerate such underhand behaviour so you might as well close your doors now!'

'What are you talking about? We did it to help you.'

'Help yourself you mean!'

'I expect a small fee for our trouble, yes, but that's all.'

'A small fee? Is that what you call taking the profit that should have been mine?'

'The cheque, and a full statement of what we sold, and for how much, should be on your desk. I don't understand why you're not grateful.'

'*And* you forgot the dog!' Then he stopped and asked, 'Cheque? What cheque?'

'We pushed it through your door along with the full statement so there wouldn't be any delay. The suggested fee for our day is up to you. If you don't think we deserved it then don't pay!' Meriel's voice was rising with her anger.

Lucy came to stand beside her. She said, 'I suggest you go back and look for it, Mr Dexter, then we'll expect a full apology.' She began to guide him towards the door. 'Your son begged us to help and now I wish we had refused.'

'What d'you mean? Teifion asked you to help? It was your idea and—'

'While you're picking up our cheque, why don't you ask him what really happened, Mr Dexter?'

'It might be an idea for you to listen occasionally instead of charging off with half the facts,' Lucy said angrily.

The man was clearly embarrassed, his face was white with shock. 'I didn't think he'd – I'll go and find out exactly what happened, and—'

'Would you like a cup of tea?' Meriel asked, concerned by the man's distress and heavy breathing.

But Lucy said, 'The café's open if you do!' She opened the door and George left, walking slowly away as though in a daze.

'That Teifion is worse than his father. Why did he lie? He knew the truth would come out.'

'He was convinced his father would either believe him, or pretend to. As Teifion once implied, lies and loyalties can be two sides of the same coin.'

'Poor Teifion,' Lucy said, with a smile. 'His defiance didn't last long, did it? Leaving home, looking for a job, telling us he was having nothing more to do with his father. I don't suppose it was easy, mind. He lacks confidence and wants only what is readily available. That's why he's so anxious to please his father, afraid it will all be taken from him.'

'All his life whatever he needed was given to him, he's never had to work or earn it. It was a lot to give up.'

'He's still a coward!'

They settled back to work and after a minute or two, Meriel asked, 'What did he mean about the dog?'

'Oh, my goodness! I forgot! There was a puppy in one of the sheds and we were asked to find it a home! The poor thing must still be there!'

Meriel offered to go and she set off for the farm that now had their advertising board on the gate with a SOLD notice across it. The farmer came out when she drove into the yard and offered a hand. 'I was coming to see you.' he said. 'I want to thank you for yesterday. Everything went better than I'd hoped and I achieved more than Mr Dexter expected. Thank you both very much. I'll recommend your firm whenever I get the chance.'

'Thank you. I'm glad we pleased you, but I've come about the dog. I'm afraid we didn't sell it and it's still in the barn.'

'No she isn't.' He gave a piercing whistle and a young collie ran out, dragging a piece of blanket, shaking it furiously. 'Come here, you young rascal,' he said, bending forward, and the puppy jumped into his arms.

'She'd make a lovely pet for you,' he said coaxingly, offering the squirming furry bundle to her. Meriel took her into her arms and admitted that it was love at first sight.

'Her name is Rascal,' she told a surprised Lucy when she carried her into the office.

–

George went back to the office and shouted for his son. 'This auction which you told me you had managed without me—' he began.

'Sorry, Dad, I thought you'd be angry so I—'

'So you lied. When I found out that it had been held by Evans and Calloway, you then told me that the business had been stolen by them going to see the farmer and telling him I'd had an accident and he'd be let down unless he accepted their help. More lies. You made me look a complete fool. I went there demanding an apology for their dishonesty but once again, the problem was with you! Tell me what really happened. Now!'

'I couldn't make it, I was too far away to drive back in time.'

'Didn't try, you mean.'

'All right, I didn't try! I contacted everyone I could think of, then I asked Meriel, hinting that it might be a good time to stop feuding.'

'And the statement and cheque?' George held out his hand.

'Oh, yes. It came by second post.'

'Did it? I was told they pushed it through the door last night.'

Teifion's shoulders drooped. 'All right, Dad. I was hoping you wouldn't find out. I thought if I could put it all through the books quickly you'd have just presumed I dealt with it.'

'Where you're concerned, all I can presume is that you'll mess everything up! What is the matter with you, boy?'

'You are!' Teifion retorted. 'I've never been able to please you no matter what I do so why should I try?'

'Because you're my son?' George put both hands on the desk and glared at him.

'Your hatred of Walter Evans is stronger than any feelings you have for me!'

'Rubbish!'

'Why d'you hate him so much?' he dared to ask. 'I'm entitled to know that much.'

'Mind your own business and get those advertisements sent off, or we'll be giving even more business to Walter's precious daughter! Now pass me that list of auction prices.'

Teifion looked suitably chastened as his father read the list. Noting the prices they'd made he nodded approval.

'A poor show, eh, Dad?' he said, hopefully.

'On the contrary, they did very well. Probably better than you'd have done. You see, Teifion, your heart isn't in it and they have the sort of enthusiasm that breeds success. They are straightforward and intelligent and you use stupid tricks. Lucky Walter Evans. I wish she were my daughter!'

'Dad!'

'One more trick like this that makes me have to apologize for you and you're out. You tried once but returned and next time I'll help you on your way. Right?' He glared at his son, his face red with fury. Calming slightly he continued, 'I'll do what I've often dreamed of doing, sell up, retire and take Frieda somewhere far away from you! I'll spend the money I've earned on someone who appreciates it. Any hope you have of inheriting the business is fading fast. Now I have to go and tell Meriel Evans that my son behaved like the imbecile he is!'

Teifion glared at his father's departing figure. Of course he wasn't enthusiastic, he hated his job. Years of being treated like an idiot by the father who promised he was keeping the estate agency for him when he was old enough, yet never giving him a chance to show what he was capable of. He should have stayed away, made more of an effort to make a new life for himself.

He told himself that if Lucy and Meriel had believed him capable of a change of heart, accepted his apology and his promise that he was a changed man, he could have succeeded. But their rejection of him at the same time seeing an opportunity to try one more time to please his father, over the sale of that man's cottage, had been too great a temptation. He had seen the possibility of making some money from the sale of that barn. A way to impress his father. But once again it had gone wrong. Ironic really that when he tried to change sides neither wanted him.

Now he simply didn't care. As soon as the business was in his hands he planned to sell up and do something he really enjoyed. By then, if he were lucky, his cheating stepmother would be long gone.

If only he could find out something about Meriel Evans to discredit her. That would make his father sit up. If she continued she would take more business from them and he'd have less to inherit when his father retired. But what? From all he had learned she had lived an exemplary life before coming to Cwm Derw, and neither she nor Lucy behaved in a dishonest way in the search for clients. Perhaps her parents had some secret in their past he might use? There had to be some way of making her leave Cwm Derw.

Making an excuse of appointments, he drove to where Meriel's parents lived and began asking around, in shops and pubs and even knocking on the door of a house they had just sold to check on their methods. There was nothing untoward. They were just what they seemed; honest business people. Perhaps there was something to be found in the register office. A family secret maybe. It seemed very unlikely he'd discover anything underhand in the way Walter Evans had found the money to start his business. From what he knew about the man he had probably done it the hard and straightforward way; worked and saved. Dragging the dregs of hope, he went into town.

As he looked in the register office to search their past he found a mystery. He was looking for the date of Meriel's birthday with idle curiosity, thinking he might go back again to where her parents were born, ask a few questions about the family, when he discovered to his disbelief that no birth had been registered in their name.

–

Leo Hopkins had heard about George's outburst after Meriel had auctioned the farm and contents and he called to see her. 'Can I do anything? Talk to him? I hope he has apologized properly.'

'Not really. He came back and muttered about his son not giving a proper explanation. He thanked us for the cheque and paid the small fee we asked for with hardly another word. I think he was ashamed of his son, but it isn't easy to admit your son is a fool, is it?'

'Maybe not, but in his case I imagine George has had plenty of practice!'

'I don't think he's a fool, he's just in the wrong life,' Lucy said.

'What on earth d'you mean?'

'He doesn't like living at home with his father and step-mother, he doesn't enjoy working for George. As I say, he's in the wrong life.'

'Then why doesn't he get out of it and find the right one?'

'Come on, having George Dexter for a father, how can he possibly have the confidence to leave and make his own way?'

'You're right. Although he did try,' Meriel said. 'He came to us expecting a pat on the back, like a small boy finally sleeping without a night light.'

Leo was looking at Meriel as he said, 'His only chance is to find a woman he'd want to please more than pleasing his father.' He continued to stare at her intently. 'Love is stronger than hatred, don't you think?'

Looking away, unsettled by the look in his eyes, she said, 'Dadda always says love is the heart of the home.'

'Yes,' Lucy agreed, still defending him, 'and Teifion has been deprived of it.'

Leo invited Meriel to lunch and they drove to a small village a few miles away, where they ate at an hotel overlooking the sea. The meal was an excellent serving of fresh trout, followed by home-made custard with delicious apple pie.

As he walked her back to the car they saw Teifion and at the same moment Mr Roberts-Price appeared riding an ancient bicycle. The man stopped and swiftly turned and rode away. Teifion stared after him and with a nod in Meriel's direction, he too turned aside.

'I can understand Teifion not stopping to say hello,' Meriel said with a laugh, 'his embarrassment is still raw, but I don't know why that man hurried away as though I threatened danger.'

'Perhaps he was running away from Teifion. Why should anyone want to avoid you?'

'But it was me he was looking at before he turned and rode off, not Teifion.'

'Forget it, I doubt if it was anything to do with either of you, or me for that matter. You don't know him, do you?'

'I think I do. Although we only met briefly, I think he's Mr Roberts-Price. Lucy sold his house and it was she who dealt with him.'

'Roberts-Price,' Leo shrugged. 'I can't say I've heard of him. He looks rather old-fashioned, dressed for church rather than a bicycle ride. He's probably old-fashioned regarding women too. You are quite beautiful, Meriel, and you dress to remind people you're a woman. A woman in a man's world. I bet his wife wears old potato sacks!'

She smiled, shaken by his compliment spoken with sincerity, not his usual jokey manner, the one she was used to. 'I remember Lucy telling me the family are devout and rather serious,' she told him.

'I'll make enquiries if you wish.'

'No, I don't think he's important. Perhaps he just remembered he'd left the kettle on the gas.' She increased her speed. 'Come on, Lucy will wonder where we've got to.'

He pulled her arm through his. 'We're so late, another five minutes can't matter.'

She glanced up and was startled to see the way he was looking at her. There was affection and something more in his expression. She was aware of a strange emotion, a kind of swelling inside her, a new kind of happiness. They walked very slowly the rest of the way.

As he drove away she was engulfed in sadness, wishing she'd asked him to stay. I'm being silly, she told herself and walked briskly into the office where Lucy was reading through the local paper looking for prospects.

After the usual greetings Meriel went to the files to remind herself of the Roberts-Prices' new address. It wasn't far from where she had seen him, about five or six miles away. The house was called Church Cottage, in the village of Glyndwr, and Lucy told her he and his wife were caretakers in the church.

'Mr R–P works in a shop selling religious books, and so does his son, Noah,' Lucy told her. 'Although as you know he is in the army at present. They have a daughter Martha, who works in Woolworth's on the record counter. I had a job to get even that much information from his wife, who seems afraid of people knowing too much about them. I wasn't being nosy, but sitting there I tried to make conversation, talking about people we know, looking for a connection like people usually do. An odd family, but they seem content, don't they? Loving and close.' She was about to add that she would have given a lot to be a part of such a family even though they were reserved, but she didn't. It was time to stop looking back with regret, enjoy the present and look forward to her exciting future.

The sale of the farm had been a breakthrough and although small, there was an increase in the people who came to them when they were looking for a property or wanting to sell or rent. This month looked set to be by far their best so far and they began to feel more confident in the future.

Lucy was talking to a couple who wanted to buy a small property when Gerald called in. Despite trying to look unconcerned, Lucy felt a tug of excitement deep within her. Holding it back she waited until the couple left then looked at him and said, 'Looking for a property or selling, Mr Cook?'

'Neither, Miss Calloway, I want to – take you out this evening.'

'Sorry, we only deal with property.'

'I wish you were my property,' he said softly. 'What a fool I was to let you go.'

Still calmly she said, 'Yes, Mr Cook, you were. Now, if there's nothing else, I need to get these invoices paid.'

'Please, Lucy, just a meal somewhere, or the pictures, you always loved the pictures. Or a dance? D'you still go dancing?'

'Sorry, we're far too busy. Office all day and the garden all evening.'

'Perhaps next week?'

'I doubt it, next week will be even busier.' Then she spoilt her act by laughing.

'Come on, Lucy, a few hours of your company is all I want. To hear all about what you've been doing since we last met.'

'All right, so long as it isn't a cycle ride. Or one of your father's motorbikes.'

'I'll try to borrow a car.'

'The bus will do. Monday? It's our day off.'

'But it isn't mine. I don't think I can take a day off, even for you.'

She knew this perfectly well and was teasing him and enjoying it. 'Sorry, there isn't time any other day.' She stood up, tacitly dismissing him. He left the shop, blowing a kiss, which she didn't return.

–

Meriel's parents came to stay at Badgers Brook the following weekend. Leo agreed to stay in the office with an assistant on Saturday so they could travel down early Friday evening. As usual, Meriel and Lucy were not alone. Betty Connors was visiting before she started work at the Ship and Compass, and Stella called when the post office closed with her husband Colin, to give the two young women some runner bean plants from their allotment.

The puppy was fussing around greeting everyone and bringing toys to play with.

Delightful chaos, was how Lynne described it. 'I can't believe how well the girls have settled in and become a part of the community.'

'It's the house,' Stella told her. 'It welcomes people and calms them, helps them sort out problems like no place I've ever known.'

'Calms them!' Lynne laughed as she watched the puppy running off with a cake from Bob's plate and everyone trying to get it off her.

'It's true,' Bob said, having rescued the cake and put it out of the puppy's reach. 'Geoff and Connie, who own the place, say it has always attracted people in trouble and helps them to solve their problems with its peaceful atmosphere.'

'But Meriel isn't in trouble, is she?' she asked in alarm.

'Oh no, Lynne, forget we mentioned it, I'm sure it isn't always the case,' Stella said quickly. But she stared at Meriel and wondered if the trouble was yet to come.

Gerald called at the office several times in the days that followed, usually at lunchtime when he tried to persuade Lucy to go with him one evening, to a place out of town where they could talk. Encouraged by Meriel, she finally agreed. It was a long time since she'd had a date and the memories of loving him had not completely faded.

'It will have to be Thursday,' she told him, determined not to make things easy for him. 'Come to the office when we close and we can go straight off, I don't like being out late,' she said.

He frowned. 'I think it might be best if you went by bus into Cardiff and we met there,' he said.

'What? If you can't be bothered to escort me then you can forget it!' Angrily she turned away.

'Oh, Lucy, don't be so difficult. I'll already be in Cardiff that day attending a conference on the latest motorbikes. Dad insists that I go,' he added ruefully, 'he thinks I'll enjoy it. So it would make sense for you to join me there rather than me coming all this way back then setting off again.'

With some reluctance she agreed. Meriel insisted she left the office early and went home to change and make herself ready. She went by bus to Cardiff and was at the appointed place at a quarter to six but he wasn't there. She was fifteen minutes early but didn't fancy wandering around, with the shops already closed it seemed pointless, so she decided to wait. Quarter of an hour would soon pass.

Gerald was in a room not far from where she was waiting, desperately glancing at his watch. The conference on the mechanics of a new range of engine had been boring but as he'd been asked to take the minutes in the absence of the secretary, he'd had to stay. Besides, his father would expect a blow by blow account of the day when he got home.

Aware he was going to be late he tried to leave but was stopped by the owner of a business similar to his father's and he couldn't get away. Time passed and he imagined he could hear the vibrations of seconds passing throughout his body.

Lucy was puzzled at his choice of meeting place, a quiet road outside the centre, where there were warehouses and a few abandoned premises. She looked at her watch and decided she would allow him no extra time at all. If he were late then she wouldn't be there. Tapping her foot irritably, she was beginning to wish she hadn't succumbed to the temptation of an evening out.

It was going to be a disaster. She was already edgy and ill-tempered. He should have been there, waiting for her, looking anxious. He should have shown relief when she turned the corner – ran to her joyfully – held her close, kissed her and… She pulled away from that foolish dream and glanced around her at the empty street. It wasn't going to happen.

A few minutes passed then a steady movement of people began to leave the buildings and head for the bus station and with everyone passing her she felt even more alone and foolish. They all seemed to be rushing to get home, some putting on their coats as they ran, impatient to leave their place of work, while she was wishing she was back in hers.

Was he really going to stand her up? She walked to the corner several times, beginning to worry she might be taken for a 'street walker'. The small rush of people slowed to a trickle, the quiet area seemed to be closing down and it became more silent as minutes passed. Six o'clock came and went and still she waited. She knew she was lowering her own value, admitting she wasn't worth consideration, by accepting his poor treatment. He had told her six o'clock and it was now exactly five minutes past. Still she waited.

–

Gerald suffered another delay as he went to collect his coat. Someone had taken his by mistake. It took an age to sort out the mix-up as the man had put his wallet into the wrong coat and Gerald had to wait with the caretaker until he came back to retrieve it.

At fifteen minutes past the hour and with a final glance behind her, Lucy hurried to the corner and began walking briskly to the bus station trying not to run. Now she had decided to leave she didn't want to meet him and she went by a slightly devious route, heading for the Railway Hotel, cutting through roads where there were more warehouses and fruit wholesalers before reaching the railway station with the buses standing in lines in front of it.

Crowds still gathered around the railway station, reading newspapers, standing beside luggage, looking anxiously for a familiar face. Once she thought she saw him and deviated from her route just in case. Now she really didn't want to see Gerald, or be seen by him. Too many minutes had passed and she hoped he would never know how long she had waited.

She felt so self-conscious, dreading being seen by Gerald, that she had the foolish sensation someone was about to touch her shoulder even as she stepped onto the bus. Heart racing, it was a relief when she was finally seated down and the bus was moving away.

She looked straight ahead, refusing to give the crowd one last look.

Gerald ran as fast as he could through the home-going crowd and stopped in disappointment as he reached the corner and looked down to where Lucy should have been waiting. His final delay had been caused by a man from the meeting who knew his father well. He had insisted on walking with him, stopping to chat about his boring wife and boring family.

The man was someone with whom he was supposed to discuss a good deal on the newest motorbike, but instead, without telling his father, Gerald had contacted a firm who promised a new deal repairing and selling second-hand cars. Better than motorbikes, he had thought, comfort being more important than style, these days. Family cars, that was the future. Bikes or cars, he hoped he would be far away from his father's garage one day soon. Lucy was his strongest hope of escape and he was angry with everyone for making him miss her.

Comfort was the main reason for wanting to revive the friendship with Lucy, and perhaps marry her if it meant he would be a part of the business she and her friend owned. Without the promise of an easy life, with no financial worries, she wasn't exciting enough. But she's still attracted to me, he told himself gratifyingly. I'll soon get her back. He felt a surge of superiority as he thought of her pathetic attempts to play hard to get. She was so unsophisticated.

He turned and hurried, without much hope, to the bus stop but there was no sign of Lucy in the queue that waited for the Cwm Derw bus. She'd have been tired of waiting. The fifteen minutes he had been delayed had cost him his first date. Well, he thought philosophically, the deal with the car salesman was underway and the evening was his own. Hazel Proudfoot was usually available.

He changed his mind when he got back to Cwm Derw. Perhaps he ought to try and make his excuses to Lucy. From what his parents had told him, Lucy and Meriel were building a successful business and he really liked the sound of that. It promised a life of leisure and he would be very happy if he could leave his father's small workshop.

Repairing bicycles and motorbikes, plus the occasional sale, was not the way he wanted to spend the rest of his life. Lucy, boring Lucy, was suddenly his way out, his path to better things. Running an estate agency, having clean hands, wearing smart suits and with people looking up to you, that was better than being an uninspired, uninterested mechanic whose father was still trying to teach him even the simplest procedures.

It would be easy to win Lucy back, there had never been anyone else in her life, certainly not anyone as attractive as himself. Besides, she was at an age when she couldn't be choosy. His optimism revived, he headed for Badgers Brook.

–

Teifion had travelled on the same bus and was walking in the same direction as Gerald but he didn't go as far as Badgers Brook. He stopped at his father's house having been avoiding him all day. He knew his father was angry with him and he thought he had the means of changing that. He had spent the day making enquiries but had come up with no corroboration to back up his guess that Meriel was not the child of Lynne and George Evans. But the lack of proof was not enough to stop him relating it as a good story and when he and his father were alone, Frieda having gone for a weekend with her sister in Brighton, he told him he suspected Meriel was adopted.

George said very little, his mind was on Frieda and where she might be. But he listened and wondered how he could use the information to make Meriel leave. He decided to keep the story as ammunition for use if there was any trouble between him and George Evans in the future. Meriel and Lucy had affected his sales but he had no justifiable complaints about the way they ran their office. They did search more diligently for clients but he had been doing the same and in fact he hadn't lost much income since they arrived. Although, there was a slight increase in the number of people now buying homes, rather than renting, and perhaps that was disguising his own lack of progress. After all, every house they sold meant one less for himself.

Teifion went out again. A drink at the Ship and Compass was better than staying in for one of his father's lectures.

—

Lucy went home and, hiding her humiliation, laughed as she told Meriel that, as Gerald wasn't there before the appointed time, she hadn't waited. She couldn't admit to the extra fifteen minutes she had stood in that silent, empty street and hoped.

'Good on you,' Meriel said, but she guessed her friend had been hurt by the incident. 'I'm glad you're back. I made a fatless, eggless concoction which the cookery book had the cheek to call a cake, and I want you to try it.' She bustled about making tea, talking about the few clients she had seen since Lucy's departure and giving Lucy time to recover from her disappointment.

Then there was a knock at the door and Lucy went to answer it expecting one of the neighbours, but Gerald stood there, his trilby in his hands and abject misery on his face.

'Lucy, I'm so sorry, but the meeting went on a bit and as I was one of the people in charge, I couldn't get away.'

'In charge?'

'Well, I was responsible for taking the minutes and helping with the distribution of information, and a few other things besides, you know how they intend to put the pressure on the capable ones. I simply couldn't leave until everyone else had gone.'

Lucy stood there barring his entrance, unable to decide whether or not to believe him. It was Meriel who called for him to come in. 'Come and try a piece of this cake, Gerald. It isn't too bad, is it, Lucy?' she called as she reached for her coat.

'Where are you going?' Lucy asked, as Meriel cut a couple of slices of the soft, rather sticky cake.

'I promised Kitty and Bob a taste, it was she who gave me the recipe.' Chewing her last mouthful, she mumbled that she wouldn't be long and went out.

Gerald stood just inside the door and Lucy sat down at the table and cut a slice of the cake. 'You'd better sit down as you're here,' she said ungraciously.

'I'm really sorry, Lucy. Shall we try again tomorrow?'

Lucy shook her head, but he pleaded until she agreed to give it another try.

'Same day next week. But this time I want you to meet me at the office, I don't want to go on the bus on my own and hang around in the faint hope you'll turn up.'

'I'd love to but I don't think I can. I'm working in Cardiff next week. It's a course on engines. My father still fondly hopes to make a mechanic of me one day.'

'That's all right, call and see me when you're free,' she said brightly. She reached for her coat and said, 'Sorry but I have to go and see Kitty and Bob as well, they've been helping us with the garden.'

She ushered him out of the door and he walked to the bus stop, wondering if he was too late to meet Hazel Proudfoot. His tender ego needed some attention. He stopped at the house where George Dexter lived, staring enviously at its elegance, the facade partially lit from uncurtained windows and a lamp outside the porch. It was a beautiful house with an impressive porch, there were five windows at the front, the stone front wall was covered with a creeper, which he didn't recognize, not being interested in flowers. He felt a surge of longing to own such a place. He was certain he had been meant for better things than a small terraced house and a greasy garage workshop. He would have no chance of living in a place like this if he stayed mending bicycles or even cars, he thought, as he stood, imagining himself with a glamorous wife, stepping into an expensive car parked on the wide, double entrance drive. However hard his father might try to teach him, he simply wasn't any good at the job. But married to a successful estate agent, this is what he might aspire to. He increased his speed, striding out through the darkening evening and began to think of ways to persuade Lucy they belonged together.

He called at the Ship and Compass and sat there looking around at the assorted customers with dismay. Would he end up just like these men? Sitting talking to men like themselves, convincing themselves they were happy and successful? He ordered a potato and meat pie and, eating without enthusiasm, decided that although Hazel Proudfoot was a pleasant enough companion, his only real hope of achieving the rich life he believed should be his, lay with Lucy Calloway.

Teifion was also in the pub and left at the same time as Gerald but they didn't speak. Gerald walked slowly, knowing he was on his way home to a dull evening, with his father talking about the conference, the people he'd met, followed by a conversation on engines old and new, and even more boring subjects like paint finishes. As he passed the office of Evans and Calloway in Forge Street he felt a tug of hope. He was good-looking and Lucy had been hard to discourage when he'd first met Hazel Proudfoot, so he was surely capable of winning her back? She was almost thirty, a time when most women needed to feel secure. For women, security meant a man, he thought complacently, confident she'd agree.

Teifion also walked home and was relieved to find that his father wasn't at home when he went inside. There was a note from his father, resting against the biscuit tin in the kitchen, to tell him there was a meal in the oven that would need about twenty minutes to heat. He looked at it and shuddered. At least Frieda's food was edible. He reached for the loaf and began cutting it, searching for a remnant of their cheese ration to fill the slices. The fire was low, almost out and the evening had brought a chill to the empty house. How far was this from his dream? Like Gerald, he ate without enthusiasm.

—

George was about seven miles away staring up at a dilapidated hotel. He knew he shouldn't have come. Walter's words had to be untrue; his suspicions, roused by Walter's unkind words, were no more than anxiety brought on by reminders of their age difference. The rumours that surfaced from time to time were nothing more than that, untruths made up by jealous people, envious of his happiness with a young and beautiful wife. Frieda was in Brighton as she had told him, enjoying a few days with her sister. He'd had a card from her that morning with a loving message on it. Although, a small cynical voice reminded him, that wouldn't be hard to arrange. He looked up at the building in front of him with its boarded windows and the harshly painted front door, the unwashed steps. He couldn't imagine Frieda in such a dreadful place! The door opened, its weak hinges causing it to drag noisily against the step. He darted back into the shadows and watched, promising himself he would go home as soon as these people disappeared. He studied them as they headed towards him, a man arm in arm with a woman, her high heels tapping as she hurried to keep up with his long-legged stride. Then he heard laughter and knew without doubt that it was Frieda.

'Frieda!' Without giving himself time to think, plan how to deal with the situation, he stepped out and confronted her. He was horrified at the way she was dressed. Short skirts, low-necked blouse, in spite of the cold, late evening weather.

'George, darling? How did you know I was here?' She stepped forward as though to kiss him and he backed away. 'This is my sister's fiancé, Simon, they were going to give me a lift home but I decided to stay one more night with them. Awful place, but it belongs to a friend of theirs.' She looked back as though expecting her sister to be following. 'Teresa will be along in a minute.'

'You might as well come home with me, hadn't you?' George said. His voice had a tremor, shock making his body shake.

'No, darling, you go on, we've arranged to meet a few friends. I'll tell you all about it tomorrow, love you,' she whispered and he turned away.

George drove at dangerous speed to where Walter and Lynne Evans lived and banged furiously on their door. Walter had been the first to confirm what he suspected and he ought to suffer as well. Shoot the messenger? At last he understood what that meant.

'I know your precious daughter was adopted!' he shouted as Walter opened the door and began to smile a greeting. 'There! How d'you like it? Being told some unpleasant gossip about your family? You enjoyed telling me about Frieda and I'm enjoying my revenge.' At that time he didn't care whether or not Teifion had been telling the truth, he just needed to hurt someone. He hurried away on legs that seemed to wobble, he was shaking so much he had difficulty unlocking the car door.

Walter turned and stared at Lynne, who had run to the door as the shouted words had reached her. 'Walter, he knows! What shall we do!' She was crying, tears falling and he took her in his arms.

'After all this time, and it had to be George Dexter, of all people, who learned our secret. Oh, Lynne, love, why didn't we tell her? We should have told her.'

Still sobbing, Lynne said, 'Now he knows he'll tell her. He'll never be able to keep this to himself. He'll tell our daughter.'

'I don't know what to do. I could go down, tell her now in a rush, nothing like how we dreamed of, telling her of our love, and pride. I don't think I can. Perhaps he won't tell her.'

More calmly, Lynne said, 'Oh he'll tell her, don't doubt it. Unless you can persuade him not to. Go after him, plead with him to keep quiet. It will ruin everything if she finds out like this. She'd never trust us again. Why didn't we tell her when she was young enough to cope? I daren't think what this will do to her — to us.'

Walter sat down, his face like parchment, his eyes bright and feverish. 'I'll probably be too late.'

'Please, Walter, we have to try.'

Like a frail old man, Walter got up, took the coat Lynne was offering and picked up his keys from her trembling hand. 'I'll come with you,' she said.

He didn't drive as furiously as George had done and when he reached Badgers Brook he saw to his alarm that George's car was already parked in the lane. He and Lynne ran to the path leading to Badgers Brook but as they passed his car, the door opened and George said, 'I haven't told her.'

'Thank goodness for that. George I'm ashamed of the way I told you my suspicions about your wife. I'm sorry. I was wrong.'

'No, you were right, I've just found out that what you said was true. And that was why I wanted to hurt someone. We're both capable of childish behaviour, Walter. There's malice in the best of us when we're hurt.'

Lynne was trying to subdue her sobs of relief. She got back into the car, waiting for Walter to join her.

'Thank you. I'll always be grateful to you for this, George. And I'm very sorry about your wife.' Both men had calmed down, but Walter said just too many words and ruined it. 'I suppose it was always a risk, marrying someone as young and attractive as Frieda.'

'What d'you mean?' George demanded. 'The age difference hasn't been a problem.'

'Well, she's bound to be tempted by younger people, having fun, going places. Let's face it, George, we aren't as keen on dancing and parties as we once were. She must feel she's missing out.'

'Of course she isn't missing out. I'm not an old man. I can keep her happy. Age isn't the issue!'

'Fifteen years? Give over!'

'She's content with the life I give her, living in a beautiful home, all the money she wants, plenty of clothes and holidays twice a year, what more could she want?'

Walter shrugged. 'What we had at her age I imagine.'

George had a vision of how Frieda dressed at home, with subdued colours, neat twinsets and sober skirts, very little make-up, hair held in a netted bun. Then as a sudden shocking reminder, he saw her as she had appeared that evening, with a red, revealing top and a white skirt, ridiculous red shoes and her hair loose around her heavily made-up face.

He leaped out of the car, punched Walter and burned up the path. Without knocking he went in to where Meriel and Lucy were sitting near the fire listening to comedy on the wireless. Meriel jumped up in alarm.

'Mr Dexter? What on earth is wrong?' She saw her father following, blood on his face and Lynne behind him pleading with George Dexter to stop.

Walter grabbed George's arm and pulled him towards the door, shouting, 'Haven't you harmed us enough?' Then the two men were fighting, hitting out at each other wildly and without skill. Sobbing, Lynne was begging him to say nothing. With Walter off balance following a blow, George pushed him aside making him stagger and fall against the wall, and he panted, 'Wrong, Meriel? Only that you were adopted. Only that Walter and Lynne aren't your real parents.'

Laughter flooded out from the wireless as Walter sank into a chair. Lynne ran to him, hugging him, his low groans at odds with the merriment of the wireless programme. Without a word, George walked out.

'Dad? Is this true?' Meriel whispered, hugging Lucy like a lifeline.

'I'm sorry, my darling girl, but yes, it's true.'

Lucy reached over to turn off the cruel canned laughter from the wireless that seemed to be mocking them. In the awful silence they all stared at each other like strangers, none of them knowing what to say. Walter's heavy breathing, the shifting embers of the fire and the distant sound of George's car driving off, brakes squealing as though sharing their pain, were the only sounds.

Five

Adopted, adopted, the word echoed in Meriel's head as she tried to take in the implications. Shock numbed all thought momentarily, followed by disbelief, then the comforting conviction that it was a stupid joke, then, seeing her mother's stricken expression, the terrifying realization that it was true. She wasn't the person she had always thought she was, she no longer belonged.

It seemed later that she and her parents had stared at each other in silence for an age, but in reality it could only have been seconds before Lynne gave a sob and pulled Meriel into her arms. Meriel relaxed against the well-loved warmth and wrapped her arms around her mother as though to stop herself being dragged away.

'It's true, is it?' she said softly. 'You're not my real mother?'

'Of course I'm your real mother, darling. I've cared for you and loved you with a fierce pride from the moment I first held you in my arms. How could anything change that?'

Walter was standing beside them and he reached out and put an arm around them both. 'No one could be loved more than you. Besides being our daughter, you're our best friend.'

Lucy was shaking, unable to decide whether to go or stay through the painful revelations. She finally tiptoed away towards the kitchen.

Through the haziness of her confusion, Meriel heard the kettle being filled, the gas being ignited and the normal, everyday sounds brought a return of sanity.

'Lucy's making tea, isn't that the only thing to do, drink tea and pretend everything is all right?'

'Everything *is* all right. Nothing's changed.'

'Of course everything's changed! Who am I? Where did I belong before I belonged to you?'

'You were ten days old, a tiny scrap of a thing and so beautiful. You've never belonged anywhere except with us.'

Questions flew from Meriel's mouth like barbed arrows, attacking her parents, demanding answers to questions that were hardly formed. Her emotions darted from bewilderment to fear and back again. Lynne and Walter answered them all calmly assuring her of their love and pride. 'We regret not telling you before this, darling,' Lynne said tearfully. 'We were so wrong, but really, everything is the same as it was an hour ago.'

'Except there's a part of my life about which I know nothing. And never will,' Meriel replied. Her voice was harsh with pain.

'I'm afraid that's true,' Walter admitted, 'and we'd have given anything to protect you from this.'

'D'you know why I couldn't stay with my mother? Why she didn't want me?' she demanded.

'I expect we were given a little information but I don't remember. We didn't ask,' Walter replied.

'We were so thrilled when you arrived we didn't give such questions a moment's thought,' Lynne added.

'And you and – Dadda?' She couldn't help the momentary pause before his title. 'Why did you adopt?'

It was Walter who answered. 'We couldn't have children of our own, but if we'd had a dozen, you wouldn't have been loved any less.'

'Why didn't you tell me? You've made me live a lie all these years. Everything I believed has been a lie. I should have been told.'

'You're right, we should have explained when you were a child. We did try, many times, but we were too afraid of losing you, afraid you'd hate us, step away from us and treat us like strangers.'

Lucy came in with cups of tea and handed them round, bringing tables and stools to place beside each chair. It was Lucy who refilled cups and, after listening to the stumbling and disjointed attempts at conversation, who finally suggested they parted and continued the discussion in the morning. 'I think you all need some sleep, and tomorrow everything will seem clearer.'

Without arguing, Lynne and Walter left, hugging both girls before stepping out into the darkness.

'We'll be back in the morning,' Lynne said, unable to hide her tears.

'Why not come in the evening,' Lucy said briskly. 'We need to open the office between nine and five thirty. Best we keep everything as normal as possible. We can't neglect the business, even at a time like this.' She glanced at her friend, hoping she had said the right thing. She was at a loss to know how to deal with such a painful revelation but instinct told her that normality was the best way forward.

Meriel didn't think she could ever face people again. 'How can I?' she asked Lucy when they were alone. 'I don't know who I am.'

'You are Meriel Evans, estate agent, daughter of Lynne and Walter Evans. Like your mum said, nothing has changed.'

'But George Dexter knows and so does his son. I can't believe they will keep quiet, can you?'

'So what?' She grinned then. 'I was never close to my mother and certainly not my stepfather or my stepsisters. I wouldn't complain if I learned I was a stranger.'

'Oh yes you would!' Meriel said angrily. 'No one wants to lose their family and live in a void.'

'No. That was my poor attempt at a joke. I'm sorry.' She stacked the dishes in the washing bowl and dampened down the fire. 'Come on, it's time you went to bed. Things will look different in the morning.'

Meriel went upstairs but knew she wouldn't sleep. Why hadn't she been told before? If she had grown up with the knowledge she'd have accepted it and pushed it aside. Learning now – and from the unpleasant George Dexter – made it shameful, something to be hushed up like a dirty secret. Oh, how she hated the man and his objectionable son.

Lucy went up after dealing with a few chores, moving quietly hoping her friend was asleep, but as she passed Meriel's door, Meriel called out in a hoarse whisper, 'Lucy, I don't think I can sleep, shall we have a cup of cocoa?'

'All right, I'll get it.'

'No, you get ready for bed, I'll go down. I need to move around, get chilled, then perhaps getting back into a warm bed will help to send me off.' She took the steaming cups up the stairs and sat on Lucy's bed while they drank.

'I'm all alone – or that's how I feel,' she added, as Lucy began to argue. 'Like being in the middle of a desert with nothing but sand all around, covering all I once had. Or being on a bare mountain with no one in sight, with small cracks and crannies I can't reach, that are hiding secrets about my real family that I'll never be told.'

'You wouldn't want to find them, would you? This other family?'

Meriel looked thoughtful. 'It isn't possible, but if I had the chance I doubt I'd be able to resist. But I'd like to see them without them seeing me.'

'So you can walk away if you don't like what you see?'

'No, I don't think I could walk away. I'd like to watch them, then think about it before facing them. I so desperately need to understand, but I'd like time to consider, to learn something about them – and maybe see who I might have been.'

'I'm sure the way you're brought up has a bearing on how you develop, but I really can't imagine you being anything but bright, clever and besides, your looks won't have been any different. You'd still have your beautiful blue eyes and glorious red hair. So you'd still have been you.'

Lucy continued to persuade her to talk and they were still sitting there when dawn sneaked through the curtains and birdsong began filling the air.

'A robin, a chaffinch, a blackbird, a song thrush,' Lucy reported, concentrating. Then a loud yelp startled her. Rascal was awake and ready for action.

'We might as well get up and start the day. There'll be time to give her a good walk if we go now.'

Meriel went down and released the dog from her night time captivity in the kitchen and laughed as she leapt about her feet, before running straight up the stairs to

Lucy. We're her family, she thought sadly, and she isn't happy unless we're all together.

—

George Dexter had also had a sleepless night. He had driven away filled with shame for what he had done. With those few words he had destroyed a happy family, and out of spite. His disappointment with his son and the hurt and embarrassment over his young wife's behaviour had made him unnecessarily cruel. Hadn't he harmed them enough? Yet he couldn't forget hearing those words pouring out of Walter's self-satisfied face.

He didn't go home but drove instead to an isolated beach and sat looking across at the island just a short distance from the shore, faintly visible in the darkness. As he sat there the tide came in, coming around from both sides of the island and meeting in restless white foam before moving on towards the narrow beach.

The rhythmical sound of the waves calmed him and he knew he had to go at once to see Walter and Lynne, and apologize. He doubted whether any words he could say would help, the damage was done, but he needed to try.

Teifion was making toast when he got home. 'Dad?' he queried. 'Where have you been? You must have gone out very early.' Seeing his father's solemn expression he asked, 'Is everything all right?'

'No, it isn't all right and I don't want to talk about it.'

'It isn't Frieda, is it, she's all right, is she?'

'She's having a wonderful time. We're all all right, now shut up and get and open the office before we lose even more business!'

Presuming there had been a problem with the company – about which he wasn't allowed to ask – Teifion pushed aside the breakfast he'd hardly begun and went out.

George sat staring at the wall, seeing pictures in his mind that he didn't like. Meriel's stricken expression, Walter and Lynne's distress, specially Lynne's. Then he visualized his own, distorted with spite and envy, and left the house and went to the café, where he sat in a corner and rudely ignored every attempt to start a conversation.

–

Walter and Lynne sat in their living room, the made-up fire casting a glow over the elegant room. They'd hardly spoken after the first hour, but sat there, holding hands and staring into the flames wondering how to repair the damage. As dawn broke, Lynne went out to make tea and toast which neither of them wanted. She needed the pretence of being busy.

'I know this is my fault,' she said returning with the tray. 'The past never goes away, does it?'

'It wouldn't have happened if I hadn't goaded George, reminded him of his fifty years and his wife's thirty-five.' He stared at her then. 'In all these years I never dreamed anyone would find out she isn't really ours.'

'No one else would. Just George and his need for revenge.'

'Revenge? Why would *he* want revenge? Surely that's our prerogative if anyone's?'

With an uneasy glance at him, Lynne said quickly, 'Jealousy then. Or envy. We're happy and anyone would be proud to have a daughter like ours. You only have to compare that to his situation with a straying wife and a useless son.'

'Yes, but where was my common sense? Why did I have to remind him about his unfaithful wife at that precarious moment, when I was begging a favour?'

'The way you two have always felt about each other, how could you not?' she replied with a sigh.

'Shall we have an early breakfast and go to see Meriel again? I don't want to leave it as though it's of no importance.'

'No, I think we ought to leave it until this evening as discussed, go down there and perhaps take her out for a meal at a place where we can talk.'

'Shall we phone and suggest it?'

'I don't know how she's feeling but I can't help thinking she needs time. What if Leo went down and helped in the office, gave Meriel and Lucy a day to rest. I doubt whether either of them had much sleep.'

It was still very early but Walter couldn't wait. He woke Leo, knocking on the front door, hoping he would wake Leo and not his mother. Leo had known about Meriel's parentage for several years but he was surprised and distressed to learn of George's revelation. 'I'll get there when they open the office and have had time to deal with the post. If I can persuade Meriel a day off for herself and Lucy would be a good idea. I'll stay till five thirty and tell them you'll be there soon after.'

The day was living up to April's reputation and rain threatened. It was as though the weather was joining in with the feelings of regret and anxiety. Pointlessly he wished the morning had been fine and sunny. Surely that would have helped to cheer Meriel, rather than this semi-darkness which could only add to her gloom. In the hope it would add a little brightness to her morning, he detoured calling in at Treseder's plant nurseries near Dmas

119

Powys to buy two large bunches of flowers to take with him, arriving soon after nine o'clock. The threatened rain was falling and he ran from the car to the office struggling with his umbrella and the flowers.

As he had guessed, both girls were already there and immersed in their work; Lucy typing letters and Meriel with a list in front of her, talking on the telephone.

'Leo!' Meriel said in surprise. 'What are you doing here so early?'

'I've come to bring you these,' he said, thrusting the flowers at her. 'And to mind the shop while you and Lucy take a day off. Your mam and dad suggested it might be a good idea for you both to take Rascal and go out for the day. I'm here to make sure you don't miss a client.'

Meriel stared at him. 'You know?'

Leo nodded. 'Come on, you two, you can't expect me to believe you won't enjoy a few hours of freedom.'

'It's raining.'

'Rascal won't mind a drop of rain, and I doubt whether either of you two will shrink!'

They took a lot of persuading but when Leo complained mildly that she should be able to trust him of all people to look after the shop for a few hours, they agreed and decided to go to the seaside.

'Paddling? In this weather?'

'You just reminded us that we won't shrink,' she retorted.

'Wonderful idea,' Lucy agreed. 'It's never the wrong time for a walk along the shore.'

'And the cliffs are a good place to blow cobwebs away, so they might work on shock and misery too.'

'Don't be upset, Meriel. Nothing's changed. You are still the person you were before George Dexter made his announcement. He was trying to hurt, so don't let him.'

'We'll pack a picnic,' Lucy continued. 'We can eat in the car if we can't find somewhere to shelter. Geoff and Connie go to the beach for picnics no matter what time of year. In fact, she never goes anywhere without a flask and a packet of sandwiches. She's famous for it.'

'Sounds a good idea to me,' Leo said.

Once they had gone he picked up the desk diary, admiring the neat entries, noting that there were two people calling that morning and pleased Meriel had trusted him without going into the details of the day. He spent some of the time looking through the local paper, marking any possible prospects for them to follow up.

At twelve Gerald called in and asked to talk to Lucy.

'Sorry but she and Meriel are out for the day and before you think of it, they're not to be disturbed if they're at home. Not today, they're having a quiet day to relax away from everything and everyone. Understand?'

He knew he sounded harsh but he had disliked the man on sight, considered him idle, vain and self-important and although he had no feelings for Lucy, he couldn't help wishing she would find someone more deserving of her.

At lunchtime, dashing through the now heavy rain, he went to the Ship and Compass, where Connie served hot pies and sandwiches. The bar was surprisingly full. Holidaymakers he gathered, from snatches of conversations he overheard; glad of somewhere warm and welcoming where they could shelter and start to dry off. He had noticed touring cycles parked outside and a pile of rucksacks in a corner, so he guessed many of the strangers were just passing through. Rain-soaked coats were drying on the backs of chairs, issuing a mixture of smells, mostly unpleasant. He managed to find a seat near the door and away from the dense group around the open fire.

As he ate he hoped the girls had found somewhere warm and had had a more interesting lunch than one provided in a steaming car with soggy sandwiches, and had given their picnic to the birds.

In fact, they had stayed at home. Neither the weather nor their sombre mood encouraged them to go out. At five o'clock they went to close the office and allow Leo to leave.

'Your parents will be down later,' he told them after bringing them up to date on the day's events. 'I think they're hoping you'll go out with them for a meal.' As Meriel began to shake her head, he added, 'You're upset. I can understand that, but don't forget they're devastated. They're terribly afraid of losing you, their daughter, who they love more than anything in the world. Have a thought for them, Meriel.'

When Walter and Lynne went to Badgers Brook they found the place empty, the door locked. Gerald had ignored Leo's demands to stay away and, finding them at Badgers Brook, had invited them out for a meal. He was delighted by their enthusiastic response, unaware that his offer simply meant that Meriel could be unavailable when her parents came.

Over the following days Walter and Lynne tried repeatedly to see Meriel but whenever they appeared she would walk away. When they telephoned the office, the phone was quickly passed to Lucy. Only Leo managed to spend a little time with her and even then Lucy was with them making it difficult to speak openly.

'I can't meet them, not until I've found out why I was given away. How can a mother do that?' she asked Lucy a dozen times a day. Lucy patiently listed possibilities: illness, too many in the family, poverty, or the lack of a husband – which they thought the most likely. None of them convinced Meriel that their abandonment of her was necessary.

Meriel began to depend more and more on Leo for comfort. She needed reassurance from him that her parents were coping. She needed someone who knew and understood her distress and most of all she needed affection, which he gave without hesitation. His show of affection was balm to her damaged esteem and she was hardly aware of the excuses she found to delay his leaving. There were only a few kisses at first, and a declaration of his love was accepted as from a loving friend.

Gradually the kisses became something more, affecting her in the depth of her body in a way that was wonderful and at the same time frightening. She could become so dependent on him, but if she drove him away she would have no one. She knew she had been turning further and further away from Lucy, needing her less as she needed Leo more. The ache to feel his arms around her became a hunger that left her feeling bereft when he left to return home. She said nothing to Lucy of love's awakening. Coming so soon after the news of her adoption she needed time to adjust before she revealed that Leo was more than her father's assistant and her big-brother type friend.

Lucy kept refusing Gerald's invitations, not wanting to leave Meriel alone. But he called at the house instead and would stay, talking to Lucy in the kitchen when Leo was present, sharing an hour or two listening to Lucy's records when he wasn't. Occasionally they would get up and dance to some of their favourite bands, but although she said nothing, it was clear that whatever she chose to play, Meriel thought the music inappropriate. Lively numbers like their current favourite, Count Basie's 'One O'Clock Jump', failed to lift her out of her misery and the more romantic melodies, like Harry James's 'You Made Me Love You', just made her cry. Lucy was unaware of the confusion in Meriel's heart over the apparent loss of her parents and the anxiety of the way her feelings towards Leo were changing. For the first time since they had become friends, Lucy was not the recipient of her thoughts. It was an uneasy time for them all.

Although she was sympathetic, Lucy found the evenings when Leo and Meriel talked together very lonely. She felt isolated from her friend, made to feel like an outsider. When Gerald was there he was sympathetic although he wasn't told of the problem. But gradually his visits became fewer and Lucy knew that the possibility of reviving their friendship was fading. But she couldn't abandon Meriel, she knew she had to wait until she was ready to talk to her.

Gerald was soon bored with sitting in the kitchen with Lucy when he visited. They were alone but not in a close way, he sipped the occasional cup of tea and watched the clock until he could leave. He was disappointed. Lucy's conversation was stilted, half her mind on her friend in the next room.

She only became animated when she talked about business. 'How would she like it if I talked about nothing but motorcycle engines?' he muttered to himself as he walked home one evening. The idea of marrying her for security had less and less appeal.

Lucy sometimes went to see Kitty and Bob, without explaining the reason for Meriel's absence, or to the little cluttered room behind the post office, where Stella and Colin sat with their little terrier on guard, watching to make sure Rascal didn't go near his treasures.

It was the loneliness she suffered from most and she began to be less dismissive of Gerald, not wanting to be alone evening after evening with little sign of Meriel coming out the gloom into which George Dexter's announcement had thrown her. After some time had passed, and the loneliness was making her restless, she agreed to go with Gerald to a dance.

He arrived to escort her and came with a gift of flowers, which set the evening off to a happy start. Gerald was also most attentive throughout the four hours they spent together. The music was the same as when she and her friend Jennie had enjoyed these evenings so long ago, but the crowd seemed much younger, and more animated than she wanted to be. Gerald was a moderately good dancer but they no longer 'jelled' as a couple, her instincts failing to guide her to do what he expected, and they left early. Gerald's anticipation of an exciting end to the evening was unfulfilled and he took her home and left after a light kiss on the cheek and the promise that they would 'Do this again sometime.' Gerald ran up the road to the bus stop, more like an escapee than an ardent lover.

She watched as he turned the corner; hoping for at least a wave, her disappointment was painful, he had been so casual, no invitation, just a vague 'see you sometime' end to the evening. Had she outgrown the fun she used to have? Had she let him down, been dull and boring, after his efforts to persuade her to go out with him?

Teifion stayed out of the house as much as he could. He felt more alone than he could have imagined. Neither his father nor his step-mother addressed a word to him and he drifted around the office, trying to look interested, and left, as soon as he dare, to drift around the town instead.

He often stood and watched as Meriel and Lucy dealt with a growing number of clients and wondered how Meriel was feeling. She appeared to act normally, smiling at the clients, laughing with Lucy, but he guessed that inside she was feeling wretched, as his father had intended.

One morning as Meriel walked to the bank, he ran up and walked beside her.

'Sorry for my father's outburst,' he began.

Before he could continue she turned to him and smiled.

'Don't worry, I won't tell the world about your precious step-mother's other life. I don't have your father's viciousness.'

'Thank you, I wouldn't blame you if you did. Meriel, I'm very sorry.'

'Why are you sorry? It isn't important, is it? I'm still me, whatever my parents failed to tell me.'

'You're all right about it, are you?'

'Of course. Or I will be, when I find out who my real mother is and why she gave me up.'

'You want to know?'

'Of course.'

'But she might be anything, something unpleasant I mean. Because you are beautiful and clever, it doesn't mean she will be, heavens she could be—' He faltered as she stopped and stared at him.

'Go on, Teifion, what's the worst you can think of for a mother?'

'I don't know. I was going to say she could be someone you instantly dislike, then you'd regret finding out.'

'Whatever the outcome, I want to know.'

'Then I might be able to help.'

'You know who my mother is?'

'Well, not exactly know, but I have a possibility in mind. Although I haven't checked dates or anything. It's probably just a coincidence.'

She grabbed his arm and almost dragged him into the café near the post office. She called for two teas and sat down. He sat beside her after adding two slices of cake to their order. He might as well try and take control.

'I know of a family not too far away who lost a child about the time you appeared,' he explained, 'and I wondered if – you see I noticed the man didn't seem to want to talk to you, in fact he hurried away twice on seeing you.'

'You don't mean Mr Roberts-Price, the religious man in old-fashioned clothes?' She laughed. 'How can you imagine I'm connected to him?'

'That's the point, you don't know, do you?' He'd only meant to discourage her. A neighbour was too easy, her real mother could be miles away and probably was. 'A thief, a blackmailer, a violent criminal, a murderer? You have no way of learning about your family unless you find them. Are you sure you want to search?'

'Yes.'

'Have you really thought about it?'

'I've thought about nothing else since your father blurted out the truth.'

'What about what it might do to your parents?'

'Do you mean my legal parents or my true ones?'

Ignoring that, he said, 'Think about it some more. If you find the woman who gave birth to you she could be evil, with a family who would cause serious trouble, try to get money out of your parents, your real parents, the ones who brought you up!'

She raised one eyebrow. 'Of course they might be decent, honest people. And yes. I *do* have to find them. Can't you understand that?'

After they'd hurriedly disposed of the cake and tea, he drove her to the village of Glyndwr and stopped near the church. A narrow lane passed close to the boundary and on the opposite side of it there was a cottage built of the same stone as the church. He pointed it out as the new home of Mr and Mrs Roberts-Price and family.

They sat for a while, staring at the silent cottage, not knowing what they were waiting for, Meriel anxiously aware that, perhaps, inside the place was someone who could help her find her other family. Her heart was thumping as her imagination spiralled in hopes, wild guesses and possibilities, most of which were less than happy. Could she really be something to do with the strange man and his subdued family?

She knew he worked in a book shop, a gaunt and cold figure, dealing with the running of the office and rarely meeting the public. His daughter Martha served on the record counter in Woolworth's. She had seen her there, a timid girl, thin and shy, who concentrated on the classical. How could she ever relate to them if they turned out to be her true family?

Seeing someone open the cottage door and put out empty milk bottles, Teifion got out of the car. 'Come on,' he said. 'We might as well ask. We aren't doing any good sitting staring at the place.' Meriel followed as he went across and knocked on the door. On the way to Glyndwr and several times since arriving, he had pleaded with her to change her mind about investigating the past, reminding her he could be wrong and that she might get upset for nothing. He also warned her of what she might lose, but she had refused to budge.

The door opened on the smiling face of the white-haired Roberts-Price but when he saw her, the smile vanished and he began closing the door. 'Sorry, it isn't convenient to see anyone at present.'

'Who is it, dear?' His wife came to the door and scolding him affectionately invited them inside. She gestured towards two hard chairs and stood beside her husband, waiting to hear what they wanted.

'I'm very sorry, I know this isn't the right way to set about this, but I wondered if you have any information about a child who was adopted. Meriel was born twenty-two years ago and—'

'Please leave,' the man said, taking hold of Teifion's arm.

'I know you lost a child and I wondered, it being the same date and everything, whether—'

He struggled with the man but the woman was smiling. 'Please, where are your manners, William?' she scolded him in a soft, gentle voice, touching her husband's arm. 'We lost a child, but he's not far away, he's in the church-yard the other side of the hedge.' With shaking hands she searched through a marquetry box and handed him a death certificate, dated twenty-one years previously, 1929.

'You told my father a child was lost, you didn't say it died.'

'His name was Jacob. We believe we'll meet him again. He's lost but he will be found.'

'This woman was born twenty-two years ago. Why did you ask if we were involved? That was long before we were married, in fact, my wife and I would have been no more than seventeen at the time. The idea's preposterous!'

Deeply apologetic they began to leave.

'It was my punishment,' the man said in a strangled voice as they reached the door. 'I'm the guilty one. Our beloved son paid for my sin.'

His wife stood beside him, comforting him as they left.

'How could you?' Meriel demanded. 'As if this affair hasn't caused enough misery you have to revive *their* grief. I'm ashamed of myself and you!'

'I really thought you might be their child. You have the same red hair as his wife, in fact you aren't dissimilar in other ways. Add to that his uneasiness. He seems frightened at the sight of you – you saw how he behaved when he opened the door and saw you. The date was right and my father saw an entry in their Family Bible about a lost child. I thought—'

'Thought? I don't think that's something you do very much, is it, Teifion? Half an idea and you act on it. Well, for goodness sake leave me out of any further thoughts you might have. I've enough to contend with as it is.'

'What did he mean when he said he was the guilty one, that his son died as punishment for his sins?'

'I don't know, but I do know it's nothing to do with me!'

'Strange though, I wonder what his guilty secret could be? Sins of the fathers visited upon the sons?'

'Oh, shut up and drive me back to the office.'

'You're one of the lucky ones, even though you were adopted,' he said as they drove away from the church cottage and its sad secrets. 'You had a good childhood, freedom to choose what you wanted to do, I was pressured into being what my father wanted me to be.'

'Oh, poor you. A beautiful home, plenty of money and a job where you can take time off to go on ridiculous and embarrassing visits.'

'You've never wanted to do anything except follow in your father's steps, have you? Just imagine how you'd feel if you'd had to when you hated it.'

'I'd have done something else,' she retorted flippantly.

'So easy! Except when your father is George Dexter.'

'I'm sorry, Teifion. I can understand how difficult it must have been for you. You're right, I was one of the lucky ones.'

'Things are worse now he has Frieda. I didn't trust her from the start and now she's shown him what she really thinks of him I thought she'd leave, but he can't let her go. Unless she leaves him and they divorce, the business will be hers when my father dies. Even though I dislike it I expected one day to inherit and be able to sell up and do what I really want to do.'

'Which is?'

'I'll tell you one day.'

'Since learning that I'm no relation, I don't expect to inherit anything from the man I've been calling Dadda.'

'Don't be so melodramatic! Go home, Meriel. It's where you truly belong.'

Walter and Lynne were in Walter's office, Leo was out on an appointment and Lynne was dressed in her smartest coat, hat and shoes, and beside her was a suitcase.

'What are you talking about? You can't leave me!'

'I have to.'

'But why?'

'It's all my fault, you see. Twice I've almost destroyed you, can't stay.'

'Have I made you so unhappy?'

'I've been blissfully content, no one could ask more of life than the years you've given me.'

'Then for heaven's sake stay!'

'I can't. Not now. If I leave, then perhaps George will say nothing more. He'll have achieved what he wanted and will leave you and Meriel alone. None of this will come out and Meriel will forget and come home. But while I'm here, George is likely to add yet more outbursts, let everyone know the rest of it. I couldn't cope with everyone knowing the rest, darling. I want to avoid that for you and our daughter.' It was Saturday morning, a day on which most offices closed for the day at one o'clock. Walter stood up and pulled the blind down on the door and window. 'Come on, we're going to talk about this, at Badgers Brook. Meriel will have to listen. No matter how she tries not to be, she's involved in your decision making. She'll make you see it's the wrong one.'

'But how can we convince her? We can't tell her the rest.'

'Hopefully that will not be necessary.'

Putting a notice on the desk for when Leo returned, he closed the office and drove to Cwm Derw. It was two o'clock when they parked in the lane and walked up the path, leaving the suitcases in the boot. Rascal began to bark as they approached the door and, as she came from around the side of the house, Walter guessed Meriel and Lucy were in the garden. With Rascal fussing around them they went into the garden to see Meriel and Lucy pouring teas for several neighbours.

They greeted everyone and, helping themselves to extra cups, sat and joined them. Meriel said nothing. Although the chatter seemed the same as usual, it was apparent from Meriel's silence that something was wrong and, as they became aware of the tension, the others left.

When there were just the four of them left, Meriel picked up the dog's lead and hurried out into the lane and across to the wood. Determinedly, Walter and Lynne followed. At the stream, where the badgers crossed on their nightly search for food, they insisted on her stopping. There were a few fallen logs and she sat on one far away from the rest and stared at them. She released the dog to go exploring and half smiled at her parents. She spoke calmly and almost lovingly.

'Dadda, Mam, I can't explain how I feel but I love you just as much as always. It's just that I can't sit with you and pretend nothing has happened.'

'And what exactly has happened?' Walter asked softly. 'Only George in his bitterness has told you something we should have told you ourselves, a long time ago. It's a secret we had no right to keep, a truth about you, our darling daughter, that should have been a natural part of your growing up. The truth is, Meriel, we were afraid.'

'Is my name really Meriel? Or did I have another name before you took me as your daughter?'

Ignoring the tearful question, Walter went on, 'Every time we decided the time was right, we prepared ourselves, went over the words again and again, then the moment passed and we gave ourselves another perfect moment some time in the future. Every time, the same thing happened.'

'We began to believe you'd never find out and we relaxed,' Lynne said, 'believing it was for the best for you as well as us.'

'Of all the places you could have chosen, why oh why did you choose Cwm Derw?' Walter said with a groan. He lowered his head into his hands and added, 'You should never have come here. Specially to rival George Dexter. George and I have never got on, he – well put it this way, he could never pass up a chance to hurt me.' He looked at her and gave an apologetic smile. 'I tried to stop you, remember.'

'Without telling me why,' Meriel said.

'I should have tried harder.'

'It would have happened some time whatever you did, Walter, darling,' Lynne said, gripping his hand in hers.

'And now, because of this, your mother wants to leave.'

'But why, Mam? That will add to the gossip if it comes out. It won't stop George Dexter telling anyone who'll listen, will it? Why add to the misery by leaving Dadda on his own? Let it go, it will blow over quickly if we ignore it.'

'George is angry and angry people hit out.'

'There's something you haven't told me, isn't there? Something else he can use to hurt us?' Meriel saw the glances between Lynne and Walter and felt deep concern. The explanations were vague and Meriel was left with the feeling that there were other secrets to learn, secrets in George's keeping. She persuaded them to stay the night, giving Lynne a chance to reconsider her decision, hoping that the real reason for her intended flight might be revealed.

At nine o'clock Geoff and Connie called. They knew about George's revelations from Meriel and came to see if all was now well. Meriel and Lucy were about to prepare supper, and afterwards Connie persuaded Lynne and Walter to go with them beyond the wood to where badgers were likely to be feeding, in one of Treweather's fields. When they returned, Lynne and Walter kissed both girls and went to bed.

After their unexpected walk and watching the badgers playing chase, grooming themselves and crunching through peanuts Geoff had spread for them earlier; they all slept well and Lucy was aware of them all being in a slightly more relaxed mood as they ate breakfast. Geoff had brought them some eggs from Treweather's farm – which were written off from the farm quota as allegedly being cracked. Lucy boiled them and they ate them with thin slices of bread and butter – off ration, having been exchanged, again illegally, for something in the barter chain that included many pairs of hands and had begun with two pounds of sugar.

They kissed as they parted, although still with an edge of insecurity, and Walter told them, 'Leo is coming for dinner tomorrow. Why don't you also both come for the day, bring Rascal. You know how your mother loves to fuss over people,' Walter added with an affectionate smile, helping Lynne into the car. 'Try not to worry, love, we'll probably hear nothing more about it,' Walter whispered to his wife. 'George has caused as much trouble as he could and it's unlikely he'll say more.'

Meriel waved to them as they drove off, hoping the calming atmosphere of Badgers Brook had been enough to change Lynne's mind about leaving.

The gossip in the post office was still all about the news that Meriel was an adopted child.

'So what?' Stella retorted every time this was mentioned. 'She isn't the first and won't be the last. Stop talking as though the poor girl's a criminal and tell me what you want or I'll be closing for lunch before you're served.'

—

George was a nervous man. Having made a stupid mistake and blurted out the truth about Meriel's adoption, he knew that unless a miracle happened, Walter would spread the story about his wayward wife. He had tried to discuss the possibility several times with Frieda and over breakfast he tried again. 'Why shouldn't he tell everyone? It would be a laugh, poor deluded George Dexter being cuckolded by a wife who's too young for him to handle. Great story it'll make.'

'Why should he?' Frieda said, unperturbed.

'I would in the same circumstances.'

'Fortunately for us imperfect mortals, not everyone is like you, George. Walter and Lynne might stop and think what this might do to Teifion for one thing.'

'Why should they care?'

'Because it's what most people do – care.'

'I care. I do everything I can for the people who matter to me, you and Teifion. Everything I do is for you and my son.'

'The world is wider than your wife and son, George.'

'You're dreaming if you think it won't come out about... your—'

'About my sister in Brighton?' She was laughing and for a moment anger flared in his eyes.

'It isn't a joke!'

'No, it isn't and I'm sorry, George. I've made you a promise not to see the man again and when I go to Brighton to visit my sister you will come with me.'

'The story will soon be on everyone's lips, we have to prepare for it.'

'D'you want me to go away, George?'

'You know I don't.'

'Then I'll stay, we'll face it and let it pass. I'm truly sorry for the hurt I've caused you.'

'Well, we'll see what happens, take it as it comes. Right?'

'I won't be in at lunchtime, I'm going Cardiff to do some shopping,' she said kissing him goodbye. He left for the office and Frieda carelessly put the breakfast dishes into the sink. The cleaner will deal with them later, she thought. After changing her clothes, and phoning for a taxi to take her to the station, she went out.

She caught a train to Cardiff and from there a train to Newport. It was unlikely anyone she knew would see her there, but to make sure, she and the man she had arranged to meet walked separately into a restaurant and an hour later came out together.

–

Meriel and Lucy went as arranged to spend Sunday with Walter and Lynne. The welcome was as enthusiastic as ever but Lucy was aware that something had irrevocably changed. Meriel was quiet, choosing to spend a lot of the time out of the house. They didn't visit Meriel's friends as they had previously done. Instead they went out with an equally subdued Leo, and walked through the fields and along quiet stretches of the coast where they met no one. It was almost a relief when they gathered their coats and started back to Badgers Brook. Leo was formal in his goodbye, Lucy being there made him wonder whether Meriel had only brought her to avoid being alone with him.

Lynne watched them go with a heavy heart. It might never be put right. Meriel's unconscious reaction was to punish them and herself for their dishonesty and there seemed no hope of an end to it.

'I feel so angry with George,' Walter said. 'Why did you stop me telling everyone about his wife? He doesn't deserve our loyalty after what he's done to us.'

'Old-fashioned I suppose, but I believe that two wrongs never make a right. Harming George and Frieda and Teifion won't make me feel any better. In fact I'd feel worse. This is my fault, all of it.'

'Lynne, don't say that. Any problem is ours, we share everything, remember that. Look, if you want to go away for a while I'll take you to stay with your auntie Gladys May. She isn't far away and I can bring you back as soon as you've had enough.'

'Thank you, darling. I think I'd like that.'

While she waited for a reply to the letter to her elderly godmother who had been a large part of her childhood, she tried to make a decision. She made mental lists trying to decide whether it would be better or worse for Meriel and Walter if she stayed or went away. If Walter took her to stay with her auntie she could move on from there, disappear. Surely then Meriel would come back to her father and that was what she wanted more than anything. Walter didn't deserve this estrangement. Whatever he said about troubles shared, the fault was hers and hers alone.

They drove through Newport and on impulse stopped to have a cup of coffee. It was there, unbelievably, that they bumped into Frieda and her man-friend coming out of a restaurant, arms around each other, a glow of too much food and a surfeit of wine on their faces. Frieda was wearing a smart black two-piece, high-heeled shoes and a saucy red hat.

'This isn't what it seems,' Frieda said with the cautious precision of the drunk. 'Alfie is my brother.'

Walter pulled Lynne aside for them to pass without a word. Lynne was shocked and dismayed. It would be impossible to stop Walter talking about this, and if he did, George Dexter had a few more revelations up his sleeve. Now she would definitely have to leave. It was the only way.

They drove on in silence after she had pleaded with him to remain silent. Then, as they were within a few minutes of her aunt's home she asked him to take her back. 'I'll go in and explain to her that I'll come soon, but something's happened and I can't stay.'

'You won't persuade me to keep quiet this time,' he said grimly. 'He doesn't deserve our silence after what he did.' She saw the tight expression on his face and felt afraid.

The following morning, she wrote a note, telling Walter that if he said nothing she would come home, but if he started another round of his fight with George Dexter she would not. She picked up the case which was still packed for her visit and reached for her handbag. Dammit, she must have left it in Walter's car with her warm coat. Now what was she going to do?

After a few minutes, during which she took cash from the various insurance books and the payments for the milkman and the baker, making a neat list of what she had done, she left the house. Walter could send her handbag on at a later date, there was no worry about that, but she had to leave today. He had to find her gone and know she meant it. There was no time to lose if she were to stop him threatening George and starting the worse scenario she could imagine.

A taxi took her to the village of Glyndwr and she knocked on the door of Church Cottage.

'William,' she said when he opened the door to her, 'I've never once asked you for anything, but now I need some money to go away for a while.'

Without a word he went inside, leaving her standing there and came back with an envelope containing several one pound and ten shilling notes. 'This is all I have,' he said, handing it to her.

She took three pounds and handed the rest back to him. Then she went to the bus stop without looking back.

William turned to his wife and said sadly, 'You know all this means we have to move again?'

Six

Leo looked at his mother and tried to tell her what was on his mind, but she smiled up at him, so trustingly he found it hard. How could he tell her he wanted to go away, stay in Cwm Derw for a week or two to keep an eye on the distressed Meriel? He had never left his mother before, not since his father and brother had died during the war. His three sisters had all left and were busy with their own lives and he had kept to the silent promise he'd made to stay and look after her, make sure she was never so lonely the memories would slide back and torment her.

She had never been in the house alone overnight and he knew the prospect frightened her. The time for her to cope with it had been immediately after his father's death while she was coping with so much more but his concern was too great and now it was too late and he felt committed to being there for her.

To stay with her hadn't been a difficult decision to make at the time. He hadn't imagined how things would change. Now his feelings for Meriel made his chosen responsibility less easy to accept. Now he wanted to share his love and caring with Meriel. At present Meriel needed him more than his mother. How could he explain that?

'Is something worrying you, Leo?' she asked when he moved away from her and sat near the fire, his hand smoothing the lower part of his face, which she recognized as a symptom of anxiety.

'Mam, how would you feel about my going away for a few days? You could invite Mabel Lyddiat to stay.'

There was a sharp intake of breath before she replied. 'A holiday with friends?'

'No, it's Meriel. You know she's found out she was adopted? It's upset her quite a bit and she needs someone to talk to, someone whom she knows and trusts. I think I'm the right person.'

'That's a kind thought, Leo. She'd appreciate that, you could stay in Cwm Derw and take over while she has a break? Perhaps I could come with you? There's bound to be a guest house near the office. You know the business and she would trust you to look after it. There's nothing better than a few days away from routine when there's a problem to sort.'

'No, that wouldn't be a good idea. Better to stay and face things.'

'Yes, dear, you go and help her, stay a while.'

'You wouldn't mind?' Her voice had risen slightly and he stared at her, seeing the fear she was trying to hide, knowing she was unable to face the silence of the empty house with its memories and ghosts. 'No, Mam, on second thoughts I needn't stay. Perhaps I'll just go down each day and give her a chance to rest and think.'

'Whatever you think best, Leo.' He noticed the slight change as her voice slid back down to normal. 'Whatever happens you must remind her of how much Lynne and Walter love her. That's what makes or breaks a family. Love is the heart of a home, we all know that.'

'I – I'm fond of Meriel. Very fond,' he said, glancing at her.

She met his gaze and smiled. 'Nothing would make me happier than knowing you had someone to love and care for. Meriel would be a perfect choice.'

'Oh, there's nothing like that, I just want to look after her while she copes with all this. She and I have never been more than friends.'

'The best possible start, Leo. The perfect basis for love to grow.' She hesitated a moment then said brightly, 'I'll be all right if you want to stay with her, she's the one who's important at the moment, I can understand that.'

He left the room, filled with embarrassment, and regret for saying too much. How could he even think Meriel would consider him as anything other than her father's employee? There was the age difference for one thing, and the fact that familiarity had certainly bred indifference. The recent affection and closeness was nothing more than her appreciation of his help. If she thought of him at all it was as a kindly older brother.

The garden was looking good, he thought as he cut off the heads of a few dead pansies and pulled up the sad remnants of forgotten wallflowers, grown tall, hidden behind the rainwater butt. He wondered whether he could persuade Meriel to come and see the newly planted geraniums and petunias and admire the blossom-filled rowan, that gave height to the small plot. If he invited Lucy as well, perhaps he could talk to them, manage to persuade them to call and see Lynne and Walter, begin to ease away the pain. What a pity he had spoken of her to his mother, now she would be smiling at them in that special way and making everyone feel ill at ease.

When he reached the office he found Walter in a terrible state, walking up and down, making phone calls and slamming the receiver back into its rest with more and more fury. Leo said nothing for a while but as the calls came to an end he asked, 'What's happened, is Mrs Evans all right?'

'How would I know?' She went off yesterday and I've no idea where she's gone.' The man sank into a chair and hid his face with his hands.

Leo made tea and handed him a cup. 'Tell me who you've tried and we'll try to add to the list. Later I'll try them. Perhaps she'll speak to me.'

'Why you and not me?' Walter sounded belligerent but Leo was unperturbed.

'Because for some reason you know and I don't, it's probably you she's running away from, not me. Right?'

'She blames herself for this trouble with Meriel.'

'Look, Mr Evans, I don't want to know the ins and outs of it, but let me help. Give me a list of the places you think she might be – all of them, including those you have tried. Think back on old friends, there are sure to be some you've missed.' He had a thought. 'Have you told Meriel her mother's gone away?'

'No, I don't think she'll care at the moment.'

'Then I'll call her.' He looked at Walter for permission and, accepting the nod as agreement, dialled the office of Evans and Calloway.

Lucy answered.

'Meriel isn't here at the moment. I'll tell her you've called but I can't promise she'll ring back,' she said doubt-fully.

'Tell her I'm on my way. No, tell her I'll meet you both for lunch. Tell her I insist, will you?' he asked, crossing his fingers with the optimism of a child. 'Tell her it's very important.'

For the next couple of hours he and Walter dealt methodically with the business calls, and going through the list of plans for that day regarding on-going purchases and sales. The few calls in the search for Lynne had resulted in no news. With a heavy heart Walter closed the office an hour after Leo left to meet Meriel, wishing he had gone with him.

Leo's heart was racing as he parked the car near Meriel and Lucy's office and he was afraid to look through the window to see whether both girls were there. Why had he dared to insist on Meriel being there?

He opened the door and saw a couple sitting on the customer side of the desk being attended by Lucy. Meriel was rearranging notices in the window and he was relieved when she smiled, put down what she was doing and came over to greet him.

He waited until the clients had gone then said simply, 'Meriel, your mother has left home and your father is frantic. He has no idea where she can be. Can you offer any suggestions as to where she might be?'

'Gone, without telling him where? Mam wouldn't do that. Something awful must have happened.'

'No, she packed her case and left. There's been no accident or anything like that.'

'But why has she gone?'

With a grim smile to take the sting out of his words he said, 'You aren't the only one affected by George's announcement, remember. Your parents are devastated. You are their life and they're terrified they're going to lose you.'

'They shouldn't have lied.' Meriel tried to revive her anger but the thought of her mother disappearing from her life softened the words into a whisper.

'Let's go and find some food,' Leo said, putting an arm around her shoulders. 'You and Lucy. Perhaps we'll come up with the solution. She has to be with someone you know. I can't imagine she'd go to strangers, can you?'

Lucy was reluctant to join them, but they both insisted and they went to the Ship and Compass and ordered sandwiches, none of them wanting anything more. Leo took out the list he had made of the people Walter had tried and who denied having seen Lynne. 'It doesn't mean she isn't in any of these places, mind. It's likely she has asked them to say nothing. But,' he stated at Meriel, 'if you tried, I don't think she'd refuse to speak to you. So let's go through the list and I'd like you to go back to the office and phone the most likely.'

Meriel smiled then, amused at the way Leo had taken charge. Impulsively she hugged him.

'Yes, Boss,' she said, taking up a sandwich and biting enthusiastically. With difficulty she added, 'When I've finished this though. I've just realized I'm starving.'

Leo smiled, enjoying his new role as adviser. To Lucy, he said, 'Will you manage if I take Meriel off while we find out where her mother is staying?'

'Of course I will. Gosh, this is like living through a mystery film. Meriel is Celia Johnson, you are a very handsome Trevor Howard and me, well, I'm the retired nanny who follows you around and makes sure you eat regular meals, all your greens, and drink lots of milk.'

They all laughed and soon afterwards left to return to the office. The official lunch hour was not over, so while it was unlikely they'd be disturbed, Meriel started making calls. After four failures, she found her mother. Auntie Gladys didn't have a telephone but her neighbour did and when Meriel rang she went at once to fetch her. Without any warning, Meriel found herself talking to her mother.

Both women were crying too much to make sense at first and Leo put a pencil in Meriel's hand and urged her to write down the name and address. While they were still talking he went outside and from the red call box, phoned Walter to tell him where Lynne had been found.

Stubbornly, the anger still present, Meriel refused to close the office before five thirty as she had two appointments to keep and a message to this effect was sent to Walter. So it was after seven o'clock when the car carrying Meriel and Leo, followed by another driven by Walter, arrived at Auntie Gladys's house.

It was Lynne who opened the door and ran to Meriel. She was clearly not expecting Walter and hesitated like a animal about to take flight. He held out his arms and said, 'Lynne, my love, come home.'

In the moment that followed, Meriel felt superfluous but once the couple had hugged, arms came out to envelope her in the love that bound them.

Guessing he might be needed, but staying back almost out of sight, Leo waited until they separated and began to enter the house, then he stepped forward and offered to drive Meriel back to Cwm Derw later that evening. In her euphoric state, wildly happy to be reunited with her parents, Meriel hugged him and thanked him for what he had done to help. He held her for longer than the moment justified and knew the incident would remain with him for ever. A reminder of the love that could never be.

It wasn't as easy as Meriel expected to persuade Lynne to return. Leaving her parents to talk, Meriel walked in the garden and talked to the lady she called Auntie Gladys, convinced a solution would be reached. When she went back inside it was clear that this was not the case. Lynne was adamantly refusing to go back home. She couldn't understand why Lynne had left nor why it was so difficult for her father to persuade her to return. Gladys was tight-lipped, insisting the disagreement was between Lynne and Walter and concerned no one else.

Meriel wasn't convinced. 'All this must be a result of George Dexter telling me they're not my real parents, so it has to be my concern. But I don't understand why Mam insists the blame lies with her?'

Gladys smiled, patted her hand and said nothing.

Leo drove home after promising to return for Meriel at ten o'clock. His mother had prepared a meal of fish, chips and tomatoes and he ate without tasting any of it.

'Is Meriel all right?' his mother asked as she cleared the dishes. 'Will you still need to go down to Cwm Derw?'

'I think she's forgiven her parents for not telling her, but she still needs some help.' This wasn't really true but he couldn't give up the possibility of spending a little time with her. 'I'll go tomorrow, just for a few days.'

'I'll pack your case. Just a day or so, is it?'

'Probably.' He didn't think he could justify staying for more than a couple of days. Meriel didn't need him and Walter did. After such a distressing time, Meriel wasn't the only one who needed a break. He guessed that if Walter had persuaded Lynne to go back with him, they would go away for the weekend to reassure each other everything was back to normal. 'I have to be back for the weekend,' he told his mother, and saw the smile of satisfaction she couldn't hide. 'I'll arrange to telephone the corner shop with any news, they won't mind passing on a message.'

'Stop fussing, dear, just go.' She laughed. 'I'm not a child.'

'Will you ask your friend Mabel Lyddiat to come and stay with you?'

'She'll be busy,' she replied, waving the idea aside. 'But talking about breaks, have you thought about where we'll go this summer? I know we've been there quite a few times but I do like West Wales. Aberaeron, or perhaps Aberdovey, we can drive up into the mountains, it's so beautiful.'

'Wouldn't you like to go with one of your friends for a change? A coach trip maybe? I'll treat you both, how's that? You'll enjoy meeting new people. Tell you what,' he went on when there was no reply, 'tomorrow I'll see what I can find out and you talk to Mrs Lyddiat and see what she thinks.'

'I don't think so, dear. I couldn't share a bedroom with Mabel.'

'That isn't a problem, we'll book two singles the same as when you and I go.' Avoiding looking at her, he hummed cheerfully and went to deal with some household accounts on the pretext of being busy, until it was time to go and meet Meriel.

The euphoria Meriel felt at finding her mother swiftly faded; the urgency of her parents' discussion, huddled together excluding her, was a reminder of how she had been deceived and reinforced her belief that there were other secrets untold, and she sat as far away from her parents as possible in the small room in the cottage where her 'Auntie' Gladys lived. A friend of her parents since before she had been born, Gladys had been an unofficial auntie to Meriel all of her life. Now she felt distrustful towards her as well as her parents. Their conversation made it clear she had also known and said nothing. Somehow the secret was worse than the knowledge.

She felt let down by those she loved and wondered if she would ever feel confident again. Those who knew about her adoption would have discussed it while she was blissfully ignorant, as a baby, a child and as a grown woman. The thought made her feel naked and exposed.

The revelation about her adoption had been a shock but she had the feeling there was more to come. Why was her mother finding it so difficult to go back with her father? What was she blaming herself for? Her mind was tumbling with possibilities, all of which she discarded as being too fantastic. It was a relief when Leo arrived and she could leave. She was more demonstrative than usual, thankful for his reassuring presence, grateful for having him as a loving, trusted friend. She hugged him some more when he spoke to her parents and reminded them that home was the place where they could spend time and talk things through and finally persuaded Lynne to go back with Walter.

She didn't say much on the way back to Badgers Brook, the confusion of relief and the remnants of hurt and anger bubbling up into a stew of restlessness.

'Are you all right?' Leo asked, as he pulled up in the lane.

'I don't know how I feel,' she said and moved towards him as he put an arm around her and held her close.

After a few blissful moments he opened the car door. 'Come on, let's get you inside.' He jumped out and went around to open her door. Offering a hand to help her out he continued to hold hers until the narrowness of the path made it impossible. The door opened as soon as Meriel handed Leo the key and Lucy asked at once, 'Your mam, is she all right?'

'Yes, she was staying with Auntie Gladys. And, thanks to Leo, she and Dadda have gone home.'

'Thank goodness for that. What's the matter with everyone? Teifion leaving home then going back almost straight away, now your mum doing the same thing. Come on, the kettle's on for a hot drink. You too, Leo?'

They went inside and Meriel threw her coat on a chair. The sadness was back in her eyes. She and Leo sat very close together. 'I can't understand why no one told me, and the thought of them discussing me and at the same time lying to me, makes me unable to talk to them or Auntie Gladys. How many other people knew and didn't tell me?'

'I knew,' Leo said. 'Not telling you was a way of protecting you.'

'I'm talking about people who have known all these years, you found out at the same time as I did.'

'No, your father told me years ago.'

She stared at him in disbelief, the new disappointment more painful than she could bear. She jumped up and stared at him, her eyes filled with tears. 'You knew and said nothing? Leo, I thought you were my friend. The one person I could really trust. How could you deceive me like the others?'

'I didn't look on it as deceit. It wasn't my secret to tell, was it?' He stood up and tried to hold her hands but she pushed him away. The happiness their strengthening love had brought was now draining away. He caught hold of her as she tried to run from the room and she hit him, hard.

'Stop it, Meriel, you're behaving like a crazy woman,' Lucy protested, holding her friend round the waist.

Meriel fought to hold back tears. She felt so let down. Looking at Leo's distraught face she knew she was throwing away something special but she couldn't stop. 'Go away,' she told them. 'Leave me alone. Alone is what I am and what I'm likely to stay. I haven't a family and now I haven't a friend in the world that I can trust. Even you, Lucy. You're siding with him.'

'You are being a bit unfair,' Leo said anxiously. 'Hear my side and you'll understand.'

'He's right, Meriel, you're being unreasonable. Sit down, Leo, and have another cup of tea.' Lucy struggled to keep Meriel from starting an argument. 'Some toast?'

'I don't know, perhaps I should go and leave you two to talk.'

To his disappointment, Meriel agreed. 'Yes, you should!'

'I'll come back tomorrow,' he said, gathering his jacket. 'Give you a chance to take some time off. I can stay till Friday.'

'Stay? There isn't room here, we've no beds and—'

He forced a laugh. 'No, I wouldn't expect to stay here. I phoned the bed and breakfast and booked a room.'

'Thanks for telling me.' Meriel was sarcastic. 'You obviously like secrets! When was this decided?'

'This evening, but it can easily be undecided,' he said lightly. He watched for her response but she turned away.

'Come here for breakfast then,' Lucy invited swiftly. 'We've got some real eggs.'

He glanced at Meriel who seemed quite indifferent to his decision. 'Irresistible,' he replied before setting off home. Meriel watched from the door as he walked towards the car and ignored his wave before he disappeared from sight.

'Come on, Meriel, don't let's have any more dramatics. Leo was told in confidence, so don't blame him or accuse him of lying. Don't risk losing him. You need all your friends.'

'I feel so let down.'

'Why? You can't blame your parents for being afraid. They love you and the fear of losing you must have been a daily dread.'

'Perhaps when I was young, but I'm twenty-two!'

'The longer they waited the harder it would have been. When d'you think would have been the right age? How could they suddenly say, oh, by the way, Meriel, we aren't your real parents, they didn't want you, they gave you up when you were a tiny baby. There's no easy way of announcing that to a daughter you love.'

'I want to go for a walk. Coming?'

'At this time of night? Where shall we go?'

Meriel shrugged. 'Through the wood? There's enough moonlight to find the path.'

'All right. Come on, Rascal.'

The evening was chilly but they sat on a fallen tree for a long time, and listened to the mysterious sounds of the countryside at night; squeaks as small creatures communicated with each other, rustling searches for food, almost inaudible snuffling and chomping as food was found. Rascal was held firmly on her lead to avoid too much disturbance although they guessed that most creatures were wise enough to give them a wide berth. Rascal pulled and half choked herself trying to escape the hated restriction. 'Frightening every creature for a radius of five miles,' Lucy said with a sigh. Snapping off the lead when they reached the edge of the wood, and with the excited dog darting about, nose to the ground, they left the dense trees behind them, at a point where the ground fell over steep fields, and looked at the faintly lit scene below. A ewe nearby gave a laboured cough, which sounded like a man, and they clung to each other in silence until realization came. An owl glided silently across the field as they stood looking down at abandoned farm buildings, where soon, Treweather's farm would be no more, replaced by modern housing. Only the farmhouse was still inhabited, with a few buildings occupied by chickens and ducks. Nearby, the pond glowed like a giant silver coin. They sat and the dog sat beside them, her head turning to every new sound. After a while she curled up and relaxed into sleep. The girls stayed on, enthralled by the magic of the other world; the mysterious hours of darkness.

As they walked back, Meriel told Lucy about how her feelings for Leo had changed. 'It happened so gradually that at first I couldn't believe it, but he's become more than a friend. Much, much more. I began to imagine what it would be like if he left, found someone else and knew I couldn't bear life without him. I knew he was important to me, then, when I was beginning to see a future for us, he tells me he's been lying.'

'Not deliberate lies. Even in your present belligerent mood you have to admit there is more than one type of lie. He was told something in confidence and, honest man that he is, he kept the secret that wasn't his to share.'

Just a few miles away, Leo stood leaning over a farm gate, listening to the quiet night, wishing Meriel was there to share it but doubting she ever would. The phrase 'the love that would never be' whispered on his lips and echoed around his head and he wondered if there was anything he could do to change the prospect of a lonely future.

Mrs Hopkins was sitting waiting for him when he finally reached home. She offered him a sandwich, then said sadly, 'It's no use, Leo, dear. I don't want to go away with anyone else. If you can't manage a proper holiday we'll have a few days out, and try next year, shall we?'

'If you're sure, but I'll get the information anyway,' he said, with unaccustomed firmness. Somehow he had to continue to consider his mother's wishes, make sure she wasn't in the slightest bit unhappy, but still find time for a life of his own before it was too late. Although, whether that life included Meriel, as he had dared to hope, seemed less and less likely.

–

Lucy prepared breakfast for three but Leo didn't appear. Meriel was both outwardly glad and secretly disappointed. When they opened the office they were both sleepy. The night hours sitting in the wood and watching the new day dawn had taken its toll. The breakfast of cereal and toast had been pushed aside and eventually put out for the birds, the effort of chewing seemed too much for them. Rascal had been offered her usual walk but she had refused to leave her basket. She too had been awake for much of the night.

Leo arrived at the office of Evans and Calloway at ten o'clock to find an irate client there, insisting on knowing why his enquiry had not been answered. Meriel looked at him as Leo entered but didn't speak, concentrating on the complainant.

'We need to know why the date we agreed has been changed,' the man was saying. 'We've booked the removals and people have taken days of their holidays to help us.

You can't just tell us there's been a mistake! You promised to let us know yesterday and you didn't.'

Leo sat on the desk and listened but didn't speak. Better to wait until he heard the facts or he might make things worse. For no apparent reason the man began to address him and it was soon clear that, as a man, he was presumed to be better at dealing with problems. Expressions like, 'these chits of girls', 'how can a woman expect to deal with something as complicated as buying a house?' and 'should be home looking after their families' were shouted, while Meriel looked ready to explode. When he could manage to speak, Leo put the facts before him.

'Mr... er—' He glanced at the details on the paper. 'Mr James. I know nothing about this purchase, the business belongs to Miss Evans and Miss Calloway, both of whom are fully experienced. Please calm down and explain exactly what has gone wrong and they will put it right. I'll make the tea,' he added with a wink at Lucy.

The voices slowly lowered as he went into the kitchen and made a pretence at rattling tea cups. The office door opened and closed and he peeped out to see the girls were alone. 'What happened?' he asked.

'The wrong date had been typed on one of the forms,' Lucy explained. 'There isn't a problem. Everything is exactly as we'd agreed.'

'And I bet he didn't apologize for his rudeness!'

'Did he heck! He reminded us again that some things are better left to men.'

'Where's the tea?' Meriel asked.

'Sorry, miss, but as a mere man, I couldn't find the teapot and if I had, I wouldn't have known how much tea was needed.'

Momentarily forgetting her quarrel with him, Meriel laughed, and looked for something to throw at him as he disappeared again to return with a tray of tea and biscuits.

Meriel didn't stay in the office. She made an excuse of visiting someone who telephoned searching for a property. 'I'll drive them around to see what we've got on the books.'

'None of them are suitable,' Lucy reminded her when she was given the details to note.

'I know. I just need to get out of this place,' she replied, and Leo guessed sadly that it was his presence that was the trouble. She had hardly spoken a word to him since he arrived.

'Why don't you both go?' he said. 'Your father is happy for me to stay for a day or so and you might as well make use of me now I'm here.'

'You can tell my father that I don't need help. Neither his nor yours! Lucy and I can manage perfectly well.'

There was no alternative but to pick up his briefcase and leave.

'You were unkind,' Lucy said when the car had driven away.

'Not as unkind as keeping the truth from me for all these years.'

'Come on, how many years? He isn't much older than us and can't have worked for your father for that long. He'd have done what his boss told him anyway.'

'He was fourteen when he started in the office and I was six. A long lanky boy who was what I had always dreamed of – a big brother who spoilt me rotten. I was always running to him when something good had happened and seeking his help when I met a problem. After a while it seemed as though he'd always been there.

Even before he had come to work for my father he had often helped out at the office, and had often sat with me while I chatted to him about the inconsequential events in my sheltered and safe days.'

'Lucky old you,' Lucy said softly. Although she doubted whether Meriel heard.

'So how has everything changed? Why was he no longer the older man, Dadda's assistant, my big brother designate? Why has his keeping the secret of my adoption hurt me so badly?'

'That stuff that's the heart of a home, probably,' Lucy said. 'And I don't mean the kitchen!'

–

Lucy went out with Gerald that evening and Meriel sat alone, no visitors for a change, relishing the calm quiet of the house and trying to understand her feelings. She prepared a snack for when Lucy returned and looked forward to listening to her news. She wondered if her friend was wise to meet Gerald after the disappointment of their previous engagement but knew the only way to help was to say nothing and hope that if it fell apart again, Lucy would be able to turn to her for comfort. Interfering now, offering an opinion, might harm their friendship and that was something she didn't want to risk.

It was almost eleven o'clock when Lucy burst through the door, her eyes sparkling, her face aglow.

'No need to ask if you've had a good evening,' Meriel said jumping up to attend to the kettle simmering at the side of the fire. 'Cocoa all right or is this a night for champagne?'

'Never tasted the stuff and never likely to, but I do think cocoa is a bit tame for how I feel.'

Meriel waited for her friend to expand and found herself filled with anxiety at the thought of Lucy giving herself to a man who had let her down before. She knew the house was partly the reason for her concern. It was such a restful place but there was always an air of tension apparent during the few moments Gerald came in and waited for Lucy to grab coat and bag and dash out. She would never admit her fanciful thoughts to a soul but she somehow knew the house didn't like him.

Lucy ran upstairs to put her coat away and when she came down again, Meriel had made their hot drinks and brought out a tray of biscuits and small cakes. Rascal, who had been sleeping, came to life and stared at the tray in the hope of joining in the late snack.

'I think we're returning to how we used to be before he joined the RAF. He explained how leaving like that, and facing all sorts of dangers, made him lose confidence in the future and how he is only now beginning to sort out his life.'

Meriel cynically wondered how a couple of years in the service clothing store just a few miles from home had been so traumatic, but she kept quiet and waited for Lucy to go on.

'He says he still loves me, and always will.'

'And you? How do you feel? Can you trust him?' Warning signals were riding up and down her spine and she knew she had to tread very carefully not to alienate her friend. 'Perhaps it's a bit soon to forget what happened before. Give yourself a bit more time. Play hard to get, make him work for your love.'

'No need, he's assured me that this time it will end in church with wedding bells and choirs and "happy ever after".'

'I hope so, Lucy. I do hope so.'

'You don't sound convinced.'

'Well, I'm concerned whether you both have the same feelings. I don't blame him for loving you. Besides being lovely, and gentle, you're also a woman with prospects of a good career. Who wouldn't respond if you smiled in their direction?'

'It's nothing to do with my share in our business.' The words were sharply spoken.

'Of course not. It's obvious to everyone that he's clearly smitten. No, Lucy, it's you who has to be sure. Now you no longer hide your talents behind a hairdresser's overall, there will be plenty of others on the scene if you'll give it a chance. So wait, give yourself a choice.'

Lucy patted her friend on the shoulder. 'It's too late, I've chosen Gerald.'

Was it her imagination, or did Meriel hear a sudden angry gust of wind rattle the windows?

–

Petrol rationing ended, as summer sneaked in masking its promise with chill winds and dull days. As the days lengthened, the clouds relinquished their hold and the air grew warm and was filled with the special scent of blossom. Flowers that had seemed hesitant to bloom exploded into full splendour and the second half of the month of May amazed everyone with its glory. The days continued to be long and sunny.

Teifion called at the office several times each week and gradually wore down their displeasure. He would some-times appear about ten o'clock with a few cakes still warm from the bakery, and stay a few minutes and share their mid-morning cup of tea. On other occasions he walked with them to the café or the Ship and talked to them through their lunch break.

They saw nothing of Leo, which Meriel regretted. Still avoiding her parents she was lonely, convinced that was how she would stay. She did accept phone calls from her parents but refused to see them, insisting she needed time to think, but knowing in reality she was punishing them, although she was no longer sure why.

'I know you don't understand,' she said, when an exasperated Lucy asked when she was going to stop playing the prima donna. 'I don't feel I belong, not like I used to. I can't help thinking that the bedroom I'd always thought of as mine was only a temporary shelter, that I was one of the waifs and strays who are taken in until their proper home can be found.'

One day, thinking it would break the deadlock, Lucy said 'Why don't we have a party here, invite some of the neighbours, and if it's a Sunday, we can ask Betty Connors from the pub, as well as Stella and Colin, Kitty and Bob. Leo too, and Gerald of course. Then you'd be able to relax and talk to them without firing questions and accusations at the poor couple.'

'Not Leo.'

'Oh don't be so pathetic! Of course Leo! And his mother and Uncle Tom Cobley an' all!'

'Oh, all right! If only to stop you nagging!' She was laughing, and at once they began to make lists of the things they would need.

So it was arranged for the following Sunday. 'Before Meriel can change her mind,' Lucy confided by phone to Lynne and Walter.

As usual guests came with plates of food to add to the spread. Kitty and Bob were the first to arrive and they helped take chairs and small tables out into the garden. The day wasn't perfect – May can be a moody month – but it was warm enough to sit outside in reasonable comfort.

Walter and Lynne arrived early and Leo and his excited mother were with them. Leo guided his mother to a seat at the edge of the group. He was clearly uneasy and said very little and silently hoped his mother would say even less. He badly wanted Meriel to forgive him for his unintended offence. He'd been told the truth about her adoption in confidence and still believed he'd been right not to tell her.

Connie and Geoff joined them. They sat inside for a while, talking to Meriel's parents, then, having opened up the food they had brought, they went into the garden. There seemed to Connie's sharp eye a definite division, with neighbours on one side of an invisible line and Lynne, Walter, Leo and his mother on the other. Connie insisted they stood up and moved their chairs so the group sat closer together and the two parties mixed. People stayed long after dark, the thought of work the following day forgotten. The blending of the disparate factions had eased the way to more relaxed conversations.

Lucy took out her wind-up gramophone and she and Gerald danced. Kitty and Stella dragged their unwilling husbands up to join in, but there was something in Meriel's expression that prevented Leo asking her to partner him.

In the lane, Teifion listened to the murmur of conversation and the occasional burst of laughter and felt utterly lonely. Since his father had learned of Frieda's double life he had felt even less welcome in the house where he'd lived most of his life. The strain was palpable, an awareness of invisible anger that bounced from wall to wall.

He knew he should leave home but didn't know how. He'd been used to going in and having meals put in front of him, opening a drawer to find the clothes he needed; crisp and ready to wear. How would he achieve all that if he left? Would he find a landlady willing to do everything for him as his mother, then Frieda, had done? How much would it cost? Where would he earn the money if he left his father's business?

He moved into the shadow of the trees when he heard someone coming out of Badgers Brook, chattering loudly. From the excited way they were talking it was clear they had enjoyed their evening. Envy churned his stomach. When had it all gone so wrong for him? He turned before they reached the lane and walked swiftly away.

'Wasn't that Teifion Dexter?' Bob asked, staring after the hurrying figure.

'I think it was. I wonder what he's been doing around here?' Kitty hurried towards their house, she wasn't particularly interested in the man.

'I've seen him standing looking into the window of Meriel and Lucy's office a few times. Got a crush on one of them, d'you think?'

'Poor dab if he has. There's no love lost between George Dexter and Meriel's family.'

Bob took Kitty in his arms. 'Love has a way, my dear.' He waltzed them the rest of the way home.

Leo tried several times to talk to Meriel, but every time he got close she moved away, seeing someone needing an offer of food or another drink. She wasn't going to forgive him easily. On one occasion he stepped outside and walked up the lane, to where the sound of voices and music had faded. He was angry with George Dexter for revealing the truth and wondered if there was any hope of things going back to how they were. There was a car parked beyond Walter's Hillman and he looked at the number curiously. He wasn't certain, but thought it belonged to Teifion Dexter. What was he doing around here? He waited a while, but no one came and he returned to the party. The clock told him he'd been out in the lane for more than an hour. Not even his mother had noticed his absence, he thought gloomily.

—

Betty Connors was enjoying the evening. Running a public house meant she had little time for socializing, and few friends thought to arrange such things on a Sunday, the only day she was free. She had a few part-timers to help in the bar but no one on whom to rely if she wanted more than a few hours off. Once she'd had her brother Ed to help, but he had married Elsie Clements and they were busy running their small guest house near the post office.

'Can't you find someone to take Ed's place?' Lucy asked her when she explained.

'A girl called Daphne Boyd stayed for a while but she went back home and she's now planning to leave for France with one of the twins from Treweather's farm. Finding someone suitable isn't easy. Besides the long hours and heavy work, they'd have to forgo many of their other interests. The Ship and Compass opens at the same time as most other activities.'

'D'you ever think of selling up and doing something else?'

'No, it's all I know.'

'I once thought I'd never do anything but hairdressing but look at me now, working as an estate agent, having a share of the business. Who'd have believed that?'

'I'm thrilled for you, Lucy, you've found your niche, haven't you? I found mine years ago, when I was still in my pram. Ed and I were brought up in the pub run by our parents, it's all we've ever known. I'm content there but sometimes I wish I could find a reliable assistant. Not for exotic holidays, but so I can have the occasional day off.'

Lucy looked around the garden at their assorted friends. 'Meriel and I will keep an eye open for possibilities as we go about our business. We meet a lot of people.'

'Someone as bright and capable as you would suit me perfectly,' Betty said with a laugh. 'With outsized muscles of course!'

People began to move inside as nightfall brought a chill to the air and one or two more prepared to leave. Lynne and Walter wanted to stay until the last, but it was late and there was no sign of a general exodus so they collected their coats and gathered up their now empty plates and said their goodbyes. Walter went to kiss Meriel, but she managed to put someone in the way and they both left with a continued sense of isolation. The moment of relief when he had found Lynne safe and brought her home had been short-lived. Since then they had hardly spoken to their daughter, who had refused every attempt to meet them. Even this invitation had come from Lucy and not Meriel.

At the door Leo reminded Meriel that if she or Lucy needed anything she had only to let him know.

'There's really no need. The business is fine. We know what we're doing. You don't have to come and comfort me any more either. I'm over the shock of your dishonesty,' she said firmly. 'I was never likely to collapse like some Victorian lady with vapours because of your deceit. Thank you for helping, even if we didn't need it.'

'Dishonesty and deceit? Is that how you see it? Isn't that distorting the facts? I gave your father a promise not to mention it. Dishonesty would be reneging on that, surely?'

'I don't want to argue and spoil a pleasant evening. You'd better go, your mother is by Dadda's car waiting patiently for you, she'll be getting cold. Thanks for helping, but we don't need anyone, we're fine, just Lucy and me.'

He didn't try to persuade her. How could he tell her the visits were the high spot of his days?

They said little as Walter drove home. Leo's mother, relaxed by several port wines, was fast asleep before they had driven a mile, and Leo was slouched in a corner of the back seat enveloped in gloom. They had set off with hope of at least a softening of the edges of their problems but nothing had been achieved except a reminder of how badly Meriel had been hurt.

The following day Leo did go to Cwm Derw. Walter had given him some magazines as an excuse to call. If she wouldn't see Lynne or himself, sending Leo was the next best thing.

The car he had seen the night before was parked outside George Dexter's office and Teifion was just getting out. He called to him and Teifion approached.

'What were you doing outside Meriel's house last night?'

From Teifion's expression he was about to deny it but he changed his mind and instead said. 'I went for a walk. I often do. I heard the sound of voices and wondered who was there. That's all.'

'You weren't there to cause trouble?'

'Come on, what d'you think I am? A kid who'd smash windows or kick milk bottles over?'

'I've felt like that myself, at times,' Leo admitted and Teifion stared at him, a half grin on his face.

'You have? What have you got in your life that would make you think such childish thoughts?'

'Just don't do anything to hurt Meriel or Lucy, that's all.' A sudden turn and he was striding away. What was the matter with him that he could even hint at his unhappiness to a man like Teifion Dexter?

Teifion stared after him, his mouth slightly agape. When things aren't going well, it's always a surprise to learn of others in similar straits. Lucy walked past a few minutes later and he was still standing staring across the road.

'Frightened of the traffic, are you? Waiting for someone to help you across?'

'Oh – hello, Lucy. No, I've had a surprise, that's all.' He turned to walk with her and said, 'D'you know, I don't want to cross the road because I don't want to go through the door of that office. I hate it. I've always hated it. And if you tell my father I'll kill you.' He was smiling at her and

167

at the same time wondering why he had suddenly spoken his most private thoughts aloud, and to Lucy Calloway.

'Tell him yourself and find work you do enjoy.'

'If only I could.' He straightened up as though shaking himself out of the mood.

'You can and you should. Look at the long years ahead of you stuck in a job you hate. Can you face that?'

'Ignore me, I'm talking nonsense. Forget what I said, I've had a bad start to the day, that's all it is.'

'Betty Connors wants an assistant at the Ship and Compass,' she said cheekily.

'Me, work in a pub? You must think I'm crazy, give up a place in my father's business to be a pot man? Good morning, Miss Calloway.'

She laughed out loud as he scuttled away as though in fear of his life.

Seven

The man they knew as Harry Power, who worked for Mr Lewin at Bracken Court, often passed the office. He rarely called in but always waved and occasionally came close to the door and gave them a wide-eyed cheeky wink. When he did call he usually begged a cup of tea and produced a few cakes bought from the local bakery. He came one morning, chatted amiably, asked how they were getting on. He flirted a little, seemed interested in the business, about which he seemed well informed, but after he'd gone both girls admitted that he gave nothing in return.

'He has the amazing skill of turning all of our questions into comments that don't need a reply. I wonder what he really wants?' Lucy mused. 'D'you think someone has sent him to spy on us?'

'Mr George Dexter?' Meriel added ominously.

'Or Gerald trying to work out how much we're earning!'

'Or,' Meriel added lightly, 'perhaps he's my long lost brother searching for clues about my mysterious beginnings.' She laughed, but the humour was dark.

She couldn't forget there were people out there who were her family; a mother and father, aunts, uncles, cousins maybe, and even stepbrothers or sisters. She often sat and wondered about them, thinking they might be searching for her, wishing there was a way she could reach out and help. At times she imagined them so strongly she expected the next day to be the one on which she met them all.

'When are you going to forgive your mam and dad?' Lucy asked a few days later as they opened the office door after lunch. 'You can't continue like this for ever. They love you, and you love and need them.'

'I can't stop thinking about my adoption, blaming them for their deceit. I don't know who I am and that's the worse part, not knowing where I came from or what sort of family. I could belong to criminals, or violent, quarrelsome work-shy hooligans.'

Lucy began to laugh. 'Look in the mirror and tell me, what do you see?' She opened her handbag and thrust a small mirror towards her friend. 'Whoever they were you can't honestly believe they were anything but decent people.'

'If I'd been brought up by my real family I'd be someone different though, whatever their circumstances. You must agree with that.'

'Maybe, but you'd still be beautiful, capable, business-like, kind and loving.'

'Thanks, I know you're trying to help but the truth is, I won't accept what happened until I know why. I need to know where I belong, why I was given away like an unwanted puppy. And all that's on a different level to my hurt at not being told. I have to see the people who gave me away, understand why they didn't want me.'

'My guess is that your mother was a young girl, unmarried and being offered no support from her parents. Mine wouldn't have helped me, I know that for certain, although I think yours would have supported you whatever you did.'

'I don't intend to try them on that!'

'I almost did last night. Gerald is pretty insistent and I was strongly tempted.'

'You didn't, though?' Meriel looked alarmed.

'Not this time,' Lucy replied, adding hurriedly, 'Now, let's look at the diary. I have to talk to the town hall about a lane at the back of the house in Short Street, there's an agreement that no gate will open into it as it's used by dustcarts and coalmen and they don't want any hazards blocking their way. Our prospective purchasers have a car and want to make an access. What are the chances, d'you think?'

'Nil minus! But go and try.'

'What are you doing?'

'Manning the office and making a few phone calls to hurry up the solicitor. Mark Lacy is very thorough but I wish he'd move a bit faster.'

When Lucy had gone, Meriel sat day-dreaming for a long time, trying to put faces to the family who hadn't wanted her. Was she like them? Did they have mannerisms she would recognize as her own? If she only knew who they were she might find some peace.

The tracks would have been carefully concealed so where could she begin to search? They were unlikely to live in this area. Surely for secrecy the child would be sent to grow up far away from any chance meeting? So her mother could be anywhere, even abroad, people travelled to foreign countries with greater ease these days. The distance between them could be a bus ride or hundreds of miles.

What she also had to consider was that, if her mother had been very young and unsupported, she would have made a new life for herself and wouldn't welcome a secret from her past bursting in and ruining everything. Was that something she could risk? She felt tears squeeze through her eyelids. A dirty secret, was that all she was?

'You look serious,' Leo said as he entered. 'Is it anything I can help you with?'

'Why have you come?' she asked ungraciously. 'Lucy and I manage very well without Dadda sending you to hold our hands.'

'He's concerned about you. You can understand that, can't you? He's afraid you'll refuse to talk to him, so he sends me. I have no choice but to do as he asks.' His tone echoed her own and at once she was ashamed.

'I'm sorry. But you and he both lied and I don't appreciate you trying to make up for that by offering help I don't need.'

'I don't need to apologize for what I did.'

'Then why come?'

'It's called keeping contact,' he replied, coming to sit on her desk. 'And if there's another way I can help then you only have to ask.'

'Find my real parents.'

'You know that's impossible.'

'Teifion at least tried!'

'How?' He frowned. 'I wouldn't know where to start.'

She turned in her chair to face him. 'We sold a house for someone who was moving to Glyndwr village. William Roberts-Price and family. I don't know why, but Teifion found out they had lost a child – not that it had died, but it had been "lost" – he put two and two together and made a big mistake. He took me there to face them with the suspicion I was their daughter and they were horrified. Poor man, he was so upset, and his wife soothed him and led him indoors like a child. They live in the church cottage and they seem to be very religious.'

'Surely he didn't expect it to be that easy? Many families have lost a child, so what made him think the child hadn't died of illness or accident?'

Meriel shrugged. 'I don't know, just that odd sounding word. A lost child implied something different from a child who had died, that's all. But at least he tried.'

'The law uses secrecy to protect mother and child for a good reason. Learning who she is and why she gave you up could be devastating. For the mother who probably has a family ignorant of what happened it could be destructive, surely you can see the reason for secrecy?'

'Of course I understand that. I'm not stupid!' she retorted loudly.

'Then let it lie and thank your stars you belong to Lynne and Walter Evans.'

'I do know how lucky I am! I had a wonderful childhood and nothing that I learn will take that away from me!'

'Good.' Their voices had become sharp and they glared at each other like two warring cats.

'I'm going out, I want to see someone.'

'Right. I'll stay till you get back.' Still speaking as though at the edge of quarrelling, she went out.

He looked through the diary and began noting phone numbers and addresses of people who had made enquiries about properties they hadn't bought, knowing that if another came in they would probably be interested in seeing it. He wrote several letters, deciphering Lucy's scrawl and typing efficiently on the office machine. When she returned an hour later Meriel was grateful for his help to bring them up to date. She knew she had been lax of late and it was Lucy who was doing most of the work. She was also comforted by his presence, although, she wasn't yet ready to forgive him and let him know how much she needed him in her life. That emotional see-saw was still confusing her.

At four fifteen he looked out of the window. 'Here's Lucy back and she looks pleased about something.'

Bursting through the door, breathless with excitement, Lucy said, 'I've battled and won! Permission is granted for a double gate into the lane but apart from the few moments necessary to get a car in or out it must be closed at all times and, if it causes a hazard the householders might be fined.'

'Well done, Lucy,' Meriel said, and Leo patted her on the back.

'I pointed out that this is 1950 not the dark ages and more people are able to afford a car. And with petrol no longer rationed there'll be a few more.'

'Come on,' he said, 'we obviously aren't going to be offered a cup of tea by your miserly partner, so let me take you both to the café when we close, it stays open till six o'clock.'

'We have to get back, Rascal will be needing her walk,' Meriel said sharply, and Lucy, the peace-maker, insisted he went back with them and shared their meal. Lucy had bought pasties from the baker's and with a few salad vegetables they made a satisfactory meal. Lucy insisted on dealing with the dishes and suggested Meriel showed Leo how well they were looking after the garden.

It was quite lovely, with so many summer blooms adding chaotic brightness to the borders and the vegetables in their neat rows offering contrasting symmetry and order.

'It's mainly Bob Jennings and Colin Jones who keep it looking like this,' Meriel admitted. 'Lucy and I do the weeding and some of the digging and trimming but only under their supervision. They love working here and they are all such wonderful friends. I'm so lucky to have found this place.'

'The superstition is that the place finds you and not the other way around,' Leo said.

'Where did you hear that?'

'Oh, here and there. The locals believe that Badgers Brook is where people come when they're in trouble. Are you in trouble? Meriel, if you are, then please let me help.'

'You know the things that are bothering me.'

'Why you were lied to? You'll have to work that out for yourself.'

'Who I really am.'

'That's a mystery you can't solve.'

'Will you try to help, Leo?'

'Where do I start?'

She shrugged, but missed the gleam in his eyes. He had decided to repeat the visit that Teifion had made to Mr and Mrs William Roberts-Price. Something must have made him curious, something more than them losing a child. And why had they been so upset? It was a tenuous thread but the only one he had.

He drove to the church beside which was the home of the Roberts-Price family. Surely it couldn't be this easy?

–

Teifion spent less and less time in his father's office, making excuses to go out, often not returning until late at night, when he went straight to bed. Seeing Frieda there, showing affection for his father when she had been deceiving him with another man, sickened him. He'd never liked her but hadn't been prepared for the real dislike she engendered now. Staying in the same house was becoming more and more impossible. When he caught his father's eye it was George who looked away, embarrassed at his son knowing of Frieda's double life and his pretending ignorance of it. He had to leave, but to go where, and do what?

Ignoring the food provided by his stepmother, he usually ate out, either in a café or a pub; managing without the traditional meat and two veg didn't seem like hardship compared with sitting facing Frieda and his father. One summer's evening he sat in the bar of the Ship and Compass, without a place to call home and wondering what to do about it. He was old enough to leave home; most men of his age were married with homes of their own, families and responsibilities. He justified his lack of these things by reminding himself of the difficulties he had faced. Working for his father had been a tie most people lacked and walking away meant giving up his inheritance, and giving it all to his young stepmother seemed an impossibility. Meriel had been tied to her family by love but in his case it was nearer to hatred.

Betty Connors was busy that evening and the young woman at the bar seemed inexperienced and slow. Tables and areas of the bar were filled with empty glasses and a few plates, there was hardly room to put down a newly drawn pint. Every time Betty began to clear, or asked the young girl to do so, a few more people came in and they had to serve. Without realizing how uncharacteristic of him it was, Teifion began collecting the glasses and putting trays of them on the bar.

'Thanks, Teifion,' Betty said. She leaned towards him and added, 'Daft girl this one. I have to tell her every little thing. You wouldn't watch the bar a moment, would you, while I go down and change the barrel? Ed was supposed to come and do it but he hasn't turned up. Elsie must be unwell, he can't come if she needs him.'

'Of course, but, better still, tell me what to do and I'll do it for you.'

'Best I do it this time, most flood the cellar the first time they try. But come and watch by all means.' She called to where Colin Jones was sitting and asked him to 'mind the shop' and led Teifion into the cellar. 'It's always useful to have a few people around who can change a barrel and who know where to find the drinks and cigarettes.'

He was surprised at the size of the cellar and its cleanliness. 'I'd always imagined cellars to be cobwebby places with murky corners and creepy echoes.'

'You're thinking of coal cellars, like most people. This is inspected regularly and no cobwebs are allowed, I promise you. Walls whitewashed regular and floor scrubbed every day. Very fussy about such things we have to be.'

'There's more to a pub than serving pints,' he said, watching as she carefully changed the tap on the barrel to the new one, wiping up the few drops of spillage.

She pointed out where the various drinks were stored and he asked a lot of questions. Foolishly he began to imagine himself working in such a place. As he sat finishing his drink he thought about Lucy's words. Working in a pub often meant accommodation as well. Less pay of course and fewer comforts than he was used to, the accommodation wouldn't be as grand as in his father's house but the idea was growing. It was one way by which he could leave home without too many problems. A pub would solve most of them immediately: food, a room and a job.

He wondered where he would apply for such work, and whether he would need to go away somewhere for training or would learn on the job. Was there a magazine advertising such vacancies? Or would Betty Connors know? He amused himself imagining working at the Ship and Compass. If he could face living in the same house as his stepmother for all this time, living in the same town wasn't impossible. His father rarely drank at the Ship and if he did, well it would be fun to serve him, take his money, offer him his change. With a smile he wondered whether his father would give him a tip and how generous it would be. No, somewhere further away where no one knew him, a fresh start, that was what he needed, but the idea of working in a bar still appealed.

With no experience there was doubt whether he would find a job but tomorrow he would try. Even offer to work a month without pay. When the bar closed he helped take the remaining glasses to the bar for washing and helped wipe the tables. Then he talked to Betty, explaining his desire to try something completely new.

'The work is heavy, the hours long and inconvenient if you want any sort of social life,' she warned.

'I have a feeling I'll accept the inconveniences. Give me a month's trial and I'll prove to you how capable I can be.' A little more persuasion on his part and she agreed to give him a month's trial. As he walked home and let himself into the silent house he promised himself that tomorrow Lucy would be the first person he would tell. That thought quickened his heart. Like a child at

Christmas, he wanted to go to bed immediately to make tomorrow come more quickly.

–

William Roberts-Price saw the young man coming towards the door, recognized him from Evans and Calloway, and hurried out through the back and into the lane. He almost ran up the hill towards the bus stop, where he caught a bus for the centre of town. His daughter worked in Woolworth's and he would make an excuse to call on her. The book shop he ran closed all day on Wednesdays and that was the day on which he did gardening for the vicar and a few other elderly house-holders. Today he had finished gardening early having promised the vicar he would whitewash the porch walls, but now it would have to wait.

Behind him, Leo knocked at the door and after a few minutes turned away disappointed. He had prepared a list of questions referring to the way the sale of the house had been handled, explaining they wanted to make sure their clients were satisfied with the service. He decided to call at a time when someone was more likely to be in.

He had said nothing of his intention to Meriel. Better for her not to know, as it was certain to end in another disappointment. He was closing the gate when he saw a woman approaching. She had auburn hair in an untidy bun and wore a grubby cross-over apron, long skirt and stout shoes. She carried a wooden basket in which he saw polishes and dusters and small brushes, and all this, plus the direction from which she approached, suggested she had been cleaning the church.

'Looking for me, are you?' she asked.

'Sorry to bother you. I'm from the estate agency. Evans and Calloway, just a check up to make sure you and your husband were satisfied with the way your house sale was managed.'

'Everything went smoothly, thank you, we have no complaints.' She stretched up on tiptoe to see as he wrote something unimportant and illegible on his notepad. 'I can't ask you in,' she said. 'I have to get food before we go to the evening service, you see.' She glanced towards the door and he was jolted by a sudden recognition. There had been something in that fleeting glance that reminded him of someone and he wondered if they had previously met.

Pulling himself together he said. 'No need, Mrs Roberts-Price. If you have no complaints I'll be on my way.' Although he thought about it all the way back home, and through the meal he shared with his mother, he couldn't put a name or an occasion to the face of Mrs Roberts-Price.

Making contact was all he had intended for a first visit. On another occasion he might start a conversation and slowly build up a casual friendship. Then as strangers often do, they would exchange questions and perhaps she would open up about the lost child. The plan didn't fill him with much hope but at least he was doing something to help Meriel out of her confusion and unhappiness.

–

George knew his wife was still seeing the man he had seen at the neglected hotel. She had made all the usual promises, displayed regret, shame, remorse and guilt in huge proportions but her shopping trips, from which she returned sparkling and excited, made him doubt her honesty. Now he knew of her unfaithfulness it was hard to ignore the worm of suspicion in his heart. The look of disapproval on Teifion's face was hard to take and he knew he had to sort his life out or he'd end up having no one. So one day he decided to follow her.

Teifion had an appointment the same day. Between the pub closing after lunchtime and opening for the evening session, Betty had invited him to call and have a cup of tea and discuss his idea of working in the licence trade. A month's trial was what she had agreed but she needed to know whether he was serious enough to justify so much of her time or if it was to be a temporary job, just until he and his father had sorted out their difficulties.

He said nothing to his father when George told him he would be out for most of the afternoon. He would simply close the door and leave a note explaining to prospective clients that he'd be back in an hour. In fact he was away for more than two.

He was surprised at how interested he became once Betty began talking about the Ship and Compass. From the way she talked about the customers he began to think of the place as the very heart of the streets it served.

'Like the kitchen is the heart of the home, the pub is the heart of the community,' she explained. 'All life is represented here, it's where news, both good and bad, is aired, and opinions argued out, problems solved and decisions made.' She smiled and added, 'I don't think the vicar would agree with me, mind! But although the church has its role, and it's an important one, there are aspects of life that can only be dealt with at the pub.'

While Betty made tea Teifion thought of the many times he had come to the Ship when he was happy, and when there had been a need to drown his sorrows. It was here he had come when his mother had died and when his father had remarried. It was here he had come to boast about girlfriends, and for sympathy when they had parted.

'Mrs Connors, this is what I want to do for the rest of my life,' he said, jumping up and helping her with the tray of tea.

–

George kissed Frieda goodbye and gave her some extra money for her shopping trip to Cardiff the same as he always did. From the car he saw her head for the bus stop then drove to Cardiff as fast as he dared. Parking the car he followed her on foot from the bus. She went first to the Louis restaurant on St Mary's Street and sat at a table. The room was long and narrow and unless she was facing away from the door he would find it impossible to go inside without being seen.

He decided to risk it and go in. Better to allow her to see him before she met anyone, that would be the best. No explanations would be necessary. It would be nothing more than coincidence. She had made him promise that if they tried again he would trust her and never look for evidence of her deceit. She told him she couldn't live with mistrust and if he couldn't forget and make a genuine fresh start, it was better she left. He had made that promise and had meant it, but now, a few weeks later it was impossible to keep. Her many unexplained absences caused him fears and doubts and kept him awake and if she were cheating he had to know.

He took a deep breath and opened the restaurant door to the hum of a dozen conversations; a few people lifted their heads to look. He walked a few paces and saw her sitting at a table for two, her slim body in a smart red dress – which he hadn't seen before – her blonde hair flowing in waves around her shoulders, not in its usual neat style, and he felt sickened. It was a clear signal that she was playing a different role from the one she acted out for him.

She faced away from him and didn't turn to look at who had entered. He stood, frozen into the moment. He didn't know what to do. He either had to show himself now, or walk away. If she was meeting someone quite innocently for a girls' shopping spree and saw him following, any trust would be gone. He knew it would be harder to mend their difficulties a second time and this time he would carry the guilt.

As he began to back out, the door opened and a man entered. He walked confidently to the table where Frieda sat and gasped in mock surprise. 'Fancy meeting you,' the man said loudly. 'How are you? Waiting for someone?' Frieda said something George couldn't catch and the man laughed and sat down taking both of her hands in his. It was the same man she had met before, whom she had promised never to see again. Blinded by misery, George stumbled out into the fresh air.

He was shaking as though with a fever and he went into Bwyty Hayes Island open-air snack bar and asked for a cup of coffee. Later he didn't remember drinking it or paying for it but presumed he had done both. Still shaking, his heart racing wildly, he walked back to where he had left the car.

He sat there for a long time, knowing he wasn't capable of driving back to Cwm Derw. The crowds around him began to diminish as shops began to close. The queues at the bus stops lengthened with women carrying shopping bags and girls chattering about their plans for the evening. Buses came and went and the queues filled the pavements with tightly packed and impatient passengers, all wanting to be taken home, then the numbers gradually reduced until the place was deserted.

George glanced around him. He ought to leave, calm himself and drive back and be there before Frieda. He forced himself to think about the office. Concentration was difficult but he wondered if Teifion had remembered to phone the council about the query a client had regarding trees near the house he was buying.

Irritation, both unreasonable and fierce, overcame him as he thought of Teifion. The anger he couldn't show Frieda exploded at his disappointment in his son. He isn't interested in the business, he thought, he's far too lazy. His annoyance at his son allowed him to forget the real reason for his unhappiness; blaming Teifion for his bad mood, he found he was able to face driving home.

He drove slowly, politely, allowing others priority when there was an uncertainty about a right of way, stopping to let people cross and acknowledging their thanks with a wave and a smile. When he reached Cwm Derw he was coldly calm.

He parked the car and walked into the house. Teifion was waiting for him in a hall.

'Frieda not back yet?'

'Dad, I want to leave the business. I've got a job with Betty Connors at the Ship and Compass and I'm starting straight away.'

George stared at him then his face seemed to twist, making him unrecognizable. He tried to say something that came out as a guttural moan and, in front of a startled Teifion, he fell.

Teifion knelt on the floor beside him and begged him to be all right, he said stupid things and asked stupid questions for brief moments then got up and reached for the phone, thankful they were one of the few who had one in the house. Unable to decide what to do, continuing to talk to his father reassuringly, he rang the doctor and explained what had happened. By the time Frieda arrived, soberly dressed, her hair tied back in a neat bun and carrying several shopping bags, the doctor had arrived and George was being carried into the waiting ambulance, already recovering.

Frieda wailed, insisting she was unable to go with him as hospitals terrified her. After giving her a look of real contempt, Teifion went with his father, who was by this time awake and asking for his wife.

'She's staying at home, Dad. I think it's best not to upset her, you know how nervous she is.'

'Not nervous. Loves danger. Excitement,' was George's odd response.

Teifion didn't wonder what he meant, if he'd even heard the words. He was concentrating on his father's white face and wide staring eyes, convinced he was responsible.

'It's all right, I won't leave, if you need me I'll stay,' he said, longing to hear his father tell him he was needed, valued. 'I was only a bit fed up, that's all, just thinking out loud.'

'Go,' George said quite clearly and forcefully. 'I'm selling up.'

–

News spread fast, with one or two people seeing the ambulance at the large house and guessing George was the occupant. Stella heard about it before the ambulance had even left the main road and had told a hushed group hoping to be served before closing time. Betty was there and those who came into the Ship that evening added to what they knew with what they had guessed or made up.

It was almost closing time when Teifion came into the pub, and the murmur of conversations ceased.

'Dad's going to be all right. It wasn't a heart attack, he was upset and made himself ill. And the fault was mostly mine,' he added when he spoke to Betty. 'I told him I wanted to leave and work here and he just, well, he went a dark shade of puce and sort of keeled over. He told me later he'd been angry all day about something and when I made my announcement it all flared up.'

'Did he say what made him angry?'

Teifion shook his head. 'I bet it's something to do with that stepmother of mine. She's the only one to make him lose his rag apart from me.'

'Frieda? I thought they were blissfully happy?'

'They are, but someone else made her happy too and maybe she didn't give him up as she tearfully promised. That's my guess anyway. Now, can I stay and help clear up? I want to learn every aspect of the business and cleanliness is top of the list, isn't it?'

'Thanks, but aren't you needed?'

'No, he's sleeping now.'

'And you still want to leave the business and learn the licence trade?'

'Very much so. I offered to stay, hoping in a way that he'd want me to, but he said "Go!" like that, firmly, coldly, and, well, that's what I'll do.'

'This isn't the time for decisions, Teifion.'

'For the moment my decision is made.'

'Come on then, these glasses won't jump onto the bar by themselves.'

He worked beside her for an hour and everything was shiny and clean before he left, closing the door behind him. He didn't go home, he was unwanted there and something very much like spite made him refuse to go in and answer Frieda's questions. She should have gone to the hospital, her excuses were ridiculous; as his wife, her place was beside him. He didn't know she had gone there soon after he had left or that George had refused to see her.

–

Walter searched his mind for ways of putting things right between himself and Lynne. Since her brief stay with Gladys May, she had slept in the spare room and treated him formally, as though she was the servant and he the master. It was breaking his heart.

Learning from Leo that George was in hospital didn't elicit any sympathy. 'Twice the man almost ruined our lives, Lynne and me, and if he had died I'd have felt nothing but relief.'

'Twice?' Leo queried.

'Twice! And if you think I should be sorry that the man's ill then you'll just have to be disappointed. Look at what has happened to Lynne and Meriel? They're broken-hearted, that's what! And it's all his fault. Lynne left me because of that man's rumour-mongering and even though she's home it isn't the same; she's locked away by shock and misery and it's all down to that man!'

Leo wondered about the other occasion George had caused trouble but dared not ask. 'If I took her to see Meriel, would it do any good?'

'Leo, I'm desperate, take all the time you need and try anything you can think of, just get things back to as they were.'

'About Meriel,' he said hesitantly, wondering whether he'd receive a reply or the man's fury.

'What about Meriel?'

'She wants to find her – well – her mother, and I wondered, do you have any information?'

'No and if I did I'd keep it to myself. She's our daughter and searching out her mother would bring nothing but misery. Opening Pandora's box that would be, finding out where she came from, why she was given up. She could waste years of her life looking for some family who probably haven't given her a thought in years.'

'She wants to know. She's in a vacuum at the moment, not knowing who she really is. In a complicated way she feels cheated, by you and Lynne, and by me, because we knew and didn't tell her. I thought, if I could help find them, or at least try, she'd settle again. Whoever her real parents were they couldn't have given her more happiness, she does know that much.'

'Real parents? We're her real parents. She came to us at ten days old and we couldn't love a child more. We were told nothing, just that the mother couldn't keep her.'

'No reason given?'

'None. We presumed her mother was unmarried and her parents wouldn't accept the child. Either that, or the poor mother died. Young, unmarried, let down by the father, that's most likely, don't you think?' He picked up a photograph of Meriel from his desk and his expression softened as he looked at it and wiped away imaginary dust. 'Look at her. She's so beautiful and yet someone gave her to us. What could you say if you did find her mother, eh?'

'I don't know, Walter, I just feel that we ought to search for her and find out.'

'Where do you start?'

'You know the town where she was born?'

Walter shrugged. 'I don't suppose it's far from here. Just far enough for us not to have noticed a girl carrying a child and never pushing a pram. I seem to remember being told the girl was from Dinas Powys but I don't trust my memory enough to be sure.'

They discussed it for a long time but nothing in the way of a slightest clue occurred to them. Leo continued to spend part of each day helping Meriel and Lucy and even agreeing to fill in when Lucy took a few days off to visit Gerald's parents and renew acquaintance with his family.

–

He went to look again at the cottage near the church with no intention of trying to talk to the occupants. He stared as though the stones of the walls would somehow tell him what he wanted to know.

He became aware of music coming from the church, an organ, not very well played, the same hymn tune repeated, and he guessed the musician was practising for the following Sunday. Then other music reached his ears. The Tommy Dorsey version of 'On the Sunny Side of the Street', played loudly. Curious, he went to the window and looked inside. A girl was dancing, her arms and feet flying as she sang along with the lyrics obviously enjoying herself. The music ended and was swiftly followed by 'Blue Moon', to which the girl danced holding a cushion in her arms. Smiling, Leo stepped quietly away.

'Here, what you doing snooping around?' a voice called and he turned to see the red-faced girl, still hugging her cushion.

'Sorry, miss, I was curious about the music. 'Sunny Side of the Street' is one of my favourites,' he told her.

'Just don't tell my father,' she said more quietly. 'He doesn't approve, see. I hide my records and only play them when he's out. Mum doesn't mind. Anything for peace, that's Mum.'

He waved and drove off. Anything for peace? he mused. Would that have included giving up a child her husband wouldn't accept?

–

Lucy bought a new summer coat in off-white linen, and went to check on a dress being made for her by Peter Bevan's wife, Hope. She needed to feel confident for the visit to Gerald's parents. Before their marriage, Hope had lived for a while in Badgers Brook and it was interesting to share their thoughts on the place. On the subject of attracting people in trouble, Hope was convinced. 'I went there without a thought of troubles, but when they came the calmness of the old house soothed me and it was there I met Peter. We're so happy and I know I wouldn't have coped so well without Badgers Brook to rush home to each evening.'

Lucy smiled. 'I'm the exception. My worries are well behind me. It was a good way to leave home, though,' she admitted. 'I couldn't have afforded it otherwise.'

'All is well now, isn't it?'

'Oh yes. I've never been happier. My ex-fiancé has turned up, we're together again, back where we were before the war disrupted everything.'

Wearing her new clothes gave Lucy extra confidence and she walked into Gerald's home as though the long months since her last visit had been only days. Gerald was attentive, affectionate and only a regular reference to the business she half-owned marred the few days of her visit.

'It's as though I'm not the dull, boring ex-fiancée, just a business woman with prospects,' she told Meriel when she returned to Badgers Brook on Sunday evening.

'You're imagining it,' Meriel said with a smile. 'I don't suppose they had ever imagined the quiet, capable hairdresser would become an expert in another business. They underestimated you, that's all, Lucy.'

'I hope so.'

'What d'you mean?'

'I hope he isn't marrying me for what I've achieved, with an eye on the business and the money I'll bring with me.'

'Lucy, love, you have such low esteem! He looks at you and sees what other people see, a pretty, clever young woman, and he can't believe his luck. He's proud of you, perhaps even a little in awe of you. Doesn't that feel good?'

'I suppose so, but it isn't the same as it was before.'

'Of course not, you aren't the people now that you were then. You must realize how you've changed?'

'I see him staring into nothingness as though I bore him and he's silently counting the minutes before he can escape. The only time he's at all interested is when he asks about how well the business is doing or makes remarks about the house we own which is our office. He makes me feel I'm boasting to impress him, keep him attracted to me.'

'You aren't boasting if he asks the questions.'

'I'm Lucy Calloway, not a set of figures and a bank account.'

'Doesn't he talk about his father's business that will be his one day?'

'Only to tell me how much he hates it.'

'No talk of love? Plans for engagement and marriage?'

'Some. It isn't enough, though, is it?'

'Give yourself plenty of time, Lucy. Don't rush into anything.'

As though she hadn't heard, Lucy asked, 'How can I be sure he really loves me this time?'

'He's a fool if he doesn't.'

'Or I'm the fool for thinking he does,' Lucy said quietly.

Eight

Walter sat in the silent living room that mocked him with its empty chairs, and wrote to Lynne. It was a routine to fill a page or two each evening and post it before twelve the following morning so Lynne received one every morning while she was away.

Since her short visit to Gladys May she had spent a few days of every week with her, aware, she told Walter, that the old lady was far from well and needed some extra care. Walter knew the real reason was Lynne's determination to gradually leave him, so if their secret were revealed she could slip out of his life altogether, taking any blame with her. It was breaking his heart. They had been utterly content throughout their years together, Meriel was an added joy and now the hollow empty house seemed worse than a tomb.

He no longer pleaded with her to come home, but always told her how lonely he was without her and how he missed her. Then he would write a few lines about the trivial events of his day, sometimes even describing the clients, making fun out of ordinary things, and telling her whom he had met on his regular visits to the café. He had given up applying pressure but settled for gentle hints about how she was needed. He knew from the little she told him that her days with her aunt were spent in the garden or helping with some sewing, decorating or cleaning. Mind-numbing tasks that stopped her thinking about where she ought to be, he thought sadly. How can something that happened so long ago come back and create such confusion?

He reported in detail any news he had of their daughter, such news usually coming via Leo, whom he still sent to help as it was the only way of making sure everything was well with her.

Sometimes he wrote on a picture postcard, as though he were on holiday and she was left behind. Other times he pretended she was the one on holiday and how he was longing to see her and hear all about it. He kept the comments light and hoped they made her smile. Every day he posted his message and every day he waited in vain for a reply. She usually wrote back after two or three days but he feared the time spent away from him would increase until she no longer felt the place was her home.

–

George was worried both about his health since he had collapsed in such a dramatic manner and for the business he was neglecting. His anxiety didn't help him recover from what the doctors thought was caused by panic and anger rather than a heart attack, which was what they had first suspected. He refused to see Frieda and told the nurse he wanted to see his son.

Teifion had been there constantly whenever visitors were allowed but this demand from his father, now well enough to tell him what he thought of his intention to leave the firm, made him less willing. Reluctantly, he put on his best suit and picked up the items George had asked him to take in. He was going to the hospital this time with less concern for his father's health and more for the outburst that was sure to come his way. He met the postman at the door as he was leaving and took the letters he offered.

One was from an important client. He got into the car but before setting off he thought he should read it. If it contained bad news he might be able to soften the blow by telling his father before he gave him the letter. When he opened it he groaned. This was the worst news. An important auction promised to them was being taken out of their hands and he knew that there was no way to soften that news.

'I don't care what dream you're dreaming, boy, so far as I'm concerned you can go and be a pot-boy as soon as you like, but you have to stay and see to the big auction next month,' were his father's first words when Teifion walked into the room. 'According to this lot,' he gestured disparagingly with a thumb, 'I won't be well enough to deal with it on my own and temporary staff will need a careful eye. You have to stay, understand?'

'Calm yourself, Dad, or you'll be ill again,' Teifion dared say.

'I'll be ill? I *am* ill! And I won't get better while you're playing with the job instead of getting on with it. You can't leave. It's your business and you have to be aware of that and look after it. This sale is important.'

'There'll be others,' Teifion said.

'Not many as big as this one, and what d'you mean "there'll be others"? If we make anything but a perfect job of this one people will choose other auctioneers in the future. There are plenty looking to take our place. *Every* sale is important, surely you've learned that much?'

With a nervous glance to make sure the nurses weren't far away, Teifion handed his father the letter that had come that morning. As he might have predicted, his father burst into angry demands and accusations.

'Have you phoned and asked them why they've changed their mind? Promised them a better deal? Extra advertising? More staff to help shift the goods about? Canvas cover if it's raining? That won't be expensive to hire. Transport to deliver to buyers at reduced prices?'

'The letter came as I was leaving the house. I haven't had a chance to do—'

'Then what in blazes are you doing here?'

'You – I – it was you asked to see me,' he stuttered. 'I thought it must be important.'

'Not as important as getting this agreement back, you idiot! Go home and sort it and don't come back till you have. Right? Anything there you don't understand?'

He was waving the letter about and Teifion took it, tore it through and left.

'Come back!' George shouted, leaping out of bed, grabbing the torn pages. A nurse told him to stay in bed.

'Stay in bed while my stupid son ruins my business? Get my clothes, I have to go home.'

'I'm sorry if you have problems, Mr Dexter, I really am, but you can't go until the doctor's finished his rounds.'

'Sorry for him?' the nurse whispered to a colleague. 'I'm more sorry for his son!'

Teifion went back home coldly calm. It was as though his father's anger had released him from any doubts about what he wanted to do. He packed a couple of small suit-cases, left his keys on the table and looked around him. It should have been sad leaving the place where he'd lived for most of his life but he could find no regrets, only excitement. He was like a child on the last day of term, nothing but freedom beckoned and he had a job not to shout with excitement. He drove to the pub and knocked at the side door. Betty appeared, wrapped in a waterproof overall and wearing cut-down wellington boots.

'Hello, Teifion, I won't be a minute finishing the floor, my cleaner failed to arrive again. Go in and put the kettle on, will you?'

'I've come to make a start if that's all right with you, Mrs Connors, and perhaps you'll show me how I can best help.'

'Put the kettle on,' she repeated with a grin. 'Tea first then we'll talk about who does what, right?'

She spent the morning patiently explaining the system of stock-keeping so everything was used in sequence. He seemed to understand and even suggested moving one or two items so that the most frequently used were nearer the entrance to the bar. He felt satisfied he had made the right decision, at least for the present. And Betty was encouraged to believe he would be a useful and, more to the point, an interested employee.

He didn't visit his father even though he was told he'd come home. The room Betty offered was small and sparsely furnished, old-fashioned and rather dark, but seemed to him just perfect. About the all-important auction he thought not at all.

–

George was sitting in the living room staring into space. In his hands he held a letter, telling him that Frieda had left him and he could contact her through her sister in Brighton. He wondered vaguely by how much she had emptied their bank account.

Meriel and Lucy were opening the office when a car drew up and a well-dressed and important looking man stepped out. They watched with surprise as he approached the door and walked in, head down, so the brim of his trilby shaded his face. Then he looked up, said, 'Good morning, lovely ladies,' and they saw with delight that their visitor was Harry Power. Meriel and Lucy both stood and offered him a chair.

'I represent Mr Lewin of Bracken Court,' he began rather formally then he grinned. 'I really am here on business. Interested?'

'You bet!' Lucy replied.

Meriel picked up a pen and pulled a notebook towards her, looking at him expectantly. 'Mr Lewin of Bracken Court is looking for someone to organize the auction at Rosebay Farm next month. Are you interested?' he asked them.

'Of course,' Lucy said, with what she hoped was nonchalance, and Meriel took from a drawer details of the auction they had taken over from George. He went out then and a well-dressed man of about fifty took his place, sat in the chair offered and began, 'I am putting a lot of trust in you, can you reassure me? Are you able to cope with such a large event?'

'As you can see from this previous sale, we managed to achieve and pass the expectations regarding price and we believe that was mainly down to the right prices, promising people a few bargains, bringing in the crowd.' Meriel smiled at him, hoping she showed confidence and not too many teeth. 'And of course we offer our combined expertise, there's no substitute for experience and enthusiasm, is there?'

'And this was a last-minute arrangement, remember,' Lucy said, tapping the auction details with a pencil, 'when another firm was unable to carry on. Given a whole month we are certain we can do even better.'

The man said very little and as their comments slowed and they tried to think of other telling remarks to make he stood up and offered his well-manicured hand, first to Meriel then to Lucy. 'I will send my man in with all the information you need and I expect a fast response detailing your plans. Thank you for your time. I look forward to working with you. Good day.'

Shaking with excitement the two friends watched as the man got back into the car and sat there, while from the driver's seat Harry Power jumped out with a file of papers which he handed to Meriel with a half smile and a nod. To Lucy's amusement he added a wink and blew her a kiss before retreating back to the car and driving off.

'Did you see that?' Lucy said with a grin.

'Look out, Gerald, our Lucy's waking up to how attractive she is.'

'Go on, don't be daft.' But the incident flattered her and made her smile for a long time.

'So that's what he's been doing, snooping around us buying cakes and pretending to be our friend? Checking whether we're capable of managing an auction!'

'Assessing our capabilities,' Lucy joked. 'How exciting!'

'What a cheek. Mind you, I don't mind who snoops if it means a job as good as this one,' Meriel said happily, glancing down the list of items for sale.

They saw from the details that the auction had been offered to George Dexter but they had withdrawn from the arrangement. 'I suppose that means he'll be coming here accusing us of underhand practices,' Meriel sighed.

'Ah well,' Lucy said, 'he might act like a mad dog but he's unlikely to bite!'

George didn't come in and blast away at their underhandedness at taking his client. They expected accusations of deceit and dishonesty and threats that he would complain to the relevant authorities. They prepared themselves for his outrage but in fact he didn't appear at all. It wasn't until Lucy went to the post office later that they learned that George had been in hospital.

As usual, Stella Jones had the latest information. 'Some sort of attack it was, but he's out now, came out this morning he did, against the advice of the doctors, mind. Typical of George Dexter. He thinks he knows better than the doctors.'

'What about Teifion? I suppose he's running the office? Difficult to get help at short notice but perhaps his stepmother will help.'

Stella leaned towards her even though the post office was empty apart from the two of them. 'Now there's a funny thing, Teifion isn't there. The office was closed until George got back and there's gossip about the fact his wife didn't visit him, not once.' In a deeper voice, rich with solemnity, she added, 'Something's going on if you ask me.'

Lucy didn't need to ask anyone about Frieda's apparent lack of concern, she guessed the reason was George refusing to see his wife, but she did wonder how Teifion was coping. 'Perhaps I'll walk past and see if Teifion's there.'

'He won't be.' Betty Connors had just walked in with letters to post. 'He's decided to work for me at the Ship and Compass, what d'you think of that, then, eh?'

For once Stella was speechless.

–

Harry Power called at the office the following day and filled out the details about the sale, flirting and teasing them both between meticulously clarifying the business arrangements. For several days both girls were occupied with preparations for the important auction at Rosebay Farm. There were buildings and plots of land to sell as well as assorted furniture and fittings and sundry items from homes and farms.

They had posters to design and print, advertisements to place in magazines and newspapers and the complicated catalogues to prepare and order. Selecting what items to illustrate and which to describe was something that kept them out of their beds late into the night on several occasions. They went to see the lots and decided which would be sold individually. For the first time, Meriel wished she could ask her father to advise; with many years of experience his comments would be invaluable.

–

George was furious when he realized who had been awarded the auction contract but he said nothing. He blamed his son, and also Frieda for being so troublesome that he had been less than attentive to Mr Lewen at such an important time. Walter had heard about the auction being given to Meriel and Lucy and sent word via Leo of how proud he was, offering help if any was needed. 'Congratulations,' Leo said to Meriel, after passing on her father's good wishes. He hugged them both, but it seemed to Meriel that he held her for a little longer than the occasion warranted. She was aware of a slight embarrassment as she clung even longer than he did. There was something very comforting in his warmth and obvious affection, something unsettling in the way he stared at her after releasing her from his arms, his eyes softening in a disconcerting way. She told herself it was because of her stress over the all-important auction and slight apprehension about her ability to cope. She was still hurt he had not told her about her parents.

They willingly took advantage of Leo's help and he went with them when they went to look again at the items for sale. A couple of assistants were hired for the day, and were instructed on the way the items were displayed or, in some cases, discarded. They made several visits, leaving an excited Kitty and Bob in the office to cover. The well-dressed Mr Lewen appeared occasionally, on one visit offering a photograph of the farm taken fifty years previously, as a suggestion for the cover of the contents catalogue. He said very little but seemed satisfied with their arrangements.

–

George ran the office as well as he could and, as Teifion was refusing to help, he advertised for a temporary assistant. One of the applicants was Lucy's friend, Gerald Cook. After only a few minutes George guessed he was not serious.

'I work for my father and it isn't a career I wish to spend my life developing,' Gerald began. 'I want something different.'

'What does he do?'

'He sells cars and also repairs vintage motorbikes,' Gerald replied, believing a slight exaggeration was reasonable in the circumstances. 'I do find it fascinating to restore these wonderful machines, but I want something more mentally challenging.'

'Why property? D'you consider that – challenging?' George asked with a slight edge to his voice.

'Yes, and, of course, I hope to make more money than I earn at present.' Gerald used his most charming smile. 'I want to make my way in the world. What sort of money d'you make on the average house sale? Better percentage than my father gets, I'm sure.'

'I'm sure,' George repeated. 'But like your father's business, mine has to be learned. You'd do well to stay with what you know and perhaps develop the business, taking note of the rising popularity of the motor car, don't you think? What's the mark up on selling a new car?'

'I don't know.'

'And the cost per hour of repairs?'

'I don't know.'

'A set of tyres for a Norton? A new engine for an Austin Seven? A brake cable for an Enfield?'

Gerald shook his head. 'In fact,' he said in an attempt to extricate himself, 'I leave the office side of things to my father and specialize in getting on with the work.'

George looked pointedly at his stained hands and fingernails and stood up. 'Thank you, Mr Cook, but I think you've come here simply to find out if the job offers an easy alternative to your father's honourable business.

Good day.' As useless as that son of mine, he muttered to himself, finding an assistant was not going to be easy.

He knew he should see Teifion and ask him to come back, plead with him even, and remind him of what he might lose, but he knew that with his present simmering anger he would only make things worse. With Frieda and his son away and only the morning lady, as he called Mrs Prothero, in the house to provide meals he decided to close the office and eat at the Ship and Compass. He had seen no one apart from a few clients since he came out of hospital but guessed the gossip would be out about his wife leaving, his neighbours laughing at him for believing he could keep a woman so many years his junior. Frieda had taken all her things and was gone. Unless he could persuade Teifion to come back he would be quite alone. He had to face people soon or he'd become a recluse, hiding his shame and embarrassment behind the office door.

That the news was out he did not doubt; one or two people had passed the office and unable to hide their delight at his embarrassment had smiled knowingly through the glass. As though he were a strange animal in a zoo, he thought angrily. The gossip merchants would be having a great time gathered in groups, their shoulders slightly hunched as they shared the latest rumours and guesses, and embroidered the facts. Leaving Mrs Prothero with instructions about taking a message if the phone should ring, he stepped out, shoulders back and wearing a haughty expression he hoped might discourage idle questions, he crossed the road and went to the Ship.

After the bright sun of the early June day it was dark inside and took a moment or two for his eyes to adjust. When they did he gave a gasp of horror. Teifion was behind the bar with Betty, laughing as he served Bob Jennings and Colin Jones. He turned abruptly and walked out. First Frieda letting him down in the most cruel way then walking away, and now his son abandoning him for a job, with Betty Connors!

He went to the café to settle for whatever they had to offer, filled with self-pity. He had never been a popular man. His first wife had gradually become a stranger after Teifion was born, sleeping in his bed but with such obvious dislike that even that familiarity had faded and died.

When she passed away a few years later his feelings had been resentment rather than grief, hating himself for allowing her to waste his best years. He had blamed Teifion. If he hadn't been born she might have been different, or he could have left her, found someone else. But a son, a promise of continuity for the business had been strong reasons for staying. For what? No son, a second wife who had betrayed him, and between them they had made him a laughing stock. His mind twisted then and he saw clearly that the one who had ruined his life was not his wife, or Teifion or even Frieda. Walter Evans had made everything go wrong for him. All those years ago. He had destroyed any chance of happiness by stealing his girl.

—

Gerald was not unhappy about George's curt dismissal of him. He hadn't wanted the job but, as George had guessed, he had hoped to discover what prospects there were as an auctioneer and estate agent. If he were to accept a life with the boring Lucy Calloway, he wanted to make sure it was worthwhile. Money was a compensation for many things, including being married to someone as dull as Lucy.

Cheerfully he went to Badgers Brook to see whether Lucy was at home. They often went back to the house for lunch, preferring the garden to the noisy café when the weather was kind.

Lucy was at that moment standing at the top of a ladder, thankful she was wearing pedal-pushers to protect her modesty. The house was, for once, without visitors. Stella seemed to sense when they were at home and make an excuse to call, and Bob and Colin often came to work on the peaceful garden they treated like their own.

She handed down the remnants of a squirrel's nest to Meriel. They had been warned that although squirrels were charming, they weren't recommended as roof-dwellers. So now the occupants had fled and before they could add to the nesting material ready for the winter, Bob had promised to block up the hole the busy little creatures had found.

When Gerald called to see Lucy, on the pretext of delivering spares in the neighbourhood, there had been no reply to his knocking. The little dog came running around from the back of the house but, after a few short barks, had run back again. Shrieks of laughter, plus the dog's excited yelps, led him around to the garden.

Seeing Lucy pausing cautiously halfway down the ladder, he misunderstood what was going on and made an offer of help, to be the man of action. 'Come down, darling, you could fall. I'll go up and do whatever's necessary.'

Dutiful expression on her face, Lucy descended the ladder and watched as he climbed up. 'Now, what do you want me to do?' he asked looking down.

'Whatever you like, Gerald, I was on my way down having moved a squirrel's nest from the roof.' She and Meriel laughed as he came down giving them a rueful smile.

'All right, I was showing off, but I do think it's dangerous for you to do things like that. Please call me and let me help. I can't have you harming yourself, Lucy, you're too precious.' He put an arm around her and a warmth he hadn't felt before startled him with its promise.

She gazed up at him, her eyes full of mischief and the closeness of her and the look in her eyes excited him. Perhaps she wasn't the dull, shy creature he'd known. Perhaps she had changed and he had been too self-centred to have noticed. While Meriel was walking towards the kitchen, he kissed her, held her close. 'Don't take chances,' he whispered, running his lips across her cheek, under her chin, down to the pulse beating her throat, before putting his hands on the sides of her face, staring deeply into her beautiful greeny-blue eyes and blending his lips with hers. Breathlessly he said, 'Precious, precious girl. I care too much to want you hurt, dear Lucy.'

He was sincere for the first time since they had rediscovered each other, but to Lucy the words, although spoken from the heart, sounded false and she doubted him and felt her growing love for him shrinking away, disappointment fused with unexpected relief.

—

The preparations for the sale were progressing well and Leo couldn't find many excuses to visit Cwm Derw. One day he phoned and asked if he could bring his mother and take them out to lunch. 'Or we could bring a picnic, Mam would enjoy that, if you don't think that's too miserly on my part?'

'A picnic will be fun. Yes, we'd love that. It will have to be Sunday, of course. Is that all right?'

'Of course. It's the only free day. Er, Meriel, can I invite your father too? Your mother is still spending a lot of time with Auntie Gladys and he's very lonely with only the cleaner, and she's usually in the house when he isn't. Please? It will mean so much to him.'

'Let's make it a party. Connie and Geoff, and Betty Connors. Then there won't be any embarrassing pleas for me to go home, will there?'

'Sounds good to me. Have you heard from your mother?'

'No,' she snapped. 'I haven't found out who she is yet!'

'Silly girl, you know I mean your true mother, Lynne Evans. She's spending a lot of time with your Auntie Gladys.'

'She isn't my real aunt either. More lies.'

Leo didn't argue. 'See you on Sunday then?'

'Sunday.'

'I can't wait.' He tried to put some meaning into the simple phrase but even to him it sounded trite. 'I'm really looking forward to seeing you,' he added and that sounded even worse.

As usual, there were more people than planned when Sunday came. At eleven o'clock Kitty, Bob, Stella and Colin arrived with some ancient hampers and new shopping baskets filled with assorted packages and they set off in a convoy of cars. Betty had brought Teifion, and Gerald had heard about it and invited himself.

They headed for Connie and Geoff's favourite beach, a fairly isolated spot near the village of Sully and the small town of Penarth. The tide was on its way out and at one o'clock, Meriel and Lucy suggested walking across the slippery rock of the causeway and spending a brief time on the island. Leo at once offered to go with them. Gerald assured them he wanted to, but declined. As he wore good leather shoes that might spoil, he decided to walk on the coastal road instead. He persuaded Lucy to go with him and it was only Leo and Meriel who set off, while an anxious Walter watched from the narrow stony beach.

Meriel and Leo confided in each other their concerns about Lucy, probably because it was a safe subject. They were unhappy about Lucy's involvement with a man neither of them found appealing. The shared worry gave them a closeness that had been lacking. Then the uneven surface, causing them to slip and stumble on the wet rocks, changed the mood. Joking about the tide suddenly turning, or the possibility of facing a monster escaped from Loch Ness, relaxed them. Within a few yards of starting out they were two friends on a fun day out.

There was laughter in the air as Meriel and Leo walked, jumped and made their way to the island's beach facing them. They couldn't keep to a straight line, lurching around pools and areas where the rocks were slippery underfoot, stopping occasionally to examine the small creatures waiting for the tide to return, moving briskly at times, even crawling occasionally and holding hands whenever the need was there, and often when it was not. The sun had already dried much of the route but there were places where they had to take care and Leo's hand was always waiting for hers.

They climbed halfway up the grassy slope in view of the shore, where rabbits hopped about in apparent indifference to the visitors, and waved to Walter and the others.

'Ten minutes then we'll start back.' Leo said, checking his watch.

'Come on, there's plenty of time yet.'

'Once the tide comes around the sides of the island the path is very dangerous and I'm not going to risk anything happening to you.'

'At least let's walk to the top and look at the other side.'

'The cliffs are steep there, not a gentle slope.'

'Come on. I promise to hold your hand, Uncle Leo,' she teased.

He stared at her.

She looked at him, he was so familiar yet not the same. Reliable and always there, as before, but no longer the man who had seemed a part of her father's generation when she had been small, a man who she knew so well, yet didn't know at all. He smiled at her, his skin flushed into a bronze glow by the summer sun, brown hair blowing in the soft breeze and a shiver of recognition passed through her.

'It's a long time since you called me Uncle Leo,' he said quietly.

'It's a long time since I thought of you like that,' she said. Then to break the breathless moment she ran away from him up to the highest point and he ran after her, his thoughts in confusion, not knowing what to say.

A few minutes later, the crowd on the beach were waving to them as they walked back down the grassy slope, slightly apart.

'I think it's time for lunch,' Leo said, waving back. 'They have a fire going, Connie brought a kettle and I suspect we're in for some smoke-flavoured tea.'

They were faster on the return, Leo's hand was there but she didn't reach out for it as readily, even when she slipped and her foot went into a pool. Something had happened and she didn't know how to handle it. She just knew that her body was crying out for something and nothing would be the same ever again.

–

Lynne read Walter's latest note in which he mentioned the planned picnic and felt ashamed of her continuing fear of going home. He was so lonely and was being punished for something not his fault. She was the guilty one, even though so many years had passed, that fact remained. She was afraid of gossip, convinced that if she were to open her mouth she would say something that would allow that truth to emerge and ruin everything they had built. If Meriel learned of her sordid part in it all, she'd walk away from them, and that would be more than Walter could bear. Better for her to hurt him by staying away.

She heard the clatter of dishes as Auntie Gladys set the table for breakfast, and she walked into the kitchen and reached for the loaf. 'Tomatoes?' she suggested and the smiling face of her mother's greatest friend nodded.

'It's such a treat having you here. I never bother with anything more than toast,' she said. 'Although, I don't want you staying for too long, mind. That husband of yours needs you more than I do. Is that another letter?'

'Every day, he's never failed to write, has he?'

'Go home, lovely girl. It's where you belong.'

'I can't, Gladie, I can't risk Meriel finding out. Why on earth did she have to live in Cwm Derw? Of all the places she might have chosen, why did she pick on the one place that spelled danger?'

'That's life, the only thing you can expect is the unexpected. The only way to deal with it is to face it and that's what you have to do, my dear.'

'Tell her the whole story, you mean?'

'No, there's no need for that. Just explain about how unhappy you and her father were knowing you couldn't have a child and how happy you've been since you were given the gift of a daughter. Why her family couldn't keep her is best left for her to guess. She's bound to be near the truth, that her mother was too young and was offered no support from her family. Tell her that, remind her how much you and Walter love her, and while you're at it, tell Walter how much you love and need him too.'

While they ate breakfast Lynne was quiet and Gladys said nothing more to distract her. She had said her piece and must now allow it to germinate. Later, she put some newly ironed laundry in Lynne's room and pointedly placed the suitcase she had brought with her beside the bed.

Walter was at home when the taxi arrived. Uninterested, he listened as the engine idled and door slammed but didn't leave his chair. Then the sound of the key in the lock made him sit up. Meriel! It must be Meriel, with a smile he opened the door to the hall. Tears welled in his eyes as Lynne ran into his arms.

'I'm home, darling, and this time it's for good. No more silly games, I promise. What we have to face we'll face together.'

–

Leo knew he was playing a dangerous game by trying to solve the mystery of Meriel's true parentage. The odd family with their old-fashioned clothes and subdued manner were more unlikely every time he thought of them, how could they be even remotely related to the bright, lively Meriel? But there were questions he was interested in having answered and he needed to be absolutely sure they were unconnected before searching further afield. Although where he would start on a new enquiry he had no idea.

Without much hope he went to the church beside which the Roberts-Price family lived and looked around the gravestones in the churchyard. He didn't know why, he had no plan in his mind, he was just looking for the name Roberts-Price. Although how that would help he hadn't the faintest idea, but he looked anyway.

A man wearing the cassock and collar of a clergyman appeared and stood watching as he walked up and down the rows of stones. When the route took him over to the church doorway the man spoke. 'Can I help, sir?'

'Not really. I don't even know what I'm looking for myself!' He smiled and offered a hand. 'I'm killing time really and I saw several graves with the name Price and Roberts, and wondered whether they were local names. I know there is a gentleman in the cottage across the lane called Mr William Roberts-Price, that's all.'

'They moved here quite recently. You're a friend?'

'Not even that. I'm a friend of the young lady, Miss Calloway, who sold their house for them and we've met a couple of times.'

'It seems they're moving again. Sad when people can't settle.'

'Do you know why?'

The man shook his head. 'It sometimes means people are running away, trying to escape their problems, forgetting that the problem is often within themselves and therefore will travel with them.' He straightened up as though regretting his remarks and said swiftly, 'Not that I'm saying this is the case with these good people. I think they want to do something worthwhile with their lives and haven't quite decided what that should be.'

'I wish them luck, whatever it is,' Leo said. 'Most pleasant talking to you, sir, good day.' He tilted his hat as he left.

Leo drove back to the office and told Meriel that the Roberts-Prices were moving again. 'It might be worth calling to see whether you can help find them a house.' He looked at Meriel. 'Best Lucy goes as they know her, don't you think?'

'I don't know why their name keeps cropping up,' Meriel said. 'Since Teifion had the crazy idea they might be related to me they seem to be hovering around at the edge of my life.'

'In that case, forget it. They're probably looking too far afield for you to help anyway.' He placed his hands on the desk in front of Meriel. 'Now, how about coming home with me? Mam has promised a casserole and fresh vegetables.'

Meriel was about to decline, she had been uneasy in his presence since the Sunday picnic. But he pleaded and assured her his mother would have been working all day preparing for her visit and would be disappointed.

'Thank you, I'd love to come.'

'Lucy?' he questioned.

Lucy shook her head. 'I'm meeting Gerald. Besides, Rascal will want her walk and some supper.'

'I'll follow you in my car,' she said, 'simpler if I can drive myself home.'

'Not tonight. We'll go together.' Excitement showed in his eyes and she tried to avoid looking at him. She must be under some sort of spell, imagining he could be something more than a lifelong friend, her father's assistant, yet the strange tension that was far from unpleasant wouldn't be denied.

She didn't go home and change, just freshened herself in the small washroom behind the office and set off with a slightly uneasy heart. She avoided touching him, dropping the office keys into his palm for him to lock up, refusing his hand to help her into the car. She was afraid his skin against her own would be like electricity, she was so aware of his presence. What was happening to her?

She leapt out before he could come around and open the door for her and ran into the house calling for Mrs Hopkins. At the door to the living room she stopped. Both of her parents were there, Walter's arm around Lynne, both smiling happily. Walter opened his other arm and waggled his fingers for her to join them. Lynne did the same and by the time Leo appeared, they were hugging as though they would never let go.

Nine

They eventually calmed down and rose to eat the meal Mrs Hopkins had prepared. Meriel kept glancing at her mother. Lynne had changed; she had lost weight and was very pale. It was as though the revelations she had tried for so long to hide had brought on an illness. Watching her mother she was aware of a lessening of her own pain. How much harder it had been for Lynne and her father to have been faced with her anger and resentment.

Feeling renewed happiness she wanted to hug Leo, thank him for his persistence in making her face up to the situation, but her awareness of him as an attractive and desirable man stopped her. Instead she hugged his mother.

Leaving her parents talking to Mrs Hopkins, Meriel found herself in the kitchen, with Leo standing with tea towel at the ready, preparing to wash the dishes. Then his mother bustled in and sent him out of the room. Laughingly he went, complaining about being bullied. Meriel began to wash the dishes, tense and uneasy. Why hadn't he stayed and shared the task?

'He's been a wonderful son,' Mrs Hopkins said as she took charge of the tea towel. 'When his father and older brother died he was still a boy. With my hardly realizing his sacrifices he took on the role of deputy father to his sisters and gave up the lovely years of fun and friendships, flirting and courting. That happy time passed him by and

I regret my blindness – my selfishness – in not seeing it.'
She glanced at Meriel and said, 'Now, I think perhaps he
was simply waiting for that special person to find him.'

'Don't you mean for him to find her?'

'Oh no. He found her a long time ago.'

Meriel didn't reply, she wasn't sure what was meant.
Was there someone special in his life, someone who wasn't
aware of his love? Or tied up and unable to accept it?
The thought depressed her and she excused herself as soon
as the dishes were washed and went back into the living
room.

Lynne and Walter were sitting close together. Leo
walked in through the french windows, arms filled with
roses, which he gave to Lynne. He disappeared again and
Meriel followed him. He picked up secateurs and began
cutting a second bunch. 'These are for you,' he said.
'Would you like to choose?'

'Whatever you give me will be perfect,' she said, staring
at him as he concentrated on his task. When he was
satisfied with his selection they sat for a while in the seat
beneath the rowan tree and he talked about the flowers he
grew and asked her advice about changes to the layout of
the beds. She couldn't think of such mundane problems
and just nodded and smiled as he described his plans for
the autumn. She was wondering about the mysterious
woman in his life and inventing reasons for them not
wanting to reveal their love and marry. She felt a sadness
wrap around her and went inside, where the sight of her
parents lifted her spirits even if it failed to cheer her out
of her growing melancholy.

Drinks were offered and the mood of celebration
was revived and lasted until it was time to leave. Leo
drove her home but she avoided conversation apart from

thanking him for the part he played in getting her family together again. She feigned tiredness and closed her eyes to discourage anything more and when he stopped in the lane beside the path to Badgers Brook he didn't suggest going in.

'I have to get back,' he said, 'but I'm so glad it worked out well. You're very fortunate, Meriel, having so many people who love you.'

'I know,' she said, reaching for the door handle. He got out and walked around to open the door for her and for a moment they stood close together before he kissed her lightly on the cheek and turned away.

She waved as he drove off although he wouldn't have been able to see in the darkness, then forcing excitement, she ran into the house calling for Lucy to tell her about the wonderful evening.

'I feel so ashamed,' she admitted when they were sipping their late-night drink. 'Leo managed to put it all into perspective and I'm determined to forget about why I was given away and just be grateful that it was Mam and Dadda who adopted me.'

'You were very lucky,' Lucy agreed.

'As for George Dexter, he's a bitter man for whatever reason, and is best ignored.'

'You have good reason to be grateful to Leo,' Lucy reminded her softly and Meriel frowned and looked away.

–

Teifion had an unexpected visit from his father. He was putting the tables back after Betty had washed the floor in the bar when there was a knock at the side door. The prepared smile left his face as his father pushed him aside and walked in.

'I have to go away for a few days and I need you to cover the office,' he announced.

'Sorry, Dad, but I can't let Betty down. I've only been here a little while and I need her to know I'm reliable.'

'Reliable? You? Not a word I'd use for you! Come on, for once in your life do something to help me. I'm your father. It's the family business involved, you can't refuse to help.'

'Where are you going?'

'None of your business.'

'Sorry I can't help. I work here now and I'm enjoying it.' He suggested one or two people who might help but was adamant in his refusal to let Betty down. George shouted a stream of insults and stormed out. Getting into the car he set off for Brighton, determined to bring Frieda back.

With his heart racing, Teifion closed and bolted the door, feeling guilty but at the same time knowing his response had been the right one.

–

Leo didn't appear over the following days, although he phoned the office and asked how the plans for the auction were progressing. Her father also called and her mother asked if she could come down and meet them for lunch. 'Mum, we're so busy we wouldn't enjoy it. Can we make it next week? We're so anxious for everything to go well.'

'Of course. I understand how important this one is. I've been through a few such events with your father, remember,' she said with a laugh. 'Do you need Dadda's help? Or Leo's? They've both offered, but will only come if asked.'

'I think I'd rather we did it on our own, just for this one.'

'We understand, darling. Good luck with everything. I know you'll do well.'

Lucy was concerned about whether they had enough people to help but when Gerald called and offered to assist, she refused. 'Experienced help is what we want,' she explained, 'not people who will get in the way. Even the furniture shifters need to know what's expected of them.'

'I wouldn't want to move things,' he said in mock horror. 'I was thinking more an administrative role, writing down what's sold, the prices for each item and working out commission, I'm more suited to such things.'

'I'm sure you are,' Meriel said with a glance at Lucy.

'Gerald has dreams of becoming a part of all this, if you and he marry,' Meriel whispered to her friend later, 'so watch him.' She was smiling but although the words were light-heartedly spoken, she was serious.

'I won't let him take any of our worries away from us! We need them all!' Lucy too spoke jocularly but like Meriel, she was aware of the possible danger. Gerald was looking for a comfortable life and she wondered if that was all he saw when he looked at her, and uttered words of love. She found him attractive and there was something safe about being one of a loving couple. It promised a fulfilled life in the future, a home, children, someone there in good times and bad.

She had no illusions about his loving her and wondered, rather sadly, just how important love was to this thirty-year-old who desperately wanted a wife and a comfortable home.

The time since the war ended, when they had not been together, was fading from her memory, and the earlier years when they had been engaged no longer seemed separated by that emptiness but a continuing part of their long relationship. So many years to look back on plus the selective memories of someone half in love, made it hard to think of giving him up. She wondered sadly how many other people settled for second best. Was Gerald falling into that category? And, in Gerald's eyes, was she?

She was woken from her reverie by Teifion walking into the office. 'Lucy, I have an idea.'

'Is it something I'll like? If so sit down and tell me,' she said. 'If it's a favour then you'll have to wait until after the weekend, we're busy.'

'That's it! I'm free on Saturday as Ed Connors is helping Betty. I've got the whole day off. Lucky eh? I can come and give a hand. My years of experience are at your disposal! And, I don't want paying. And, in case you're in any doubt, I won't be representing my father, just helping you.'

'Why are you having the day off? Saturday's a busy day at the Ship, surely?'

He didn't tell her how he had pleaded for the time, wanting the excuse to share the day with her. 'Betty says I've worked so hard, doing much more than I'm paid for so I can have the day off. I'm free on Friday too, at least between opening hours, so if there's any setting up, I'm your man.' After a brief discussion with Meriel his offer was accepted.

George was predictably furious when he returned and stormed at his son, who seemed unaffected by the tirade of words although in fact he hated upsetting his father, afraid of seeing him collapse again in that frightening way.

Frieda was home again and acting the part of the loving wife whenever they were in company. In private she and

George rarely spoke to each other. She had insisted that her affair would continue as she couldn't live with George unless she had what she called her freedom. She agreed to return to George and play the part of 'the dutiful wife'. The words were cruel. What he wanted was a loyal, loving and truthful wife, a partner in everything he did, and a 'dutiful' wife was as far away from that as he could imagine. By her occasional appearances in Cwm Derw and her pretence at being his loving wife he would at least have had some pride left, and sadly, he had settled for that.

He stopped going home at lunchtime whether Frieda was at home or not, either going to the café or for a snack at the Ship and Compass. Betty made him a few sandwiches and, with a pint, he was content with that. He took a daily paper and hid behind it, using it as a screen to avoid conversation with other customers. He was in no mood for polite chatter. The jovial businessman, everyone's friend, was a part he played in the office and shed every time he stepped out of its door. Let down by his wife and with a son who refused to work for him, Walter's face, smiling contentedly, lurked at the edges of his mind as he tried to hold back on the anger that threatened to consume him.

He stayed at the office late each evening and some-times called once again at the pub for a leisurely pint before going home. He found some savage satisfaction in watching his son being pleasant to unimportant people, although he always made sure it was Betty who served him. There was always a meal waiting and sometimes Frieda had eaten hers and he ate alone. Somehow he found that satisfying too. Punishing himself seemed a bitter kind of pleasure when he was unable to punish Frieda – or Walter Evans.

He often passed the office of Evans and Calloway and childishly wished he could throw something at the window, destroy Walter's daughter's success, smash it into oblivion. To add to his misery the place always seemed busy. It was rare to pass when there was no one there. Often several people filled the small space, looking at the houses on offer or at the desk, presumably making enquiries about a house move. 'Upstarts,' he said aloud and someone passing looked at him and hurried away, alarmed by his red, angry complexion.

–

Between opening hours and the necessary work behind the scenes at the Ship, Teifion went through the arrangements for the sale with Meriel and Lucy. He didn't interfere, apart from offering a few helpful suggestions, upon which they acted. He and Lucy seemed to get along surprisingly well, with her having so recently considered him as one of the enemy, and Meriel wondered how Gerald would feel about their companionship.

Gerald's feelings were alarm and resentment. He decided that it would be a sensible move to propose. A partnership between Lucy and Teifion would be so convenient it had to be stopped before either of them realized it.

Having made up his mind he hated to delay but knew the important sale was filling Lucy's and Meriel's days and their minds, and he wouldn't receive a good hearing. Instead he planned an evening purporting to celebrate the success of the auction but in fact it would be an evening on which he would propose.

His father had arranged for him to go to London for a few days to attend a sale of old vehicles including several motorbikes. He had a list of models in which his father was interested and the prices he expected to pay. At the same time Gerald intended to gather leaflets and information on the latest cars, in the hope of persuading his father to concentrate on selling new machines rather than dirty-fingered repairs to old bikes which he hated and his father loved. Polishing new body work, persuading the wealthy to part with their cash was far more his style.

He booked a table for dinner in an out-of-town hotel for the evening following the auction and ordered flowers and a gift of Joy perfume to be delivered to the table. The price of the perfume nearly gave him a heart attack as he handed over the money in a shop in London, but he concentrated on looking nonchalant, hoping the tic at the side of his face didn't show. He knew he had to imply generosity and the promise of an attentive and adoring husband, he had to convince her she would be putting her life in safe hands. He had a moment of doubt when he wondered if Lucy would actually know the value of his gift, but decided he could accidentally let slip the price to make sure she understood.

–

Although they worked together for just a few days, Lucy had become used to Teifion's presence. When he arrived she would glance up and nod a welcome then they would begin discussing the various arrangements. Together they sorted out many small problems that occurred. Meriel was amused and a little worried, wondering whether Teifion was reporting back their plans to his father, who seethed with anger over his lost business.

Confidence in him was revived when they walked to the office early one morning and saw several of their posters advertising the sale had been fly-posted around the streets. One, to which Teifion proudly pointed, was on George Dexter's office window. Meriel wondered how the man would react when he noticed it.

'Best we never find out,' Lucy said with a chuckle.

Meriel and Lucy were up very early on the day of the sale. Leo had arrived at five thirty to find them up and awaiting his arrival before eating a simple breakfast of tea, toast and jam. To their surprise Teifion walked in just before six. They had expected him to be one of the later arrivals, forgetting momentarily his own experience of days like today.

They were on their way by six thirty, arriving to find men already at work spreading out the garden items and farm equipment in the grounds around the barn where the auction would take place, and adding labels carrying the lot numbers. The well-dressed Mr Lewen was there, suitably dressed in corduroys and a thick jumper and on his feet instead of highly polished shoes he wore work-manlike wellingtons, which were cleaner than those seen in a shop window, Meriel noted with amusement. Harry Power was there too and he waved as he dashed past on an ancient bicycle, carrying a paperboy's sack filled with leaflets, around his neck.

The grounds and the two barns being used for the sale were soon filling up with people examining the varied items. Most carried catalogues and were marking lots on which they would later bid. Any nervousness Meriel and Lucy had felt in the past few days quickly left them and they went around, planning their route as they went, intending to step outside for some of the larger and more expensive items.

On time precisely, Meriel and Lucy hugged each other before they went to the desk to begin. Their hearts were thumping painfully yet they both appeared calm. They sat at the desk, side by side, with Lucy following the lists, noting the successful bidders and the agreed price and at times directing the men who were to display the pieces as they came up.

Leo stood near and Teifion waited beside the desk out of sight within the crowd, ready if he should be needed to move anything or help to display them. In the entrance, squeezing himself into the already densely packed barn, George found a place from where he could watch Meriel and Lucy but not be seen.

The barn where they were to begin had been filled to capacity long before they were to start with many more standing outside craning their necks to listen to Meriel's clear voice, noting the progress on their catalogues with a moving finger sliding down the page.

Bids came fast as the more interesting items of furniture were sold first and almost without being truly aware of the sums involved, Meriel knew the prices were slightly above what she had hoped. A collection obviously from a child's nursery, produced a spate of bids and she felt the usual excitement as the prices rose. After years without such luxuries, even now, five years after the war had ended, there was an excitement as fine old rocking horses, dolls and dolls' houses, prams and clothes plus other paraphernalia went under the hammer.

When they stopped for lunch she and Lucy did a rough estimate and were encouraged by the sales so far. Teifion went to the tea tent and brought them each a plate of sandwiches and a sticky bun, which Lucy declared she was too excited to eat, but ate them anyway.

Harry Power cycled past, this time eating a doughnut. With a thumb stabbing the air he called, 'Well done, ladies, you're doing well.'

'What did you expect?' Lucy shouted through a mouthful of crumbs. 'We're the best!'

Meriel hushed her. 'Don't tempt fate, we've a long way to go yet!'

'It seems to be going well,' Leo said, bringing his sandwiches and joining them. 'I think this one is going to break records. You haven't started on the farm equipment yet and already the money's pouring in.' He had stayed in the background, just watching in case of trouble. They were a good-tempered crowd but just occasionally there could be an argument between two bidders getting out of hand and he was ready to deal with any unpleasantness. But whether because of two women being in charge or because there were plenty of bargains for all, there were no moments of anxiety for him. He had relaxed and watched with immense pride at the way Meriel dealt with the long and tiring day.

Walter and Lynne were there too but like Leo, they kept very much in the background, soaking up the atmosphere and swelling with pride at their capable and talented daughter. Her adoption was forgotten in the thrill of the moment as on so many occasions in the past. She was their daughter, their wonderful girl. They were happily unaware of George looking at them with envy and hatred.

Meriel and Lucy watched as the men helped the purchasers with their goods, heaving the heavy and awkward lots on to waiting lorries, fastening the dockets on to their clipboards duly signed. Lucy's eyes were sparkling. 'This is wonderful, Meriel. I can't imagine ever wanting to do anything else, can you?'

The rest of the day went well, with higher than expected prices being achieved for almost all the goods. With Leo and Teifion offering help, seeming to do what was needed before being asked, they moved from one barn to the next, carrying their precious lists and notebooks. The table and chairs arrived ahead of them, from barn to barn then out into the grounds to dispose of the last of the collection. There were still many shortages and the opportunity to buy second-hand some of the equipment they couldn't otherwise afford had brought farmers and smallholders from miles away.

There was no sign of the crowd diminishing; as the day went on some left but more continued to arrive. The auction moved outside; there were several pieces of stone statuary, everything from birdbaths and planters to huge full-sized figures of men and women on plinths, towering over the crowd. There was no initial bid for a collection of dog kennel, basket and bowl, but Meriel's father began to bid and eventually bought the lot for Rascal. Tennis rackets, croquet sets, picnic tables, deckchairs, curtains, the place was a treasure trove that had tempted unbeliev-able crowds.

Meriel knew that Leo's reminders about extra advert-ising, his persuasions to widen the area she had intended to canvass with leaflets and posters, had been a large part of the day's success. Teifion too had been a valuable addi-tion to the wonderful auction and catching a glimpse of George and remembering the poster Teifion had stuck on his window, they laughed and waved at him. Lowering his head George hurried away.

It was after eight o'clock before they could leave. Lynne had already disappeared and her father told her she was making sure there was a meal waiting for them all at Badgers Brook. Leaving the temporarily employed workmen to finish clearing up, and arranging for the few curtains and oddments to be disposed off, a weary Meriel and Lucy walked towards the cars. Meriel smiled as she heard Leo warning the men to 'Make sure there's nothing more than a few flattened grasses to show we've been here.'

'They've been marvellous,' Lucy said. 'They all worked so hard and with remarkable efficiency considering they'd never done this before. Even Mr Slick-Dresser Henry Lewen can't complain.' Lucy said with a sigh. 'What a day!'

'Henry? Is that his name?' Meriel asked, amused.

'Yes, doesn't it sound exactly right for him?'

'You ought to refer to him as Henry, that'll upset your Gerald.'

'Is he *my* Gerald?'

'Do you want him to be?'

'Come on, get into the car, I'm suddenly starving.'

Leo ran up, having gone back to discuss the success of the sale with Mr Lewen, to gauge his opinion on the day. 'He was smiling widely and proclaimed himself more than delighted with the day,' he reported to them. He hugged Lucy, then Meriel, holding her just a little longer, telling her she was wonderful.

Meriel felt the tiredness falling from her and wallowed in his praise. With an arm still around her he walked her over to Walter and repeated his comments about the owners' delight. Meriel was sorry when the weight of his arm left her and they got into the cars.

Leo and Teifion had been invited to join them for supper and Lynne had a casserole warming and some bread crisping in the fire oven. With fresh fruit offered as dessert they considered it a feast.

Lucy was about to sit and begin when there was a knock at the door. A very agitated Gerald stood there asking for Lucy.

'Come in, we can find another plateful,' Meriel said, but he refused. She was aware then of his anxious expression and asked, 'Gerald? Is something wrong?'

'Yes, er no, not exactly. I booked a meal for us and when I went to find Lucy she was still busy, then I was told she'd gone. We're late but we can still make it if I phone to explain.'

Lucy appeared and when he explained she shook her head. 'Sorry, Gerald, but I'm too tired. We're going to eat then collapse.'

'But it's arranged, something rather special to congratulate you on today. From what I've been told you were wonderful. Amazing.'

'At the moment all I feel is exhaustion. Can we make it another day?'

'Please, Lucy. It's important to me.' He gave a half-smile and added, 'The flowers won't be as fresh tomorrow. Flowers and a special gift for a special lady.'

She looked at him, the expression of devotion as his eyes stared into hers, the pleading tone, his hands reaching out and holding hers and suddenly she knew. He was going to propose. Panic filled her, both pleasure and pain. How much she had wanted this but now she was unsure. She had changed, her life had been transformed; marriage and children and a lifetime of Gerald no longer encapsulated her entire world.

'Gerald, it's a kind thought and normally I'd love to come but tonight I wouldn't be good company, I'd be sneaking glances at my watch, wondering how soon we can leave. You don't deserve that. Please, let's make it another day, shall we?'

His shoulders drooped and his hands fell to his sides, a picture of utter dejection. Once more his actions were genuine but again, Lucy found his behaviour unconvincing.

She went back into the kitchen where her meal had been put into the oven to keep warm, looking very thoughtful. She brightened and joined in the conversations and good-humoured laughter and said nothing of what had happened.

It wasn't until everyone had gone and they were making their traditional hot drink to take up to bed that she told Meriel what she suspected. '"Flowers" he said, and a special gift. I'm sure he was going to ask me to marry him.'

'And why doesn't that thrill you?' Meriel asked softly. 'Why aren't you bright-eyed and glowing with happiness?'

'I no longer want to trust my life to him and I don't really know why. Once it was all I dreamed of.'

'You were an assistant in the hairdresser's then, look at you now!'

'That's the trouble. I'm no longer that nervous girl afraid of being left on the shelf, desperate to say yes to a proposal of marriage.'

'Being successful in a business doesn't preclude you from everything else – at least, I hope not!' she joked.

'No, but perhaps it makes Gerald consider me a better prospect.'

'A prospect? That's what we call someone offering business.'

'Perhaps that's what I am. To Gerald. Offering him a share of all this, something that belongs to you and me.'

'Nonsense, he isn't that stupid.'

'Neither am I. Meriel, will you do something for me, a big favour?'

'Of course.'

'Will you hint to Gerald that I'm leaving Evans and Calloway? Just a hint that I'm not pulling my weight, and that we're to part company?'

'I can't do that! Someone might believe it and it isn't true, you're an equal partner. I can't lie about such a thing.'

'Please, just for a while. Just a hint, to Gerald. Then we'll see whether he changes his mind, about the flowers and the special gift for a special lady. Please?'

'All right, I'll try but don't expect me to be convincing. I'm not a natural liar.'

'This cocoa is cold,' Lucy said.

'Then make some more, you useless apology for a partner.' The attempt at a joke fell flat and Meriel pleaded again for Lucy not to make her lie.

Lucy was adamant. 'I have to know,' she said.

'If you will go to such lengths, you can't be too sure of your own feelings.'

'That's the problem, I no longer am.'

—

Gerald went to the hotel and collected the flowers and the perfume and went home. This wasn't going to be as easy as expected. He'd been so sure she'd collapse into his arms and say — Yes. He passed his father's coat in the hallway and the slight smell of petrol and grease wafted towards him. He felt choked by it. He had to persuade Lucy to marry him. Becoming a partner and eventually running an estate agency was his only hope of escaping from his father's garage.

–

Escaping from his father's business was also on Teifion's mind. After leaving Badgers Brook he was helping Betty to clear the last of the glasses and bottles away, his mind filled with the day and evening he had spent with Lucy and Meriel. He was surprised that, having been disenchanted with the business when he had worked for his father, he had found the day filled with excitement. Looking back he couldn't remember ever being happier. Yet the business was exactly the same. The only variations were Lucy and Meriel, instead of his father and the people who had worked for him over the years. How could he have been so bored in such a fascinating profession?

'Something on your mind, young Teifion?' Betty asked. 'Only that's the same glass you've been drying for the last ten minutes.'

'Sorry, Betty. I've been thinking about the auction. Lucy and Meriel are very good, they made a real success of the day. I enjoyed it far more than I'd expected. Why wasn't it as interesting when I worked for Dad?'

'You needed to spread your wings. Perhaps you'll go back one day and be a part of it again.'

He shook his head. 'I don't think so. I enjoyed it because of Lucy and Meriel.'

'But mainly Lucy?' she asked, her head on one side like a bird searching for titbits.

He shook his head deprecatingly. 'Lucy has her Gerald.'

'Since when would a bit of competition stop a full-blooded Welshman?'

He grinned and put the last glass in its place.

'It's Sunday tomorrow,' she reminded him. 'A day off. Why don't you call at Badgers Brook and see if they've recovered?'

Meriel and Lucy slept late and it was the impatient yelps of Rascal that eventually brought them downstairs, heavy-eyed, to be greeted by the young dog demanding to go outside. Lucy was first up and she went to the kitchen to make tea. As she lit the flame under the kettle, her thoughts were twisting and turning with images of a wedding with Gerald at her side, interspersed with visions of future house valuations, and auctions in which she stood beside Meriel and Leo, with the shadowy presence of Teifion close by.

As Meriel emerged from her room and followed her into the kitchen she was sitting staring at the kettle that was beginning to sing.

'Have you changed your mind about testing Gerald?' Meriel asked with a yawn. 'I know it's bothering you. I didn't sleep very well even though I was desperately tired and I heard you creep down sometime after midnight to make another hot drink.'

'I can't explain why, but when he talks of love and caring and all that stuff, he isn't convincing. I can't afford to make a mistake and although I know it's dishonest and I'm asking you to share the lie, I have to know before I can decide how I feel. Does that make sense to you?'

'As much as anything makes sense through this fuzzy, overtaxed brain of mine this morning. Wasn't it a marvellous experience, Lucy?'

They drank their tea still wearing dressing-gowns, in the garden, closing their eyes against the sun and wallowing in the joy of having a free day to recover from the past hectic week. Slowly they came to and having decided on baked potatoes for lunch with whatever they could find to have with them, they scrubbed some, allowing a couple extra in case of visitors, put them in the oven, dressed themselves and went back into the garden.

It was there Gerald found them when he arrived at midday. The dog warned of a visitor and they looked towards the corner of the house without getting up. Both girls felt dismay on seeing him put his head around and call to them; Meriel knowing she had to prepare her story and Lucy because she didn't know how she should feel.

He brought a huge bouquet of flowers from behind him with a flourish and on one knee handed them to Lucy. She panicked. Surely he wasn't going to propose there and then, in front of Meriel?

'Get up, Gerald, we had a heavy dew this morning,' she said in a squeaky voice. Laughing, Meriel went in to make coffee.

'Are you feeling recovered?' he asked, taking the seat vacated by Meriel.

'Not really. I don't think I can do that very often. I found it all too exhausting. Hairdressing was far easier.'

He laughed and ruffled her hair. 'You wouldn't go back to that, surely?'

She shrugged, glanced towards the door through which Meriel was carrying a tray.

'Who knows what the future holds, Gerald?'

'You aren't serious, about not enjoying your success? I'll always help when things get hectic. You can rely on me, always.'

She didn't reply, just moved to make a space between newspapers and notebooks for the tray. There was an uneasiness as they sat sipping coffee, conversation stilted, and he wondered what had gone wrong. He wasn't invited to stay for lunch as he had hoped, and when Lucy went inside he asked Meriel if anything was wrong. 'You haven't argued, have you? You seem to get on so well.'

'Things haven't been right for a while,' Meriel said, crossing her fingers as she lied. 'Yesterday was the final disaster. Papers missing, a client not given the correct statement, accounts muddled up, some goods not paid for, information not passed on. Thank goodness Teifion and Leo were on hand. It's no good pretending, Gerald, Lucy isn't cut out for this complicated business.'

'She wasn't joking then, when she hinted about going back to hairdressing?'

She took him to the shed where the hairdressing equipment they had bought had been stored, and silently shrugged. 'It was always a possibility, or why did she buy this? Thank goodness she'll have you to support her. You do plan to propose, don't you? She'll need a loving partner to console her when she's told to leave. Even though she's expecting it. it will still be a shock and disappointment. She'll need you, Gerald, very much.'

He didn't stay very long after Meriel's bombshell and the conversation was stilted. He filled the silences with idle flattery and gentle enquiries, most of which Lucy avoided answering. With a cursory kiss he left and Lucy watched him go, in no doubt about his change of heart. She felt tears well in her eyes and she turned away from Meriel's sympathetic face.

'Best I know. There's no point in kidding myself I was loved for my brains, my bubbling personality and outstanding beauty, eh?'

'Baked potatoes and salad for lunch, come on. It's just you and me. Until someone comes along who'll love us for all those things.'

A call from the side of the house alerted them to visitors and without their usual delight they turned, half expecting to see Gerald again. 'I'm not stopping,' Teifion assured them, misunderstanding their glum expressions. 'I just called to ask how you're feeling after yesterday. I met Gerald on my way and he seemed to think it wasn't as good as we all thought. What went wrong?'

'Everything's fine,' Meriel said. 'It was a very successful day, thanks to Lucy, and you and Leo and all the rest.'

'Then what's up with Gloomy Gerald?'

Lucy laughed. 'I'll tell you one day, not now.'

Teifion stared at her and saw she was blushing, then he looked pointedly at the flowers. 'A proposal?' he mouthed at Meriel, who shook her head.

'She turned him down? Thank goodness for that. I'd hate to think of someone as talented and lovely as Lucy stuck with someone like Gerald Cook, wouldn't you?'

He didn't stay for lunch, as Betty had food prepared, and Lucy stared after him as he walked down the path to the lane stopping to wave and blow a kiss as he went back to the Ship and Compass, whistling cheerfully.

'I think Gerald proposed and was turned down,' he told Betty happily, as he went through the side door of the Sunday-silent pub.

The following weeks settled down to the usual mixture of enquiries and occasional sales and Lucy was aware of the rarity of Gerald's appearances. The 'special gift for a special lady' hadn't appeared and the flowers faded and died.

'I was right, wasn't I?' she said to Meriel as they gathered their papers and set off for work one morning. 'Gerald hasn't been beating the door down to see me since we made him think I was about to be sacked.'

'It could be coincidence, he might be ill or something.'

'We have a telephone and so does his father.'

'Perhaps he's waiting for you to use it,' Meriel suggested with a smile.

'It's very hurtful, to know he only wanted me when he thought I was brilliant and successful and on the way to making a fortune.'

'Hardly a fortune.'

'Better than an assistant hairdresser. More prestige in being a business woman and that's what he admires – besides the money.'

'Don't be too sure, give it a few more days.'

Teifion called in as soon as the office opened and they talked about many things and Gerald was pushed, just a little way, out of her thoughts. Teifion had a few hours off each morning and offered to come and help. 'Perhaps noting any new addresses in your files? Checking the local papers for prospects?'

'Thanks, that will be useful. We both have appointments this afternoon, different times but it eats into the routine work. And we try not to work all evening.'

'We can't anyway. Living in Badgers Brook means the evenings are filled with visitors, and we don't want that to change,' Meriel said.

'Has Leo been lately?' he asked.

Meriel shook her head, laughing to hide her disappointment from Teifion and Lucy. 'He'll come if we need him but I think that, at last, Dadda and he both know we're managing perfectly well.'

Lucy stared at her friend, aware that she was not the only one feeling the loss of someone they had hoped was dependable. Meriel was wondering how she could encourage Leo to call. She was still confused by her growing affection, it made her vulnerable to embarrassment. She couldn't admit she simply wanted to see him. She needed a good reason to ask for his help, a genuine difficulty would protect herself from possible humiliation.

Lucy's cold provided her with the excuse she needed. Lucy awoke one morning with a headache and a streaming nose. A cough threatened. her eyes were reluctant to open and her legs felt weak. Meriel insisted her friend stayed home and rested. 'It's the only thing to do, spoil yourself for a day or so. I'll manage, there's your Teifion, he'll help us.'

'He isn't *my* Teifion!' Lucy protested weakly.

'Funny how he enjoyed spiting his father, isn't it?' Meriel mused. 'Him helping us must make George very angry. First we steal customers from him, then make him face up to his wife's misbehaviour and now we've stolen his son.'

During a phone call to her father, Meriel casually mentioned Lucy's illness. She heard muffled remarks as her father covered the phone, then he said, 'Leo's on his way.'

'There's no need,' she protested weakly, before happily replacing the phone. Her smile faded as she wondered how best to bring the conversation around to his secret love.

Teifion had left by the time Leo arrived and, as it was almost lunchtime, they closed the office and took a few treats back to Badgers Brook to coax Lucy to eat.

During the afternoon, Leo checked through the accounts and the prospects for the following few days and noticed a few pencil crosses on many of the pages. Tiny marks almost invisible. He frowned as he was assured by Meriel that neither she nor Lucy had made them. So what were they for?

'Perhaps Teifion was making another list. He seems very keen on double-checking so we don't miss a chance of a sale. He's very helpful,' Meriel said. 'And,' she added in a whisper, 'I think he's rather sweet on our Lucy.'

'Watch him, Meriel. Remember who his father is.'

Lucy came back the following day, insisting she was feeling well enough to work, and for the first time since the auction, Teifion didn't appear. At five o'clock, as the office was about to close, there was a telephone call from a solicitor telling them Mr George Dexter would like to make an offer to buy their business.

Ten

Lucy collapsed onto the desk in a distressed state. 'I'm stupid and vain,' she wailed at Meriel when the news of George's offer had sunk in. 'I thought Teifion was a friend and all the time he was spying for his father. Oh, Meriel, I've ruined everything. I really thought he helped because he liked me. How stupid is that?'

'Come on, we're going home,' Meriel said, her eyes blazing with anger and a little fear. Could he persuade them to sell? He was capable of making things so difficult they would be glad to. Lies and rumours, leaking secrets, they had been his weapons in the past, and could be again. With that determined expression he so often wore on his face he could threaten to buy them, or destroy them. Destroying them might take a bit longer but would cost him nothing.

In a spate of activity they closed the office, pushing papers carelessly into drawers and filing cabinets, ignoring the ringing of the phone as they locked the door behind them. Whoever it was could wait. They had to get out of the place, escape to the safety of Badgers Brook and think what to do.

Lucy drove back to the lane and they let themselves into the house in silence. Meriel began preparing their meal and Lucy stood outside, staring at nothing, her mind aching with the pain and humiliation of knowing she had let Meriel down. What was wrong with her that she believed men could like her for herself? She had believed Gerald loved her and twice he had let her down. She felt tears fill her eyes as she remembered the flattery of him asking for a second chance. His recent disappearance was proof enough of his lack of love. Now she had encouraged Teifion – against Meriel's instincts – to work beside her, allowed him to gather information which he had passed on to his father.

Meriel called her from the doorway. 'Come and eat, Lucy, then we'll decide what to do. Dadda will help. Don't worry,' she said as Lucy still didn't move, 'we aren't a company suitable for a takeover, that's for the big league. All George can do is spread rumours that we're in a difficult situation financially and hope the public will do the rest. We can make sure people know the truth. Come on, let's eat, then drive to Barry and talk to Dadda.'

'Best I stay here,' Lucy said, turning to go inside. 'I'm the cause of this.'

'Rubbish. What could Teifion have told his father that he couldn't have found out easily some other way?'

'Ironic isn't it, us trying to convince Gerald I was being sacked? I didn't dream it would happen.'

'Lucy, you're talking rubbish. We're partners and if there's a problem – and we don't know that there is – then we'll deal with it together.'

They ate in the garden, sitting in the sun and relaxing in its warmth. As they were about to get up and set off to talk to Walter and Lynne, they had a visitor. Teifion came around the corner, bent almost double in his haste, a hand held up to stop them talking.

'Please, let me talk first,' he pleaded. 'I heard about Dad's offer at five o'clock and tried to phone you.'

'Go away, Teifion.' Lucy said, rising from her chair.

'I know you're upset and you believe the worst, but I have never discussed Evans and Calloway business with my father. It's important that you believe that. I helped because I really enjoyed the business for the first time in my life, felt the excitement of a prospect and the thrills when things went well.'

'Just go,' Meriel said, with an exaggerated sigh.

Ignoring her, he went on, 'That auction was the most exciting day and I felt a part of it. A part of it! I've never felt that before. The business is called Ace, it was always referred to as George Dexter and Son, but it belonged to Dad, and I never belonged. Never.' He paused for breath and they stared at him unable to reply.

He flopped down in a garden chair, his eyes bright, his face flushed with emotion. 'Dad told me he'll close you down once he's bought you out. I told him I'd never speak to him again if he tried to.'

Meriel and Lucy exchanged glances and Meriel handed him a glass of home-made lemonade. 'Are you telling us the truth?' she asked coldly.

'I am. Making the break and leaving Dad's business was scary but turned out to be the best thing I ever did. I enjoy working with Betty Connors at the Ship and Compass. Using my spare time to help you, using my hard-won experience in an estate agency, I've enjoyed it for the first time. It has opened my eyes to a better future.'

'Like me, Teifion, you're an only child and you have a moral duty to support your father.'

'I used to think so but not now.'

'So you think working in a pub is what you were intended to do?' Meriel asked.

'Or take over our business and earn a pat on the head from your father?' Lucy added cynically.

He stood up and walked towards her. 'Lucy, I'd never hurt you. I hoped we'd become friends, something more than friends now you've given that Gerald creep the heave-ho.'

'I didn't. He left me,' Lucy said honestly.

'More fool him. Lucy, please believe I didn't cheat on you and Meriel. It's important that you believe me.'

Without another word Meriel took out the page which had been marked in several places with a cross. 'Can you tell us what these crosses mean? Are they points of interest to pass on to your father?'

From his inside pocket he took out a sheet of paper which he handed to her. She read it quickly, it was a brief letter asking the editor of their local newspaper to read and consider the enclosed article. She shook the solitary page and, still in silence, quirked an enquiring eyebrow as she passed it to Lucy.

'I've been preparing a piece about you two. Young women who had started a business usually run by men, and making a success of it. I'm not completely satisfied with it yet, and the crosses on that report were marking the words in hundreds to give me an idea of the length I needed. Nothing more sinister, I promise. I didn't intend sending it until you two approved,' he added.

'Sorry,' Lucy said. 'It was instinctive to blame you for your father's behaviour. I was wrong.' Her apology was echoed by Meriel and he was invited to stay.

'Anyone home?' a voice called and Walter and Lynne came around the corner of the house.

'Perhaps I'd better go,' Teifion said.

'If you're afraid of more questions, then yes, you should hurry away before they start!' Lucy said, as Meriel went across to meet her parents. Teifion glared at her with some defiance, and sat down.

When explanations were over and Walter told them how he had heard George's latest move from a friend, Lucy said, 'Teifion has been working with us but insists he knew nothing about this.'

'He's probably right. George has been telling people that the business is insolvent and about to collapse and he's buying it as a surprise for his son.'

They decided on an increase in their advertising and Walter applauded Teifion's idea of writing an article about the enterprising friends and their new and thriving business. 'A successful business run by two beautiful young women is news and worthy of a mention.' He took Lynne's hand and added, 'We're so very proud of you, love.'

An unbidden thought entered Meriel's mind and she wondered whether her real mother would be proud of her too. Although she had told her parents she had abandoned hope of finding her mother, the need to know and her curiosity wouldn't go away.

Walter and Lynne left about nine o'clock, leaving three more relaxed people still sitting in the garden. Teifion left soon after and when Meriel and Lucy finally went to bed the shock had eased from them, the house made its small comforting sounds as night settled around them, and they slept.

–

Leo still clung to the curiosity about Meriel's family too although he tried to keep his thoughts about them to himself. He walked past a book shop specializing in religious literature one morning and saw William Roberts-Price inside, serving a young woman. He went in and began to say hello but the man looked up and at once shuffled back out of sight.

When another assistant appeared Leo asked, 'Was that Mr Roberts-Price? I'd like a word, please.'

'I'm sorry, he has had to go out on an errand. Can you try later?'

Leo tried twice more but each time he was told that the man was unavailable. He drove to the cottage near the church where the family lived and knocked the door, unsure what he was going to say, but hoping to have an explanation of the man's reluctance to speak to him. The door was opened by a stranger who told him the family had moved away and he didn't have a forwarding address.

Later that week he called into a café for a cup of tea and saw the young woman from the book shop. He involved her in conversation and once the introductory politenesses were over he asked about her boss. 'I don't think he likes me,' Leo said conspiratorially. 'I must represent something he doesn't approve of.'

'I have to admit he doesn't approve of very much at all,' she confided, adding, 'it wouldn't have been personal, he keeps very much to himself. You could try talking to his daughter, she's more chatty, not that that's very difficult,' she added with a laugh. 'She works in Woolworth's on the record counter. She loves serving young people and enjoys modern music and the latest comedy records but she isn't allowed to buy any. Her father won't allow them to have a wireless let alone a gramophone! Can you believe that? He doesn't approve of her working there either, but at least she shows some spirit and defies him.'

'Good on her,' he said. He stood to leave and thanked the girl for trying to help. When he tried the record counter Miss Price – without the Roberts – was at lunch.

Putting aside any worries about the time he was wasting, he went back later on but the girl wasn't there. A few days later, when he was calling in the area he again asked for Miss Price but this time he was told she had left and the family had moved away.

As he walked away, Leo wondered if the family were still in the area. The daughter had left her job on the record counter and the family no longer lived in Church Cottage. Everything seemed to suggest that William Roberts-Price insisted on complete obedience. He felt a brief sympathy for the daughter who had tried to make up her own mind. He wondered where she was and what she was doing. Perhaps the girl from the book shop could once again help?

–

Teifion was worried about what his father might do to harm the business of Meriel and Lucy. He didn't go to see him, having decided that any contact might be miscon-strued and he was afraid Lucy would think the worst. When he saw his father and Frieda coming into the bar the following evening he walked to the far end, hoping Betty would serve them, but he couldn't escape.

'A pint of your best, please, Teifion, and a sherry for Frieda.'

Teifion served the order without a word and avoided looking into his father's eyes. He took the money he offered, put the change in front of him and moved to serve someone else. George smiled and pushed the change towards him. 'Keep the change, *barman*, I expect you can do with it.'

Teifion pushed it back to his father so fiercely it fell to the floor. Neither made any attempt to collect it.

'You'd better come and pack up the rest of your clothes and things,' Frieda said. 'We're having some rooms decorated and we need to clear as much as we can.' She touched his hand lightly and added, 'Tomorrow afternoon when you close after the lunch session. All right?'

'All right,' he said, glancing at his father, who was smiling at some unspoken joke. He knew it wasn't humour to be shared, *he* was the butt of his father's cynical amusement. His face reddened as he felt the embarrassment he'd so often caused him in the past.

–

When they closed the pub at two o'clock the next day, he went to the office and told Lucy where he was going and why.

'I quite understand.'

'Does that mean you believe me?'

'I don't think your father needs your help to harm us. He can manage well enough on his own.'

'I'll come back as soon as I've finished,' he promised.

He walked past his father's office and tried to see whether his father was there but the July sun was bright and the reflection restricted his view. He hoped George would not be at home.

There were only two hours before he needed to be back at the Ship but he dawdled as he went to the house he still called home, stopping to look over a farm gate, to count trees and lamp posts and chimney pots. Anything to delay the visit in which he might have to face his father.

Frieda saw him coming and opened the door. She led him straight into the living room where piles of clothes covered the chairs and a couple of boxes were open revealing many of his possessions, some forgotten since childhood.

'Frieda! What am I supposed to do with all this? I've only a small room at the Ship.'

She shrugged. 'Your father asked me to collect it all up and ask you to get rid of it. We're refurbishing two of the rooms and what was once your bedroom is one of them.'

'Put it all in the shed. I can't sort it out now. I'll need to have a few hours to go through it all and decide where I can dispose of it. I have to be back in an hour.'

'Then you should have come earlier, shouldn't you?' George said from the doorway.

'Oh, throw it all away!' Teifion said, startled by George's sudden appearance. 'I don't want anything from you, not even my clothes. I'll manage on what I took with me.'

'Cellarman, barman, you won't need much in the way of smart clothes.'

'That's right. What does it matter what I wear? Who looks at a cellarman?'

'Come on, boy, don't you think you've sulked long enough? We want you to come home.'

'I'm happier where I am.' He looked properly at his father for the first time and he felt a shock of alarm. The unusual pallor around the eyes made them look deepset and large. The high spots of colour on the cheeks and the way the skin on his face had become loose and lined had aged him. Was he ill? Was that the reason for asking him to come back? Did he have a real need for him? George's words seemed to confirm his concerned thoughts.

'Are you all right, Dad?'

'Are you pretending to care?'

'I just thought that if you aren't well – it might be why you want me back.'

'The truth is, son, I'm thinking about retiring. Frieda and I want to move down to Bournemouth, somewhere pleasant and warm. The business was always intended to be yours. Come home and take over. I'll persuade Meriel Evans to sell her paltry attempt to ruin it and you can have Lucy working for you. Wouldn't that make you happy?'

For a moment his heart leapt with excitement, but he showed no joy. He calmly repeated his last words. 'I'm happier where I am.'

'Evans and Calloway are losing their reputation, you know. Quick to rise and quicker to fall, that's the fate of amateurs.'

'If that is true then it's your doing. And how can you call Meriel an amateur?'

'What else can we call Lucy?'

'She's keen and a fast learner.'

'Then ask her to come and work here, for you.'

'You're really going to leave?'

'I said so, didn't I?'

'When?'

'Soon, probably in the spring.'

'I don't believe you.'

George walked across to the table and picked up a leaflet. 'We're acting for that Roberts-Price family, you know the ones who sold their house through Evans and Calloway? Odd that they aren't going through them to buy, isn't it? Could it mean they aren't as good as they suppose?'

'I wouldn't read anything into what that man does.'

'Know them well, do you?'

'Not really, I thought for a while they were—'

George tilted his head curiously and waited. Teifion saw no reason to prevaricate. After all, the story had been disproved. 'For a time I thought they might be Meriel's real parents. Since you told everyone she was adopted and ruined her peace of mind, I tried to find her real mother but I failed.

'I approached the family but they are nothing to do with Meriel, thank goodness. She thought it might make it easier to bear once she knew where she came from, why her mother didn't keep her. You really shouldn't have done that, Dad. It was cruel.'

'What made you think it was the Roberts-Price couple? From what I know of them they're hardly the type to abandon a child.'

'I was wrong and before you ask, I haven't been able to discover anything about her adoption. If I had, you'd be the last one I'd tell. You almost destroyed her telling everyone the truth.'

George shook his head and tutted slowly. Then he smiled and patted his son's shoulder as though amused at the rantings of a child. 'Oh, how I've missed you. Come home. Please, Teifion. Come back and make us laugh again. The place isn't the same without you, is it, Frieda?'

The words seemed condescending to Teifion, as though he were stupid, good for a laugh, and unworldly and incapable of surviving outside his father's care. He stood up and kicked at the boxes holding his childhood memories and went out. 'If you don't want the business sell it, and leave Meriel and Lucy alone!' he shouted back.

George didn't call after him. He looked at Frieda thoughtfully. 'Now I wonder whether it would be worth visiting the Roberts-Price family? Letting them presume I know more than I actually do is a ploy that often works.'

'This is all very boring, George. I agreed to stay with you but on certain conditions, remember, and one of them is forgetting this need for revenge against Meriel and Lucy.'

'Come on, Frieda, I've agreed to our moving, haven't I? Can't I have a little fun before we do?'

'Why d'you hate her so much? It's a side of you I don't like at all.'

'I don't hate Meriel, it's her father who always gets in my way.'

–

Teifion was filled with doubts. Mistrusting his father was a habit, but perhaps this time he really did need help. He certainly looked unwell but he doubted his promise that retirement was imminent. George Dexter, Estate Agent and Auctioneer, would always be his life and if he took over, his father would never be able to stay away. He'd be unable to refrain from interfering and telling him how hopeless he was, criticizing him, humiliating him until the day he died.

There was no one to talk to. He could hardly discuss taking on a rival business with Lucy, and Betty would probably remind him that his loyalty lay with his father. Perhaps Leo might offer a solution? He was far enough away from the situation to give an honest opinion.

Back at the Ship and Compass after he dealt with the routine tasks and they had eaten, a few minutes before the doors opened for the evening, he wrote a short note to Leo, marking it private and addressing it care of Walter's office.

Gerald was unhappy. He looked at his grease-stained hands, at the blackness under his fingernails, and pulled a face. The oilcan on the bench seemed like a symbol of his misery, he picked it up and threw it against the wall where it clanged and clattered before landing in the corner on a pile of spare parts.

Life was definitely passing him by. It seemed to have happened in a matter of weeks. There he was, playing with the idea of marrying Lucy, giving up on the distasteful occupation his father had planned for him and dreaming of a life married to a wealthy woman.

He now knew he'd been misinformed about Lucy leaving. He didn't understand why she'd lied and presumed it was one of her jokes. Everyone knew the business was growing and that Lucy's future was secure. But if they were married, he would be able to look after her, support her and offer help when she needed it. She wouldn't be alone when problems threatened. She was so remarkable, walking away from all she knew, taking on a new challenge and making a success of it. A feeling of pride swelled in his chest.

He sighed contentedly as he thought about Lucy, not as a way out of a future he couldn't face, but as a woman he desired. He recognized with some surprise his need to protect her and care for her. Could it be love? he mused with growing excitement. He certainly anticipated meeting her with more delight than before. And he wanted to do things for her, take her presents. The perfume was still in his drawer at home and he began to imagine a scene in which she fell into his arms with delight at his generosity. He was smiling when he bumped into his father as he went through the garage door into the workshop. His father was not.

'Have you finished the service on the B.S.A.?'

Gerald looked up in surprise hearing the anger in his father's voice. 'Well no, actually. I've been thinking about how we can expand. I was about to go through the order book to see how many cars are on order.'

'I can tell you that,' his father snapped. 'Exactly none. I don't want the business of new cars, I repair and service motorbikes. That is what we do here.'

'But I arranged to supply a new Morris to Mr Gorman.'

'I unarranged it! I passed the order on to the place in Cardiff where they're better suited to deal with such things.' As Gerald took a deep breath to complain, he went on, 'And before you say anything more, let me tell you something. I am tired of carrying you. I've paid your wages all these years and you've given nothing back. You don't even pretend to be interested. Well, it's over. I don't intend to carry you any longer. Get stuck in and help with the work that's waiting, or get out. Right out. Understand? I've had enough.' Gerald's mouth opened and closed like a stranded fish. 'And, before you say anything, your mother agrees with me. Right?'

Throwing down a rag with which he had been about to clean the work bench, he hurried out, his face like thunder. Gerald turned on his heel to follow his progress but in contrast to his father, he was smiling. So he was sacked. What a good opportunity for a fresh start. He reached for the tin of cleaning jelly, washed his hands meticulously, symbolically removing the remnants of the work from his skin, then went to change out of the hated overalls and heavy boots.

The showrooms opening up in every town, selling both second-hand cars and new models, offered him hope. After all, he had the perfect credentials. Whether he liked it or not, he was a trained mechanic, and he had the tall, broad-shouldered figure that appealed to the ladies and the easy conversation and upper-class accent, perfected over the years, that men found reassuring. Confidence and good looks, that's what a salesman needed and – as long as he was well away from his father's disapproval – he had plenty of both.

While his father and mother were discussing what had been said, he made a phone call. He spoke well and his comments about his abilities and enthusiasm impressed. An interview was arranged for later that day. Dressed in his newest suit, highly-polished shoes and an immaculate shirt and tie, he went into the yard.

He stood beside the firm's van and shook his head. It wasn't the vehicle to be seen in, not if he wanted to be taken seriously. On the pavement he hesitated, considering bus or train, and inventing reasons to explain why he hadn't arrived in the sports car he had told the interviewer he owned. George Dexter drove past and stopped.

'Any luck with a new career, Gerald?' he called, exaggerating the accent on the name.

Gerald walked across. 'I'm going into Cardiff. There's a vacancy for a salesman at one of the new car showrooms. Selling high-class vehicles will suit me better than working with Dad, repairing bikes. But how can I arrive in that thing?' He gestured towards the van.

'Get in, I'll take you,' George said, pushing open the passenger door of his MG. He drove out of town and once they were on the road to Cardiff he stopped and said, 'Better still, you can drive.'

Cautiously, determined not to damage the car, Gerald took the wheel. It was a dream to drive and unable to resist, he picked up speed on the quiet stretches and it was with regret that he slowed when they approached the town. He parked at the side of the road where there was a bus stop.

'Thanks,' he said. 'I enjoyed that.'

'Go on, drive the rest of the way, impress them. I'll be a friend who begged a ride in your smart two-seater.'

Glowing with pride, Gerald drove into the forecourt and leaped out. He straightened his tie in a nervous gesture then walked across to the office. This was the moment to impress and he determined to make them aware of how much they needed him, not how much he wanted the job. Casual and confident, those were his key words.

He was offered the job and accepted with ill-concealed amazement. The first time in his life he had applied for a vacancy and he got it. His first thought was how much he would enjoy telling his father, the second was telling Lucy.

Driving home beside George they talked about his success, laughing and joking like conspirators. 'Thanks, Mr Dexter,' Gerald said seriously. 'Driving up in this fabulous car definitely helped.'

'It probably gave you a good start. Look successful and you're halfway there,' George said.

The confidentiality of their unplanned afternoon made Gerald relax and talk of many things. He had never had anyone to confide in before and George was like a newly discovered friend. He told him about his dread of loneliness. 'To reach middle and old age alone must be the worst thing. I'd rather marry someone in haste than end up on my own. I'm past thirty and time is running out.'

'And there's no one you care for? What about Lucy Calloway?'

The success of the interview had made his earlier dreams of loving Lucy fade a little. Now he was going to be a salesman and earn lots of money, her attractions no longer fed his picture of a golden future. 'I don't think I've found the right woman yet,' he said. 'I'm fond of Lucy, very fond. But she won't fit the image I have of how my future will evolve. I need a wife who will help me build my reputation. Someone who can stand by my side and mix confidently with the best.'

George was silent for a moment then said harshly, 'Whether you realize it or not, what you need is someone you love and who loves you. There is no substitute for that.'

'Really, Mr Dexter. I wouldn't have put you down as a romantic.'

'Call it what you will, I can tell you my life has never been happy despite my success. I was young and foolish and I discarded the one love of my life. I married my first wife because her father offered me the money to start my business. My love was thrown away on the altar of greed. The man who married her is showered by my hatred every time we meet. Yet it was I who threw that love away.'

'Aren't you looking back through rose-tinted spectacles. Mr Dexter?'

'Maybe.'

'You think I should marry Lucy even though I don't think she suits my needs?'

George chuckled. 'You have to ask her first. She might say no! You aren't the only man who finds her desirable, my young friend. I suspect my son is seriously smitten.'

Gerald stepped out of the car to see his father sweeping up some iron filings in the garage yard. 'I went for an interview this afternoon. Mr Dexter gave me a lift, in fact I drove his MG most of the way. Wasn't that generous of him?'

'Did you get the job?' His father's voice was low, he didn't look at his son.

'Oh yes,' Gerald replied airily. 'I start a week on Monday.'

'Good,' was the abrupt reply.

'Don't you want to know what and where?'

'A salesman in a car showroom?'

'How did you know?'

His father pointed to a small Fiat parked outside the yard. 'It isn't grand or even very impressive but it's yours if you want it. You'll need transport and you can always hope they'll think you an eccentric.'

'I don't understand—'

'It's a parting gift.'

'Thanks, I'll be glad of—' But his father walked off without another word.

The excitement of the day fell from Gerald like an icy garment, spreading a chill as it went. He'd been so pleased with the interview and the friendliness of George Dexter, it was as though the day had opened a door onto a brand new start, but with hardly a word, his father's attitude spoilt it all. A parting gift? Where was he supposed to go?

His father went into the house and said to his wife, 'That was the hardest thing I've ever done in my life. We've spoilt him and I just hope it isn't too late for him to stand on his own feet.'

In need of comfort and praise, Gerald went to Badgers Brook to see Lucy to tell her about the new job, but even that fell flat as there were several people there, including Teifion Dexter, who seemed completely uninterested in his news. Even Teifion seemed bored when told of his father's kindness when he went for the interview. Lucy asked polite questions but showed no real interest in his replies. He was aware of sitting outside a close circle of friends, being in a place of which he had no part. He didn't stay long. Better to talk to Lucy when they were on their own. After he gave her that bottle of perfume. She would listen to him then.

–

Leo was surprised to receive Teifion's letter and he opened it with Walter looking over his shoulder and they read it together.

> *Please forgive me for involving you in my problem, but I believe my father is ill. He denies it but tells me he is to retire and move to the south coast of England. He wants me to take over the business and threatens to close down Evans and Calloway. He promises to employ Lucy as my assistant and I have to admit here that the thought of working with Lucy is something that strongly appeals, but not at the expense of harming either her or Meriel. If I go back to help my father, Lucy will believe I have betrayed them and this is something I don't want to happen.*
>
> *My instinct is to ignore all this, I dread the thought of going back to work for him, but I am worried in case my father really is unwell and this*

is his way of asking for my help. What sort of a son would I be if I did nothing? Frieda is not the type to care for a sick person.

I don't know what to do and would appreciate the opportunity to talk to you about it.

Will you phone me at the Ship and let me know if you agree to help?

Walter read the letter a second time and said, 'I believe the boy's genuine, what do you think?'

'What also jumps out of the page is his feelings for Lucy. I think that if I go, you should come with me.' And so it was agreed. Leo rang Teifion and arranged to meet him at the weekend, when he, Walter and Lynne could include a visit to Badgers Brook.

–

Without mentioning it to Walter, Leo went to the Religious Books shop and invited the young girl assistant to have lunch with him. 'I'm visiting a client and I need to eat and prefer not to eat alone,' he explained. She accepted with obvious pleasure and led him to a café where a long list of choices turned out to be chips with anything you fancied. As they ate he was thinking that they would have done better to buy from Gwennie Flint's and eat chips straight from the paper, sitting on a park bench. But he hadn't come expecting haute cuisine, he wanted to find out where the Roberts-Price family had gone.

Apart from listing her opinions about the dull boring family to which her friend had the misfortune to belong, he learned little. The town to which the family had moved was Bridgend and the street she thought might be something to do with a castle or something medieval but she remembered nothing more.

'She promised to write, but I don't think she will,' she said. 'And I won't be devastated if I never see her again. Can you believe she's not allowed to go to dances, or the pictures, she can't listen to the wireless or buy records – at least when the old man is around. I sold her a record player,' she confided, 'and she keeps it hidden, only playing her records when he's safely out of the way.'

Leo remembered with sadness the view of the young girl dancing alone, her reedy voice singing along with the lyrics, trying to put some gaiety into that sombre house.

'What a life, eh?' the girl went on. 'That job in Woolworth's was her best chance of having fun but her miserable father made her leave and move away. And,' she added, her eyes wild with disbelief, 'she has to go to church three times every Sunday. I ask you, what sort of a nineteen-year-old girl accepts that these days? A drip, that's what sort of girl. I was glad when she left.'

'But I thought, as you work in a shop selling religious books, you'd understand?'

'Understand? Do I heck! I took the job to fill in until I'm old enough to join the ATS. It sounds good when they ask what I've been doing, see.'

Leo thanked her for her time, wished her luck in her future career and went back to the car. It had all been an utter waste of time. Or had it?

On a whim he went to Bridgend and asked if there were any religious book shops in the area and was told of two. At the first he struck lucky. He stood in the doorway pretending to look at the books displayed on a stand, and as his eyes became accustomed to the dark interior, there behind the counter he saw the unmistakable stooped form of Mr Roberts-Price. Hoping he hadn't been seen, he walked swiftly away.

After a phone call giving Walter untrue reasons for his delay, he sat near the shop in his car and waited. At five o'clock the shop door closed and a few moments later, during which time Leo wondered whether the staff had left by a back door and he'd missed his quarry, three people came out. The door was locked by Mr Roberts-Price then rattled to make sure it was properly secure. Heart racing, Leo started the engine.

The man didn't go far. In the street behind the book shop he went into a door beside a bakery. The daughter went in a few minutes after him, dressed in a long ill-fitting dress and flat sandals, her hair straight, unevenly cut and reaching her shoulders. Leo found it hard to believe she was approaching twenty.

Hunger was tormenting him but he waited for an hour but no one came out again. He drove back to Barry, satisfied he had found their new home. He still didn't know how he would use the information, but felt reassured by having it.

–

Lucy woke the next morning and felt her head jar painfully as she lifted it from the pillow. A tightness around her throat and a tickle that quickly developed into a cough and she knew she had caught another unseasonal cold. She had always been susceptible to these and wondered what to do about it. Kitty recommended oranges, lots of oranges. Stella in the post office advocated lemon juice and blackcurrant jam. When she went downstairs, where Meriel was already up and setting the table for breakfast, she was sent straight back to bed.

When she protested, Meriel said, 'The best way of getting rid of a cold is to rest, and besides, our clients wouldn't be pleased if you passed it on.'

Teifion heard at lunchtime from someone who had called at the office and as soon as the pub closed he went to see Meriel. 'Can I do anything, go and see her and take Lucozade or Tizer?' he offered.

'Best to let her rest,' she said after thanking him.

'Then can I do something here?' There was a brief silence and he added, 'That's if you trust me.'

She smiled, and gestured towards Lucy's chair.

When they closed the office at five, he went with her to Badgers Brook and to their surprise, when they reached the door they heard voices and laughter. 'Gerald!' Teifion said pulling a face. 'Perhaps I won't stay after all.'

'Don't be so defeatist,' Meriel said, pushing him through the kitchen.

'Gerald's got himself a job,' Lucy's muffled voice reported.

'Two jobs, isn't that going to be difficult?' Teifion asked.

'My father and I have parted company. I phoned about a position and went to Cardiff for an interview. They were very impressed, especially as your father let me drive myself there in his MG,' he added, watching for Teifion's reaction. 'I start work on Monday as a car salesman.'

'Does this mean you'll be moving?' Meriel asked. 'If you've been kicked out by your father you won't want to go on living there, will you?'

'What d'you mean? My father didn't kick me out, I found a better way of earning my living.'

'We had an enquiry today, from a neighbour and he said your father told you to go. What's that if it isn't being kicked out?' Meriel asked sweetly.

Teifion laughed at the man's discomfort and looked at Lucy, relieved to see she was sharing it.

Gerald realized with alarm that Meriel was right, he would have to find somewhere else to live. Leaving home! How would he manage, unless Lucy agreed to marry him? Sharing Badgers Brook with her and Meriel wouldn't be too bad, until he got on his feet and could afford something better. He touched the house key in his pocket. He'd better get home fast before his father presumed he wouldn't be back. He had visions of seeing his clothes piled up on the doorstep. All appeared normal when he returned, his parents were listening to the wireless and he muttered goodnight and went to bed with a sigh of relief. He wasn't ready to move out, he wondered vaguely if he ever would. Despite George's wise words, Lucy's charms didn't give the situation that much urgency, he admitted sadly.

–

When Leo eventually reached the office, Walter and Lynne were there although it was after closing time.

'Where have you been all day?' Walter asked.

'I'm sorry but something happened and I had to deal with it. I'll make up my time. Sorry I couldn't let you know how long I'd be.'

'I asked where have you been.'

Leo looked at his employer and lowered his head. 'It's private,' he said.

'Nothing to do with our daughter?'

From Walter and Lynne's expression Leo knew it was pointless to lie. 'Meriel was devastated when George Dexter told her you were her adoptive parents. Since then she has tried to accept it, but feels she won't be able to until she finds her other family and is told why they gave her away. She wants to see the family she was born into and find out who she is. I can understand that.'

'You've been investigating, even though you know we didn't want this?'

'Not investigating, I didn't know where to begin. More like excluding someone from her possibilities.'

'And did you? Exclude these people from her possibilities?'

'Not really. I just don't know. The family in question doesn't seem the right sort, but – I'm sorry but I really think she needs to know. All I have decided is to investigate this one lead and if it's wrong, as I think it is, that will be an end to it. I really don't know any other place to search.'

'Finding a connection with a Bible-thumping bore, how will that help her?' Walter growled and in alarm Lynne spoke over Walter's words hoping Leo had failed to hear them and realize their import. 'We don't know who she was, Leo, we aren't allowed to know,' she shouted to block out the words. 'Our guesses won't help anyone, and guessing is all we can do.'

'We were never told,' Walter insisted. 'Secrecy protects the mother as well as the child. We don't even know the town in which she was born. Believe me, there are no clues to help us even if we wanted to find out where she belonged before we took her into our lives. Please, Leo, let this rest.'

He felt shame for upsetting them but Walter's outburst, his angry mention of the 'Bible-thumping' family gave him a sick feeling in the pit of his stomach which he hoped he'd managed to hide. Lynne said they had no idea, so perhaps Walter was hinting that he knew where his enquires had led him, nothing more than that.

'Please, Leo,' Walter said, 'if we mean anything to you, Lynne, Meriel and me, please drop it.'

'I'm sorry I've upset you,' he said. 'I apologize to you both.'

Lynne stood up and went to the door, Walter following. She turned and said, 'This is not the way to make her notice you, Leo. There are better, kinder means to attract her attention than this.'

Startled, he stared at her.

Walter attempted a smile and quirked an eyebrow. 'Don't think we haven't noticed how much you care for her. You've seen her grow from a gawky schoolgirl into a lovely woman – your feelings for her changing too.'

'Nothing would delight us more than you and our daughter getting close. It's our dearest wish.' Lynne said as she opened the office door and stepped out. 'Good night. Come on, Walter, darling, let's leave him to think about things. We'll talk about it again tomorrow.'

'Just remember what happened to Pandora when she opened that box,' Walter remarked grimly as they left.

Were they warning him he would lose Meriel if he didn't agree? He had never been a man to evade trouble, had always thought it best to face it head on. He knew he wouldn't rest before talking to Meriel. He had to ask her one more time if she really wanted to take the risk of knowing the truth. His loyalty was to her. Walter's displeasure was a risk he had to take. He called briefly to tell his mother he wouldn't be home until very late then drove once more to Badgers Brook. He was unaware of Walter making the same decision.

–

Lucy was in a chair, wrapped up and dosed with lot lemon juice and blackcurrant jam – delivered earlier by Stella. Meriel was listening to the wireless turned low and the fire was slowly sifting down to its end. A peaceful scene and what Leo had to say would probably ruin it.

He was offered a cup of tea and when they were seated, he said, 'Meriel, are you sure you want to find your first family? They might not want to find you, remember. You could cause them a great deal of hurt. And you could find the truth upsetting, too. Wouldn't you be happier just living with vague dreams? After all, you could invent a family and make them what you want them to be. Rich, poor, clever, successful or the village idiots, happy or miserable, town or country, tall or short, fat or thin, knock-kneed, toothless—' He stopped and looked at her, hoping his words had raised her spirits.

'Leo, I have tried to forget it, I really have, but I must know. Even if they are the worst people I can imagine, I need to know where I came from and why I was abandoned.' She lifted her head and looked at him, her eyes filled with suspicion. 'You know, don't you! You know!'

He carefully explained his reasons and the way the investigation had taken him. Then he told her of the slip made by her father that his mother couldn't quite cover up.

'Who are they?' she whispered and he held her close, her heart beating wildly against his own.

'I'm whistling in the wind here, I'm not at all convinced,' he began, 'I haven't spoken to them, faced them with it.'

'Tell me!'

'It was Teifion's initial idea that you are the daughter of the Roberts-Price family and I'm now beginning to believe he was right. I have no proof, just a few odd hints, their behaviour when they see you, their leaving Church Cottage so soon after moving there, and making their daughter move with them, give up her job and start again. They're running away from something, at least, he is, but I have nothing more concrete than that. I wish I hadn't started this. All I've done is upset you and your parents and none of you deserve it.'

She gave a groan and whispered. 'I believe I knew. There was always something odd about the way he was with me. He avoided me and ran off whenever I appeared, or pedalled off on that creaky old bike, and there was the strangeness of them all. Belonging to them, being their dark unspoken secret, was one of my worst dreams. I was the explanation of their oddness. I was the reason they lived surrounded by secrecy. They suffered shame and guilt from my being born which was made worse by then giving me away.'

'None of the shame rests with you, remember that. You are innocent of anything sad or shameful. You are Meriel Evans and that baby was the end of a tragedy and the beginning of something wonderful.'

A knock at the door and Walter walked in. 'So he's told you then?'

Still clinging to Leo, Meriel could only nod.

'Then let this be an end to it. I pray you'll never learn the rest. If you have any feelings for us at all, finish this now. Forget the Roberts-Price family and let it go. If you carry on with this you will destroy your mother. Is that what you want?'

'There's more?' Meriel gasped.

'For heaven's sake, Meriel, let it rest!'

Walter turned and went out, running down the path to the lane. Through the open door they heard the sound of the engine as he drove away.

Lucy, wrapped like a cocoon, forgotten by them all, peered out from the blankets.

'That wasn't very sensible, was it? Telling you there's more and demanding you don't try to find out what it might be. Red rag to a bull, that is!'

Eleven

Leo was at the office waiting for Walter the following morning. He had been unable to sleep and at five thirty had gone for a walk to Watchtower Bay and around the lake. He had met no one and was thankful he hadn't needed to make polite, inane comments on the hour or the weather. He valued the silence as he tried to decide what he would say to his boss.

Should he offer to resign? That was the worst thing; his loyalty and support for Meriel might result in him leaving the job he had enjoyed since leaving school. He didn't regret supporting Meriel but wished the outcome had been a failure to find her first family instead of her having to face the sad Roberts-Price family and search for echoes of herself in them.

He stood when Walter walked in and began to apologize. 'I'm so sorry about this. I had no idea it would be so painful. I so wanted to help her and I thought that if I made enquiries. and assured her there was no connection between the Roberts-Prices and her, that she'd give up, but now she insists on seeing them for herself. I honestly thought any enquiries I made would come to nothing. I'm truly sorry.' When Walter took off his jacket and began to look through the mail without saying a word, he went on, 'I'll quite understand if you want me to leave. I don't want to, but if it's what you and Mrs Evans would like – if it would help.'

'How would it help me to lose an able assistant? Have you any idea how difficult it is to find experienced staff?'

'Then I can stay?'

'Of course,' Walter said gruffly. He attempted a smile and added, 'Meriel would kill me if I sacked you, wouldn't she?'

'Thank you.'

'You'd better take some more unofficial holiday and go and see if she's all right.'

'What d'you want me to say – to do?'

'Leo, I've known you since you were a toddler. If I can't trust you to do the right thing now, when will I ever?'

'She will want to meet them.'

'Then go with her. Help her to understand, will you?'

Still stricken with guilt, seeing the strain on Walter's face and knowing he was at least partly responsible, made the prospect of talking to Meriel difficult. Should he discourage her from trying to talk to the Roberts–Price family? Or would that make her go there alone and face whatever happened without support?

When he reached Cwm Derw he didn't go straight to the office but sat in the café, nursing a cup of tea he didn't really want, playing with a scone he couldn't eat, trying to clear his mind, calm himself for the difficult interview ahead. He reached Evans and Calloway as Meriel was making a cup of coffee in the room behind the office. 'Make that two, will you?' he called.

'Oh Leo!' she sighed, coming to greet him. 'I'm so glad you've come. Pandora's box this certainly is. What can I do to make it all right again?'

'What d'you want to do?' he asked, holding her close.

'Truthfully?'

'Truthfully,' he replied.

'I want to talk to Mr and Mrs Roberts-Price.'

'Then that's what we'll do.'

Leo phoned the Ship and spoke to Teifion, who arrived at two thirty and after a brief explanation agreed to stay until five o'clock. Meriel and Leo drove to Bridgend and went into the shop selling religious literature and asked to speak to Mr Roberts-Price. The assistant came out of the back room and told them the boss was out. 'He won't be back today,' she said after acknowledging Leo with a smile. 'There's a publishers' conference or something. Can I give him a message?'

'You don't know where his daughter is working, I suppose?' Leo asked.

'In a shoe shop – and hating it! It's next to the cinema. There's a musical on there this week.' Leo thanked her and they left.

'I think we should try and find the daughter,' Leo said. 'Her name is Martha, she's nineteen but looks about fifteen.'

'What is she like?'

'Old-fashioned and childlike, very much under her father's thumb I'd guess. But under that subdued and obedient appearance I think there's quiet defiance.' He told her about the time he had peered into the cottage near the church and saw her dancing and singing to lively music from her gramophone. 'She obviously has some spirit, in spite of her parents' rigid upbringing.' He saw her hopeful look and wished he'd said nothing. To build up her dreams, probably falsely, would add to her distress.

'I'd better ring Teifion in case we aren't back,' she told him, still smiling as she imagined the girl who might be her half-sister. 'We might be a long time, so I'll tell him to close the office at five.' She turned to Leo walking beside her, his hand under her arm, and pointed to a phone box. 'He's been very kind to us, hasn't he? It's as though he's trying to make up for his father's behaviour. Being your father doesn't make a man perfect, does it?'

'You don't have many complaints about your own, do you?'

'None at all. I couldn't have asked for more. He and Mam have given me a wonderful life. I love them and I'm grateful.'

'So why are you going on with this, knowing it's hurting them?'

She pushed his hand from her arm and linked arms. 'It probably sounds silly, but for one thing I'd be afraid to marry, because I don't know what I've inherited, perhaps some dreadful disease I could pass on to my children, or some human weakness that might show itself. Oh, I don't know! Call it curiosity if you like! I thought I knew who I was, but when George told everyone I was an adopted child, that Walter and Lynne Evans are not my real parents, he took away everything of importance.'

'Except their love for you.'

'That isn't why I'm doing this.'

'Then what is the real reason for this crusade?'

'Nothing specific. I just need to know, to see whether I recognize anything of myself in any of them.'

'If – and it's a big *if* – if they are your missing family, the soldier you told me about, who threatened you with the police when you were sorting out his parents' shed – he could be a half-brother.'

'And the sad little girl you describe will be my sister.' She squeezed his arm. 'Nothing will change my love for

273

my parents, that has never been in doubt, even during those first awful moments. Nor has your friendship been anything but true.'

It wasn't what she wanted to say and neither was it what he wanted to hear and they went towards the shoe shop a little sadder for it having been said.

They stood outside the shop for a few minutes, both afraid of what they might learn. Looking through the window, the interior was too dark for them to see whether the place was busy, and finally they went inside the rather gloomy shop with its heavy smell of leather.

'We need to talk to your father,' Leo said to the brown-haired dull-looking girl who came to assist them. Meriel stared, wide-eyed, at the unattractive stranger who might be a relation. Surely this must be a mistake?

'Will he be at home this evening?' Leo asked.

'Who shall I say is calling?'

'My name is Leo Hopkins, but he won't know me. I'd rather not say what it's about, it's rather confidential.'

The girl shrugged and walked away. A moment later from the room behind the shop music could be heard and as she stood close to the doorway, watching for a customer, they saw her feet, in their high-heeled sandals, were tapping in time to the music and her lips were moving silently following the words. A wartime favourite, 'Don't Sit Under the Apple Tree, With Anyone Else But Me'. It seemed they were already forgotten.

Somehow Leo's hand had wriggled up and was holding hers again. She knew it was only for reassurance, that he was aware of the anxieties she would face very soon. But it felt so right and the warmth of him travelled through her veins and made her feel safe. She wondered if he felt the same or whether, to him, she was still that young girl, his boss's daughter.

–

Gerald was enjoying his new position. Although he hadn't actually made a sale, he had been allowed to approach customers and cope with the preliminary chat, admiring the vehicle, telling the customer he was clearly a man of discernment. As soon as a real interest was shown he introduced him to the boss, who gave the practised spiel and told the customer how easy it was to buy using hire-purchase.

He found himself boasting about Lucy quite often. His girlfriend ran her own business, he told anyone he wanted to impress. She was an estate agent and auctioneer. She must be a remarkable woman, was the frequent response, and he agreed with more and more pride. That it saved him admitting his father mended motorbikes was a bonus. Until one day when he gave his name to someone who wanted to meet him for a drink after work. The man was obviously wealthy, buying a new car for his wife.

'Cook, you say? Not related to Arthur Cook, are you?'

Before Gerald could make up some story about a distant uncle, the man went on, 'Marvellous man. There isn't anyone else this side of Birmingham or nearer than London who can do what he does. My first motorbike was offered for scrap, but it was all I could afford. A Norton it was. Nothing more than a wreck to be honest, but Arthur Cook restored it to perfection. The parts he couldn't find he made in that small workshop of his. The man's a genius.'

'He's my father,' Gerald said, still with doubts about whether he should admit it. After all, a mechanic wasn't on the same level as this man with his smart, expensive suit and clean hands.

'You must be thrilled to have a father like Arthur Cook. Wait till I tell my father. Tell him Peter Drew was asking about him.'

Guilt made Gerald stutter as he promised to tell his father he had met him. It was very confusing. Later, he asked his boss if he had heard of Arthur Cook, a restorer of motor cycles, and the man admitted he hadn't heard of him. That made Gerald feel much better. The man had been talking rubbish.

He was glad of something to tell his father, though. He had ignored the request to leave home and had continued to use his bedroom, but his parents were making it clear they didn't want him there. Any attempts at conversation were quickly snubbed and at least this little snippet of his exciting new job would be of interest. He repeated the name for fear he'd forget it.

A few days later his boss suggested he invited Lucy to lunch. 'I'll bring the wife and we can get to know each other.'

He wrote to Lucy and asked her to meet him.

–

At five o'clock as Teifion was closing her office door back in Cwm Derw, Meriel stood beside Leo and watched the door at the side of the bakery in Bridgend, for the appearance of William Roberts-Price. He arrived with the girl they knew was his daughter, at a quarter to six and unlocked the front door. Meriel noted that the shoes the girl now wore were heavy brown lace-ups.

As the door was about to shut the sad looking couple inside, they called and ran across. They saw momentary fear shadow the man's face and he moved the door as though he was about to close it against them. Then he relented and said, 'You'd better come in.'

They were shown into what the man called the parlour, a cold impersonal room furnished with a polished table around which there were four elegant and precisely placed chairs. An armchair stood on either side of an empty grate, each with a pristine cushion carefully arranged. Heavy dark-green curtains hung at the window almost obliterating the light. Meriel sat on an armchair and Leo stood beside her. Mr Roberts-Price excused himself and said he would be a moment, and left them. Uneasy, unable to sit still, Meriel stood up beside Leo, close together in the cold, comfortless room.

When the door reopened it was his daughter who came in. She held out a hand, saying, 'I'm Martha. Who are you?' she asked in a whisper. 'Father seems very upset by your visit. Is he in trouble?'

'No trouble, I promise you,' Leo said, putting an arm around Meriel's shoulders. 'Trouble is the last thing we want.'

Martha's parents came in then and sent her out to make tea.

'We don't want to upset you,' Meriel said hesitantly, 'I just need to know – can you tell me – is there any truth in the story that I am your daughter?' They were such a sad couple and living in a sad house that she willed them to say no, the idea was a nonsense.

'You are our daughter,' the man said, and his wife nodded agreement, and Meriel felt her whole body begin to shake. The room spun around her and she would have fallen if Leo hadn't been holding her. She was shivering violently and Leo lowered her gently into one of the

277

stiff armchairs and wrapped her in his coat. He spoke soothingly to her and kept reassuring her that everything would be all right, he'd take her home and stay with her until she had recovered.

Mr Roberts-Price left the room and came back with a drink of water, his wife knelt down beside Meriel and rubbed warmth into the girl's hands. Slowly the room righted itself and her eyes focused. She looked properly for the first time at the woman who had given her life. She had the same colour hair as herself but it was carelessly arranged, dragged back into a loose plait that stretched down her back, almost to her waist.

'I didn't really think it would be true,' she whispered to Leo. 'For all my talk, I wasn't prepared for this.'

The couple stood near them and said nothing as Leo continued to talk to her in a low voice. Meriel looked at them, he with his old-fashioned clothes like a person from another time, and the woman who was her mother, wearing a homemade cotton dress and apron, dark colours, plain design. Fashion and attractiveness were forbidden strangers in this house, she thought miserably, and happiness too. How could this be true?

The family members she had met were all wrapped in some shameful embarrassment, hiding behind plainness, apologizing to the world, ashamed to be seen. Surely it couldn't be because of her birth and abandonment? After almost twenty-three years the wounds must have healed?

'Please don't discuss this in front or our daughter – our other daughter.'

'As you wish,' Leo answered for her.

'Can we meet somewhere and talk it through?'

Having heard the last remark and seeing an opportunity, Martha put the tea tray down and asked, 'May I go to the pictures, Mother? It's nothing violent or wicked.'

'Just this once,' her father said. The young woman skipped off like a ten-year-old.

'My wife and I knew this day must come, so you might as well hear our shameful secret. Keeping it is now impossible.'

Meriel reached for Leo's hand as he went on, 'Ellie gave birth to you when we were only seventeen. We weren't allowed to marry and were separated. Our child' – he stared at Meriel with his sad eyes for a long moment – 'was given up for adoption. A year later we had defied them once again and our son Jacob was born. This time our families accepted that we loved each other and allowed us to marry.'

'That's a lovely story,' Meriel said softly, her voice quivering with emotion. 'I'm so relieved. You can't imagine how many unhappy stories I've invented since I learned of my adoption.'

'The story didn't end there. A year on we had a second daughter, Martha, and our son died. We felt it was punishment for our behaviour, flouting the teaching of the Bible. Even though we were gifted of a second son, who is now eighteen, we didn't feel forgiven.'

Meriel didn't know what to say. Leo offered her his hand to rise. 'Thank you, Mr and Mrs Roberts-Price. We are most grateful to you for talking to us and explaining why you couldn't be parents to Meriel. I think I should take her home now.'

'Yes, thank you both. It was not knowing, you see? I didn't know who I was any more.'

Mrs Roberts-Price opened a drawer in the table and brought out a locked box. From it she took some papers, many yellow and faded. 'We were fortunate, knowing you were loved and being given a good life.' She began spreading out the contents of the box and Meriel saw they were photographs and school reports and some newspaper cuttings showing various sports day events and stepping closer she recognized they were all about herself. She looked at the woman who was her mother and frowned.

'Your new mother was thoughtful and generous,' Ellie told her. 'Lynne Evans found out who we were and over the twenty-two years and ten and a half months, has sent news of you.'

'Anonymously of course,' her husband added, 'but we knew who was sending them. Such a kind, generous woman to allow us to share in your special moments.'

Meriel still felt a bit light-headed as they walked to the car. She was tearful but Leo didn't speak, he held her, silently comforting her, knowing this wasn't the time for an inquest into the strange visit. That would come later when she had been through it all in her mind.

–

At home, Walter was edgy, waiting for Leo to telephone to tell him how the dreaded visit had gone. Instead it was Meriel who rang, from the office when they called to glance through Teifion's notes for a quick update on the day's happenings. 'Dadda, I've seen them and I understand why they couldn't look after me.'

'We were so lucky that they had to part with you,' Walter said. 'You've brought us so much joy over the years we can never thank them enough.'

'I don't think they want thanks, but they're grateful for Mam's kindness in sending regular reports on my progress. Wasn't that a wonderful thing to do? They're such a sad little family.'

'Regular reports?'

'Yes, you know, Mam sent school reports and pieces of news and— Oh no. Don't tell me you didn't know!'

'I didn't know.'

'You aren't angry?'

He was bewildered and hurt that he'd not been included in Lynne's secret, but he said, 'Hurt? How could I be? Such thoughtfulness is typical of your mother.'

'Dadda, let's make an end to these secrets. Talk to Mam, tell her you're pleased she helped them to keep contact.'

'I am pleased, it was a generous thing to do. And you're right. There'll be no more secrets, my darling girl.' But behind his back his fingers were painfully crossed.

There was still one secret and that must never be revealed.

–

Leo went back with Meriel to Badgers Brook, where Lucy was up and preparing a meal insisting she would be well enough to work the following day. As they ate Meriel told her all they had learned. With coffee beside them Leo and Meriel talked about the day and the strangeness of the family they had met.

'It's as though they're punishing themselves for loving each other,' Lucy surmised. 'Keeping that daughter of theirs on a short leash too, for fear she'll be as wayward as they once were. If I were her I'd run away and join a group of gypsies, exchange the prison of that home for the freedom of the road.'

'The saddest thing is, it's probably too late.' She held Leo's hand and said, 'I feel ashamed to say this, but didn't I have a lucky escape, being brought up by Mam and Dadda instead of being inhibited and choked by their guilt?'

'But if they'd kept you they wouldn't have felt guilty.'

'Oh yes they would. Some other reason would have been found, it's what they are. So afraid of life and of making mistakes they don't do anything that has the slightest risk. They're ashamed and wrapped up in guilt and fearing a God who is loving and forgiving.'

'Perhaps knowing the secret is out will help them. They might learn from it.'

'Well,' Lucy said with a glimmer of mischief in her eyes, 'it seems you two have learned a lot today, not the least about yourselves.'

Leo let Meriel's hand go and stared at Lucy. 'Don't mind me,' Lucy said with a chuckle. 'I'm going to wash the dishes and it will take me a very long time!'

Embarrassed by Lucy's remarks, afraid Meriel might not have been pleased at the implications, Leo kissed her lightly on the cheek, called 'Goodnight' to Lucy, and left. Meriel's spirits sank. A joke, a hint that he was fond of her and he had run away. She ran down the path and stopped him as he got into the car.

'I'll want to see them again, will you come?' she asked.

'Of course I'll come. We're friends, aren't we? You know I'll do anything to help.'

'That's very *friendly* of you. Although it's probably nothing more than trying to please the boss!' she retorted as she hurried back inside.

–

As it seemed to be the day for sorting out people's problems even if not his own, Leo went to the Ship and Compass. The bar was quiet. Betty was chatting to Bob and Colin, a couple sat near the fire and Teifion was emptying a tray of washed glasses and putting them in their places. Leo ordered a beer and engaged him in a discussion about his father.

He didn't know the facts about Teifion's childhood and knew he couldn't really contribute, but as in most cases, all the man needed was someone to listen. He wondered doubtfully if he could keep his thoughts away from Meriel long enough to be any use.

'My father wants me to go back to the business and I can't,' Teifion began.

'Why, it's yours, isn't it? Shouldn't you be there to keep up with it all?'

'Lots of reasons why I want to stay away, most of them boiling down to my father's attitude.'

'We all have problems with parents at some time, we usually grow out of it,' Leo offered.

'I was never happy at home and looking back I've spent all my life trying to please him. Making him proud of me was impossible – I learned that at a very young age – but I tried to please him, convinced that would be enough. Now I've come to my senses and realize nothing will change. I'm not sure what I'll do with my life but it will be independent of my father.'

'You'll tell him that?'

'He won't listen,' he replied dolefully, rubbing at a glass that was already shining. 'The strange thing is, the job wasn't the problem. I've really enjoyed it since working with Lucy – and Meriel, of course.'

'Of course.' He smiled. 'Lucy being the real draw?'

'I like her very much, but I don't think we have a future, that's something else my father has ruined for me. How can she trust me after the way he's treated them?'

'If it were me, I'd stay away, but you know your father better than I and you must decide.'

'What if he's ill?'

'That is a sticky one, but he has a wife, that would be her problem to solve, wouldn't it?'

When he left, Leo wasn't sure if he had helped, but had always believed that speaking the words aloud was always better than having them going round and round in the head. He wondered if Lucy was aware of Teifion's growing attraction but his thoughts soon returned to Meriel and how she was coping with the dramatic developments.

A note was handed in to the Ship the following morning. It was from George asking Teifion to go home as there was something urgent to discuss. The note was brief but hinted that he, George, needed help.

Determined to be firm, explain to his father that his interests were no longer with the family business, he set off an hour before opening time. He had hardly reached the gate before hearing voices raised in anger punctuated by the alarming sounds of smashing glass. He began to run up the drive but was almost knocked off his feet by his father running from the house. He was panting, red in the face and blind to everything except his urgent need to get away.

He began to run after him but was stopped by the slamming of the front door. He turned to see Frieda coming out of the house dragging a couple of suitcases. Ignoring him, she went to the gate and got into a taxi as the driver came up and collected the suitcases.

Before he could gather his wits and decide what to do, Teifion heard his father's powerful car leaving the garage. He had to leap onto the lawn to avoid being knocked aside. The taxi had gone and he stood there like a half-melted statue until the sound of it faded away. He was panting almost as much as his father had been.

Using his key he went into the house wondering what he'd find. He opened the door to chaos. Furniture had been pushed over, every ornament he could see was smashed, as were the fine crystal glasses from the shelves. Picture frames no longer contained glass, and even the curtains had been pulled from their pole. A vase of flowers leaned drunkenly against the wall above the fireplace and water dripped musically onto the metal fire tools below.

His first thought as he stood gazing at the damage was that neither of the participants had been harmed. He gingerly picked up the phone and told Betty what had happened.

'I'll get in touch with the woman who used to be the housekeeper,' she promised, and in less than ten minutes, while he stood bemused, she arrived.

The capable woman took charge and between them they cleared up the dangerous glass, threw out the broken items and put the room back in some semblance of order.

Teifion sat there for a long time after the housekeeper had gone, wondering where his father was and whether he'd be back. Eventually he wrote a note and went back to the Ship.

He went back to the house several times before he went to bed but there was no sign of his return. Days passed and there was still no word. He began to worry and even enquired at the hospital but no one had reported an accident. The office opened daily with George's assistant in charge and gradually his alarm subsided and he settled back into the daily routine. 'He'll be in touch when he needs me,' he told Betty, with a nonchalance he didn't feel. 'Meanwhile the office will manage without him.'

—

Unable to find his father and aware that Meriel needed some time off, having been told of the meeting with her first parents, Teifion spent as much time as he could at the office with Lucy. She showed him the letter from Gerald inviting her to lunch. 'I'm not keen to meet him or his boss. He's hardly been near since hearing that rumour about me leaving the firm and I've been ill with a cold and not a word. Now this. Why would I want to go all the way into Cardiff to meet him and let him show off to his boss about how clever I am? He's been telling him I own this business, can you believe that? He's nothing but a poseur, and that's all this is, he'll pretend we're close and boast about me as though the business has nothing to do with Meriel's expertise.'

'He doesn't know you if he thinks you'll let him get away with it!'

She smiled and said, 'Won't he be upset if I tell his boss I'm an unqualified hairdresser, usually employed sweeping up and shampooing hair and helping Meriel with menial jobs?'

'You wouldn't dare! Or perhaps you would!'

'Poor Gerald, he has a built in snobbery button.'

'What if I meet you after the lunch and we go for a walk in Sophia Gardens, find a café for tea and perhaps go to the pictures, make a day of it?'

'It will probably rain if Gerald is involved,' she said gloomily.

'I'll bring an umbrella!'

'I'll tell him it will have to be in two weeks' time, as we're very busy.'

'Fine by me. Just tell me when. Betty Connors will let me have a day off.'

George appeared later that day and Teifion went to the end of the bar to serve him, wondering whether to ask questions or wait until his father explained what had happened.

'Thanks for clearing up the mess,' George said, but there was no remorse in his voice and his eyes were clear of any apology. 'Frieda really went mad that day.'

'Are you all right? You look a bit feverish.'

'Of course I'm all right. What's the matter with you?'

'And that,' Teifion told Betty, 'was the best explanation I can hope for. What's the matter with the man?'

'Pride,' Betty said succinctly. 'He won't let go of that till he's in his coffin!'

―

Walter was busy and without Leo helping he didn't have time to go home for lunch. A phone call to Lynne brought her to the office with a wicker picnic hamper filled with small delicacies. 'Not good to rush a heavy meal, darling,' she said, spreading out tiny sausage rolls, sandwiches, fruit and some small cakes.

'Have you heard anything more from Leo or Meriel?' she asked as he finished the last of the fruit.

'I told Leo not to phone, but to concentrate on our daughter.'

'I'm so afraid we'll lose her love, Walter. This has upset her so much.'

'Love isn't a limited quantity, silly girl! There's always more if there's someone to give it to. If we'd had another daughter we'd love them both and there wouldn't be less for Meriel, would there? Or any less for you,' he added.

'Such a pity I wasn't able to give you children.'

'I haven't felt the lack of them. Meriel has been such a joy.'

'Will she still be there, after this?'

'I don't doubt it for a single moment. Now, shall we have a cup of coffee together, before I get back to this sale of shop contents?' He pointed to a muddle of papers beside the neat list he was making. 'It's a wool shop closed down and for sale. I don't know anything about wool and knitting patterns.'

'Let me help, darling, let's see what I remember, knit one, make one, purl two, slip one, knit two together—' Laughter came easily.

It was almost six o'clock when he closed the office door and they set off home. At exactly the same time, Meriel and Leo were knocking on the door beside the baker's shop in Bridgend.

Their intention was not to go in, but to invite the family to visit them at Badgers Brook.

The daughter was invited too and on the following Saturday evening, they arrived, getting off the bus wearing stiff, obviously best outfits used only rarely and carrying with them a whiff of moth deterrent. Meriel had told her parents what they had planned but both had declined to appear. Lucy was there, but Teifion was working at the Ship.

Conversation was difficult at first, but Martha and Lucy were soon discussing the music of Glenn Miller and Tommy Dorsey and the songs of Hoagy Carmichael, amid disapproving glances from her father. Having to avoid the subjects of music and books and the wireless and the cinema, Meriel struggled to find a basis for discussion and time stood still, the conversation dragging 'like wading through deep water wearing a long serge skirt', she remarked to Kitty and Bob later.

The only time there was any animation in the sad couple was when they talked about the work they did for their church. Although Meriel was impressed with the industry as they told her of the fund raising and sick visiting and voluntary help they provided, it was a monologue rather than a conversation.

She and Lucy were honest in their admiration for the way they spent their lives in the service of others but after a while found even that was hard, running out of new ways of describing their genuine admiration. Everyone was relieved when it was time for them to leave. Lucy and Meriel both offered to drive them home but they insisted on catching the bus.

'They never stop punishing themselves, do they?' Lucy remarked as they waved them goodbye and went back to start on the dishes.

–

George drove from the hotel where he was staying to the shabby house where Meriel had first met Frieda. He knew his wife was there and he was prepared for another row as he made a final attempt to persuade her to come back home.

She opened the door and at once the face of the man for whom she had repeatedly left him, appeared over her shoulder.

'Don't come in if you intend starting another row,' she said and the man's arm came around her shoulder.

George lowered his head, relaxed his shoulders as though in defeat and said, 'I just want to see if we can come to some arrangement, that's all. If not, then I'll go and you can start divorce proceedings as soon as you like.' She opened the door wider and allowed him to enter.

'If you're sure you'll be all right, I'll go for a walk and leave you to talk,' the man said.

Frieda looked at George, who said, 'I don't hit women, if that's what you mean!'

When the door had screeched to a close behind the man, he sat near her on a filthy chair and said, 'Cards on the table. We can't go on like this and I think you at least owe me a full explanation. This isn't just an affair, is it?' He looked around the drab room and the ill-matched chairs, the stained walls. 'For once in your life tell me the truth.'

'He was my first love, but he became ill and went away. We lost touch and I found out afterwards he thought he was going to die and didn't want me involved. He lost his way for various reasons, mostly the lack of a job and no money. He turned to crime and ended up in prison. Three times he was sentenced to prison, each term longer than the last. He'd been about to give up, knowing he couldn't cope with another and, well, we met again and I've been helping him. And before you ask, yes, we're lovers. I never stopped loving him, you see.'

'So our marriage is a joke?'

'No, George, never that. But after we met again, I couldn't leave him, not even for you.'

'Now I know, will you come back and pretend? I'm beginning to realize that pride isn't enough, but if it's all I have then it's better than nothing.'

He was aware of a pain in his chest but managed to hide it. This was his last chance and he couldn't risk losing her in spite of all she'd told him. No one else need know, not even Teifion, he told himself, at least people would believe that he, George Dexter, was able to keep his pretty young wife.

'Give me my pride,' he said, knowing he had to get out before he collapsed.

'Give me a few days to get a decent place for him to live and I'll come back,' she said.

'Thank you,' he replied with more humility than he'd shown in his entire life. She put his breathlessness down to emotion. He drove himself straight to hospital and still breathless and in pain, stopped at the gates. Then he changed his mind and drove away. A few more days, just until Frieda came back, so people would know she was home again.

He drove home and went to bed. That's all he needed, a couple of quiet days. Then he would talk to Teifion, remind him of where his loyalties lay.

-

William and Ellie Roberts-Price came to Badgers Brook several times after that first difficult visit, bringing photographs of their son, Jacob. Meriel still found the visits difficult and was relieved when Leo managed to be there too.

Then Martha came on her own. Less self-conscious without the presence of her father she explained how much she had enjoyed working on the record counter and talking to the young people who crowded around every Saturday to listen, buy and discuss the latest releases. 'I was supposed to be the one with knowledge about the classical stuff but I prefer dance music,' she explained. She lifted her legs and pointed to the heavy lace-up shoes she wore. 'I hide these shoes which Father insists I wear and put on some really smart sandals, and dance to the rhythm like the rest.'

'If you enjoyed it so much, why did you leave and get a job in a shoe shop?' Meriel asked.

'Father didn't like me working there and when we moved he said it was too far from home. There were buses, but he wasn't willing.'

'How old are you?' Lucy asked pointedly.

'Obviously not old enough!' was the reply.

One evening in September, while Meriel and Leo took the parents for a walk through the wood and down to the remnants of Treweather's farm with its chickens and a few sheep, Lucy and Martha discussed hair. 'I think your hair would wave a little if you took some of the weight off it with a good cut,' Lucy said.

'I can't! Father won't allow it.'

'How old are you, Martha?' Lucy repeated the question with a sigh.

'Nearly twenty.'

'Can he forbid you to have your hair cut?'

'He says while I'm under his roof—'

'There's the solution. Find another roof!'

'I'd love to stay here with you and Meriel,' she said wistfully.

Lucy shook her head. 'That would be changing one bolt hole for another. If you leave it has to be to make your own way. A room wouldn't cost very much and you might find another girl to share with you. Nothing's impossible and that's a lesson I was late learning. I made the mistake of staying too long with my parents and if it hadn't been for Meriel, I might still be there.'

'My brother Noah is in the army and he told me that when he's finished his time he won't be coming back.'

'What will he do?'

'He's clever with accounts, book-keeping and office management. He wanted to go to college and study accountancy, but Father refused, said it was not for people like us. Noah said he doesn't care if he sweeps the roads, he isn't coming home.'

Lucy thought the saddest thing was that Martha's father would be happier if his son swept roads than if he did something with prestige and a good salary.

She dug out the hairdressing equipment she had rather foolishly bought and, with Martha behaving like a frightened mouse, styled her surprisingly thick and healthy hair; washing it and drying it and leaving it silky and clean. When Lucy held up a mirror and Martha saw herself with the sleek, shining glory where there had been a dull lacklustre curtain behind which she had hidden, she stared in silence for a long time.

'Look at the lovely young woman you've been hiding,' Lucy whispered. 'You've come out of the shadows.'

'Father will kill me! He won't let me be seen until it's grown back,' she wailed fiddling with the ribbons with which her hair had previously been held.

Lucy was alarmed. Had she really made difficulties for her? Persuading her to leave home, revealing herself as an attractive young woman, alienating her from the safe security of her family? Then Meriel came in with Mr and Mrs Roberts-Price and it was too late to change anything.

'What have you done?' the girl's father demanded. Running forward, her mother hugged her and said, 'Oh

Martha. Look at you! Two beautiful daughters I produced. I can't believe it. You look lovely.' Ignoring the puffed out anger of her husband she turned to Lucy. 'Thank you, you're very clever.'

'I didn't have to do much, the beauty was always there.'

They didn't stay any longer; pulling on the coat he had discarded only a moment before, and ignoring the meal set out for them, William Roberts-Price indicated his desire to leave and in silence, Martha and her mother collected their things. Meriel and Lucy walked up to the end of the lane with them and waited for the bus. Although the women made brief comments in an attempt to lighten the mood, the atmosphere was awkward. It was a relief when the bus rumbled into view and they waved goodbye. Martha was the last to mount and she whispered a thank you to Lucy, adding, 'I'm going to see if I can get my old job back. I'll bury these awful shoes and I'll start looking for a place to live. Can I write and let you know how I get on?'

'Please do. I wish you luck,' Lucy whispered back.

When the bus had disappeared Lucy turned to her friend and wailed, her hands over her mouth, her eyes wide. 'Oh Meriel, what have I done?'

'Made the poor girl see herself for the first time?'

'I talked to her about her leaving home and she's such an innocent she'll get into terrible trouble and it'll be my fault!'

'If she's my half-sister, then she'll cope!' Meriel replied. Then her eyes widened.

'D'you know I keep forgetting she's not a half-sister but a full one, both of her parents are mine too. And I have a full blood-brother called Noah. I wonder what they would have called me? D'you think names influence what you become? Would I have been the same if I'd been brought up by them and called Penitent?'

'There's no such name.'

'You'd be surprised. Martha's second name is Goodness. Noah's was to be Servant of God but the vicar refused, according to Martha.'

'Come on, Penitent, let's have a cup of tea.'

They were still up talking over the events of the evening when there was a knock at the door. Leo called out and came in.

'I saw there was a light on. I wouldn't have knocked otherwise,' he said. 'Come on then, how did it go?'

'I'm ashamed to say that again I feel nothing but relief that they gave me to Mam and Dadda,' Meriel said. 'I'd have certainly been a non-achiever if I'd been brought up in that inhibiting, unhappy atmosphere, where guilt is worn like a badge almost with pride. Does that make me a terrible person, d'you think?'

'It makes me realize how important it is to consider your responsibilities when you have a child. How important it is for them to be free to make their own choices.'

'You want children, Leo?' Lucy asked.

'I want a family very much. Doesn't everyone?' He spoke lightly but he was looking at Meriel.

'I'll go and make the cocoa, then,' Lucy said with a chuckle. 'Let you get the preliminaries done.'

'What did she mean by that?' Meriel said, looking at him and seeing love in his eyes reflecting her own.

'I think she means this.' Leo offered his hands and, lifting her from her chair, enfolded her in his arms and kissed her.

Behind them Lucy stepped through the doorway and stepped back quickly, her face creased in a wide smile and her fingers firmly crossed. 'Come on, Rascal,' she whispered to the dog. 'Tonight you're going to have an extra walk. A long one I think.'

—

On the day Lucy had arranged to meet Gerald in Cardiff for lunch with his employers, Teifion watched as she set off with some apprehension in his heart. She was going in by bus, partly because Meriel might need the car and partly so he could meet her and drive her home. He marvelled at how much she had changed since first arriving at the new premises with Meriel. At first he automatically disliked her, she was a rival to his father and loyalty had then been strong, now he couldn't imagine life without her.

He fervently hoped she wouldn't be beguiled by Gerald; he was clever, a natural flirt and attractive to the ladies, and, he knew how to impress. They had known each other for a long time, even been engaged for a while and although Gerald didn't appear to be an ardent lover, there might still be a part of Lucy's heart he was capable of reaching.

He refilled the bar, cleaned the cellar and polished the copper pipes and all the time he was thinking about the lunch, visualizing Gerald at his most charming wondering if Lucy could be won over by Gerald's flattery, or whether she was planning to have a little fun at his expense.

Before he left, he went back in to make sure Betty and the part-time assistant had all they needed and when the phone rang he waved and began to leave. At the door he was called back to be told that his father was on his way to hospital suffering from a suspected heart attack.

He knew the name of the restaurant where Lucy was meeting Gerald and telephoned to leave a message to tell Lucy about his father and explain that he wouldn't be there to meet her as arranged. The young woman who took the message seemed vague about the name but promised to find her.

—

Outside the restaurant, a taxi pulled up and Lucy stepped out followed by Gerald and another couple. At the last moment the booking had been changed and they had eaten at an hotel.

'He isn't here yet,' Lucy said, looking around the busy street.

'I'll wait with you, shall I?' Gerald looked at his boss. 'If that's all right with you, sir?'

'There's no need, he's sure to be here in a minute.' She glanced at her watch. He was already late, but only by a few minutes. He was probably walking around as he waited for her to arrive. She insisted on Gerald leaving and managed to avoid his attempt at a kiss before he went off with Mr and Mrs Harris. She pretended not to see him turn and wave. Where was Teifion?

What was it about her and Cardiff? Was she about to face another embarrassing wait and a self-conscious walk back to the bus stop? Half an hour later she went into a nearby café for coffee, half an hour after that she went home.

She wasn't angry as when Gerald had left her standing on the street. She was concerned. Something was wrong.

An accident maybe? Alarmed, she rang the Ship but Betty wasn't there. She tried the office but Meriel had heard nothing, but promised to try and find out. With a feeling of dread, she ran to the bus stop wishing she had used the car.

Twelve

As she rode home on the bus, Lucy wasn't angry; she was worried. She began to imagine every kind of accident and disaster. She knew Teifion wouldn't have let her down without a good reason. She got off the bus at the end of the lane and started walking towards Badgers Brook when she saw Meriel coming to meet her.

'What's happened? Why aren't you in the office?' she asked with dread.

'It's George Dexter, he's had a heart attack and is in hospital.'

Guilty relief flooded Lucy's mind, grateful nothing had happened to Teifion. 'So that's why he didn't meet me.'

'Teifion left a message for you at the restaurant, where have you been?'

'Plans were changed, we went to an hotel so the message didn't reach me. I waited for more than an hour then came home. D'you think I should go there?'

'I'm sure Teifion would be glad to see you. It sounds serious.'

'I think I need a cup of tea first, then I'll drive to the hospital and see if there's anything I can do.'

They walked back down the lane, where after several days of wind and rain, there were already signs of autumn, with leaves beginning to curl and wither, and grasses yellowing and drooping to allow their seeds to fall.

'I love it here,' Lucy said. 'Every time I come home it's a reminder of how lucky I am and how fortunate we are to live in that wonderful house.'

'The legend is that no one stays longer than they need to sort out their problems. D'you think that's right?'

'If it is, then perhaps I'll be moving out one day. I have the feeling that Teifion and I will marry – not that he's asked me,' she added, colouring with embarrassment. 'I might be wrong. I just feel that even after all that's happened, we belong together.'

'Then you'd better get to the hospital fast, so he knows you support him, even with that unpleasant father of his!'

Teifion was sitting in the corridor outside the ward and he ran to her and hugged her.

'Thanks for coming, I'm sorry about our ruined after-noon. You got my message?' he asked rhetorically, and was surprised when she shook her head.

'I waited an hour then came home. Meriel met me at the bus stop and told me what happened.'

'I'm so sorry. You must have been very angry.'

'Angry? Of course not. I was afraid you'd been hurt or something. I knew you wouldn't let me down without good reason.'

'Reason. Now there's a word that isn't in Dad's vocab-ulary!' They sat together, hand in hand, while he told her all he knew about his father's condition.

'He won't see me,' he said. 'I went in and asked whether Frieda has been told. He said no, that she'd gone back to her previous life, then told me to go.'

'What was her – previous life?' Lucy asked.

'She worked in a dance hall and sang with the band. Apparently, the pianist was a man called Kit Keys, a made-up name of course, but it sounded good. They were more than friends – still are, I gather.'

'This is the man she's been seeing? In that shabby house? Why didn't she marry him?'

'He already had a wife and three children.'

A nurse came out and told them that his father wanted to see him and with a frown, he nodded and followed the nurse back into the ward. Lucy stood at the door and watched as Teifion went to his father's bedside. George was propped up on several pillows. He was obviously talking although she couldn't hear what was being said, but she guessed from Teifion's nervously shifting feet that it was nothing pleasant. Two minutes and he was back.

'How is he?' Lucy asked, touching his arm.

'Breathless but telling me off for not manning the office instead of coming here.' He gave a wry smile. 'I reminded him I no longer worked there and he just glared at me. Illness doesn't change anything, does it?'

'Frieda ought to be told. D'you know where she is?'

'I think I can find her, but should I?'

'I can't decide for you, but if it were me, I'd let her know.'

The simplest thing was to go to the house where Frieda had been staying and, leaving Lucy at the hospital, he drove there following Meriel's directions. Frieda carelessly tidied herself by putting on fresh make-up and combing her hair then followed him out to the car. On the way to the hospital Teifion explained that he was disobeying his father's wishes. 'Be prepared,' he warned. 'Your reception might not be warm.'

'I can't believe he wouldn't want to see me at a time like this.'

The nurse led her straight into the ward and Teifion sat beside Lucy with fingers prominently crossed. Only a minute passed before he gestured to the doors through which Frieda came, trying to wipe tears from her eyes.

'He told me to go back to my piano player,' she said.

'Come back to the house,' Lucy suggested. 'None of us can do anything here.'

Trying to take her mind off George's abrupt dismissal, Lucy told her about Meriel's success in finding her real parents.

'Telling Meriel about her birth was such a cruel thing to do. What pleasure does he get from hurting people? I don't understand.' As Teifion began to speak she went on, 'I know I deserve his treatment of me. I married him without loving him, still loving another man. I was flattered by his attention and he's still an attractive man – and wealthy. I thought I'd make it a success. I really intended to do everything I could to make him happy.'

'And in the process made yourself very miserable,' Teifion said. 'He's my father, so I automatically disliked you, took his side when he complained about the trivial things he thought of as personal attacks, but I've always had a sneaking suspicion that you deserved better.'

'Thank you,' she said tearfully.

When they reached Badgers Brook, Meriel was listening to a Glenn Miller recording on the wireless, there was a freshly baked loaf on the table and a pot of rabbit stew simmering on the hob. Frieda felt the weight of misery lifted from her as she sat near the fire while Meriel set extra places at the table.

They talked about many things but not at all about George. Frieda told them stories about her time in the dance hall and they discussed their favourite music, then

Frieda's eyes became heavy and when Teifion had gone to make his apologies to Betty Connors, Meriel and Lucy made up a bed. Frieda fell asleep as soon as she closed her eyes.

The following morning, after hearing about the illness of his old adversary, Walter drove to the hospital to see him. George kept him waiting for twenty minutes then told him he could only spare five minutes as he had his solicitor coming to discuss something important.

'Cutting your wife and son out of your will, are you? Leaving your money to a cat's home?'

'What I do with my money isn't your business, Walter Evans! You need to take care of your own affairs. No,' he said, his dark eyes glinting with what could have been pleasure but Walter thought more likely to be malice. 'I've written a letter and I want to make sure it goes to the right person if I should die before I can deliver it myself. It's time the truth came out.'

Without another word, Walter turned on his heels, threw the fruit he had brought towards the sick man and stormed towards the door. 'Do what you wish, George, but nothing will help. You ruined your life. Not me. No one else can be blamed however hard you try. Your mess and misery is all down to you! How can you even think of creating more?'

A nurse stood up from the desk and hurried towards Walter. 'Please, this is a hospital, I have to ask you to leave.'

'Don't worry, I'm going. This man is poisoning the air, as he's tried to poison everything else.' The agitated nurse followed him to the exit and closed the doors after him. George Dexter clearly wasn't a man blessed with many friends, she thought with some surprise. Such a charming man, and handsome too.

Frieda woke completely refreshed, and hungry. There were eggs from the farm, illegal of course, but better tasting for that. Boiled eggs followed by rounds of toast and jam was the best meal she'd had in ages, she told them, as she poured herself a second cup of tea.

'You go off to your office and if I may, I'll stay here today and relax. There's something very calming about this house, isn't there?' Putting her cup and saucer on a small table she sat on the couch and slid down among the cushions and was asleep again before Meriel and Lucy left the house. Rascal hopped up beside her and resting his chin on her feet, slept too.

At the office, Meriel opened the post and read out a letter asking them to organize another auction. The letter was from the man they had worked for a few weeks previously, Mr Lewen.

'Yippee,' Meriel said inelegantly, dancing around the room.

'Well done you,' Lucy said, taking her hands and dancing with her.

'Well done us,' Meriel said as the door opened and they tried to behave more soberly.

'Is this a party? Can I come?' her father asked with a huge smile. 'Good news?'

'Dadda, it's another large auction, the same people as before. Farm and contents. It seems farmers are being offered high prices for building land and the government needs more houses, so approval is readily given.'

'Many farmers are selling because their sons are refusing to follow them,' Lucy remarked. 'Some blame the war years followed by two years' National Service which has apparently unsettled them, shown them a wider world and offered greater choices.'

'Still, it means business for us,' Meriel said, 'and I can't pretend to be sorry.'

'Well done you two. Wait till I tell your mother! We're so proud of you both. Would you like to borrow Leo?'

'Yes please,' Meriel said at once. 'I mean, only if you can spare him.'

Walter chuckled. 'From what he's been telling me, he won't need much persuading.'

—

Martha had become a regular visitor to Badgers Brook and she came on the day Frieda was staying. Meriel and Lucy were starting to prepare a meal for a still-sleepy Frieda when there was a rather timid knock at the door. 'Martha,' Meriel whispered and went to invite her in. She had brought a bag of rather squashed cakes and, as she hoped, was invited to stay.

It was Lucy she usually spent most time with, talking about hairdressing and fashion, but when she learned that Frieda had been a singer with a dance band she transferred her attention to her. Her blue eyes were round with wonder as she coaxed Frieda to tell her about life behind the scenes, laughing in disbelief when she was told that it was quite hard work.

'What a fabulous way to spend your life, being an entertainer,' she uttered admiringly. 'I wish I had a talent.'

'Everyone has a talent, even if it isn't one of the most talked about,' Frieda told her, amused by the girl's intensity. 'What's wrong with being a successful shop assistant, knowing your stock thoroughly and being able to help and advise your customers? I wouldn't have the patience you need for work like that.'

'Selling is only a job.'

'So is singing when you've done it for a long time. Everything becomes routine after a while.' She was lying, it had been a wonderful experience and if her voice hadn't failed she might still be up there on stage and loving it.

'I suppose selling records was a sort of talent,' Martha said thoughtfully. 'I was quite good at it, getting to know the bands and singers and latest recordings, being able to find customers what they want. Sometimes they'd hum a few bars of music and ask me to identify it and usually, I could.'

'There you are, a talent without doubt,' Frieda agreed.

Aware of how she was trying to help the girl who was her sister, Meriel smiled and mouthed her silent thanks.

'It was hard though,' Martha went on, 'father not allowing us to have a wireless and forbidding me to play my records.'

'You mean you didn't hear all the latest tunes at home, yet managed to keep up with the latest? That's impressive.'

When the girl had gone, Frieda asked why a wireless had been forbidden. 'The man who is my father,' Meriel said, her usual way of referring to William Roberts-Price, 'is rather strict. Afraid of anything that might lead his daughter into trouble. Dancing would never be allowed.'

'Can't we do anything?'

Meriel looked at her thoughtfully. 'I suppose we could try.'

They went together to the rooms behind the bakery and at once asked Mr and Mrs Roberts-Price if they would have any objection to them renting a wireless for their daughter. 'She's extremely knowledgeable about music, both popular and classical,' Meriel told them as they gazed at her in shock. 'And a great asset when she worked on the record counter.'

'She should be encouraged,' Frieda added. 'Did you know she tried to get her job back? The vacancy you made her create has unfortunately been filled. Such a waste of your daughter's talent, her replacement is nowhere near as clever. There are other shops though and I think I might persuade one of them to give her a trial.' She smiled and added, 'I was in the music business myself, you see, and I still have friends in high places.'

The man had been struggling to speak but each time, either Meriel or Frieda stopped him. Finally he raised a protesting hand and said, 'We do not wish our daughter to be involved in anything like this. She is settled in the shoe shop and the manager reports that her behaviour is excellent.'

'Good behaviour is what you hope for from criminals,' Frieda said sadly, 'not young girls who've done nothing wrong.'

The man stood up and walked towards the door. 'Thank you for calling. I'll bear in mind what you say.'

'We've been dismissed like naughty children outside the headmaster's study,' Frieda whispered, choking with laughter.

–

'I think it's time I went home,' Frieda said a few days later. 'I'm in control and thoroughly rested thanks to a few days with you two, but I have to try and pick up the threads of my life sometime and the longer I stay here the harder it will be to leave.'

'Where will you go?' Meriel asked. 'I mean, where's home?'

Sadly Frieda shrugged. 'I'm not sure. Not with George – not at the moment anyway, not till we've talked and I've made a few promises, he's made that clear. I don't want to go back to my sister, Brighton is too far away. So it's the awful house where you and I first met,' she said with a wry smile. 'I don't know where Kit has gone. I've tried all the usual places but no one has heard from him. I'm worried that he's got himself into trouble once more. After several prison sentences it's very hard to start again.'

'You can come back when you've sorted things out,' Lucy told her. 'Badgers Brook is a wonderful place to sit and think and it seems you need to do a lot of that.'

'I have to find Kit. He's disappeared from all the usual places. George promised him some money to get him started, you see. Enough for a few weeks' rent on a room, some clothes, an opportunity to get himself a job so he won't be tempted to do anything illegal. If he stays away from the area where he's known, where his so-called friends tempt him with offers of "just-one-more-job", he stands a good chance of staying out of trouble.'

'Then that explains it, he's getting a new life and as soon as he's settled he'll contact you.'

'Maybe.' She sounded doubtful. 'I have to find him, make sure George did what he promised. Then, once George is out of hospital I'll do what I agreed and go back home and this time, play the part of the dutiful wife.'

'He's expecting you to go back then?' Lucy said. 'He implied to Teifion that you and he are separated.'

'He blusters, but he wouldn't be able to face the failure of us separating. So many people would love to see our marriage fail. Considering he's a man who enjoys spreading unpleasant gossip he has a morbid dread of being at the receiving end!'

Meriel had a word with Lucy then offered to go with her to see Kit. Frieda drove and when they pulled up outside the rundown building Meriel wondered what they would find inside. The place had an eerie feel as they opened the ill-fitting front door and stepped inside.

The stairs were uncarpeted but had been scrubbed clean, the air was sweeter than expected and she saw, as they passed, that several doors had been recently painted and bore name plates. The tenants were more particular than the landlord, she guessed.

They went through a door bearing the name Martin, and Meriel was even more surprised when she entered a comfortable, albeit a sparsely furnished, room. There was a fire laid ready to light in the polished grate and two armchairs stood facing it. A wind-up gramophone stood in a corner with a sliding pile of records beside it. There were two gas lights sprouting from the walls but each had a broken mantle. A glass lay smashed in a corner lying in a puddle of its contents.

Evidence of a struggle immediately became apparent, A kicked-in door led to a bedroom and when they went inside they saw the bed tipped up and its cover ripped, a wardrobe door hanging on its hinges, a table on its side in a corner with drawers emptied onto the floor.

'What's happened?' Meriel gasped. A small kitchen led out from the living room and with bated breath they pushed open the door and peered in, but it was empty, the solitary cupboard was apparently untouched, its neatly stacked contents visible through the open door.

Frieda sank into a chair and said, 'He's had a visit – from the police probably. Either George didn't do what he promised me, or Kit couldn't wait and went off to do that "one more job" convinced it would give him what he needed.'

'Come on,' Meriel said peremptorily, 'We have to go to the police station and find out what happened.' Slowly Frieda did what she was bidden. It was with relief that Meriel left the building that seemed, despite the efforts of its tenants, to be bereft of all hope. To their surprise they saw a policeman walking towards the house but he was unable to help, even though Frieda gave the man's real name. The officer stood at the corner as they drove away.

'Is there anywhere else you can try?' Meriel asked.

'Only his wife and children and I refuse to cause them more distress by going to see them. I've hurt them enough. Can I come back with you to Badgers Brook?'

'Of course.'

'Tomorrow I'll insist on talking to George. As usual, whatever trouble I find, he's at the centre of it.'

—

George was feeling more able to sort out his life and the promise of a return home had him making demands in his usual manner. He sent for Teifion and sat tapping his fingers irritably while he waited for him when visiting time came round.

'Where have you been?' he demanded, even though his son was among the first few to walk into the ward. 'I need to get a few things organized for when I get home.'

'Hello, Dad, how are you feeling?' Teifion asked sarcastically.

'I haven't got time for all that. Listen to me, you'll have to go in and run the office. The boy who I employed to learn the business isn't any use and I need you to oversee all that's going on and report back to me. Right?'

'No it isn't,' Teifion replied quietly. 'I work for Betty Connors and I've no intention of letting her down. You'll have to learn to trust the people who are employed by you. I no longer am.'

George began a long string of invective, telling Teifion how useless and stupid he was and what a failure for a son he'd had to put up with all these years. Teifion saw the nurse running towards them and he left the ward without another word. He was shaking and sat on a bench near the doors to the ward, from where he heard his father shouting and the nurses trying to calm him down.

As he stood to leave, one of the nurses came out. 'If you'll wait a few more minutes you can go back in. I think he wants to talk to you.'

As she went back through the swing doors she turned to see Teifion striding away down the corridor. When she told George that his son had gone, he demanded that they telephoned Leo Hopkins. It was against the rules but he was in such a state they did as he requested.

–

Teifion went to see Lucy and told her about the distressing visit and what his father had demanded.

'He never asks. He shouts and his commands are interspersed with reminders of my stupidity and uselessness. Why should I help him?'

'What will you do?' Lucy felt this was a test, both of his loyalty to his father and to herself, aware that he had information about their business that George would benefit from knowing. 'However he treats you, he is your father and the business will be yours one day, won't it? Shouldn't you look after it for those reasons?'

'I'm staying at the Ship and Compass with Betty, and in between, if you still want me and trust me, I'll come and help you and Meriel in any way I can.'

'At least ring the hospital and ask how he is.'

He rang and the nurse came to the phone and asked him to return to the hospital as his father wished to see him. 'Tell him I'm very sorry but I'm needed by my employer,' he replied.

–

During a cold wet Sunday afternoon, allowing for the times the Roberts-Prices would be attending church, Meriel and Lucy went to the flat alongside the bakery in Bridgend and knocked on the door. There was no reply and they decided to wait.

'They must be home soon, there's nowhere to go on a Sunday, especially in weather like this,' Meriel said. There were no cafes open so they stood in a doorway opposite and waited, with mackintoshes draped around them, cold, wet shoes chilling them, stockings clinging to their legs, wondering how long they could stand the discomfort.

They saw Martha's parents coming and stepped out. Martha wasn't with them. Before her husband could speak, her mother said, 'Oh, just look at the state of you both! Come in and let us dry you off.'

'Where's Martha?' Meriel asked.

'Not very well, she has a nasty cold, as you will too if you don't get yourself warmed.'

'We seem to be suffering with the same thing,' Mr Roberts-Price added as he searched for his key. 'We had to leave the meeting we were attending much earlier than planned.'

'Come in quietly if you will,' his wife whispered. 'If she's sleeping I'd rather not wake her.'

To their surprise the sounds of a popular cowboy song greeted them as the door softly opened. Immediately Mr Roberts-Price began to run up the stairs but Meriel held him with a hand on his arm. He looked outraged but his wife pleaded with him to stay. Their daughter was singing along to a record, her thin, reedy voice attempting an American accent making Meriel and Lucy grin.

'I'm an old cow-hand, from the Rio Grande—'

Slowly they went up the stairs and peered through the door. They listened as the record ended and heard Martha's now unaccompanied voice singing 'Yippy I oke I aye – yip yip yip – yippy I oke I aye.' Pushing the door slightly they could see her dancing around, wearing an ancient hat and drumming an imaginary guitar. Meriel glanced at the couple who were her parents and slowly, oh so slowly they began to smile.

They crept back down the stairs, breath held as though to prevent the wood creaking, and noisily opened and closed the front door.

'We're back, Martha, we seem to have a cold too so we came back a little early. Meriel and Lucy are here.'

Meriel and Lucy called up the stairs and took a long time removing their sodden coats and shoes while above, a scuffle suggested that Martha was putting her records out of sight.

'We heard singing as we came in,' Martha stared as her father spoke, afraid to reply. To her disbelief, he went on, 'It sounded very good, and such a cheerful tune. Perhaps you'll sing it for us sometime?'

Like a child threatened with a hiding, Martha looked at her mother, who said, 'Yes dear, we were really impressed. First Meriel and Lucy, and then Frieda telling us we have a talented daughter, we must try to find you a more suitable job than selling shoes, it's such a waste of your talents.'

Meriel and Lucy didn't stay long, happy to leave Martha and her parents to talk. They promised to ask Frieda to try and persuade one of the music stores to give her a job, convinced that the girl's reputation would have gone before her. They reached Badgers Brook as the dull day had turned into a dark evening but the weather couldn't deaden the excitement and hope they felt for Martha's future.

–

Frieda tried all the most likely places in her search for Kit Keys. In despair she went to the hospital to see George.

'Of course I didn't send him any money,' he told her. 'I wrote to him though, telling him what a disgusting apology for a man he was, treating his wife like a chattel and me like a fool. And you – like the tart you are.'

'Where is he?' she asked, her voice trembling with fear and dread.

'In prison facing a charge of aggravated burglary. He insisted he was innocent, that it was a frame, isn't that what they call it, your criminal friends?'

She went to the police station and asked to see him but she was told it was impossible at present. Offering to stand bail for him, she was told that it would almost certainly be denied. Tearfully, she returned once again to Badgers Brook.

It was with curiosity and some trepidation that Leo went to see George. He was sitting in a chair beside his bed, holding a pile of papers on which he was scribbling notes and instructions for his anxious assistant who stood beside him.

'You wanted to see me, Mr Dexter. I can spare you ten minutes.' Leo refused to be treated like the young man who stood nervously beside him.

'Two will do!' He searched among his papers and handed Leo a sealed letter. 'Private and personal for Mr Walter Evans. It's an apology. I want him to have it about six next Sunday evening, when he can share the moment with his wife.'

Leo thanked him and went out. In the corridor he stopped and stared at the envelope. Could the man really be saying he was sorry for the distress he'd caused? It was very unlikely. He toyed with the idea of steaming it open and reading it but knew it would be impossible to disguise the fact and besides, he had no right to interfere. Thoughtfully he put it in his pocket. Perhaps George has been told his health was giving concern and he wanted to settle things while he still had time, he mused. But an apology from George Dexter to Walter Evans? That still sounded unconvincing.

In the ward, George took out an identical envelope and handed it to his assistant. 'This one must go to Miss Meriel Evans at Evans and Calloway,' he said. There was a glint in his eye as he handed it over. 'Deliver it to Badgers Brook at six next Sunday evening, when they can savour it at leisure. Keep it safe, mind, and don't show it to anyone else.'

Teifion rang the hospital daily to enquire about his father's progress but didn't visit. He continued to work at the Ship doing much more than he needed to do, keeping busy in an attempt to stop thinking about his father. Between the shifts at the pub he helped Meriel and Lucy, grateful that they trusted him with the details of their day-to-day dealings and even occasionally taking his advice.

'If only the shadow of my father weren't there threatening to do what he can to ruin everything, I'd be completely happy,' he said to Lucy as they sat in the office drinking tea and enjoying a cake brought in by Kitty and Bob. 'I don't want him to disappear, I just want him to accept that my life is with you and—' he hesitated and stared at her. 'Lucy, our friendship, our affection for each other has travelled a rocky road, but it's brought us to this happy moment.'

'Yes, Teifion, we are happy, aren't we?'

'We could be even happier. Lucy, you know I love you. Can you forget my father and all that's gone before and marry me?' She stared at him but didn't reply and he went on. 'I'm not after a share in your business, I'm content to stay at the Ship and help here when I can. I don't want anything from my father. Frieda, or whoever he chooses to give it to, can have it all. I have enough money to give us a start and somehow we can find a place of our own where we can create an atmosphere as peaceful as Badgers Brook and be blissfully content. Will you marry me?'

They were still wrapped in each other's arms when Meriel returned and words were unnecessary, their eyes said it all.

The following day Teifion spoke to Lucy again. Meriel and Leo were included in their discussion and their plans were made.

–

Leo didn't wait until the Sunday evening to hand the letter to Walter. It seemed to be burning against his skin, so worried was he about what it might contain. He showed it to Walter on Saturday, explained George's instructions and after a brief hesitation Walter took it and broke it open.

Leo left him to it and went to his desk in the outer office but a loud wail startled him and he ran in. 'Here, you might as well read it,' Walter said and Leo, seeing his white, shocked face and trembling hands, took the pages of writing and led the distressed man to a chair.

'Are you sure?' he asked. 'Shall I ring Lynne to come? Or shall I drive you home?'

'Read it.'

It wasn't very long, barely two pages in George's scrawling handwriting. It stated coldly that he, George, had been Lynne's lover before she had married Walter who was then, and always would be, second best. Amid the blustering and boasting, Leo gathered that when Lynne became pregnant she had begged George for his help but he had refused to marry her and face sniggers about wedding dates and birth dates. Instead he had forced her to have an abortion.

'Lynne became very ill,' Walter said. 'Her parents weren't told and she stayed with her Auntie Gladys May. George showed no concern, or even enquired about her.'

'Was the – the operation – the reason your wife couldn't have a child?' he asked.

'Operation? A backstreet butcher more like.'

'What I don't understand,' Leo said with a frown, 'is why he's sending you this letter if you already knew about it? What could be his reason if it isn't to upset you?' Then he jumped out of his chair and the two men stared at each other in horror.

'Meriel! He's written to Meriel too!'

'You go to Lynne and stay with her in case she's had a letter,' Leo said. 'I'll drive to find Meriel and if there's a letter I'll stop her opening it.'

'How will you do that?' Walter stared at Leo like a trusting child.

'I don't know how but I will.'

–

George's assistant was going out for the day on Sunday and, hoping his employer wouldn't find out, he delivered the letter to the office on Saturday morning. Like her father, Meriel opened it at once, ignoring his request to wait until the following evening. She stared at the pages in disbelief and Lucy ran to see what was wrong.

'It's about my mother, Lynne I mean. Before she and Dadda married, she was expecting a baby and George Dexter was the father. He says she adored him so much that when he asked her to have an abortion she agreed, and—' she threw the hated letter towards Lucy, locked herself in the kitchen and howled.

When she had read the letter Lucy called through the door. 'Meriel, it says at the end he's sent a similar letter to your parents, shouldn't you go to them? They'll need you there. You must go to them. We'll close the office and I'll come too but I'll stay out of the way while you talk,' All this through a closed door and with no response from her friend. Foolishly and almost without thought, she knocked on the door insisting she needed to make some tea. The door opened and a tearful Meriel stood there. After a brief hug, Lucy filled the kettle and set the tray for tea. Making tea in a crisis, she decided, was something to do with your hands, and a pretence that you're helping when there's no way of helping at all.

They drank a cup of tea as though it was expected of them and set off. 'I'll drive,' Lucy said. 'I'm the calmest.'

'No!' Meriel snatched the keys from Lucy's hand and strode out, leaving Lucy to lock up. She drove carefully through the town but when she reached the open countryside she pressed harder on the accelerator and drove wide as they reached left-hand corners better to see ahead. Lucy gripped her seat and prayed.

–

Walter insisted on going with Leo, and when Leo offered to drive, Walter refused. He wasn't capable of just sitting. He needed to see Meriel and to do that had to get himself there; this wasn't a moment to rely on someone else, even someone as involved as Leo.

The weather was brighter and this had brought out a few more motorists. He tapped his fingers irritably on the steering wheel every time he had to pause at a junction or wait while a car manoeuvred into a parking spot. Leo warned him not to be impatient. 'We need to get there fast, but still in one piece,' he reminded him. His words were ignored and as soon as they were past the hazard Walter increased his speed.

As the road narrowed, a cyclist appeared from a rough track and Walter had to swerve to avoid hitting him. Leo pointed to a lay-by a bit further on and told Walter to pull in. 'I really think it's best if I drive,' he said and to his relief Walter agreed.

It was as they were changing seats that a car approached and slowed to pass them. Joyfully, they recognized the driver. 'Meriel!' they called as her brakes squealed and she began to reverse back to them.

'We have to talk about George's latest bombshell. Lynne mustn't know about the letters. Some secrets should never be told,' Walter called.

'How did you know I'd received a letter?'

'I guessed how his devious mind works. George gave a copy to Leo to deliver to me and I read it today.'

'Leo? You delivered the letter from George Dexter and didn't check it before giving it to Dadda?'

'He said it was an apology.'

Without another word she slipped into gear and drove away.

They were facing the opposite direction and it took a while before they could turn and set off to catch her up.

Walter ignored Leo's plea to drive and set off in pursuit, cutting corners, overtaking dangerously until at last they saw her in the distance. The road went downhill then up and they could see her about halfway up the other side. Walter increased speed as they went down to gather speed for the rise and were soon close on her tail. He flashed lights and sounded the horn to persuade her to stop but she ignored him.

Lucy was frightened. Meriel was crying and with tears in her eyes she must surely lack the ability to make high-speed decisions? It was when they took a sharp corner that she lost control. Fortunately she'd slowed to take the blind turning but unable to straighten up in time for the double bend she ploughed off the road and into some bushes. Branches slowed the car's descent into the field below until it was standing on its bonnet among greenery. Lucy reached across and turned off the engine. The silence after the chase had a sort of dream quality.

Stiffly, amazed to find they were unharmed, they struggled out of the car and stared around them. Again, like part of a dream sequence, voices reached them and they heard rustling accompanying the voices as Walter and Leo scrambled down to reach them.

Cries of relief and hugs and halting explanations followed before they were helped back up on to the road. The got into Walter's Hillman, Leo sat in the driving seat with no question of anyone disagreeing. Walter sat in the back with Meriel, holding her as though he would never let her go, and a still shaking Lucy sat beside Leo.

Lucy gestured back the way they had come, reporting that there was a café on the main road they were approaching. Turning the car cautiously, Leo headed in the direction they had come. They parked outside the large café, where a line of lorries stood, their crews taking a welcome break, but they didn't all go in. Leo went to use the telephone and report an accident, and a few murmured voices around him made him aware that he'd been overheard. He assured them that no one was hurt, and the car was off the road and causing no hazard to other drivers.

'This isn't the place to talk about what's happened,' he said, when he went back to the car. 'I suggest we drive back to Badgers Brook.' Without questioning his decision, that was what they did.

Strangely there didn't seem much to say once they were settled in the living room with the fire burning and food prepared. George had done his worst and they had survived. Sadly, Leo was aware that Meriel was avoiding him, refusing to look at him and ignoring him when he spoke. She was angry with him for delivering the letter, yet he'd had no alternative.

'Leo should never have shown you that letter,' she said to her father when they were temporarily alone. 'Anything from George Dexter was bound to have meant trouble. He must have known that.'

'Leo will always be honest and he had no right to keep a letter addressed to me. I'd think less of him if he had. So would you if you'd think about it.'

Teifion arrived at ten thirty having been told Lucy and Meriel had been involved in an accident. In the way of small towns, someone had heard it from someone, who'd met a lorry driver who had been in the café and had recognized Meriel and Lucy in the car.

He was relieved to see neither girl was hurt, but insisted they had a fire lit in their bedrooms and hot water bottles between their sheets. He and Leo dealt with these comforts to the silent amusement of Walter.

'I don't want your mother to know about the letters,' he said. 'There's been too much agony caused already by looking back. It was a terrible time for her but it's been overlaid with so much happiness that it no longer matters.'

Meriel handed him a box of matches and together they set the letters on fire, held them until the flames caught hold, then dropped them into the grate where they smouldered until they were no more than black ashes.

Walter went to see George the following day. He was sitting up in bed and smiled maliciously as Walter approached his bed. A nurse watched anxiously from the table in the middle of the ward.

'Was it worth it, George?' Walter began.

'I've always hated you,' George replied. 'You took what should have been mine.'

'I loved her, you wanted to possess.'

'You stole her, tempted her when she was at her most vulnerable.'

'What a fine state you're in.' Walter's voice was deep with apparent sympathy and the nurse relaxed. 'All alone, your son preferring to work in a pub than run your business, no longer wanting to be a part of your life.'

'I was a strong father and he couldn't take it.'

'You were controlling and critical. Unable to hide your disappointment that he didn't grow up into a carbon copy of you.'

'Shut up!'

'My darling daughter was given freedom to grow. She didn't live with resentment and disappointment, she was nurtured with love.'

'Love is for weaklings.'

'Is that why you have a wife who can't live in the same house as you?'

'She let me down as you well know!'

'You've neglected them both, spending too much of your energy seeking revenge for something that didn't happen, something out of your imagination. That's why your life is such a mess.'

'I've told Meriel everything! See how well your love will deal with that! She has a letter too.'

'I know,' Walter replied. 'We burned them together on the fire at Badgers Brook.'

After he'd gone George demanded his clothes and insisted on signing himself out.

—

Meriel and Lucy began making preparations for the farm sale. They designed posters and ordered copies, they visited the place and made lists of the items to be included, and all the time, Meriel wondered how she would cope when she met her mother, knowing what she knew. Would she be able to hide that knowledge from her and act normally? Or would the secret show on her face? Lucy reassured her several times then ignored her worries, knowing her words weren't needed. But she was aware of her friend's anxiety and tried to think of a way to help. One morning as they opened the door to see Kitty and Bob waving, then later, had a visit from Stella bringing a few cakes she had made, the idea came.

'Let's have a party. That's always the best way to deal with something like this. It will be good to fill the house with friends, and an opportunity for you and your parents to put George and his wicked letters behind you.'

Meriel put aside the notes she was making in her neat hand and nodded. 'Let's make it a week next Sunday. Something special to celebrate then, eh?'

'Fantastic! What about your other parents? Won't Sunday be a difficult day for them?'

'We'll invite them and leave it up to them.' Sales business put aside, they at once began to make new lists of things they needed to do, people they wanted to invite.

Lucy was relieved to see her friend was more animated than she had been for several days.

'We won't invite Gerald and my first move must be to tell him I'm going to marry Teifion,' she said. In fact Gerald had already heard the news from Teifion.

He and Gerald had met in the Ship, where Teifion was serving at the bar. Gerald approached him rather diffidently and asked, 'Is Lucy well?'

'That's a formal query about a friend of many years.' Teifion stared at him curiously. 'Unless you heard about the accident she and Meriel had a few days ago?'

Gerald coughed in an embarrassed way, aware he had never bothered to find out if they were safe. 'I had heard,' he admitted, 'but working in Cardiff and being so busy,' he let the words fall and Teifion stared at him in disgust.

'To think that she might have married you. What a disaster that would have been.'

'Lucy will marry me and when the time is right I'll ask her. She'll be happy being the wife of a successful salesman.'

'You're too late, she's going to marry me.' Teifion handed him his drink, snatched the money from the bar and walked away. Gerald sipped his drink nonchalantly. Plenty more women about and he really deserved better than Lucy. She really wasn't the type to fit the new, exciting life that was opening up for him.

—

George was back in the office but finding it hard. He was constantly tired yet was unable to sleep. Frieda had phoned offering help but had been told to stay away, so she continued to live at Badgers Brook, helping by cleaning and cooking for the two friends; a fact that increased his anger.

His assistant did all he could to please him at work and his housekeeper made things comfortable for him at home but once she had gone the hours dragged by in utter loneliness, although he still refused to admit the loneliness was of his own making. He thought about Walter, Lynne and Meriel and wished he could think of a way to destroy their happiness. Between them they had ruined his. This was a distortion of the facts, but his weary mind believed it utterly.

–

One Saturday morning, Meriel and Lucy dressed with extra care but they didn't go into the office. Leaving a happy Kitty and Bob in charge, they set off in Teifion's car, their own still being under repair, and headed for Cardiff buzzing with excitement.

They pulled up at the register office and an excited threesome stepped out. Leo and his mother were waiting for them and they went inside. Half an hour later, Mr and Mrs Teifion Dexter emerged and they all drove back to Badgers Brook.

Lucy and Teifion had discussed their plans with Meriel and all had agreed that with Lucy's family so indifferent and George being so unreasonable and likely to spoil the day, it was best to arrange a small ceremony with as few people as possible being told.

They were negotiating to buy a small terraced house not far from the High Street and had arranged for its decoration. Until then, they would take a room in the bed and breakfast establishment belonging to Betty's brother and his wife.

Betty Connors had left to open the Ship but she had given them a wedding cake and several plates of sandwiches and some tiny decorated cakes. Frieda had set everything out and with Kitty and Bob joining them when the office closed at one o'clock, the simple celebratory meal took place. The small wedding cake was cut to enable a photograph to be taken but otherwise untouched, intended for the party on the following day when the news would become public.

–

George heard the news via his assistant who had heard it at the post office, Stella Jones being the recipient of all that went on in Cwm Derw. Ignoring the pain that had settled in his chest, he went to the garage and started the car. He drove towards Badgers Brook without any clear idea of what he intended.

He reached the turning, slowing down as a bus lumbered past, then without waiting to see whether his way was clear, he swerved into the lane. A car was approaching and he braked suddenly, his heart racing with the shock of it. He pulled up onto the grass verge near the gate, turned off the engine and heard laughter and music coming from the house. Anger consumed him and he sat there unable to decide what he could do. He wanted to tell Teifion what he thought of him for arranging his wedding in secret, and he tried to prepare what he would say, but the words wouldn't come.

–

Teifion and Lucy were the first to leave, intending to visit George and tell him what they had done. They walked to the gate shrugging on their coats with confetti falling from their clothes and laughing in sheer happiness and stopped as they saw George sitting in his car on the grass verge.

Apprehensively Teifion tapped on the window. 'Dad?' he shouted. He called again but George didn't respond.

When Teifion opened the door he realized his father was dead.

They ran back inside and Leo drove to the phone box to call the doctor, the police also came and the day which had started out in happiness and joyful expectation, ended in guilt, grief and sadness. Amid all the regrets and recriminations Teifion said, 'He even had to spoil today for me.' And was immediately ashamed.

The idea of a party on the following day was abhorrent and they left messages to let people know it was cancelled. Sunday passed in a series of visitors all wanting to tell Teifion how sorry they were. Most referred obliquely to the loss of his father, the comments were regret for his ruined wedding day.

Walter and Lynne came and offered sincere congratulations to the couple, bringing some beautiful bedding as a wedding gift for when they moved into their home. Meriel greeted her mother with the same affection, momentarily forgetting George's final spiteful act. He had done his worst and they had survived.

To their surprise Mr and Mrs Roberts-Price came with Martha and their soldier son, Noah. No one had thought to tell them the party had been cancelled. They stayed and shared their meal, offering sympathy to Teifion, shaking hands nervously with Walter and Lynne, then departed. Martha managed to have a word with Lucy to tell her she had her job back, and was allowed to keep her gramophone and was happy.

The will reading was awaited with bated breath after the sombre funeral had taken place. Teifion was expecting nothing and beside him Frieda sat expecting the same. A bitter man to the end, they knew George had undoubtedly willed away his money and business to some obscure relative or to a charity, as he had threatened many times.

The solicitor attended the funeral which took place at George's home with tea and sandwiches provided by his housekeeper as he had requested. Afterwards he called Teifion and Frieda into another room.

The will was very brief and surprising.

'The business is left to my son, Teifion, for him to run or to sell as he wishes,' the man read. 'My house is for my wife Frieda and all monies remaining after all accounts are settled will be divided between them.'

'I won't take your home,' Frieda said at once, putting a hand on her stepson's arm. 'It's your home and should always be yours.'

'Of course not! Thank you for such a wonderfully kind thought but I would never take it. It's yours and you can sell it and buy yourself a place where you'll be happy.' Lucy hugged her, agreeing with her husband.

'What will you do?' Lucy asked Teifion.

Would he take over his father's business and compete with Evans and Calloway? she wondered.

'Sell it of course,' he said. 'My loyalties are with you.'

Meriel, Teifion and Lucy walked back to the office where once again a proud Kitty and Bob had been left in charge. The place had been closed as a mark of respect but Kitty was delighted to tell them there had been two phone calls and one caller to whom she had given some leaflets and allowed to leave a name and an address. 'George Dexter would have understood,' she defended.

Things began to settle down and, with Lucy no longer living there, Meriel was glad to have Frieda staying. When she eventually left, Badgers Brook would seem very empty. A week later, Frieda announced that she was going to stay with her sister. 'Not a cover for meeting Kit this time. I really am going to Brighton,' she said wryly.

–

Meriel sat in her dressing-gown, stoking up the fire and making the flames dance around the walls. The dancing reflections peopled the room with a pretence of company but did nothing to expel her loneliness. When there was a knock at the door she leapt up to answer it, thankful for a visitor to fill a few minutes.

'Hello, Meriel,' Leo said. He didn't walk in but stood there, the lights playing shadows across his face so she failed to read his expression.

'Well?' she demanded peremptorily, unwilling to show how pleased she was to see him. 'Are you coming in?'

'No, you are coming out,' he said.

'What, dressed like this?' she opened her arms to display her dressing-gown.

'If you wish, although I'd prefer you wore something more suitable.'

'Suitable for what? Where are you intending to take me?'

'Through the woods to watch the badgers. We've just got time to test the wind and find a suitable place to sit.'

Bemused she changed into trousers and dark coat and they walked across the lane and into the dark trees. He took her hand and occasionally shone a torch to guide her until they were sitting on a low branch some distance from where the badgers had trodden their path across the brook.

An hour later, having seen about eight badgers set off on their nightly foraging trip; chasing, mock-fighting, happy to be free to wander, he took her into his arms and said, 'I've always loved you and waited for you to love me. Now, despite your occasional huffs—'

'I don't huff,' she protested.

His teeth glistened as he smiled in the darkness and he said, 'In spite of your occasional "huffs", I now think you do. Marry me.'

'I don't know, there's so much to arrange and—'

He silenced her with a kiss.

She laughed, hugging him so close, feeling so good in his arms, utterly content. 'It seems I have a very determined man in my life so what can I say? Except, yes.'